THE FALL OF THE SPANISH INQUISITION

A Fantasy By
Daniel Rosenfeld

ROSENFELD BOOK PUBLISHING

3

To Joan, my wife and best friend.   Thank you for your support and encouragement.

With all my love,
Daniel

PREFACE

I n the year 1492, the Spanish Crown issued an expulsion order for all Jews then living in Spain. The story I am about to tell relates to three branches of one family. One family branch lived in Barcelona, which was in Aragon, the second in Toledo, Castile, and the third in Lisbon, Portugal.

It is estimated that 400,000 Jews lived in Spain and Portugal in those days. The number may have even been higher. Unfortunately, no known statistics exist. What we do know is the fact that despite the endless pogroms against the Jews throughout the years, many held prominent positions in the government. However, the best-known positions afforded the Jews by the Crown were those of Tax Collectors. It was also a known fact that Jews, as a group, paid to the Crown over 20% of all taxes collected in Spain and Portugal. This particular fact helped many Jewish communities in different parts of Spain and Portugal obtain official intervention by the Crown to secure their existence. However, the influence of the Catholic Church kept growing with time and as it grew and strengthened, various monarchs became powerless against it.

Opinions differ as to when and how the Jewish ghettos of Spain came into being. It is believed that the first Jewish ghetto was established in Castile in a town called Murcia in the year 1272. Jews were forced to live in these ghettos mainly to facilitate the Crown's ability to guard them from mob attacks.

The Abulafia family was a very large one. It was Moise Abulafia who first came to Castile in the year 958 soon after the Moors completed their conquest of Spain and Portugal. Moise Abulafia was a well-known merchant in Alexandria, Egypt before moving to Spain. He left two of his sons in Alexandria to run his family business and traveled to Spain to seek new business horizons. On the way to Spain he also set up one of his sons in Tangier, thus expanding his reach over the North African continent.

As his business enterprises grew in Castile, his brother Meir settled in Barcelona, which was a leading port-city in Aragon, and his brother Chaim settled in neighboring Lisbon, Portugal. Since Aragon, Castile and Portugal were three separate monarchies, the Abulafias built a solid business, which covered the entire Iberian Peninsula.

As coincidence would have it, the descendants of both Moise and Meir celebrated their Bar Mitzva on the same day, December 13, 1474. On that same day, Princess Isabella's coronation as Queen of Castile after the death of her brother, King Enrique, took place. The ceremony of the joint Bar Mitzva was planned for and celebrated in Toledo, which had by far the greatest and most prominent Synagogue in Spain.

David was the descendent of Moise and Reuven descended from Meir. David lived in Toledo and Reuven in Barcelona. While the descendents of Chaim continued to live and work in Portugal, they weren't overly close to their Spanish kin except for business. David and Reuven became very close and their lives began to intertwine through an exchange of letters, followed by clandestine activity against the Church.

At the end of their Bar Mitzva ceremony, David and Reuven were sat next to each other in the great hall of the Toledo Synagogue where a meal of unprecedented grandeur was served to hundreds of guests. It was then the two young men vowed to correspond and officially called each other 'brother'.

And they remained brothers for the rest of their lives.

I wish to point out to the reader that all historical data provided in this book, until such time as the Abulafia cousins began their clandestine fight against the Church, is common knowledge. However, the part of the story which begins with their underground operations against the Inquisition and the Church, is PURE FANTASY.

PART ONE
The letters

Sunday, 14th of December, 1474

Dear brother Reuven,

> *You haven't left Toledo yet and I'm already writing to you. My mother tucked me in and as usual form kissed my forehead with much affection and prayer. "Sleep well, my son, for today you had a most exciting day. This day, the day of your Bar Mitzva, you will have to remember forever. You cannot erase or forget this day for as long as you live. Your Rabbi has taught you that you are considered a man as of the day of your Bar Mitzva. You must follow your father's footsteps. You must be a man of integrity as he is. Learn the family business and always conduct yourself fairly and justly unto others. I will always pray for you and ask God Almighty to watch out for you. But, first, you must watch out for yourself. Remember, Im Ein Ani Li Mi Li?" Another kiss was deposited on my forehead and she left my room. I was too overwhelmed to answer her. I love my mother dearly.*

> *I was too excited to sleep, so I got out of bed and am writing to you. I'm planning to give you my first letter on the day of your departure. You may read it while traveling.*

> *This was truly a day I shall remember for the rest of my life. I didn't need her to remind me. First and foremost in my thoughts was getting to know you. The last and only time we saw each other, before our joint Bar Mitzva celebration, was about seven years ago when my parents took me with them to Barcelona for the unveiling of your grandfather's tombstone. I remember that voyage well. I loved watching the horses when my father allowed me to sit next to the wagon's driver. I felt like a man - touching the reins. As much as I pleaded with the driver, he wouldn't let me hold them.*

> *I also remember your parents taking both of us to the Barcelona synagogue for the Sabbath morning prayers. What left me with an awkward feeling of incomprehension was the Rabbi's sermon. Do you recall it? He was talking about the growing strife among the general population of Barcelona and the growing hate for the Jews. He said that as the land was being redeemed from the Moors, who captured Aragon over four hundred years ago, the Christian people began to divert their hate toward the Jews. They were disturbed by the fact that Jews were on good terms with the Muslim Moors, as well as their desire to convert people of other faiths to Catholicism.*

I also recall your father telling mine they should develop new ways to communicate because the Aragonian Christians would make it impossible to deal with merchants in Moorish countries. And, I vividly remember you telling your father that he conducted business with Jews in Moorish countries and not with Muslims or Christians. Your father laughed and said you'd be a great businessman one day. Of course, I didn't understand a thing they were talking about. Now, I believe I know more or less what they meant.

I cannot help but wonder why there are so many kingdoms in Aragon and Castile. Everybody speaks the same language. Isn't it time all kingdoms unite under one flag if they want to kick the Moors out of the rest of our peninsula? I hear that fighting still continues in the south and it is hoped that soon the Moorish Muslims will be completely thrown out of Castile.

I wish I were older and could better understand what is going on. I hear my father say that thanks to the good years when the Moors ruled Castile and Aragon business was extremely good, now that they are gone most connections with our family in North Africa and Palestine are on hold. Apparently, the Muslims respected or tolerated the Jews. He believes the Church is becoming more aggressive as far as the Christian religion is concerned, and fears we'll be forced to convert. I don't exactly understand how you can convert people? Do you?

I'm getting sleepy now, so I'll go to bed. But, before I do, I want you to know that I love you and that I'm very happy our families decided to hold this joint Bar Mitzva ceremony and celebration in Toledo. I wish you a happy and pleasant voyage and hope our next encounter will not be in the too distant future.

Yours,
David.

Saturday, 20th of December, 1474

Dear Brother David,

The letter you gave me on the day of my departure from Toledo was a great comfort to me. I read it many times during the long journey to Barcelona. It was only last night that we returned home. The weather was bad. It rained most of the time. Even though I'm tired from this ordeal, I can't postpone my writing to you.

As soon as we set foot in our house, our maid delivered a notice received while we were away. It directed my father and all male children to attend Church today and begin the conversion process. My father is hysterical. We have to leave in about an hour. I'm frightened. What does it mean to convert? Do you think the king wants us to become Christians? I'm going to ask my father many questions. I suddenly feel 'grown up' and want to understand the truth.

My father is calling me. I'll continue this letter when I return.

We've just returned from Church. We had to sit with many people I hadn't known before and had to listen to the sermon presented by a priest. He spoke of righteousness and salvation. He reminded the audience that Jesus died for all people. I was terribly confused. At the end of the sermon the priest asked my father to join him in his private chambers. My father was told he could not postpone conversion any more. The priest told him that the pressure placed on him was beyond bearing and if all the remaining Jews of Barcelona did not convert immediately, they would be subject to massacre by the mobs. My father handed him a pouch, which I knew contained a great deal of money. The priest took it willingly, pocketed it and said, "My dear Mr. Abulafia, I won't be able to help you any more. The Bishop told me in no uncertain terms that your family must convert immediately as have many of the Jews in this city. You are recognized as one of the leading Jews in Aragon, and your refusal to convert holds up many of your followers. The Bishop also told me that should you refuse to convert by the end of this week, he would direct the mobs to destroy your family and its fortunes. I am telling you all of this because I have always been a friend of your family. You know that. I personally do not believe in violence as I do not believe in forceful conversion. I believe conversion should come from a man's heart. But I cannot fight the Church and its powerful organization. As a friend I beg you to convert."

I heard my father say to the priest, "I would like to have one day to consider your message. I'll call on you tomorrow evening." We then left the Church and walked home. My father didn't say a word during the walk. I saw his face. It was completely distorted from anger. I didn't dare speak to him.

As soon as we returned home, he summoned my mother and they locked themselves in the drawing room. I knocked on the door, opened it and said, "Father, I've never seen you so upset. I hear many things about the problems of the Jews and now I hear that we must convert. Please explain to me what is going on. I was told only last week that as of my Bar Mitzva I'm considered a man. Please don't lock me out of the discussion you are about to hold with my mother."

"Son," he said, "you are very perceptive and I'm very proud of you. You may stay and listen." He continued. "We have two alternatives. We can convert or leave Barcelona. I will never forget the story my father told me when I was a child about the great massacre, which took place in this city and throughout Aragon in 1391. I have a feeling it may happen again. It seems money will not buy our freedom anymore. It is true that over twenty thousand Jews have already converted. Chaim Sasson, our accountant, tells me that he and his family go to church every Sunday and participate in all Christian prayers. He told me all about the many days of preaching and teachings of the Catholic religion they had to attend, and their oath to live as pure Christians. However, he did emphasize that all that is a pure façade and only meant for the outside Christian world to see. He stated that they celebrate all the Jewish holidays in secret, in the privacy of their home, and pray to our God every day without fail. He also told me he had given me this information in complete confidence and if the Church knew about his continued observance of the Jewish religion, he would be hung as a sinner."

"I cannot bear seeing you under such pressure and torment," my mother said. Suddenly, she turned to me. "Reuven, you are my only child. I could not bear more children for your father. I cannot continue to live in fear. Your father and I have been talking of nothing else but the living conditions of Jews in Aragon. The situation seems to be worse in other parts of the country. So far we have managed to pay our way out of it, and so far we've done our best to keep you away from our predicament. But as you said, you are now a man and you indeed have the right and should know what is going on."

My father took the conversation over. "My son, it pains me to no end to have to say this. I would rather die than have to go through conversion to Christianity, but I have you to consider. You are young and your entire life is in front of you. There is no reason for you to die. Many Jews preferred to die rather than convert. I do not find dying a useful method, for attitudes change, and Kings change as governments change. Jewish history is full of changing conditions. The day will come when we will surface again."

"Are you saying that we should convert?" my mother asked.

"I'm saying we have no other alternative. Do you want to face death? Do you want to see your son killed?" he insisted.

"Of course not!" she said. "If over twenty thousand Jews have already converted, what would three more matter?"

"Son, I know this is entirely contrary to all my teachings. I am ashamed to have to say this and ask you, can you live with deceit, because we'll have to appear to be Christians at all times when in our hearts we shall remain Jews?" His eyes were full of tears. He suddenly got up, lifted his hands towards heaven and shouted, "God, why are you doing this to us? The Jews of Aragon have been observant Jews all their lives. What have we done to deserve this?" He fell to his chair. I've never seen my father so distraught. I crossed over to him, and laid my hand on his shoulder. "Father, you've been my guiding light. I love you with all my heart. I promise I'll keep my mouth shut and do what needs to be done. You can count on me. One day, we shall come back with a vengeance. I promise you that I shall dedicate my life to the Jewish cause. I know I'm very young, but I'll grow up and fight."

My mother grabbed me and hugged me with all her strength. A minute later my father joined us, and the three of us stood immobilized. I began to see a new world developing right under my nose. I don't know what it is, as yet, but I'll figure it out.

My dear brother David, it seems we are faced with a dilemma of grand proportions. My father said that the situation in Castile would worsen too. Could you possibly write and tell me about your area? I'm very curious. Mother told me the reason my Bar Mitzva was held in Toledo was not just because the synagogue there is greater, but that it was decided not to draw too much attention to our synagogue in Barcelona. My parents kept so much away from me, but probably for a good reason.

I'm sorry if this letter sounds confusing. I know I'm confused. It's so difficult to understand why people are so brutal to each other when all of us have but a certain number of years to live on this earth. I must say, I suddenly feel I have aged all at once. I cannot watch my parents live with such agony.

If conversion will ease their lives, so be it. I'll learn to live with it like many others. But I swear to you, here and now, that I shall fight it when I grow older and can stand on my own two feet. I don't know how, but I will. I have vowed to fight this conversion business.

I'll write more after my father's meeting with the priest tomorrow. Meanwhile, I'll sign and seal this letter for the courier. Please remind me to your parents.

Yours,
Reuven

Wednesday, 21st of January 1475

Dear Brother Reuven,

Your letter of the 20th of December was quite an eye opener. I'm sorry it took so long for it to arrive. My father's courier who travels between our Toledo, Barcelona and Lisbon offices tells of a great deal of strife in the countryside. Since he crisscrosses the country, I asked him many questions. He says that the nobles, who are the landowners, exploit the peasants. The peasants are paid very little for their work, and out of their pay they are obliged to pay a hefty tax to the crown. In actuality, the peasants are robbed blindly. On top of this the peasants are forcefully recruited to the crown's armies to fight the Moors. The nobles live in unheard of luxury and the people live in pure poverty and misery.

The crown and its government seek Jews to fill important positions because Jews are better educated and literate. This enhances the people's hatred towards us. In particular, the crown uses Jews as tax collectors. Jews are also faced with growing hatred by the Church, which helps direct people's anger to them. On occasion, the crown sends troops to protect the Jews, but often too late and after the mobs had looted Jewish property. There were many instances in which Jews have also been killed. At the same time, the Church wants to cleanse the population of Castile and Aragon of its non-Christians and uses coercion to do so. The Church and its priests in high positions impose forceful demands for conversion to Catholicism - all in the name of God. In Castile, just as in Aragon, the courier tells me, thousands of Jews and Muslims who did not escape have converted. Here they are called 'New Christians'.

I had a lengthy conversation with my father after receiving your letter and my talk with the courier. My father tells me the only reason that Jews in Toledo have not been hurt as badly as in other parts of the country is because the seat of government is in this city. The crown is well aware of the fact that we Jews provide the much-needed merchandise for the country and its war effort. It's also important to remember that we pay back a great part of the profit as taxes.

Nevertheless, the Church in Toledo is increasing its power and my father said that in the not too distant future the Church would control the State. When that happens, all of us will be subjected to the same conversion demands as in other parts of the country. The general situation for Jews in both Castile and Aragon will become bleaker with time. According to my father there is talk that Castile and Aragon will unite under one King and Queen. If you recall, Princess Isabella's coronation took place on the day of our Bar Mitzva. She is married to King Ferdinand of Aragon. It is also said that she is a religious fanatic. Should the rumors become reality, we might face unheard of troubles.

I too wish that I was older, but perhaps our age has advantages which will help us overcome some of the difficult days that lay ahead. Your observation about the tolerant relations with the Jews by the Muslim Moors while they ruled Castile and Aragon, is possibly because the Muslims saw us as foreigners in this land. Also, we must take into account the possibility that they recognized the Jews as the descendents of Abraham, their patriarch. We should not forget that the Jews were the only ones in this peninsula who spoke Arabic as well as Spanish. We are the people who served as interpreters during the many years of the Moorish rule.

Despite all that, my father tells me that on many occasions, when mobs attacked Jewish neighborhoods, killed and looted, Muslim people joined the attackers. This part is really confusing, but I have to believe that Muslims who remained in this country are also subjected to demands for conversion. I can't help wondering how they feel about it.

I'm also told that similar problems are brewing in Portugal. We have had very little personal contact with our family in Lisbon. Most of the contacts are purely commercial. I feel the need to know more about the branch of our family there. I'm very curious. Aren't you?

Please write soon. In these days of uncertainty I want to share with you everything that happens in my life just as you did in your letter.
I remain waiting with much fear and anxiety.
> *Yours,*
> *David*

Friday, 10th of February, 1475

My brother David,

I'm ashamed, I have been shamed and I am disgraced from head to toe. This morning I was baptized in the central Barcelona Catholic Church. Father Julio Aristez conducted the ceremony, and as of this coming Monday I will be attending a local Catholic school under the direction of some Bishop whose name escapes me. My parents were also baptized, but in a different Church. They'll have to attend instruction for conversion three times a week, and the entire family will have to attend Sunday mass at the local church. My father will have to register our attendance in some office every week.

As long as Zevulun ben Yishai remains our family's courier, I can trust him with my letters. The day he stops or disappears I'll stop telling you about my true feelings for fear of being caught by the Church's investigators. My father warned me that we must appear to be pure Christians. Any variation sends us immediately to death. Since I've become interested and understand better what is going on, and what we Jews are faced with, I'm determined to stay alive. The main reason is that when I grow older, I will do everything in my power to fight the Church. As of this moment I don't know how, but I vowed to fight and I will stand by this vow. When the time comes, I'd like you to join me in my quest.

Every day after dark, when all candles are extinguished, and our house appears to have retired for the night, my father, mother and myself get together in the dark living room and pray to our God, the God of Abraham, Jacob and Itzhak.

My father recites portions of the Torah and all of us pledge ourselves to our God of Gods. We also ask forgiveness for the sin we have committed. My father hid all our holy books in a special case, which was sealed between two walls. He is the only one who knows where they are hidden. Our house has been redecorated with various pictures of Christ, a statue of Jesus on the cross and a number of New Testament books on our bookshelves. If you walked into our house, you wouldn't recognize it. I'm having a very hard time explaining my feelings to you, as I do not know where to begin. I feel that I've been violated.

I swear I will never forgive them for what they have done to us. One day, with the help of God, I will fight them to death. I'm making a list of the names and addresses of Jewish children who are in the same predicament as me. As we grow older, I will organize ourselves and somehow wage battle against the Church and its merciless treatment of Jews who have done nothing but enhance the well being of this country.

David, I am too angry to continue. Please forgive me. I will write soon.

Yours,
Reuven

Monday, 20th of February, 1475

My dear brother David,

It's been over a week since I wrote to you. I was very upset at the time of my last writing. I am still upset at this moment. I fear I'll remain angry and disturbed for years to come. It's not easy to live with deception. I keep observing my father, who is my guiding light, and feel extremely sorry for him. I know he tries to put on a good face, but as soon as he returns home, he's in deep depression. He seems to be coming out of his misery when he recites the bible and tells me stories I heard many times before. I cannot see his face in the dark, but I can feel it in his voice. My mother tries very hard to console him, but to no avail. He always had a prominent seat by the Eastern wall in our synagogue and now he cannot set foot there. If he's seen anywhere near the synagogue, his life will be endangered.

They call us 'New Christians', and my father said last night that the Church is going to segregate us from all other Christians because we, the New Christians, are still not pure enough for them. He also said he finds it amazing that the jails are full of 'Old Christians' who were sentenced for every crime ever created by man, and there isn't one Jew among them. He stated that the idea of creating a pure Christian society is absurd. "Look at the number of people they hang every day, in the public square. They kill people as though they themselves are God. Instead of finding ways to help those who cannot help themselves, they kill them. It's absolutely pathetic," my father concluded.

He doesn't know it, but my father adds more reasons for me to want to revolt, and God willing I will. Last Sunday, when we went to mass, I even swore by their God that I would revolt and fight the Church for what they've done and are still doing to innocent people.

I am consumed with rage. I can't help it. Someone has to take action, and I swear to you, David, I will.
Please write soon. I am desperate to have a good word from you.

With much affection, I am yours,
Reuven

Wednesday, 15th of February, 1475

Dear brother Reuven,

Your letter of the 10th hit me very hard. I feel your pain. Please forgive me, but due to the severity of your news I had to share it with my father. He couldn't stop crying. He asked me to keep the news from my mother. She's not feeling well these days. My father is very concerned about her. He is afraid that such news might kill her.

Reuven, what can we do to stop this madness? After all, we are only thirteen years old. If adults cannot do anything, what role might we play? I agree with you wholeheartedly that someone, somehow, must do something to stop this madness. Yesterday, my father sent me to pick up a parcel from one of his clients. I passed by Plaza Mayor, the main market square, and saw two people hanging from a tree. It was said the two committed heresy. Can you imagine, if I want to kill someone, all I have to do is report the person to the Church and state that I witnessed him commit heresy. He would be sentenced to death by the Church's court. My father said that priests act as hangmen. Can you imagine men of the cloth killing people?

By the way, as you know, our families have had very little, if any contact with our family in Lisbon on a personal level. My father does not know the cause. I'm determined to correct the situation. I've written a letter to one of my uncles in Lisbon, as I'm very curious about them. I have rewritten that letter for you. I will keep you informed if he returns my courtesy.

As result of your letter and the information I'm uncovering, I asked my father why is it that we are hated. He tells me that hate for the Jews dates back over a thousand years. There are many reasons for it. When the Babylonians conquered the Land of Israel, and destroyed the Temple in Jerusalem, they removed all the learned men and settled them in various parts of their world. You know of this story from the Bible. By removing the learned men from Israel, the diaspora was established for the first time. The Babylonians believed that once the elite of the population had been removed, the rest of the people wouldn't be able to revolt against them. The learned men who suddenly appeared in many foreign cities did not assimilate, mainly due to their religion. Our learned and wise men were literate and were immediately put to work by the emperors. They automatically became the target of jealousy and hate. Years later, under the guidance of our prophets, they rebuilt the Temple, only to be destroyed once more by the Romans. Again, learned and wise men were taken away. History repeated itself. The Jews of the diaspora clung to their religion with fervor while the heathen of Europe took on Christianity. In order to convert the Jews to Christianity, many of the clergies began to fabricate stories - the most famous being that it was the Jews who killed Jesus Christ. The Jews were pushed into new corners. As the years progressed, the Church began to build up power, and eventually began to influence kings and emperors. However, not all kings and emperors treated Jews badly. There were good years and there were bad years. But, hate for the Jews persisted and grew. Soon enough some of the rulers began using the Jews as bait for their political problems or aspirations. As an example, here in Castile and even in Aragon, from 1348 to 1351 there was a great Black Death. Scores of people died from the plague. The masses were told the Jews were to blame even though Jews died at an alarming rate from the same disease. Years later, the Jews were still held responsible for the death of their Christian neighbors, and mobs, directed by the Church, attacked Jewish communities, killing innocent men, women and children, and looted their homes.

Of course, now there exists a new twist to our problem. Members of the Church want all people to be Catholics, and pure Catholics at that. I don't believe for one moment that even if we converted we'll ever be recognized as pure Catholics. Furthermore, I don't think most Christians are pure. I don't believe any human being can be absolutely pure. Human nature tells you otherwise. This entire subject of Catholic Puritanism is insane. The question is, how to fight it? In this respect, I'm with you all the way. You may count on me.

Please write soon.

With all my love,
David

Wednesday, 15th of February, 1475

Dear Uncle Mordechai, Lisbon, Portugal

I hope and pray that our family courier will deliver this letter to you. I don't know whether you are aware of me. I'm a descendent of Moise Abulafia who settled in Toledo about five hundred years ago. Two months ago I celebrated my Bar Mitzva ceremony together with my cousin, Reuven, from Barcelona.

My father tells me that our family branch, which settled in Lisbon at the same period as my ancestors, never kept much of a personal relationship with the others in Castile and Aragon except for business purposes.

I'm wondering if there are young boys and girls my age in your family, as I would like to correct the mistakes of years gone by. Would you be kind enough to write to me on this subject? I would greatly appreciate it.

Very truly yours,
David Abulafia
Toledo, Castile

Tuesday, 3rd of March, 1475

Dear brother David,

Your letter was most inspiring especially because you agreed to join me in action against the barbaric Church.

I've begun to ask my father many questions about the history of the Jews in Aragon. I believe you are already ahead of me. I feel we need to know our history in detail by the time we take action. Also, let's start compiling a list of people involved in the brutal behavior of the Catholic Church. We must educate ourselves about the workings of the Church and its emissaries of death.

Now that I'm attending the leading Catholic school in Barcelona, I'll attempt to reach the top. I'll become their highest honor student in religion in order to beat them from within. I cannot explain it, but I feel as though some power has taken me over and is giving me the determination to fight for the Jews of this country. I'm thinking of revenge and change.

There are rumors about certain changes in the monarchy of Castile. You are much closer to the situation in Toledo. Please find out and write to me. This Isabella worries me, as it is common knowledge she is a religious fanatic. Apparently, she has her own priest who guides her. Let's do our homework, and let us be prepared.

My father just walked in. I'm going to have a long talk with him tonight before I continue with this letter.

I'm back. His first remark to my many questions was, "What has come over you so suddenly? I've never known you to be so inquisitive."
"I've suddenly been transformed into a Catholic against my will, just as against yours. I know I'm very young and not knowledgeable in many areas and issues concerning life, but we are forced to be what we are not. I feel it is in my destiny to fight for change. I can hardly explain the frame of mind that has gripped me. I can only tell you I'm determined with my entire body and soul to fight barbaric and outmoded ways of life. I'm appalled that men of the cloth kill innocent people in the name of God. Everything I've learned to date from our Bible tells me differently. Now, that I am attending a Catholic school, I can tell you that they, too, study the Old Testament. Our

teacher priest said the Old Testament and the Ten Commandments are the basis for the New Testament. If that is the case, they are not following the basic commandment, which states; 'thou shalt not kill'. And, where does it say in the Bible that one religion should convert another or die?" I responded.

My father listened to me carefully. I could see his face in the candlelight quite clearly. He was amazed and perhaps a little shocked at my words. He didn't respond immediately, as he usually does. This time, he sat there thinking for a few moments. "Reuven, you just said something that bothers me a great deal. You stated that some mysterious power is guiding you to fight the Church. None of us can fight the Church. We Jews have been passive in foreign lands for a number of reasons. First and foremost, we are minorities in the lands of others. We are better educated. We are masters in mathematics, medicine and trade. We speak a number of languages, and have followed the tradition of not mixing or assimilating with non-Jews. Secondly, with the exception of fighting for our freedom in the Land of Israel, Jews have never taken to arms to fight in or for other nations. We are pacifists by nature and by our education and beliefs. As to the forced conversion, we have three alternatives. One, we can leave Aragon and settle elsewhere. Second, we can die for 'Kidush Hashem' (Holiness of the Lord) and third, we can convert. I personally don't believe in dying for Kidush Hashem because it makes no sense, and I don't believe God wants us to die for him. It is true that we can leave and settle somewhere else, but the situation throughout Europe is not much different. The power of the Church is growing everywhere at an alarming rate. Christianity is the first religion to force itself on the heathen and masses. For some reason the Church feels it must be the guiding light of all people, and that there is no other God but theirs. Because the masses of the previous centuries lived by their sword as they still do, they are very brutal people, and killing means little to them. Therefore, what is left is conversion. That was why I decided to convert. However, since I am and have been a good Jew all my life, just as my ancestors were, I will continue to practice my religion in secret. If there is a God, and I believe there is, he will appreciate what I'm doing. Also, as history has shown us, rulers change. And with such change comes social change. One day we'll return to live as Jews, in the open and without fear. When the time comes, me, you, or maybe your children will cast off the façade of conversion."

My father is a very clever man and his knowledge of the world is remarkable. Yet there were some points in his remarks which I couldn't accept. "Father, I listened very carefully to every word you spoke and I admire you for it. However, young as I am, I cannot see change coming by itself, nor do I want to wait until change comes. It could very well be that change will never take place-what then? Meanwhile, hundreds, and perhaps thousands of Jews are killed. Also, why should our children, and our children's children, as well as ourselves in the present, have to suffer and live in deceit? That is why I'm determined to fight for our rights."

"My dear son," he said, "you are so young and you speak like a man. Life is not that simple. To fight the Church you will need more than an army. Please drop this whole crazy idea. I truly understand your anguish and the thought of fighting evil, which I'm sure crossed many a mind. The bottom line is that we have no power. Our only alternative is to wait it out."

I decided not to push the conversation further because I totally disagreed with him. There are many ways to fight the Church, and by God, I shall.

I can't think of anything else to write at this time. As you can sense, I am consumed with thoughts of the future.

Reuven

Friday, 13th of March, 1475

Dear brother Reuven,

I took your advice and began grilling my father about the past. Interestingly enough, he seems to have similar opinions to your father. I suppose the Abulafias are born of the same flesh and blood. He said that Catholicism developed in the sixth century and took Europe over. He also said that while many differences existed between the various clergy, they were all united in one mission, and that was to convert every person on earth to their faith. He wasn't certain as to when the brutality factor entered the scene, but it has been going on for generations. The degree of force and brutality differed from country to country, and endless deceitful tactics were used.

Over the years, tens of thousands of Jews were brutally handled and massacred, their properties vandalized and looted, and all in the name of God. What amazes him is that Jews suffered for centuries and are still suffering with no end in sight. Yet the Jewish population in general keeps growing in numbers. The biggest difficulty, in his opinion, is that the masses have been taught to believe the Jews use Christian blood when celebrating their holidays, of stealing Holy Water from the Churches, and so on. The heads of the Catholic Church, the Cardinals, Bishops and clergy deliberately and with malice inform their audiences that Jews are the messengers of the Devil, the Jews killed Jesus, and the like.

Having read the description of the conversation you held with your father, and listening to mine on the suffering of the Jews, I tend to agree with you that we need to fight the Church. The problem is that it's not only the Church we have to fight, but we'll have to change public opinion as well. I can't think of how to achieve such an objective at this moment, but I'm sure it'll come to us in due course.

I think it's a good idea to learn the history of the Jews in Castile and Aragon, as well as in other countries. It will be helpful in the future. It just cannot be that Jews are persecuted endlessly in every corner of the world. I can't remember any acts of violence against the Jews in Toledo during the past ten years. On occasion I heard my parents talk of things I couldn't understand, but I do not recall having had to hide or run away. My father also told me about the 1391 riots, the killings and the looting of homes. It was quite clear then, as it is today, that the Church was and is using the masses to intimidate the Jews. The Church knows it cannot reach all the Jews at all times, but is working systematically on conversion. Look at the pressure they put on your family, the threats your father had to live with, followed by his decision to convert. I can't help wonder when it will happen to us in Toledo, and what my father will do. In a sense you were lucky that the local priest warned your father.

My father tells me that Jews who converted are also called 'Marranos' and that a great majority practice our religion in secret. In some parts of the country they are called 'Conversos'. He believes the Church is becoming more aware of this and plans to take steps against Marranos who are caught. He also said something about what is known as "The Holy Office." I'm going to find out what this Holy Office is and tell you in my next letter.

Yours,
David

Thursday, 2nd of April, 1475

My dear brother David,

As soon as I received your letter, I decided to investigate the Holy Office you mentioned. My father tells me the Catholic Church created this office for the purpose of punishing Christians who committed heresy. He seems to believe that the first office was established in the early part of the thirteenth century in France. At the time, this office dealt strictly with Christians. It was not active against Jews or other minorities. At some point this office was renamed 'Inquisition' and began to fight sorcery which was quite common in those days. It also began to look into blasphemy and decided that the Jews were a blasphemous race. Slowly this Inquisition expanded its jurisdiction to cover areas other than those for which it was created. A number of Popes over the years did not agree with its functions, but despite various objections it grew, and became more forceful and powerful. In fact, the Inquisition has become extremely powerful in Castile and Aragon, mainly because of the Marranos, and what they call the 'New Christians'. It is rumored that the Inquisition is functioning without the pope's consent. Queen Isabella is apparently seeking such permission. As you know, Queen Isabella is a devout Catholic, and it's known she has a private clergy attending to her exclusively. This clergy is as fanatic as she is.

Jews are not the only ones forced to convert; so are the Moors who were left in our countries. The Inquisition apparently claims that many Moor converts are leaning toward Judaism. This entire subject is extremely complicated. Frankly, I cannot understand how anyone expects a human being to make a change in his beliefs overnight. Furthermore, every man should be entitled to decide how he wants to live his life. Our people were slaves in Egypt for hundreds of years. It was during their exodus from Egypt, on the way to the future Land of Israel that true religious thought and practice developed. The morals which were instilled in us two thousand years ago, are also the basis of Christianity. Why is it that they hound us? We did not kill their Jesus! He was a Jew his entire life.

Friday, 3rd of April, 1475

I was unable to continue my letter last night. My father brought up the subject of Passover, which starts next Thursday. We decided that mother should bake only three matzot on the eve of the Sedder. The three matzot will be used during the Sedder, and we'll forego eating it during the rest of the week. Of course, we'll conduct the Sedder in the dark. Father says that Inquisition investigators will surely pass through our neighborhood to do their dirty work.

As we've discussed previously, it's of the utmost importance that we learn as much as possible about the history of the Jews in Aragon and Castile. It will become extremely difficult for me to do so since I'm supposed to be a 'pure Catholic', (Ha! Ha!) This burden will have to fall on you. My only source of information is my father. You still have a broader frontier. I pray it stays that way.

Yours,
Reuven

Sunday, April 19th, 1475

Dear brother Reuven,

We've just finished our Sedder ceremony and I hasten to write you. Zevulun delivered your letter of the 2nd yesterday. I imagine he rushed back as he too wanted to be with his family for the holidays. I'm concerned about him because he spends most of his time on the road. Travel in these horse-driven wagons is not very pleasant. And, there is much strife between the nobles who fight each other from time to time. I also know that he carries on his person large sums of money, and may be subject to robbery. Father says he has been doing this kind of work for years and has his methods. I hope he's right. I also can't help but think about the fact that he visits your father's place of business and might be subject to investigation by the Inquisition.

I spent some time with our Rabbi after school, and his words about the Holy Office and the Inquisition were quite similar to your father's. The situation in Toledo seems to be quite the same. He did say, however, that Queen Isabella, while an ardent Catholic, recognizes the value of the Jews to the Crown. He also mentioned a priest by the name of Tomas de Torquemada, who is her confessor and known to be the most radical of all clergy. The Rabbi believes that this Torquemada will eventually influence Isabella more.

When I returned home, I asked my father about Isabella. He brought with him a briefcase full of papers and accounts and said he would give me some time later. His story about Isabella goes as follows: "Isabella was coronated Queen of Castile and Leon on the 13th of December, the same day as our Bar Mitzva, two days after the death of her half brother, King Enrique. She was already married to Ferdinand of Aragon. This marriage took place in 1469 against the king's wishes. Isabella was very popular with most of the Castile's nobility as she was with the higher members of the Church. It was decided to rush her coronation in order to force failure on her immediate competitor, Princess Juana.

"Isabella is fair skinned and blond, which is unusual for Castilians. It is believed her ancestors came from the north. She is known for her gentility, piety, and generosity. Some say she has a country manner, which most people like. She is a firm supporter of the ongoing push to oust the Muslim Moor invaders from the country."

Another subject I approached was the 'Marranos' issue. It is said that tens of thousands of Jews who converted after the riots of 1391 were called Marranos. In some places converted Jews and Muslims are also called 'New Christians'. Frankly, I don't understand the difference between the two. It seems the Inquisition has learned that too many Marranos are secretly practicing the Jewish religion and traditions, thus its interest in purifying them. Another factor is that many Marranos hold important high positions in the government. This causes jealousy and hate. I'm told that in 1449, long before we were born, there were serious riots in Toledo against the Marranos. It was then the government and other institutions enacted the statutes of the 'purity of blood'. Apparently there were many discussions and arguments within the Church itself. A number of clergies said that once a Jew has been baptized, he was no longer a Jew. Others said a Jew could never be pure of his evil characteristics. The latter must have won because the Church and the Inquisition are constantly growing in power.

What I'm afraid of is that their power would grow even further, to a new level, higher than the Crown and its government. Should that happen, we are doomed.

Just as one of our ancestors migrated to Castile in 958, why don't we leave this country and settle elsewhere? Our family certainly has the financial resources. There must be other places on earth where we could live in peace. What makes our people want to stay here? Do you have any idea?

My mother is not well these days. Both my father and I are deeply concerned about her. How are your parents holding up? Please tell me about the school you are attending. Everything in our Hebrew school remains the same.

Yours as always,
David

Sunday, 3rd of May, 1475

Dear brother David,

Our correspondence delights me endlessly. I hope it will never stop. However, I'm developing the feeling that these good days will come to an end as the Inquisition tightens its activities against the Jews, Marranos and Conversos. One of our teacher priests keeps reminding us almost daily about the need to purify the people of Aragon and Castile. He says it's God will that the people are completely free of sinners and Jews, who are the emissaries of the Devil.

He is right about one thing. I am going to be the Devil who will haunt his life to death when the time comes. Where does the Church pick up such idiotic ideas? The priest tells the class that Jews use the blood of Christian babies they steal and slaughter to make Matza for their Passover holiday, and soap. Can you imagine such fabrication? How can teachers stand in front of innocent children and feed them such lies? If any one should be accused of being the Devil, they're the ones. I had to bite my tongue so hard it actually bled. I was ready to explode, but managed to control myself. I remembered what my father told me. "Now is the time to be brave, now is the time to swallow pride, for it will give us the spiritual and physical strength to continue."

My father is right. Had I responded, I would have been thrown in jail, and who knows what might have happened to me? What flashed through my mind was, "Control yourself, and you'll be around to fight them." I almost blew it. You cannot imagine how difficult it is to listen to this garbage day in and day out. The masses on the street, as you certainly know, are illiterate and totally uneducated. They swallow statements made by their priests who are not ashamed to use Church platforms for passing these deceitful lies. The truth is that we Jews are far cleaner in thought and behavior than they will ever be.

At school we are fed with the New Testament every day - in fact most of the day. There is virtually no other study than scriptures. Everything we study relates to the Catholic Church and its gospels. What I find fascinating is that none of those gospels preached deceit. How can they be so hypocritical? And how can they teach such nasty lies? I am young and very inexperienced by comparison to our learned Rabbis. I've never heard any Rabbi say a single bad word about Christianity. Have you?

It's great suffering for me to continue in this Catholic school. Regrettably, I have no alternative, for I have to honor my father. I will continue in silence and work hard to beat any other student in the study of Catholicism. I will eventually use every bit of knowledge against them. I'm filled with desire for vengeance, and, by God, I will let them have it one day.

Last Sunday after mass, the most disgusting hour I have to spend, we strolled along the waterfront. I kept looking at ships anchored off the port of Barcelona. I felt jealous. I wanted to be on one of them and sail away. I was watching my father, who speaks very little lately, and felt that similar thoughts were going through his mind. My mother is also depressed. I wonder how long we'll be able to live double lives? Even though I'm depressed internally, on the outside I'm quite cheerful because I'm developing a plan for the future. I've never been more determined in my life than I am this day. I swear to you that the day will come when I'll lead the fight against the Church and the Inquisition.

I almost forgot. In yesterday's class we were told that two Marranos were sentenced to death because they were heard making blasphemous statements against the Church. Can you believe this? What Marrano in his right mind would make blasphemous statements in public? All they're doing is instilling fear into innocent people. The frightened and intimidated convert, and the irony is that such Conversos are still not accepted as Christians. What an exercise in futility!

I miss you very much and hope some day soon we'll be together.

Yours,
Reuven

Saturday, 30th of May, 1475

Dear brother Reuven,

Your letter of the 3rd, which I just received, was a real shocker. I'm appalled at the teachings of the Catholic school. It is beyond my understanding why the Church considers such malice. I'm sure the Pope and other members of the Papal hierarchy have a pretty good knowledge of our religion. The Jewish problem, as it's called, is not new. What I believe to be the real intention of the Church is to convert all people to Catholicism by any means possible. I discussed this subject with my father and our Rabbi extensively. Both believe that originally, as Christianity developed and grew, it encountered people in the old Roman Empire who were heathen. It could very well be that those heathen people got attracted to Christianity because Rome was on a decline and there was no one else to worship. Christianity filled a growing vacuum. Eventually, Catholicism was introduced and somehow the Catholics began preying on the masses. With time, as they grew further, it became a passion to convert everybody to Christianity. The Jews had a well-established religion long before Christianity and its people did not possess the emptiness, or the necessity, to replace their faith. However, the zealous New Christians of the time found an easy prey, and as they kept on growing, they developed the thinking that they had to convert every one by hook or by crook. What we are witnessing today is the enhanced continuation of the early concept. This enhancement gave birth to radical and fanatic methods to accomplish their goal.

I was horrified when the Rabbi told me about Yochanan Avitai, father of four. His family converted last year and his school age children attend one of the local Catholic schools. He was arrested a few days ago by the Inquisition and charged with heresy. He was sentenced to twenty years in prison with hard labor. No one knows where he is. For all intents and purposes the community believes he is dead. His family was left without any means of support. Money is being collected for their survival. The Rabbi said that many Morranos and Jews are in various Inquisition jails throughout Castile.

I'm beginning to get concerned about my father. He tells me the Crown needs him since he supplies some of the most needed materials for its war effort against the remnants of the Moors. I questioned him about the future; "What happens when the Castilians drive the Moors out and they no longer need your services?" His answer was, "God will guide me."

I believe in God with all my heart, but I can't see how he will help my father when he isn't helping any other Jew. Somehow I have the same feeling our Hebrews had in Egypt when they were falling under the pressure of hard labor and slavery. The Bible tells us they were crying out to God for help and he did not hear them. How much longer are we earmarked for torture, persecution, intimidation and life of fear?

It's interesting to note that while the Muslim Moors occupied Castile and Aragon, Jews lived in relative peace, as Jews live in peace in most Muslim Mediterranean countries. The Jews always were, and still are the greatest contributors to economic stability and growth. They pay the highest taxes, and are responsible citizens. The Christians, on the other hand, who want to convert the Jews and the Moors to Catholicism, exploit the peasants and the masses. Animals are treated better. They claim that by conversion the converted will become better human beings and the whole society will become pure. It is absolutely amazing that the Church is more interested in the nobles, landowners, and the Crown than in the masses. You only have to look at the living conditions of the masses. They live like pigs while nobility lives in unheard of luxury and comfort. The hypocrisy of the men of the cloth is beyond understanding.

It is the Church and the Inquisition that incite the masses to attack the Jews and loot their properties. They are told Jews are responsible for their plight. The trouble is that the masses are superstitious and ignorant. They believe every word coming out of the Church. Until the masses are better educated, we will see no change. Do you agree?

As you can see, I'm getting caught in your net. There is no question in my mind that change is needed. Regrettably, we'll have to fight for that change. Talking and promoting change will be considered heresy and blasphemous by the Inquisition. The Holy Office recognizes only one change and that is purification of the blood of all citizens. Its mind is set on conversion and creating a pure Catholic society. This will not happen in our time or any other.

It is a well-known fact that the great majority of Conversos practice Jewish religious traditions in secret. The Inquisition cannot fight hundreds of thousands of people. They can torture some here and some there. They can hang a few, they can burn a few, but there is no way they can get to everyone. I believe that they know it, and that's why they are using methods of unheard cruelty. They want to submit the entire non-Catholic population to a life of intimidation and fear so that they convert. This, of course, is not the end either. The clergy claim that those who converted will never be rid of their impure characteristics. If that is the case, what is the point of conversion?

It's extremely confusing. My father and our Rabbi cannot understand why I've become so inquisitive lately. The Rabbi thought my questions were very good ones, but felt bad he couldn't provide me with answers that made sense.

Please write as soon as you can. I'm extremely interested in what's going on in your school and life.

Yours,
David

Sunday, 22nd of June, 1475

My dear brother David,

You're certainly doing your homework. I'm very proud of you. Unfortunately, I'm limited. I have to depend on my father who hasn't been in a good mood since his conversion. He is very depressed. He keeps telling my mother and me life is not worth living any more. I suggested he leave Aragon.

"You talk as though you want me to leave without you," he said.

"That is absolutely so," I responded.

"I'm not following you at all. If I leave, you and your mother will have to join me," he said.

"My mother can join you, but I'm not leaving. As soon as I'm able, I will step out and fight this cruel regime, this Inquisition," I declared.

"And you believe I'll let you do this?"

"This is the one and only time in my life I will not honor your order. I vowed to dedicate my life to fight the barbaric Inquisition and the Crown if necessary, and I will keep my vow."

"I can have our Rabbi release you from your vow before we leave, if we decide to leave."

"There isn't a Rabbi in the world who can release me from my vow. I told you before, there is a power in me I can't explain. This power tells me that I will lead the revolt against the Inquisition."

"You are insane, my son. You don't know what you're talking about. The Inquisition is a government in itself. It possesses power over too many individuals in every office--Crown or government. They use the same tactics against their own people--frightening them with burning in hell and the Devil."

"Father, you and the rest of the world cannot convince me to change my mind. I am terribly sorry I'm talking to you in this unpleasant manner. I truly feel terribly about it. However, someone has to make a stand and I'm destined to do just that. One day you will hail me for what I have done."

"If you don't get killed in the process, and I live long enough," he said with much sorrow.

"Father, one day you'll be very proud of me, and I promise that I will not get killed. This strength, this message that I'm getting is telling me I will succeed. I know I will succeed."

"Son, I love you too much. It's your mother I'm worried about. I don't know how she'll take all this. I admit I'm entertaining the thought of

running away. I don't know how much longer I'll be able to play this game. If I decide to escape this miserable country, I will leave you a substantial amount of money. Our family has a huge fortune in Egypt, and I can always receive my share."

"I'm very proud of you, father," I said. "If you leave, I'll continue my studies in the Catholic school. I'll tell them I refused to leave with you because I want to become a true Catholic. I'll play the greatest act of these times. I need to learn everything about them so I can beat them from within."

"I'm at a loss for words. Whatever you do, may God bless you and be with you."

We stopped talking. My father was lost in thought. I've never seen him so depressed. I'll keep prodding my parents to leave Barcelona. The problem is I don't know where they should be going. The decision to leave and the destination is entirely up to him. He knows more about the world of business than I do. I decided to push my luck.

"Father, you said the family has a large fortune in Egypt. Are the Jews safe there?"

"As far as I know the Jews have no problems in Egypt. No one is trying to convert them and they are treated as any other people. In fact, it's interesting that you bring up Egypt. Alexandria, which is the main port-city, has a mixed population of Egyptians, Greeks, Italians, Arab traders and Jews. There is no known discrimination against anyone."

"I suggest you go there. I cannot see a reason for your continuing to live in this country under conditions which take away your dignity and pride," I insisted.

"I'll certainly think about it," he replied.

Please forgive me if I'm repeating myself, but I can't seem to shake off my parents' tragedy. It's the conversion to Catholicism that is killing them. Even though I hate the forced situation I find myself in, I'm far less depressed because I have a cause to follow. My father said something of great interest. He said if he departs Aragon, he'd leave me a large sum of money. I need to think hard where to hide it. It will have to be accessible. It goes without saying that our distinguished authorities would love to get their hands on it.

I'll write more next time. It has been a long and difficult day. I miss you terribly.

Yours,
Reuven

Thursday, 17th of July, 1475

Dear brother Reuven,

Last Sunday, a mob of about a hundred people attacked our central synagogue in Toledo. They came rushing in through the front door carrying axes and other iron instruments and began breaking up the benches. Our Rabbi pleaded with them to stop, but they didn't. Someone struck him down. He managed to get up, walked over to the wooden structure which holds the Torah scrolls, and stood in front of it. The mob continued to demolish everything in sight. As they drew near him, someone shouted at the Rabbi to get out of the way. He opened the door so the Torah scrolls could be seen, and thundered, "These are the Books of God, which Jesus studied and prayed. He will put his curse on you for blasphemy." The mob stopped in its tracks. Someone said something, and they departed in total silence.

There were about twenty of us boys in the adjacent room studying the Talmud when this occurred. The noise of the breakage brought us to the side door and we witnessed the whole thing. I was shaken and fearful for the Rabbi who stood gallantly in front of the Torahs. I saw some kids my age among the adults, and thinking of you in the midst of the chaos I decided to talk to at least one of them. I quickly ran out the rear door, circled the synagogue building, and caught up with them as they were leaving. I recognized one of the boys and called him over.

"The priest sent us after concluding the morning's mass," he answered my question.

I'm wondering whether peaceful Toledo is about to change. After answering my question, he ran off. I ran back and found the Rabbi standing in front of the Torah scrolls praying. The other children decided to go home. I waited until the Rabbi stopped and approached him in silence. He grabbed me and held me close. Finally he said a few words I couldn't understand. He was still in shock. The synagogue looked like a battle zone. Everything in sight was demolished with the exception of the House of the Torah and the eternal light above it.

It's so difficult to understand how people can do a thing like this. How can a priest, using his church platform to remind people of things like humility and love deliver an inciting sermon that drive his people into acts of violence? Isn't a sermon intended to remind people of humility, love, and the like? I went home and told my father about the attack. He ran out saying he was going to check on the Rabbi. Time for the evening prayer arrived and he had not returned. My mother was pacing the floor, looking out every minute, but he was nowhere in sight. We were very worried. I offered to go to the synagogue, but she wouldn't let me. In fact, I was afraid to leave her alone in the house. Father did not return until midmorning the following day.

"As I arrived at the synagogue, I was arrested by Inquisition investigators and taken to the City Prison," he said. "I tried to find out why they were arresting me only to be slapped in the face. I was told to keep my mouth shut."

"Are you all right?" my mother asked. "I was worried. I didn't sleep all night. David wanted to go out and look for you but I wouldn't let him. Why did they arrest you? You haven't done anything wrong!"

Father took her in his arms and hugged her. "There's nothing to worry about. They kept me in a cell for a few hours. One of the Inquisition priests came to see me at 5 o'clock this morning and gave me a personal sermon. He said I should consider conversion to Catholicism, because my God will not help me. For the world to continue, all people have to purify their souls under the umbrella of the Catholic Church. I told him I would think about it. He left and I remained in the cell without any food or water. A few hours later one of the guards unlocked the door and told me I was free, so here I am."

"This doesn't sound like your worries are over," I said.
"They need me. Don't worry," he proclaimed.
"I'd like to show you something," I said. I went to my room and brought all the letters you had written me. Your letters were kept in chronological order. "Please read these letters." He made himself comfortable on the sofa and began reading. My mother wanted to say something but I pulled her out of the room.
A while later he called me. "Son, close the door behind you. We need to talk. I don't want your mother in on this conversation."
"What is it, father?"
"First and foremost, I want you to destroy these letters immediately. If the inquisitors search this house, we are doomed. Use your mother's wood oven in the kitchen to burn them. Do it now and then return here," he ordered.
I rushed to the kitchen and burned your letters. Tears were running down my cheeks. I love every one of them. You cannot imagine how much your letters mean to me. But thinking about my father's orders, I quickly came to the conclusion that he was right. Now that he was arrested, there is no telling what comes next. It's obvious the Inquisition checks with the Crown to ascertain that persons of great value to the State do not get lost. The Crown

still has some authority over the Inquisition. The question is when the reverse will occur. I returned to the living room.

"From now on you burn every letter as soon as you've read it. Is that clear? I don't need to tell you the danger these letters pose. Reuven and his family are Conversos. I doubt I'll ever submit to conversion. I would rather die." He stared straight into my eyes.

"Father, what are you saying!" I cried. "You can't be serious. Look at Reuven's parents. It's more important to stay alive right now."

"I realize how this is stressful for you," he said. "It is for me too, but I will not convert. Reuven's father sees things differently. Each person has his own vision on life. Either way, I still have time. The situation in Toledo is far better than in most places due to the fact that the Crown's main offices and government seat are here. All of us have a great deal to think about. Meanwhile, I want you to be very careful. Above all, do not talk with other pupils in school about any of this. All of us must keep a watchful eye on the authorities."

"No one knows about my correspondence with Reuven, and I'll keep it that way. Zevulun knows about the letters, but not their contents. He is just the company's courier."

"I am not worried about Zevulun. He has been a trusted employee of ours for many years. I'll have to advise him about the letters so in case he's stopped, he deals with them as he does with the money," father said.

My heart was very heavy and I couldn't continue talking. I'm sure he was relieved when I asked to be excused. I know he feels awful. It seems all of us are in a terrible predicament. I can't imagine why we don't pick up and leave.

Please write soon. I'm desperate.

Yours,
David

Saturday, 16th of August, 1475

Dear brother David,

I feel bad it took me so long to write. I was locked up in the Church basement for a week. I was punished because I didn't want to cooperate with my priest teacher. Two weeks ago I was called to the priest's office. He was unusually sweet to me and offered candy. I refused, saying sweet things disagree with my digestive system. He started by complimenting me on the excellent work I've been doing, pointing out specific homework assignments. He added that my work surpassed all other students in my class and that he was particularly pleased I recognized Jesus as the true Lord Savior. I was wondering what he was buttering me up for, and finally it came. He wanted me to confirm to the class that Jews use the blood of stolen Christian children for religious purposes. The conversation went like this:

"My dear Mark" (I forgot to tell you they changed my name to "Mark" when I was enrolled in the Catholic school), I'm the happiest priest in Barcelona because you've recognized Jesus. Your writings in school and your prayers are truly heart warming. You have become a true Christian, and as such, I need your help." He paused for a moment. My mind was racing in different directions all at once. "I'd like you to confirm to the class, when I ask you, that it is true Jews steal little Christian boys, slaughter them, and use their blood for various religious rituals."

"I'm a true believer in Jesus," I declared in response. "I'm convinced beyond any doubt that he is our Lord and Master. It was Jesus who taught his pupils to love each other, to be honest, and abide by the Ten Commandments. I cannot lie. I will always speak the truth because that is what he wanted. True, I was born of the Jewish faith, but I have never seen or heard of any such atrocities as you describe. I will do anything for the Church but lie. It is absolutely against my conscience to speak untruths."

"You claim you love Jesus, yet you won't do what I ask of you for him? I'm shocked. It is Jesus who wants all of us to join his faith and be pure in our blood and soul."
"I don't understand the logic," I said. "Our Lord Jesus who taught love, charity, and purity could not have possibly wanted any of us to lie, not even for him. There must be better ways to reach the masses than through lies."

"I will not discuss this any further with you. You have just proven you're not a true Christian. I will have to punish you. You'll be placed in the Church's cellar for one week and remain there in the dark. You will meet with your confessor once a day during this week. You will also be flogged twelve times every morning before breakfast." He called one of his assistants and gave him instructions.

I was locked up as he instructed for one full week. I was flogged each morning and had to spend time with my confessor.
"Please confess your sins, my child," he began.
"I have nothing to confess, for I have not sinned. I was asked to tell lies in the name of the Church. Had I lied, as instructed, only then would I have committed sin," I said firmly every single day.
"My child," the Confessor said gently, "The Church is our life. Jesus wants all of us to be pure. We have to do everything in our power to make his wish come true."
"I'm convinced that if Jesus were here this moment, he would agree with me," I responded. "If he were here, he would not pursue his mission in life the way the Church and the Inquisition do. He would be ashamed of you."
"You are blasphemous of the Church," the Confessor snapped. "Do you know how blasphemous people are punished by the Inquisition?"
"I heard. My father told me," I said. "But to me it is blasphemous to lie."

The week was over and the priest didn't do anything else to me. He must have bragged about my outstanding work to his superiors and was embarrassed to suddenly show failure. It could also be he realized that forced lies were not the best tool. It's hard to say. The point is, I survived, and I shall continue in my quest.
When the week was over, I was permitted to go home to my"Catholic parents", as the priest put it. My insides were turning over with laughter. I'm learning to be an actor, and I think my acting is superb.

I was very sorry to read in your letter about the destruction in the Toledo synagogue and your father's arrest. Just as I thought, the Inquisition is gathering strength and power. Who knows what they'll do next. I doubt there'll be a place to hide in this country. As I've written before, my father is extremely depressed. I'm encouraging him to leave Aragon. I hope he will for his sake. I know it's very difficult for him to leave me behind. I'll continue to work on him. I hope I'll succeed.
I came across some interesting letters in the Church library. A monk living in Cordoba wrote these letters about two hundred years ago. Of course, I only have one side of the correspondence. I didn't find the answering letters. Cordoba, as you surely know, was the capital city of Andalusia, and among the first territories to be conquered by the Berber invaders in 711. The main theme of the discussions in the letters was conversion to Islam. It appeared certain segments in the Muslim government were pushing for conversion to Islam while others were tolerant of the Christians and Jews. Muslim citizens were exempt from taxes, but all others carried

the burden of taxation. Both Christianity and Islam were relatively young religions at the time and the letters didn't mention forced conversions. I wonder what makes the Christians so ardent in their quest to convert the rest of the world to Christianity. Jews developed their religion long before Jesus and Mohammad, and never tried or forced their foreign citizens to convert. In fact, the Bible tells us of the importance to treat non-Jews well. It is explicitly discussed in the story of the exodus from Egypt.

I shall bid farewell and will look forward to your letter.
Yours,
Reuven

Monday, 22nd of September, 1475

Dear Brother Reuven,

Your ordeal with the priest touched a nerve in my heart. We knew all along the Church was lying. The question is how to convince the masses otherwise? The problem, as I see it, is that the masses are totally uneducated, illiterate, and superstitious. They look up to their priests whom they believe represent the Almighty, and swallow every word they say. It's indeed tragic that the Catholic Church feels the necessity to convert every person on earth. What gives one group the right to force another? Aren't we all made in the image of the Almighty, as the Bible tells us? Aren't all people equal in the eyes of God?

At least the week in the cellar passed and is now behind you. The only question running through my mind is what your priest will do next. "Once a liar, always a liar," I heard my father say. I suggest you continue to be an exemplary student. It might throw him off.

The situation in Toledo is worsening. The Inquisition has arrested a number of Jews for different periods of time. One is Victor Hacohen, an old friend of my parents. I overheard them talking a few days ago. Mr. Hacohen was tortured for six days in a row. The Inquisition built special chambers in the basement of their building and equipped them with various machines which inflict intolerable pain. My father said that their victims are tortured three or four times a day, day in and day out. At some point the victim breaks down and confesses to anything or agrees to convert. It's a shame Jesus is not alive to see how his disciples operate in his name. If you think about it for a moment, the priests, who are the torturers, and their victims both lie to achieve their goals. In my view, the priests will have to answer to God some day. They not only lie to themselves and others, but also inflict undue and undeserved pain, suffering, and punishment upon innocent people.

Mr. Hacohen was thrown out of the Inquisition building onto the street. He lay there for hours. By pure luck a passerby recognized him and alerted his family. There is no medicine that can help his pain. He is completely bruised and vandalized, physically and mentally. My father went to visit him last night. "Father, how is Mr. Hacohen?" I asked.
"How do you know I went to visit him?"
"I overheard your conversation with mother."

"Aren't you forgetting your manners?"

"Father, we are living in a time of rage. You can't keep me out of it. I have to know what's going on, and I have to become involved."

"You're so young and so innocent... I want you to stay that way."

"I witnessed the destruction of our synagogue. I was right there! The Rabbi was lucky he didn't get killed. The Inquisition arrests and tortures people, my relatives in Barcelona have converted, like thousands of others, and you're telling me to remain innocent?" I protested.

"Attacks and pogroms against the Jews have taken place over the past thousand years in varying degrees. We'll overcome this one too."

"I can't believe what I'm hearing, father. It seems to me our world is falling apart. Yesterday Mr. Hacohen - tomorrow it could very well be you!"

"What do you expect me to do?"

"Maybe a delegation of Jewish leaders should ask for an audience with the Queen. You have to try to convince her the Church's methods won't lead to the change it seeks."

"That's a pretty good idea," he said. "I'll suggest it to the Chief Rabbi."

"I heard you say a number of Jews were arrested. You seem to know Mr. Hacohen. Who are the others? Their families may need help."

"This is very thoughtful of you, my son. I'll attend to it immediately."

My father left the house. I was happy to have given him some ideas. He returned a few hours later.

"All of the arrested were released after days of torture when they agreed to repent -- I'm not clear as to whom and for what. None of them was able to hold a conversation. They were in uncontrollable pain. I asked the Rabbi to form a group of women who would check on the families of the tortured and provide whatever help is needed. The Rabbi also said he had sent an official request for an audience with Queen Isabella. He and you must think alike."

"Let's pray our Rabbi will succeed in his mission," I said.

In a few days we'll begin to celebrate Rosh Hashana. I will pray hard and ask God to help his people. I feel bad that you can't celebrate our holidays in the open. How terrible it must be for your parents. Write soon.

Yours,
David

Tuesday, 28th of October, 1475

Dear brother David,

Our business courier, Zevulun ben Yishai, told my father his runs to Barcelona wouldn't be as frequent. He claims soldiers of different noble estates are searching wagons for gold and jewelry. He always suspected robbery and had a special compartment built in the body of the wagon. In that compartment he carries money and documents and most probably our letters.

It's been over two months since I've written to you. So much has happened since my last letter. I wish you were around the corner. I miss you so much. I'm very tired of playing this Catholic game even though there are times when I enjoy the success of my acting. As long as I'm allowed to sleep at home, I can see my parents and enjoy their company. So far, they've been good Catholics on the outside. They completed their education in a brand new religion and are going to their confessors regularly. I, too, have to go to my confessor -- at least once a week. The funny thing is I truly have nothing to confess for all I do is study, eat, and sleep. Had I confessed my future plans I would have been put to death at the stake. The latest news is that lately persons sentenced to death by the Inquisition will be burned alive. They have a new name for it -- "Auto-de-fe." My father told me a number of people have been sentenced to death, and it looks as though harsh sentences are becoming more common. He also said some of the victims are being strangled first. Can you imagine killing somebody in cold blood? How does a killer sleep at night? I know I sound different. When I lead the revolution, I'm sure people will have to be killed. However, I'm not planning to kill innocent ones. My victims will have to have been connected with the Inquisition's killing machine and the Church.

At this moment killing disgusts me, but when the time comes, I'll be vicious, I promise you that. The shame that engulfed me since I was baptized has not left for a single moment. I feel violated. I've never known shame before, but now I live with it day and night. My parents, too, especially my father, are shamed. He made the decision to convert for reasons we discussed before, but I believe his decision will kill him unless he leaves Aragon and settles in a country where he can practice Judaism in the open. The clandestine Jewish activities make it twice as difficult because he has to watch the windows and the doors. Inquisition investigators are constantly in Jewish and Marrano neighborhoods, searching. On occasion they burst into someone's house, and from time to time you see them dragging people away. Some never return.

Life at home is not the way it used to be. The joy and happiness that were always in the air are gone. We don't talk much. My father is depressed most of the time except for the moments he prays in silence. The only time I see a smile on his face is when he's in a trance. It's heart breaking to watch him. The more my mother tries to console him, the worse he gets. He doesn't want to be reminded.

Coincidentally, your letter was delivered when I was visiting my father in his office. For some reason, our school closed after our midday meal. I found him alone and decided it was the opportunity I was waiting for.

"Father, are you surprised to see me?"

"Oh! Yes, my son, come on in."

"Our priest stopped classes at noon and sent us home without any explanation. I decided to pay you a visit."

"That's very nice of you. Come sit next to me."

I sat down and took his hand.

"Father, I've been looking for this opportunity for some time. I don't want to talk at home because I don't want mother to be hurt any more than she already is. I know she's not taking the situation very well. Actually, I sense deterioration in both of you. I frankly don't understand why you should suffer."

"Son," he interrupted me, "You are the reason. We feel we can't leave this country without you."

"Suppose I promise to join you as soon as I've accomplished my mission. Would that make a difference?"

"What do you mean by 'as soon'? Won't it take years? You're just going on fourteen."

"That's true, but I plan to get started in about a year's time. It could be sooner if the Inquisition enhances its program as they seem to be doing."

"What program, son?"

"Torturing and killing Jews. Father, please don't question my plans. I have it all mapped out. I want you to leave Aragon. It will facilitate my actions and will keep you and mother safe."

"Why would your actions create danger for us?"

"Because I'll have to leave school. At that moment you'll face great danger. The Inquisition may come after you, looking for me. You may be arrested and tortured."

"You have it all planned out, don't you?"

"Yes father, I do. I want you to leave Aragon. I'll miss you terribly, but it will be the root of my strength to do what I have to."

"I've never seen you this determined," he remarked, "and at such a young age."

"Age has very little to do with this. In fact, my age will probably help me because they'll never suspect a young boy could do the things I plan to do."

"You frighten me, son. But I must admit there has to be some mysterious reason for all of this. I'm beginning to feel your intentions. Let's say your mother and I leave Aragon. What will you do?"

"After you've left, I'll tell my priest that when I got home, I discovered you'd left the country. Then I'll tell him I decided to become a monk and ask to be placed in a monastery. I'm sure he'll be happy to comply. Enroute to the monastery, I'll disappear, or soon after, depending on circumstances."

"And what will you live on?" he fretted.

"I'm counting on you for that. You told me you would leave a large sum of money. If you do that, I'll be able to get by easily, and you'll know I won't go hungry."

"I'd like to discuss this with your mother. I promise to speak to her tonight. Stay away from the drawing room this evening until I call you."

I was elated. I knew I was on the right track and at the starting point of my mission. That evening, after supper, I went to my room and waited. I was called about two hours later.

"Sit down, son," my father ordered. My mother was crying. She tried to hide her tears unsuccessfully. "Your mother and I decided to leave Aragon. I'll leave for you five thousand gold ducats. This amount should suffice you for a lifetime. In my opinion, whatever you're planning to do should not last more than a few years. When your operation is over, either we come back, or you join us. Will you promise us?"

"I'll swear to it, father," I said. "Where can you hide the money so it's safe and I can reach it?"

"I have an idea," he said. "We'll place the metal box with the money inside the grave of one of my employees who died last year. Do you remember Juan de la Rosa, the man who has worked in our company since my father's days? His grave is in the cemetery adjacent to the monastery of San Christopher. This monastery is located on the hill west of the city, about an hour by wagon. I'll take you there tomorrow night, immediately after supper, when it's dark," he said.

"Thank you, father," I said. "One day you'll be able to claim that the calamity of the Inquisition was terminated by your action." I bent over to kiss him and my mother. I had a lump in my throat for a few minutes, temporarily at a loss for words. David, the decision has been made.

Tomorrow night I'll travel with my father to the San Christopher cemetery and all the monetary arrangements will be made. Our revolution will be properly financed.

Before leaving the drawing room I asked my father about the business. He said he'd ask his uncle Joseph to take over for as long as he can. He also said he would be writing a letter to your father.

I'll keep you informed. If for some reason you don't hear from me in three months, I'll leave a note wrapped in oilpaper behind the tombstone of Juan de la Rosa as to my whereabouts. The note will be buried in the ground. Dig for it.

I love you endlessly and can hardly wait for the day you and I will lead the revolt against the Inquisition.

Yours as ever,
Reuven

P.S.   Do not write to me until you receive my next letter with specific instructions.

Once my parents leave, I'll advise you how to communicate with me.

Friday, 28th of November, 1475

My dear and beloved brother David,

I have great news for you. My parents left for Alexandria a week ago on a freight ship. They did not take any of their possessions except some clothing and money. Gold ducat coins were placed in bottles labeled 'red wine' and a shipment of wine left for Alexandria on the same ship. My father gave power of attorney to Zevulun to sell his house, and the proceeds will be delivered to you. Save it in a safe place and don't tell anyone about it - not even your parents.

At my request, I was placed in the San Christopher monastery. I rushed to my priest hysterically after my parents' departure. I told him I was abandoned and my decision was to become a monk. I evoked Jesus' name many times and declared I wanted to sacrifice my life to the Lord. Within two days my transfer was arranged and I'm presently the happiest monk alive. The only problem in the monastery is that I have to be up for prayer at precisely 5 o'clock in the morning. Being young, I'm not required to attend midnight mass. How delightful! Also, you'll be pleased to know that five thousand gold dukats are safely in their hiding place behind the tombstone, in a metal box. I suggest we place messages to each other inside this box when necessary.

Please tell Zevulun you wish to speak to him every time he delivers a letter. It's imperative that you know when his runs terminate. I must be able to communicate with you, as you're my only link to the outside world.

This is going to be a short letter - I don't have much time. I told the friar in charge of the monastery that my family donated a wagon and a horse and I wanted to deliver the gift in person. That's how I got into Barcelona this morning. I'm planning to become their deliveryman. Hopefully, they'll agree. I think I'll have various privileges due to my age, which I plan to use to the limit.

Fortunately, they allow visitors at the monastery. I've asked Zevulun to visit me each time he comes to Barcelona. I told him to be sure to bring useful donations for the monks who have nothing but the robes they wear. As you know, Zevulun is very creative.

> *Yours, with great hopes for the future,*
> *Reuven*

Saturday, 13th of December, 1475

My dear brother Reuven,

My anxiety is now mostly over since you advised me of your parents' departure. I'm also pleased that you're situated in the monastery and away from the deceitful priest. Your information will be kept in my mind and heart forever. You can count on it. I hope and pray Zevulun will be with us for a long time.

Today is our birthday and I'm thinking much of you. It is a day I shall celebrate in my heart, for we are apart. Tonight I'll say a special prayer for you. I will pray that you and I unite soon.

The past year has witnessed many events. I'm particularly pleased both of us have come to recognize the reality of the Jewish condition in its true light. Both our parents shielded us from the true morality of the Church and its Inquisition. Our eyes have been opened to the suffering of our people. I am delighted that you developed in me the desire to fight the injustice. While I'm not a fighter by nature, I've come to the conclusion that someone has to fight for the rights of our people. Fighting is not only done with a sword, but also by the mind. The two of us will fight and succeed in our mission - otherwise our people will suffer forever.

My father is more on edge since he received your father's note. I believe your parents' departure raised many thoughts in his mind, as the situation in Toledo is worsening. I know he got your father's note the same day I received your letter. That evening I had a chat with him.

"Father, Reuven wrote that his parents left Barcelona for Alexandria. I'm shocked."

"So am I," he said in a somber voice. "My entire world seems to be falling apart. Where is Reuven, and why didn't he leave with his parents?"

"I don't have the answer to that," I lied. "Why is your world falling apart?"

"Because of what is going on in Toledo. I fear that we'll soon become the target of the Inquisition. Lately they are beginning to focus their attention on the well to do Jews in this city. And, as I told you in the past, I will not convert. They cannot force me."

"In that event, why wait? Leave Castile, and go elsewhere. Why wait for the axe to fall?" I said.

"It's really difficult to explain, for I cannot resolve my feelings. Maybe I'm waiting for the axe to fall, in which event I will make up my mind," he said.

"Isn't this rather odd for a successful businessman? You make many business decisions, yet you can't decide on a crucial issue that involves your life and the lives of those you love?"

"Perhaps that's the main reason I was looking for," he said. "What will all the people who depend on me for a living do if I'm gone?"

"Father, this is not a normal situation. You do what you have to do. I'm sure if you left, most of your trusted employees will leave with you, or soon after. And perhaps you should approach the closest ones to discuss this matter," I suggested.

"I need to think about it. It's quite complex to pick up and go. There are shipments of merchandise on the way to Castile, and there are obligations of all kinds I need to keep. I am a man of my word," he pointed out.

"Father, this is not the time to place your integrity in front of reality. Jews have been converting by the thousands. Many have left and many have been imprisoned for indefinite periods. Also, quite a few have disappeared altogether. You keep telling me the situation has worsened. If in your view the condition of the Jews and the Marranos will only get bleaker, then wait for what?"

"I don't have an answer, son," he said. "I have a great deal of thinking to do. I know I still have time. And, by the way, our Rabbi had his audience with Queen Isabella today. I plan to visit him tomorrow morning."

There wasn't much else I could do or say. I went to bed and prayed. I'm going to continue this letter after I find out about the Rabbi's visit with the Queen.

Sunday, 14th of December, 1475

The Rabbi reported a very grim meeting with Queen Isabella. He said that no sooner had he begun to speak than Tomas de Torquemada, the Queen's confessor, Catholic guide, and counselor, interrupted the meeting and spoke harshly to him. He accused the Jews of blasphemy, of being impure people who believe in the devil. The Rabbi reminded him that Jesus was a Jew and that Jews contributed more to Castile than any other minority. He tried to tell him that converting people was a myth - people believe in their heart in the faith they were born with -- and reminded him of the Church's problem with the Marranos.

Torquemada became more offensive. He told the Queen that as a devout Catholic she shouldn't be found so close to a Jew who is none other than the Devil. The Queen got up from her throne and walked away at Torquemada's insistence. The Rabbi left soon after. His mission was a total failure. My father thinks the Rabbi's visit will probably enhance the

Inquisition's actions against the Jews. It's so difficult to understand Torquemada.

As soon as my father reported about the failed audience with the Queen, I said, "Father, I believe you now have the answer to your dilemma."

"I'm going to wait a few days and see what happens," he left the room.

He probably didn't want to continue discussing this miserable subject. I can't blame him. I'm very upset that he's disturbed and afraid to take action. I can't penetrate his mind -- God knows I tried. I'll continue writing when I know of Zevulun's next trip to Barcelona.

Friday, 26th of December, 1475

About noontime yesterday, Christmas Day, hundreds of people, the greatest mob ever seen, descended on our Jewish quarter. The mob went from house to house and systematically destroyed everything in sight. Items of value were looted, and a number of houses were burned. Many Jews were killed or injured. Fortunately, we were not home. My father must have had a premonition and took my mother and me out. The carriage took us to the neighboring village of Azulas, which overlooks the central mountains. We settled in one of the local inns, empty at this time of year. I hid this letter on my person and that's why it was saved. In reality we didn't know what happened until we returned home this evening.

Our house was not touched. My father could not explain why. Later he found out that the houses of the other prominent Jews were not destroyed or looted either.

"Isn't this signaling something?" I queried.

"It certainly does, my son," he said. "I'm not sure yet what it signals, but it certainly looks that way."

"Are you going to sit around and wait until it's too late?"

"The first thing we're going to do is make sure our money is well hidden so that each of us can have access to it if and when necessary," he said. "The dilemma is where to find a safe place."

"I have an idea," I said. "At the inn in Azulas I was wandering around the building since it was empty. In the attic I found an opening in the floor which could serve as a safe place. A metal box could easily slide underneath the floor and no one will ever know it's there. I would also like to suggest that to be on the safe side you place money in three different locations, just like Abraham did."

"I like your thinking, son. Let's think of two other places."

We sat in silence, trying to find a solution. Suddenly my mother suggested the stone covered ground next to the water cistern in the back yard of our house. We walked out and checked the area.

"Perfect," my father said; "we now have two places, with one left to be discovered."

"Perhaps the third is the money you take with you when you leave Castile," I suggested.

"You won't relent, will you? Why is it you keep pushing me to leave Castile?"

"Because I see trouble looming. The onslaught of the mob followed almost immediately the failed audience with the queen. It's sending a very clear message."

"Over the years we've had many attacks by mobs. In fact, mob attacks on Jews have been taking place with regularity for more than a thousand years. There isn't a country in which Jews were not molested. We can't keep running for the rest of our lives," he stated.

"These are not just attacks you can forget. There is more to it than destroy and loot. The Inquisition has an objective in mind, a very clear one at that. They want all of us to become Catholics, and it looks as though they will stop at nothing," I said.

"For a young man your age you put up a man's argument."

"I am a man. Remember, I was Bar Mitzvaed a year ago," I declared.

"If we decide to leave, where would you like to go?" he asked.

"I'm not going anywhere," I said. "You and mother are."

"This is crazy talk. First of all, I'm not going anywhere, and second of all, if we go, you are coming with us."

I didn't find it necessary to continue this discussion and changed the subject.

"All right, shouldn't you find out why the homes of prominent Jews were not touched? I believe the answer to this question will help you in making up your mind," I said.

"You are absolutely right," he agreed. "I will attend to this matter immediately."

I decided to let matters cool off for a few days because my father was consumed with worries and problems. I went to our synagogue's school every day while the Jewish quarter was putting its life back together. My father gave shelter to three children while their parents were trying to find a new residence. It became impossible to talk about private matters without having foreign ears listen to the conversation.

A few days passed and my father called me aside. "David, I have two boxes full of gold dukats ready. Tonight, when the others are sleeping, you and I will bury one box next to the cistern, and on Friday all of us will go to the inn in Azulas. The third box will be left with Zevulun. It will be hidden in the body of his wagon, which will be disabled and left in his barn. No one will bother with a broken wagon. He will fix another wagon for his trips.

I'm still unable to send this letter as Zevulun has gone to Lisbon and I am awaiting his return. Perhaps he'll bring back a letter from our relatives there. I'm very curious about them. In the meanwhile, we buried one metal box containing thousands of gold dukats under the stone flooring of the cistern, and this past weekend we placed the second box in the attic of the Andazuz inn. The third box was placed in the body of Zevulun's broken up wagon. My father also gave me a belt with seventy-five gold dukats, and from now on I'm wearing it under my garments at all times.

My father's inquiries as to why the houses of prominent Jews were not vandalized have not yet born fruit. Only one a Yehoshua Elkayam, told him he was approached by one of the local priests inquiring about his plans to convert. I suppose not all priests are alike. I tend to believe that some priests do not approve of the Inquisition's brutal ways. Perhaps I'm dreaming, but it's difficult to believe that every single one of them is an animal.

Our trip to Azulas was very pleasant. It was cold, but the sky was clear, the sun shone in all its glory, and sent some warming rays. The inn's manager was very happy to see us and gave us his best accommodations. He also prepared an excellent meal. Late at night I showed my father the hiding place in the attic, and the metal box fit in perfectly. Unless the building is torn apart, I don't think anyone could possibly find it.

Upon our return we found Zevulun in our living room. Our maid had him wait since we were due back that evening. He waited patiently. I can finally give him my letter. He believes he'll be on his way to Barcelona in two days' time.

Write immediately before he returns to Toledo. Stay strong. I'll be with you soon.

Much love,
David

Monday, 12th of January, 1476

Dear brother David,

I'm writing this letter in a great hurry. Zevulun is waiting for it in the library. I was anxiously awaiting his visit. He came dressed as a priest. I almost passed out when I saw him. He certainly is a master of disguise! The monks showed him in and called me. I was told a priest from my former Catholic school had come to visit. I stopped wondering who it was when I saw his face. He suggested we take a walk. That was a great idea. It allowed us to talk freely without fear.

As you can imagine, I was terribly anxious to read your letter, which I did as we were walking away from the monastery. You have certainly made a great deal of progress. Your parents are going through the same hell my parents experienced. I wonder whether your father will make a different decision.

"You and David are extremely close," he said. "What ties the two of you together?"

"Now that my parents have left Barcelona I can tell you the truth. I believe you'll be able to help us in our cause. What I'm about to tell you must remain a dark secret. Only if you swear to secrecy will I tell you my plans."

"I've been a trusted employee in your father's business for over forty years. In fact, he told me all about your plans before he left Aragon. I swore I would do everything in my power to help you. I also swore to guard you with my life if necessary," he revealed.

At first, I was shocked and surprised, but soon became overjoyed. Zevulun could become an important member of our group. "My dear Zevulun, I would trust you with my life. I've known you since I was a baby, and I truly appreciate your willingness to assist. At time it may become dangerous. I'll call on you to perform odd missions. As you now know, I am determined to fight the Inquisition. I'm determined to bring it to complete destruction. I'm willing to give all my time and effort and take every risk in accomplishing this objective. David will join us as soon as we begin. I don't like the latest developments in Toledo, and I have a feeling many changes are about to take place in Castile's capital city."

"I have a grand idea," Zevulun said. "As you know, I am a master of disguise. I'm also a first class magician. I enjoy playing tricks, and I think I can be of help. My idea is rather simple. I'll move with my wife into a gentile neighborhood on the other side of town. I'll rent a house. I'll be known as a

priest who moved to Barcelona from Cordoba. My wife will change her appearance and will be presented as my housekeeper. I'll tell her I'm masquerading as a priest due to circumstances, which she will surely understand. In this form we'll be able to help you at all times. The money from the sale of your father's house should last many years."

"Excellent idea. I love it. Please attend to it immediately. Also, it'll get you out of trouble with the Inquisition. But aren't you forgetting something?"

"I don't think so..."

"Oh Yes! You forgot you'll need a name change," I said.

"You are absolutely right. From now on I am Father Carlos Ramirez from Cordoba," Zevulun said with a smile.

Zevulun left and promised to return as soon as possible. He agreed that leaving Toledo and appearing as a priest in Barcelona would also help him escape the searching eyes of the Inquisition in Castile.

I've been mapping the area around the monastery, churches in the city, and all locations the Inquisition operates. I suggest you do the same in Toledo. Once we start operations we'll have to recruit young men in all major cities in Castile and Aragon so we can strike in more than one place at once. I can't write any more as Zevulun - sorry, Carlos Ramirez - has to leave. God bless.

Yours,
Reuven

Monday, 2nd of February 1476

Dear brother Reuven,

I was delighted to read that Zevulun (Carlos) intended to move to Barcelona. I had a long conversation with him. "I'm extremely happy you'll be moving to Barcelona, and even more happy you'll join our effort to fight the Inquisition," I declared.

"It will be my distinct pleasure to help the Abulafia family. As you know, I lived many years in Toledo and am very familiar with most of the Jewish community. I'm well aware of your father's dilemma, as I was of Reuven's. In my opinion, the Inquisition is gradually increasing its power and with it its brutal ways. I'm sure many Jews are wondering, why someone doesn't stand up and fight. The problem, as I see it, is that we're not a fighting, or militant people. It will take a real leader, a Moses, to take the Jews out of Catholic slavery. I can feel in my bones that Reuven is going to be our 'Moses'."

"I'm glad you believe as I do. We definitely need a leader, and we must fight and uproot the evils of the Inquisition."

We discussed a number of possibilities at great length. As to the situation in Toledo, he said the following: "It's very grim. More people are being arrested than ever before. Most of the prisoners are tortured, and some have been sentenced to death. I'm going to find out more now that I'm masquerading as a priest. Your father is extremely concerned about the arrest of some of the prominent Jews. He suspects the Inquisition is taking a new direction."

This was how my conversation with Zevulun went. On another matter, my father told me most of the prominent Jews in Toledo met yesterday in one of the local inns and discussed the Inquisition's growing pressure. Apparently two more members of the community were arrested and disappeared without trace. Their wives went to the Inquisition's office to inquire about their husbands and were thrown out viciously. The subject of conversion was discussed at length. They agreed conversion is a very personal issue and that each man should decide for himself. Many of the men attending the meeting agreed with my father- they would rather die than convert. I can't imagine why these men haven't left Toledo. I keep asking myself, what is it that keeps them attached to this city?

As the adults planned a meeting, I decided to call a meeting of my own. I arranged for all the students attending our Hebrew school to meet. The stories I heard were identical to my own. There wasn't one boy who didn't experience the same discussions about conversion, shame, pride, belief in God, how to live with yourself after conversion, and the Inquisition with its hate and brutality. The recent attacks and killings by the masses were also discussed.

I asked if anyone was willing to fight, and a few hands went up. I made mental notes of their names.

I need to discuss with my father the money cache, which was placed in the broken-up wagon. If Zevulun sells his house, we need to find a new home for the box.

I send you all my love. Stay strong.

Yours,
David

Friday, 3rd of March, 1476

My dear brother David,

Life in the monastery is not too bad, that is if you want to devote your entire self to God. The monks pray together five times a day, which includes a midnight session. They eat, sleep and perform minor roles around the grounds. Some monks grow vegetables and attend to the fruit trees, which grow in a large orchard outside the building premises. Most of the fruit is sold on the Barcelona market to fund the meager needs of the monk population.

So far, they've been very nice to me. Every day, three hours are devoted to study of the scriptures. They have quite an interesting library, with many old historical books and records. I'm allowed to use it as I please. Lately, I've been sent to town on various missions. In most cases I deliver and receive letters. All correspondence is with Church officials and on occasion one or two of the Crown's offices. I can hardly wait for Zevulun's return, as I'm sure he would know how to open these letters and reseal them properly. There's no question we'll find valuable information in many of them.

When Zevulun returns to Barcelona and has settled, I'll begin our operations. I've made very specific and careful plans, which I won't disclose in this letter. I'll tell you when we meet face to face.

The truth is that despite being kept busy at the monastery, I feel very lonely. I miss my parents very much and wonder how they're doing. I hope they arrived safely in Alexandria. I believe my parents were in Egypt on a visit when I was four years old. Our trusted housekeeper, Teresa, took care of me while they were gone. I remember that month well because I played all kinds of tricks on this loving old lady. She accepted my games and tricks with love and care.

But, above all, I miss you. It has been well over a year since we saw each other. My love for you keeps growing just as my desire to fight these brutal priests. Every night before I fall asleep I think of you and pray for you. My anxiety is overwhelming, not only to see you and be with you, but also to start operations. I know we'll make a great team. I'm as committed as ever to our cause. The burning desire to fight the Inquisition and the Church has not left me for a single moment. I feel I'm living for it. I think of actions and plans every moment of my day and night. I'm determined to bring them to their knees and destroy them.

Tension in Barcelona is high. I heard of various mob attacks on Jews and Marranos. You'd think the poor souls who converted would be left in peace, but that isn't the case. A few nights ago I was very restless. I got up and walked around the grounds to cool my temper. I suddenly heard voices and decided investigate. I approached one of the sheds from which the voices were heard. The speaker had a voice I hadn't heard before. He described at length the mischief and devilish characteristics of the Jews. At each category of mischief he emphasized the impure blood the Jews have running in their veins. I haven't heard so many lies in my life. It's impossible to comprehend how adult people, and men of the cloth in particular, believe such things. Of all people in the world, they are the ones who know our religion through the study of the Old Testament. I don't believe they are blind to the Jewish ways of education and religious observation. They are well aware that Jews are educated, literate, and hard working people. Where does all this hate come from? And, if they hate our faith so much that they can't live with it, why don't they expel us from their country? The absurdity of conversion is beyond words since they don't accept the converted as Christians either. They give them a name, 'Conversos' or 'Marranos' and keep them segregated. The poor converts are attacked and looted just the same as the Jews. If purity of faith is what they seek, the departure of the Jews would solve their problems.

I suppose that rationalizing the situation isn't going to get me anywhere. Life here is different. It never ceases to amaze me that religiously educated adults, men who've been taught the ways of Christ, go about calmly torturing other human beings. I can tell you one thing and that is the day nears when their hate will be turned on themselves. I can feel it in my bones.

I'm afraid I strayed from the subject. The meeting came to an end after the speaker instructed them to participate in the next planned demonstration against the Jews, to be held on Saturday of the following week. The demonstration was planned to start at the central church and culminate at the main synagogue building in Barcelona. I already know what happens at the end of a demonstration; mobs attack Jewish homes, vandalize, loot and kill. I will sneak into the city and warn the Rabbi.

Can't wait to see you. I miss you, as always. Soon, very soon we'll be together.

Yours,
Reuven

Wednesday, 1ˢᵗ of April, 1476

My dear brother Reuven,

Your letter of March 3ʳᵈ was an eye opener. I can't agree with you more. Their hate, their seeking of purity, their lies and brutality cannot be described or understood. But since the audience with the Crown has failed, and as the Inquisition demonstrates constant increase in brutality in order to attain its goals, we must act.

The situation in Toledo, once a relatively peaceful city, is just as bad as Barcelona. My father, who has business connections all over Castile and Aragon, tells me tension is on the rise everywhere. There isn't a single municipality where Jews are not attacked, imprisoned and tortured. It's obvious that the Church's machinery is spreading its hate and action at a greater speed. The protection the Crown used to provide is evaporating. I suspect that the emissaries of the Church are reaching the Crown's soldiers.

Terrible news just reached us. The Inquisition arrested Toledo's Chief Rabbi. At first he was thought to have taken a trip to a neighboring town. He was tortured for three days and allowed to return home to repent. My father was told that he can barely talk and that his entire body is screaming with pain.

It is said for every bad news, there is good news, too. A letter was just brought to me from Lisbon. It reads:

Dear Cousin David, (I have no idea why I'm called cousin)

My father showed me your letter that inquired about your relatives in Lisbon. My name is Miriam Abulafia, I'm fifteen years old and I too am anxious to learn about our family. I asked my parents numerous times but never got a clear answer. I'm aware of the long business relationship between the Abulafia families in various parts of Castile and Aragon, as well as North Africa. I was born in Lisbon, as were all my ancestors. I've never been out of Portugal. I'm an only child. Fortunately, my father has a number of brothers and the Abulafia name will continue. I'd like very much to learn more about your family. Please write to me. I realize we need to wait until our business couriers deliver letters, so it will be a long while until I hear from you. Please write soon.

Yours,
Miriam

Well, it's a beginning. I have always been curious about the Lisbon branch of the family. I'll write to her soon.

Zevulun informed me that he rented his house in Toledo. He'll be leaving for Cordoba with his wife in a day or two. As you know, he has no children. The move shouldn't be too difficult for him. His wife will become our courier from now on. Fortunately, she looks like any other well-bred Castilian woman. She must be sixty years old, perhaps older. No one will suspect her of anything. To me, she looks like an ancient replica of womanhood. She's a lovely lady, though. She was always nice to me.

Zevulun will change into priest's habit before he reaches Cordoba; from then on he'll masquerade as a priest until our fight is over. As you know, Cordoba is in the hands of the Moors. He plans to smuggle himself into that territory and establish a residence. A few months later he'll return to Barcelona as an escaped priest. By that time he'll have created a trail so that if investigated, he will appear to be authentic. He believes the Church will have a hard time investigating anything behind enemy lines. Zevulun is very clever at those things. He knows what he's doing. I'm told the Inquisition does not operate in Andalusia. However, Queen Isabella is determined to conquer Cordoba, which is the capital of Andalusia, and once her armies defeat the Moors, the Inquisition will surely move in.

I recall asking my father some time ago why we weren't moving to Cordoba or Granada. His answer was that Isabella and Ferdinand were planning an all out war on the Moors and will soon take military action to oust the Muslims. He believed the Crown would succeed in conquering the rest of the peninsula. If that happens, the Jews who moved there will be hated even more.

Please write soon. I'm anxious for your news.
Yours,
David

Friday, 3rd of April 1476

Dear cousin Miriam,

I was delighted to receive your letter. Since childhood I heard about the Abulafias of Portugal, but unfortunately there is no personal contact. I'd very much like to change that.

I am attending Hebrew school in Toledo, and will graduate in two years. The City of Toledo, my hometown, was rather peaceful due to the fact that it is the capital city of Castile. However, all of a sudden the masses erupted against the Jews. The Church and its Inquisition want every Jew converted to Christianity. Jews live in constant fear. Members of the Inquisition arrest, torture and kill people who refuse to convert. Lately, Jewish homes have been attacked by mobs; looting and killing have become commonplace. The Crown no longer protects us. I'm trying to get my parents to leave Castile, but they refuse.

My family has been engaged in trade and commerce for generations. We import vital merchandise needed by the Crown and export Castilian and Aragonian goods to other countries. The family business is very successful and I hope the same is true at your end.

I don't want to bore you with too many details in my first letter. Please write soon as I'm anxious to get to know you and your family. Hopefully, we'll bring us all closer together.

Yours,
David

Monday, 11th of May, 1476

Dear brother David,

You are confirming what I suspected for a long time. There is no question that the Church and the Inquisition are increasing their power, step by step. The Crown is falling more and more under their wings. The only reason the Crown took so long is because the Jews as a group pay over twenty percent of its total tax revenue. If you eliminate the Jews, the Crown will suffer major losses. The Church, of course, is not concerned with economic issues. Its sole interest is in Catholic purity.

As I wrote in my last letter, I managed to get into the city and made my way to the Rabbi's house. I dressed in my regular clothes under my monk's cloak and at an appropriate moment snuck into a deserted alley, took off the cloak, and put it in a sack I carried. The Rabbi's wife was at home. I told her of the coming demonstration and suggested the Jewish community leave their homes early Saturday, taking with them all valuables, and return at sundown. I told her who I was. I wanted to be sure she didn't think this was a prank.

You should have heard the monks when they returned from their first demonstration. They kept talking for hours about the mob not finding anybody. They could not imagine how the Jews had disappeared. The mob vandalized many homes and one of the synagogues. A great deal of property was destroyed, but at least no lives were lost.

I haven't been sleeping well lately. When I'm restless, I get up and walk inside the monastery complex. Last night, well after midnight, I was taking my usual stroll. No one was to be seen. After their midnight mass, the monks are very tired and will sleep soundly until 5 o'clock in the morning when they are awakened.
This time I decided to check the offices of the monastery's administration. On the prior's desk I found a letter signed by none other than Tomas de Torquemada. I looked in the drawers and found some other letters. Fortunately, there was a full moon and I had sufficient light to read some of them. As I was reading, an idea struck me. I will have Zevulun fabricate letters with Torquemada's seal and signature which contradict his previous orders. We'll also produce letters signed and sealed by the Queen. The letters will be addressed to different Cardinals, Bishops and priests, as well as certain dignitaries. We'll create a huge confusion. When Torquemada changes his seal, so will we. No one will suspect a monk.

I'm anxiously waiting Zevulun's return. I'm on pins and needles. I desperately want to begin our operations. In this respect I want you by my side. It's not clear yet whether I should leave the monastery and make our headquarters some place else, or use the monastery. When Zevulun returns I'll discuss this matter with him.

As you can see I'm pondering how we should begin our operations, and, of course, when. Maybe you could find an excuse to come visit me when Zevulun returns. The three of us would then decide.

Please come to Barcelona.

Yours,
Reuven

Saturday, 6th of June, 1476

Dear brother Reuven,

Zevulun's wife delivered a letter he had written from Cordoba. I must admit he is a true master of disguise. According to the letter he established himself in Sardona, a suburb of Cordoba. He began calling on local churches claiming to represent Cardinal Pedro Gonzalez de Mendoza, a close advisor to Queen Isabella. He told the priests the Cardinal was very anxious to know how they were doing under Moorish rule now that their territory has shrunk significantly. He was on a fact-finding mission for the Holy Office. He asked the clergy he met to write letters to their family and members of the Church in Castile and Aragon and promised to take the risk of smuggling them when he leaves. He already has dozens of letters, but the key is that he established an excellent rapport with the priesthood of Cordoba. He said he'd be leaving around the 20th of June and plans to meet with his wife in Barcelona early July.

Saving the lives of our brethren was a wonderful act on your part. I'm sure the mob was baffled. They very much enjoy assaulting innocent and defenseless people, and of course, to loot to their hearts' content. It's truly amazing how the Church condones stealing. The jails of Castile and Aragon are full of thieves. But it is absolutely legal to steal from Jews. What hypocrisy!

I too would like nothing more than to be with you; however, the situation in Toledo is very bad. I doubt my father will give me permission to leave at this time. Every Jewish family in this city is now living in constant fear. The situation is so bad that some people are selling their homes for the price of a wagon. Most people are afraid to leave because of the many robberies and noble infighting between the estates. Soldiers from both sides are poorly paid and supplement their needs by stealing and robbing. The Queen hesitates to send her troops to fight certain nobles because she's more interested in getting the Moors out of the country. Rumor has it that the Crown is planning a major assault on the Moors in Leon territory.

I'll let you know as soon as my father makes a decision. Zevulun's wife makes a great courier. I just feel sorry for the tremendous sacrifice she is making. It's not a simple journey. The discomfort of travel can leave your bones and body in shambles.

Am already looking for your next letter. As always,

Yours,
David

Thursday, 2nd of July, 1476

Dear brother David,

Zevulun finally arrived today. As usual, the monastery looks favorably upon visits made by the clergy. Zevulun makes one beautiful priest. His black habit and age make him look extremely appropriate. We went out for a stroll and talked at length about the future.

He is planning to rent a house in the heart of the city. His wife will be introduced to neighbors as his housekeeper. He feels his residence could be used as our headquarters for a while. After a few months our headquarters should be moved elsewhere. We discussed the fabrication of letters and he agrees with the concept. I need you here. There are many issues to discuss, and we must make decisions. After all, Aragon and Castile are quite big. There are many cities, and the Inquisition is active in every one of them. We need to map our plan so that they are attacked everywhere, not just in Barcelona. We must recruit more young men. There is so much to do and so little time. It would truly be wonderful if you could join us. Please find a way.

Yours,
Reuven

PART TWO
The Revolution

CHAPTER ONE

On Monday, 3rd of August, 1476, four Inquisition investigators burst into David's parents' house at supper time and arrested his father and mother. The investigators, priests who worked exclusively for the Inquisition, wearing their usual black habits, dragged them out of the house despite protests. David's father was wacked over the head and his mother brutally handled. David rushed to push one of the priests away, but was knocked to the ground. He lost consciousness for a while. When the housekeeper awakened him his parents and priests were gone. He wanted to run out after them, but the housekeeper held him back.

"You cannot chase these people," she said, holding him firmly. "They will kill you."

"I can't let it happen," David screamed. "Not my parents."

"You must calm down, David. We have no information," she said somberly.

"How can I calm down? You know what they do to Jews," howled David, still at the top of his lungs.

"We need to pray. God willing your father's importance to the Crown will help," the housekeeper offered.

"The Crown! That's a joke!" David yelled. "If they as much as touch a hair I'll kill them, I swear!"

"David, please, you must calm yourself. We don't know anything yet. Screaming like this will only bring the investigators back here. You must be patient," she pleaded.

As he appeared to calm a bit, the housekeeper loosened her grip. Instantly David pushed her aside and dashed out of the house. She called after him, but to no avail. He ran down the street and headed towards the Inquisition building. He slowed down as he neared it, and suddenly stopped in his tracks. He stood about a block away when he saw more Jews being dragged in. He recognized some of them. He counted ten priests doing the dirty work. He hid in the shadow of a house and contemplated his next steps.

"If you so much as touch one of my parents, I swear to God Almighty I will kill every one of you," he vowed in his heart.

He stood there for quite some time, frozen with confusion, fear, hate and vengeance. Suddenly, he tore away and ran straight into the Inquisition's building.

"Where are my parents? What have you done to them?" He screamed at a priest who came across him.

"Stop screaming," the priest ordered and slapped him hard on his face. "One more word out of you and you'll burn in hell." He grabbed David's hand and dragging him forcefully locked him in one of the cells.

David fell to the floor, cursing aloud. The cell was dark. He didn't know whether anyone else was there. He tried to adjust his eyes to the darkness, but couldn't see a thing. He found one of the walls and began circling the cell. It was a small cell, not larger than the size of two wagons.

"Is anyone here?" he asked. Total silence surrounded him. He tried to feel his way across, but soon realized he was alone in the cell. He sat down on the floor in a corner and stared into the darkness. Time passed, but he had no sense of it. He was in a trance.

He was awakened from his nightmare when the steel door opened. Sudden light hit his eyes and blinded him for a moment. Two priests pulled him from his sitting position and propelled him out.

"Where are my parents? I want to see them," David yelled.

"Shut up," one of the priests commanded and slapped his face hard. He almost lost his balance. "One more word out of you, and we'll put you back in the dark cell for a whole week."

Realizing who he was dealing with, David's mind brought him face to face with reality. *"Keep calm,"* he instructed himself. *"The less violent you are, less force will be used against you."*

The priests took him to the Church of Santiago del Arrabal in Toledo. Another priest was standing at the Alter.

"Father Jesus, please baptize this little Jew," one of his arresting priests said.

Upon hearing the priest's instructions, David turned wild, jumped out of the priest's grip, kicked them both in the shins, and ran out. The two priests took off after him as soon as the surprise of David's move wore off. David, being much younger, and having had a head start, turned into the alley on the left of the Church and quickly hid behind the walls of an adjacent house. The priests ran into the street, filled with pedestrians going to work. David stayed behind the wall a few hours before making his move.

The sun was high above his head when he began feeling safe. He peeked out but saw no one. He decided to make his way in the narrow street behind the houses. He jumped a few walls and fences and eventually found his way home. He kept looking back every so often and carefully examined every face which came his way. The housekeeper was very happy to see him. "Thank God you're all right. I was worried about you."

"The bastards arrested me last night when I asked about my parents, and locked me up in a dark cell. This morning they took me to the Church of Santiago del Arrabal and wanted to baptize me, but I managed to escape. Fortunately, they have no idea who I am. I wasn't asked for my name," David said.

"There's no word from your parents, or anybody else for that matter," the housekeeper stated. "I'm afraid to go out and ask."

"I'm going to spy on the house of Inquisition until I find a way to communicate with my parents," David announced.

"Have you eaten anything?"

"I haven't eaten a thing. Let me have some food as quickly as possible. I don't want to lose a minute."

The housekeeper took her time to prepare a meal. He washed up, walked into the kitchen, and sat at the table. His heart was heavy and his thoughts were with his parents. He had a bad feeling about their arrest. He already knew his father's position on conversion, which most probably would lead to a catastrophic end. *Maybe at the last minute my father will come to his senses,* David hoped.

Despite his depressed and lonely mood, and despite his tremendous longing for his parents, he ate heartily since he was very hungry. Sometimes he had a hard time swallowing, but decided to eat so that he could spend the rest of the day and night if necessary to watch the Inquisition. He took some food with him and left the house. A minute later he returned and changed into the most rugged old clothes he had.

He slowed his pace considerably as he approached the Inquisition area, looking, for inconspicuous place he could hide comfortably. Fortunately, there were many people in the narrow street and a number of children were playing, too. He advanced slowly, looking and checking every direction. Diagonally across from the Inquisition he noticed a building under renovation. He climbed to the second floor. A number of men were working.

"Are you the son of the owner?" one of the workers asked.

"No," David responded, a little shocked at first, but soon collected his wits. "I'm the son of one of the maids."

The worker wasn't interested in the son of a maid. David explored the house from top to bottom and decided upon a window from which he could watch the Inquisition. He stood there for hours. A few priests came and went. The two priests who dragged him to the Church entered the building. They came out a few minutes later, each turning in a different direction. Darkness began to descend, and visibility slowly came to a halt.

"I need to find a much closer location for my spying," David thought. He descended from the second floor and moved slowly towards the Inquisition's building. There were two stores directly across from the entrance and he stationed himself in the dark hallway between the two. He observed the building's main entrance while remaining completely hidden. He was very

pleased at the discovery and remained there for hours. The night passed very slowly. There was virtually no traffic, as it got later. It also grew much colder. It was close to dawn when David decided to return home.

He walked slowly and carefully towards his home, checking every corner and every opening. He didn't want to be caught by a sentry. When he got home, he slipped into bed and slept for hours. It was past noon when he awakened. The housekeeper arrived. "Did you find out anything about your parents?"

"I didn't find a thing. I saw the priests who tried to baptize me, but no one else I knew. The streets were full of people and many horse-driven wagons and carts were coming and going all day long. I'm going to stick to my spying location until I find something or somebody who can help."

Again, he took some food and left the house. The workers had gone by the time David reached his hiding place. He climbed to the second floor and positioned himself by the window. The street traffic was no different from the previous day. Towards evening four more people were dragged into the building. He didn't recognize any of them. They were treated as badly as the others. He knew they had to be Jews. As night arrived, it became totally dark. He decided to get closer to the Inquisition's building. He quietly and carefully found his way to the stairs and descended holding onto the railing. He looked out. The street was extremely dark and he saw no one.

Candles were lit in some of the rooms inside the Inquisition's building.   He ran to the side of the building and walked into a narrow alleyway. He felt the building with the palm of his hand as he moved ahead. When he turned the corner to the rear of the building he noticed four windows at the ground level, each with steel bars. There was some light in the basement. He knelt down and moved toward the first window. He was horrified at what he saw. A man was stretched on a long narrow table. His hands and feet were tied to two machines at each end. The man was stretched to a breaking point. His head fell sideways; he was unconscious. He couldn't see his face. The sight of the stretching torture kept his eyes focused on the man, but soon he began searching other parts of the basement. Against one of the walls, four people, one next to each other were standing while their hands were handcuffed to the wall well above their heads. All four heads were hanging down. He was unable to see their faces.

He wanted to see more of the basement, and crawled to the farthest window. A number of men and women lay on the ground. Their hands and feet were tied to steel loops imbedded in the basement floor. Their backs were completely exposed and were bleeding. At first he couldn't make out their faces, but soon realized that his mother and father were among them. They were out cold. David was paralyzed with shock and fear. It took a few moments before he came to.

He was ready to jump when the steel door to the basement opened and a number of priests walked in. They took their positions and poked a sharp instrument into each body. David saw mouths move, but could not hear a thing. From time to time he saw one of the prisoners lift his head, which collapsed within a second or two. The prisoners on the floor were then flogged. Not one moved. David's blood pressure mounted. He thought his head would explode. His hand held the steel bar and he screamed and screamed. A minute later he passed out.

The sun was up when David came to. At first he thought he'd had a nightmare, but quickly realized where he was and what he'd seen. He looked around, but no one was in the back of the building. He looked in once more, but this time could barely see a thing. The light played tricks on his eyes. He got up and walked away. His mind was racing. He needed to do something to rescue his parents, but what?

Filled with grief and pain, and having lost the sense of being, he suddenly made an about face and walked back to the Inquisition's building. He walked through the front entrance and asked the first priest he saw to direct him to the office of the chief investigator.

"What is it you want, boy?" the priest said.

"You are holding my parents in the basement. Let me talk to them. I will convince them to convert," David said in a calm voice. "Your methods will never win them over."

"Who are you? And how did you get here? You were supposed to have been baptized. All the children were baptized and taken away to school," the priest stated.

"Let me talk to my parents," David said. "I will make them convert and I will willingly go to your school."

"Come with me." The priest took David by the hand and led him to the basement.

"All these Jews are not worthy of living. Their blood is tainted with sins and corruption of mind. Which of these people are your parents?" the priest asked. Seeing so many broken people and so much blood, David became nauseous and vomited. The stench was so bad that his vomiting didn't change a thing. He wiped his face and pointed to his parents. The priest dragged him forward. He soon realized that his parents had passed out. He touched his father's head and tried to bring him back to consciousness. After a few strokes David's father opened his eyes, but was unable to move.

"What are you doing here?" he whispered. "Go back home."

"Father, please agree to convert and you'll be freed," David pleaded.

"I'm already a dead man. I will not give them the pleasure."

"Think of mother," David pleaded again. His father lost consciousness once more.

The priest bent down and grabbed David by the arm. "What did your father say?" Realizing that the priest couldn't have heard a thing, David decided to lie. "He said he would convert."

The priest held David firmly as he pulled him away. "Come with me. If your parents convert I'll set them free. And you, I'll send to the Church of Santiago del Arrabal to be baptized. After that you will be sent to a Catholic school for studies. Behave well and be a good Christian. Your entire life is ahead of you. Christ will guide you."

David began to do some quick thinking. His father told him that he was a dead man. There was a message in those words. He must have been beaten so hard that his insides were gone. *"I made a serious mistake,"* David thought.

The priest led him back to his office. "Wait here. I'll be back in a minute." Observing that David was semi conscious, he felt secure leaving him alone. However, as soon as he left the room, David leaped up and dashed to the door, opening it cautiously. No one was in the hallway. He ran out of the building with lightning speed and disappeared in the crowd. He ran all the way home and instructed the housekeeper to leave immediately. "Take your things and get out of here fast. The Inquisition's men will be here shortly looking for me. If they catch you, you'll be in trouble." He rushed to his parents' bedroom. He took the box, containing his mother's jewelry, clothing from his room, stashed everything in a sack and ran out. The housekeeper was out the door two minutes later.

Holding the sack over his shoulder, he walked briskly out of the Jewish neighborhood and made his way to the house across from the Inquisition. The sun had set, but David paid no attention. He sat on the floor and began contemplating his future.

"As terrible and horrific this situation is, I must collect my senses," he spoke to himself. *"I must remember Reuven and our commitment to fight the Inquisition. I cannot fight the power of the Church by myself, and neither can he. We need an army of people. I will have to recruit boys who were forcefully baptized and taken to the Catholic school. That is where I'll start. But right now I need to find out about my parents."*

David's heart sunk with grief and loneliness. He knew of other people who were tortured and brutalized by the Inquisition, but it didn't have the same effect. *"Whatever my commitment to the cause of revolution against the Church and its Inquisition was, from now on it will multiply a hundred fold,"* David vowed. *"I will not rest until this Inquisition and its practices are out of our lives. If I have to sacrifice my life, so be it."*

Time passed and he remained sitting in the same position. He was immobilized in thought and in body. He remained in a trance from which he emerged when the first rays of the sun touched his cold body. He got up and checked the entire house in search of a suitable hiding place. He couldn't find any and decided to leave. He waited by the front entrance until he saw people in the street. He snuck out and made his way to the nearby Tajo River. He walked along the bank until he came upon a small orchard, and sat down under a tree. He was very tired and fell asleep leaning against the tree. He slept for hours. When he woke, he was hungry and thirsty. He got up, stretched, and walked back towards the city. He decided to check out his father's place of business. He stopped at one of the stores and bought a loaf of bread and cheese as well as a leather container, which he filled with water from one of the many fountains in the city.

He slowed down as he neared the business district. It was very quiet and only a handful of people could be seen. He hid each time he saw someone approaching. He reached into his money belt where he kept the keys his father had given him, selected a key and opened the gate.

No one was inside. The place looked neat and well cared for. He lit a candle and entered his father's office. He went through the big desk, checking every drawer and filed folders. He needed a safe place for his mother's jewelry, but decided against leaving it in the office. *"Surely, the Crown's tax collectors will be here soon and will confiscate everything in sight."* He walked out the back door and discovered a neatly laid stone floor. He had never been behind the building and was surprised at its size. There were three huge trees at the far end of the yard. He climbed one and hid the jewelry box inside a large, thick fork in the tree. He tied the box carefully and descended. Returning to his father's office, he opened the safe and took out all the available cash, which was considerable. He filled his money belt to its brim, and seeing nothing else of interest, left the building.

David was surprised at the number of people walking towards Plaza Mayor and decided to follow them. He asked one of the boys he saw where they were going.
"We were told that this evening six sinner Jews would be burned to death. My father said that watching the Devil burn would give us salvation," the boy responded. David was shocked. Even though he wasn't planning to talk to anyone, his mind was paralyzed. He walked on with the crowd until he arrived at the center plaza. Thousands of people were there in wait for the 'show'. With the sack over his shoulder, he pushed his way to the front line. A big circle of cut lumber surrounded a number of poles set firmly in the middle. The crowd was extremely noisy. Religious shouts were heard from every direction. It was completely dark, but from time to time a sliver of moonlight penetrated broken clouds floating above.

The noise suddenly increased to an ear piercing level when a number of priests appeared bringing in their victims. None of the victims could walk. They had to be dragged or held up and carried. To his shocked eyes David saw his father, who was unconscious, being carried and tied in a standing position to one of the poles. His mother was wide-awake, but her face totally distorted. David began to scream, but the noise and shouts of the crowd around him drowned his young voice. The others were also tied and the priests began a series of inaudible prayers and quotations. Minutes later one of the priests poured some liquid over the wood and lit it. Within less than a minute the entire stake was on fire. The screams of the burned people would never leave him for the rest of his life.

"I shall kill every one of you," David yelled at the priests, but no one heard him. The level of the screams and joyful shouts of the crowd of thousands was so great that his scream for vengeance was drowned. The screaming of the burned victims subsided. The fire began to burn down as the wood turned red. David took a good look at every one of the eight priests who had brought their victims and performed the brutal and heartless murder, and cast their image in his memory.

The crowd began to disperse and the priests walked back to the Inquisition building. David followed them from a distance and entered the house across the street. He remained by the front door and waited. After a while, two of the priests walked out. David followed them to their residence, which was a small house about ten minutes away. He turned around and walked home. No one was there. The house was undisturbed. He picked one of the large carving knives, stuck it in his belt, and covered it with the jacket he was wearing.

"I will kill you one by one, I swear to God," he said, as he proceeded towards the priests' residence. David waited a good hour in the shadow of a tree until the last candle in the house flickered out. He carefully entered the house. There were very few rooms, and it was quite easy to find the bedrooms. One of the priests was lying on his back snoring. David took out the knife and brought it to the man's throat. With his other hand he woke the priest. As soon as the priest opened his eyes, David said, *"For killing my parents, you will die like a dog."* The priest began lifting himself, but as he did, so did the knife, which David held firmly. It penetrated his throat. Blood gushed out from his severed jugular vein. He fell back, dead. David then went to the other bedroom. This time he didn't bother to wake the priest. He stabbed him through the heart several times. He wiped and cleaned the blade on the bed sheet, put it back in his belt, and left the house.

David made his way to the house across the street from the Inquisition, sat down on the floor in one of the rooms, leaned against the wall, and fell asleep. He felt no remorse. His mind was clear and determined. He woke up as the first rays of sunshine were making their way to earth. He ate some of the bread and cheese and drank some water. He decided to leave the building before the workers arrived, as he did not want to arouse their suspicion. He walked into a second hand clothing store and bought used garments, of much lesser quality than those he was wearing. He wanted to appear a poor boy in every way. When he got to the orchard where he'd rested a day earlier, he dirtied his garments with mud and leaves.

At nightfall, he retracted his steps to the house of Inquisition and hid in the same doorway as the night before. Soon after, a priest left the building. David followed him. This time he didn't wait until the priest had reached his home. As soon as the priest turned into one of the alleys, David took out his knife, caught up with him, and stabbed him through the heart. The priest was dead before he hit the ground. David wiped the blade on the dead man's cloak and walked back to his hiding place.

No one entered the building and no one left. Well after midnight the building fell into darkness as the last candles were extinguished. It was obvious that a number of priests slept in the Inquisition building. David waited another hour before he entered the building. No one was at the entrance. He went from room to room. On the third floor of the building he located the bedrooms. He entered one by one and stabbed to death each occupant in his sleep except for the last room. In this room he tied the man's legs to the bedpost. David stood behind him with his knife poking the man's back.

"Don't move, otherwise the knife will stab your back," David said in a disguised voice. "Listen carefully. I am the Devil. You've been killing innocent people and burning them to death. All the priests in this cursed building are already dead. I am leaving you alive to tell the story to others. If you so much as touch another human being, I shall kill you, too." The priest was paralyzed. David cut off his ears and stabbed his hands. The priest was bleeding profusely when David left the building. He ran in the direction of the orchard and stayed there for two days and two nights.

For the first time in three days, David finally began to think. Up to that point he had simply functioned in cold-blooded revenge. *"I started the Revolution,"* he said loudly. *"Reuven will be proud of me."* He waited for night before leaving for the Jewish quarter. He was determined to see if anyone he knew was still there. He walked briskly, passing from street to street. Most of the houses were dark. Very few houses showed candlelight, but they weren't any he knew. He snuck into his home through the rear door and found that the house had been ransacked and looted. Except for heavy furniture, almost everything was taken. On the front door of the house he found a note stating that the house had been confiscated and henceforth belonged to the Crown. He went to check other neighboring houses to find the same kind of note posted. *"If you think you can benefit from Jewish property belonging to innocent people you killed, you are critically wrong,"* David said. He walked from house to house and set them on fire. Within minutes the sky was red with flames from more than a dozen houses. He returned to the orchard and slept until morning.

When the new day arrived, David picked up his sack and walked back to the city. He stopped a few blocks from the Inquisition building. There was a great deal of activity in the building. Sentries of the Crown, were guarding the entrance. Priests were running in and out. Among the visitors to the building David noticed a few military officers. He was pleased and decided to make his way to Barcelona.

He searched and found a trading barn which sold wagons and horses. He bought a horse and wagon and ordered the tradesman to fill it with hay. He also bought a container and filled it with fresh water. He then proceeded to buy dry food, which should last him a few days, and departed Toledo. As he left the city he saw a number of beggars seeking a ride. *"This is perfect,"* he said, and invited four to join him. He directed three into the wagon and asked the fourth to sit next to him on the driver's bench. He placed the knife next to his left thigh, just in case.

The journey to Barcelona took eight days. The dirt road was well-traveled. On occasion he came across other wagons and odd-looking passenger coaches. There were trade houses along the way. David soon realized they were carefully spaced. In each station he could buy food, clothing, exchange horses, and rest. Thus far the beggars hardly talked to each other. They had no provisions of their own and David was happy to share his meager supply with them. That was a mistake, as it led them to believe he had money.

During the second night of his journey his mind finally began to clear.   The cold-blooded killing of the priests and burning the houses, confiscated by the Crown surfaced. *"As far as the priests go, I have absolutely no regrets. They killed my parents in cold blood and they deserved the same death. I wish I could have killed them in public so that a similar crowd of people could have cheered their departure from earth,"* he thought. It was the burning of Jewish homes that weighed heavily on his mind. But after much thought he decided he did the right thing. *"Why should the Crown inherit the homes of innocent people it allowed to be murdered?* He finally convinced himself that burning Jewish houses was also justified.

His thoughts were at that point when he heard one of the beggars moving slowly towards him. He slept away from them, as he had nothing in common with his passengers. He was merely using them so as not to be seen alone. David grasped the knife by his side and held it firmly in his hand. He slitted his eyes and waited. The beggar came close and looked carefully at David. Believing him asleep, he began to frisk David, who suddenly lurched forward and stabbed the beggar in his chest. The beggar fell on his back, motionless. One of his lungs was severed and blood was gushing from the wound. David wiped the knife on his dirty garment and pulled his body to the nearby ravine. He covered it with loose branches and leaves and returned to his sleeping place. However, sleep did not come. He was wound up from the beggar's stealing attempt and the stabbing. He lay on the ground, eyes open, looking at the stars above. The sky was clear, not a cloud in view, and a full moon delivered its beautiful silver rays. He got up when he saw the first red lining on the eastern horizon. He placed the reins on the horse, brought him to the wagon, hitched him up and off he rode before the other beggars woke.

It was a beautiful August day. The weather was perfect, the days warm and the nights just a trifle cooler. The journey finally became routine. David was happy he'd learned how to saddle a horse, hitch it to the wagon, and how to treat it. So far he didn't have to exchange horses, since he wasn't racing it. He allowed the horse to move at its own pace. Today, however, he was pushing the horse hard, as he wanted to get away from last night's episode. The horse took it well, and David was convinced that his horse actually enjoyed the speed.

David passed a small farming village lodged between a river and a hill. He pulled the horse off the dirt road and stopped by the river bank. He got off the wagon, took off his boots, and let the gentle touch of the waters caress his feet. He sat on a large tree trunk which had fallen into the river and enjoyed the moment. A young girl approached him. At first he didn't notice her. She stood next to him, staring at the water. It was her soft voice that brought him back to reality.

"Are you from these parts?" she asked.

"No, I'm from Toledo," David answered when he recovered from the initial surprise. He looked at her. "Where are you from?"

"I live in this village," she pointed to the right. "I'm an orphan. My master took me from an orphanage in Barcelona. He promised the matron he would give me a good home, but all he has done is turn me into his servant."

"Won't he be looking for you?"

"He's still sleeping. He got drunk last night. I doubled the medicine powder he is taking. He will sleep until sundown," she said.

David got his feet out of the water and dried them with a rag. He put on his socks and boots. "You're putting on dirty socks," she remarked.

"I know, but I have no other socks with me," he responded and began to observe the young girl's beautiful eyes. "What's your name?"

"People around here call me Dulce, but my real name is Anna. Will you call me Anna? I hate when they call me Dulce."

"How old are you, Anna?"

"I'll be fifteen in December."

"So will I," David said. "Do you know what day in December?"

"Of course I know," she laughed, tossing her hair back, "December thirteenth."

"I'll be damned," David said in shocked surprise. "Me too."

"What's your name?" she asked.

"My name is David."

"Isn't that a Jewish name?"

Surprised at the question, his mind began to race for the right answer. It occurred to him that she might be Jewish, too.

"Yes, it is a Jewish name," He finally came out with it.

"Don't be afraid," she said, "I'm a Converso. My parents converted about three years ago, but were caught celebrating Rosh Hashana in secret. They were executed by the Inquisition."

David lost his voice. He was in total awe. It took him a long moment to get over her statement. He suddenly grabbed Anna and held her close to his chest. She did not object. He felt certain that she welcomed his embrace. He kissed her forehead and moved a step back. "My parents were burned to death by the Inquisition a week ago." He collapsed to the ground as he uttered those words and began to cry. It was the first time he had cried for his parents. His eyes opened to a stream of tears.

It was her turn to be shocked. She knelt over him and held him, caressing his hair.

"My God," she said, "how awful. Where are you going?"

"I'm headed to Barcelona," he sobbed.

"Will you take me with you?" she asked.

David lifted his head and stared at her. Her loving face reminded him of his mother. He looked into her eyes, lifted his hand, and touched her beautiful shiny black hair. "I'd be very happy if you came with me. I have no one in this world except my cousin Reuven. I must to tell you, though; I'm committed to fighting the Inquisition. Living with me may be dangerous and risky."

"Your fate will be mine. If you live, I'll live. If you die, so will I," she said calmly. "The coincidence is beyond belief -- my parents and yours both killed by the Inquisition. I was full of hate and vengeance, but what was I to do? I was found on the streets begging for food when a sentry took me to the Catholic orphanage. They sell children like merchandise." It was her turn to cry.

David took her into his arms and hugged her. "You miss your parents, don't you?" he asked. "I'll protect you. Come with me. We may have some difficult days, but, by God, we'll bring these animals to their knees."

Her smile and joy at hearing his remarks overcame her and she kissed his cheek. "Go get your things," he ordered, "we'll leave immediately."

Anna ran off. David took the reins in his hands and directed the horse towards her house. By the time he got there, she was out the door with a large sack over her shoulder. "I'm going for some food," she said, "I'll be out in a minute. He's still out cold."

Anna emerged with a basket full of fruit, vegetables, and bread. David helped her onto the driver's bench, placed the bag inside the wagon, and off they went.

"I killed every one of the priests who burned my parents," David paused. "I have never done anything like this in my life. I was enraged. I screamed and yelled, but I couldn't do anything. The wild cheers of that blood-thirsty crowd will never leave me as long as I live."

"You actually watched them die?" she blurted. "How terrible."

"I didn't know what to do. I was in a daze. I'm sure I was afraid of the priests and the shocking scenery. I know I was screaming and shouting. I even remember cursing, but before I realized two of the victims were my parents, the fire was set. I vowed then and there I would kill every one of them, and I did."

"I'm very proud of you," Anna said. "It shows you are a man of character. I will always remember that." They rode in silence for a while.

"What did it feel like killing another man?"

"I really can't tell. I was burning with vengeance. The sight of my dying parents in the worst possible way turned my blood to ice. I had no feeling whatsoever. I vowed to kill them and I did. There were no feelings involved, no thoughts, and later, absolutely no remorse."

"I wish I had your strength and determination. However, I don't know how they died. Some woman told me about their fate, and I ran away. I wandered a few days on the streets of Barcelona. I was dirty, hungry and miserable. I was totally lost. The orphanage seemed like a good place, but I soon found out the children were being used. The man who bought me lost his wife. He turned me into his servant. I cooked his meals, washed his clothes and cleaned his house. I was lucky he didn't molest me sexually," she said.

"Molest you?" David asked. He had no idea what she was talking about. Sex was a forbidden subject, and he didn't know the first thing about it.

"You know," she said, "when men make out with women."

"I'm afraid I don't know a thing about the subject. At my parents house this sort of thing was never discussed."

"Women tend to know more about these things. My mother taught me about sex and the need to watch out for bad men since I was very young. You don't have to worry about it at all."

"I have a lot to learn. Actually, I've never sat so close to a girl, or talked to a girl for that matter. You are the first girl in my life."

"Do you have brothers or sisters?"

"No, I was an only child. I was told my mother couldn't have more children."

"How far are we going today? I'd like to get as far as possible. I'm sure he'll sleep all day because I dropped twice the amount of powder in his drink. I've done it in the past when I wanted a day's rest. Sometimes he would sleep the night and the entire following day."

"How long have you been with him?" David asked

"About a year," she replied. "Can we drive well into the night?"

"I know you want to get as far as possible, but driving at night may be dangerous. Also, the horse needs to rest. If we come across a trading post and the night is clear, I'll replace the horse and we'll be able to continue."

"May I sit closer to you?" She closed in on him before he had a chance to respond. Her touch created a sensation he had not known before. In actuality he didn't have to respond to her question, and was happy about it.

Anna talked a great deal about her childhood and her parents. She too was an only child. David enjoyed listening to her. It was obvious she missed her parents, but their death took place three years ago. While he could detect sorrow in her voice, time healed old pain. He had the feeling that having found him, she was mentally relieved.

The beggar he had stabbed suddenly came to mind. *"He is surely dead by now,"* David thought. *"The others won't bother looking for him. They did not know each other and didn't even talk during the trip. Poor souls. Who knows what their lives were like?"* His thoughts took him to Zevulun. He had not thought of him in days.

"We'll meet a man in Barcelona named Zevulun. He worked in my father's business for many years and was one of his most trusted employees. Zevulun will be known as Carlos Ramirez, a priest from Cordoba. He has vowed to work with us and will help in overthrowing the Inquisition," David suddenly announced.

"Are you sure he can be trusted?" Anna asked.

"Absolutely, I've known him since I was born. My father and Reuven's father trusted him with their lives. He was our courier for years, delivering and receiving documents and monies. He and his wife have no children. They love us. There isn't a thing in the world they won't do for us. Reuven's parents asked him to watch over their son while they were away. They left for Egypt not wanting to live as converts in Aragon. Reuven didn't leave with them because he was committed to fight the Inquisition. His parents had a hard time leaving their son behind, but could not change his mind. You will like Reuven. He's a fine boy. At the moment he is in a monastery masquerading as a monk. Once we get to Barcelona, we'll meet and decide on future action."

"You need money to mount a revolution. How are you going to do it?" Anna asked.

"We have plenty of money and we are full of ideal and spirit to fight the brutal and murderous Church. Actually, we'll need to recruit more young men and women, since we need to attack the Inquisition in various cities around the country. Fighting one city at a time will not bring the results we're seeking."

"It sounds fantastic to me," Anna said. "How can a bunch of kids fight the armies of priests and the Crown?"

"We'll fight in many ways. We already have some interesting ideas. We need to change public opinion. We have to show the masses that the

Church is lying and directing them on a wrong course. It's not the Jews who are the devils, but the Church itself and its doctrines."

"You're certainly very enthusiastic about your revolution. You talk with conviction and passion. I'll help you as you have helped me," she stated.

"Anna, this is not a matter of reciprocity. This is a matter of life and death for our Jewish brethren. Jews have been forced to convert by brutal means, by coercion, by blackmail, and by torture. Jews have been vandalized, brutalized, looted, morally destroyed and killed in cold blood. And all in the name of religion, in the name of their God, in the name of misled conviction and beliefs. Priests, who are supposed to preach the good of the Ten Commandments, morality, of loving thy neighbor, of charity and of humane behavior have turned into torturers and murderers. How can men of the cloth kill another human being, no matter what the reason? This must stop, and if we have to stop it by killing, so be it." David paused. "Your own parents were killed by the Inquisition because they wanted to practice their religion. Has anyone come back from heaven to tell us which religion is the right one, the best one, the one which leads us to salvation?"

"I'm beginning to see your point," Anna said. "I suppose being a girl no one bothered to explain things to me. You are absolutely right. What was the purpose of killing my parents? Not only do the killers have blood on their hands, they left a young girl orphaned to wonder on the streets. I must admit I haven't given enough thought to our Jewish destiny, perhaps because my parents weren't overly religious. Yes, they did practice Jewish holidays and traditions, but that was about the extent of it."

"I'm glad you're beginning to see the true light of the situation. Will you help us for the Cause?" David asked.

"I promise you, I shall help you fight for the Cause and not just for helping me. What are your plans?" she asked.

"We're going to meet Reuven and Zevulun in Barcelona and discuss our future action in depth. Once we make these decisions, we'll begin action," David responded.

"How much further is Barcelona?" she asked.

"I think it'll take us three more days."

"I'm getting tired."

"You wanted to get as far away as possible. We'll have to travel late into the night. I hope we reach a trading post soon. Our horse needs food and rest. He's slowing down, and that's the first sign he's reached his capacity."

"Look, I see a house on the horizon. Is that a trading post?"

"I believe so," David said, "There couldn't be anything else on the road. Lie down in the back and rest. Sitting on this bench for hours is extremely difficult."

David helped her jump into the wagon. He prompted the horse. It turned its head towards him as if to say, "What is it with you. Don't you know I'm tired, too?"

It took an additional two hours before the wagon reached the trading post. The sun had set. Since the sky was clear and the moon was out in force, sending its rays to illuminate the darkness, David decided to replace his horse and drive on. He paid the trader for his services, bought a few provisions, and continued on his way. Anna had slept through the entire stop. A few hours later she woke up. "David, when will we reach the trading post?" she yawned.

"We left it a few hours ago," he replied. "You were sound asleep. I replaced the horse and bought fresh food. The sky is clear and the moon is out. As long as I can see the road, we are moving ahead. Would you prepare something to eat? I don't want to stop until I'm ready to sleep."

"Where is the food?"

"Right behind me on the floor."

"I can't see a thing. It's too dark inside the wagon."

"Feel your way. You can't miss it."

Anna found the basket, took out bread and roasted meat and passed it to David.

"Make something for yourself and come sit next to me. After you've eaten I'll show you how to drive this wagon so I can sleep while we're advancing toward Barcelona," David said.

Anna ate heartily, drank some water and joined David on the driver's bench. She put her arm inside his. They rode in silence for a while. The new horse had been fed and watered before they left the trading post. It would be at least three hours before they'd have to feed it again.

"David," Anna spoke softly, "I could fall in love with you."

"What do you mean? I don't know a thing about love. My only love was for my parents," David protested.

"You're so naïve," Anna said. "Why is it that girls develop at a younger age?"

"Anna, I really have no idea what you're talking about," David said. "My parents never talked about love in the open. In fact, the only thing I know about love is what I studied in the Bible. Please change the subject. You're embarrassing me."

"It's difficult to imagine you killed anyone. You are so gentle with me." she changed the subject.

"I was taught to be gentle. People have to be gentle, respect and honor each other. This is what the Bible teaches us. Yet the Catholic Church faces us with the exact opposite. Our Rabbi asked for an audience with the Queen, and what do you think the result was? He was thrown out and days later was beaten and found dead. Can you imagine killing a man who was as clean and as righteous as our Rabbi?"

"Poor man," Anna said. "How old was he?"

"I don't know his exact age, but he was much older than my father. He was probably seventy, perhaps a little over."

"What was your father's business?" she asked

"My father's business was a branch of the Abulafia's family empire of import and export enterprises, which originated in Alexandria, Egypt. The company was involved in strategic merchandise such as iron, alloys, gold, silver and lumber. There are branches throughout North Africa, Constantinople and Lisbon. The branches in Toledo and Barcelona went out of business recently."

"You said you had all the money needed for the revolution. Where is it?"

"Don't be too curious. I told you we had the resources. Leave it at that. The less you know the better. When the time comes, you'll know more." David was cautious. "What did your father do?"

"My father was Aragon's Court tailor. All the Aragonian dignitaries and nobles had their garments custom made in my father's shop. He was a real artist at tailoring."

"That's interesting, because my father used to import fabric from Damascus. I completely forgot about the fabric business. He told me that fabric rolls were taken by camel caravans from Damascus to Alexandria and from there by ship to Barcelona."

"But your father was in Toledo," Anna said.

"True, but remember, our family business worked through a number of branches. Reuven's father operated the Barcelona branch. If the Toledo branch dealt in fabric, all orders had to be placed through that office. When merchandise arrived at the port of Barcelona, a certain portion of the import would go there and the balance would be shipped by wagons to other cities in Aragon and Castile. Zevulun took orders, delivered merchandise, received monies and delivered such monies to either the Toledo branch or Barcelona, depending on the case," David said.

"This is interesting. It's quite possible my father knew Reuven's father," Anna said.

"I'm beginning to have a hard time keeping my eyes open. Let me show you how to control the horse," David said, "that is, if you want to continue."

"I'd rather you did the driving," she said. "Let's find a place to stop. I could use more rest. I'm not used to sitting on a bench like this. My body aches a little."

David kept going until he saw an opening in the road that led to an apple orchard. He carefully maneuvered the horse when he turned and continued until the wagon was completely hidden from sight. He stopped the horse, unhitched him, and tied him to a tree. He gave him water and hay and returned to the wagon.

"Come up here and lay next to me," Anna said.

"No, that wouldn't be proper."

"Don't be silly. Where are you going to rest, on the ground? Come up here." David was too tired to think. He reluctantly climbed onto the wagon and lay on the hay next to Anna. She moved closer until her body touched his. At first he resisted, but she held him firmly. He fell asleep instantly.

When they awoke in the morning, the sun was high. They thought it was still dawn because the big apple trees and the wagon's top hid the sunrays.

David felt rested and got up anyhow, to find that they had slept half the day. Anna prepared a breakfast of bread, cheese and olives. Hungry, they ate in silence, and drank water. David checked on the horse, gave him water too, and more hay. When the horse had its fill, David hitched it to the wagon and put on the reins. He walked out to the dirt road, and seeing no one, drove the wagon out and continued on to Barcelona.

Anna was getting used to the driver's bench and complained less. She kept holding David's arm. She felt more secure that way. As to David, he began to enjoy the bodily contact. He had a hard time understanding the sensation of his feelings, as he had never experienced them previously.

"How much further is Barcelona?" Anna was anxious.

"I'd say two more days. It usually takes eight days if you make brief nightly stops. We lost half the morning today. It'll be dark in about four hours. At night we cannot maintain good speed. Even though the horse follows the road, he slows down quite a bit when it's dark," David said.

"I need to wash. I feel so dirty. My hair is a mess, too," she announced.

"We could stop on the river's bank, if you like. There's a river flowing near this road about a day's ride from the city," David said.

"That will be wonderful," she said joyfully, "I have to wash myself and change clothes. I want to look pretty for you."

That took David into another unfamiliar orbit.

"What do you mean by looking pretty for me?" he asked.

"You poor thing," she said, "You really don't have a clue about woman – man relationships, do you?"

"Let's stop talking about these things. You're embarrassing me," David said. "I like you a lot the way you are."

"We're making great progress," she announced.

"What progress? What are you talking about?" he blurted.

"Man observes woman, woman observes man, and each develops an impression of the other. That is how relationships start. If one does not create an impression on the other, one moves on. When a man tells a woman that he likes her, that makes her happy, and if she likes him in return, a relationship develops. Think about your parents for a moment. Their being together was a relationship. Each cared for the other. Each tried to please the other. Each enjoyed the other's looks, and each liked and enjoyed being touched by the other. I enjoy holding your arm. Do you enjoy my holding you? Tell me honestly," Anna said.

"Again, you are embarrassing me," David repeated.

"There is nothing wrong talking about your feelings," she said. "In fact, it'll make you feel better. You'll be less shy and it will turn you into a man."

At hearing Anna's words, David turned his head and looked at her for a long time, as though seeing her for the first time. He had never spoken to a girl before. At school there were no girls. He didn't have a sister, and the only women he knew were his mother and the housekeeper. When he saw girls on the street he usually turned his head the other way. *"I have to be a man to do what I'm set to do in the near future,"* he thought, *"perhaps this is where I should begin."*

"You've turned silent suddenly. Do you want me to stop talking about these things?" she asked.

"Oh no!" Davis exclaimed, "I need to learn about the facts of life. I was sheltered as most boys are in this country."

"Would you like an apple?" Anna asked. "While you were caring for the horse, I picked some apples this morning."

They ate apples in silence. David thought about relationships. This was the first time in his life that he was thrown into a situation where he had a woman companion. He thought about his body touching hers and her arm holding his. He couldn't figure out the sensation that engulfed him. He thought it extremely rude, but soon changed his mind. He remembered seeing his father touch his mother, and vice versa.

His thoughts were shattered by the approach of some horsemen in armor. He was motioned to stop. "What are you carrying in the wagon?" a soldier asked.

"Just hay and water," David answered politely.

"Who is this girl with you?"

"My sister."

"Where are you headed?"

"To visit our brother. He is a monk in San Christopher monastery in Barcelona."

"You are not lying to us, are you, boy?"

"Oh no, sir," David responded. "Take a look for yourself, there's nothing in the wagon but hay and our food." The soldier sent one of his men who searched the wagon and affirmed David's claim.

"What is your name?"

"My name is Jesus and this is my sister Margarita. May we continue?"

"Do you have any money?"

"And how do you suppose two poor children would have money. All I have is two brass bits, which my father gave me," David spoke with conviction.

"Be on your way," the soldier ordered loudly, and rode off with his men.

"You were magnificent," Anna declared.

"I've been rehearsing such encounters many times since I left Toledo. We're lucky they didn't accost us. Zevulun told me many stories about soldiers attacking travelers on these roads. Apparently, they're paid poorly and rob passengers to supplement their income. He also told me of soldiers belonging to one estate fighting other landowners."

"Have you met any other soldiers since you left Toledo?" she asked.

"No, this was the first time. I did give a ride to four beggars when I left Toledo, thinking that having passengers would help, but that was a grave mistake. One of them tried to rob me at night. I had to stab him. I hid his body in a nearby ravine and left in a hurry," David recounted somberly.

"You certainly have had all kinds of experiences during the last few weeks," she said; "I hope that from now on life will be better for you."

"I doubt it very much. You're forgetting we are about to launch a revolution against the Church. You didn't think I was joking with you, or did you?" David asked.

"Frankly, at first, I didn't know what to make of your statements, but now I know you are serious. I can see that you think fast and are on your toes. You responded to the soldiers quickly, and were convincing. You spoke like a grown man. I was frozen when they stopped us. I didn't know what to think. I'm glad you handled it so well."

"Anna, there's going to be a lot of action after we decide on our course. Be assured that many missions will be dangerous. We may put our lives at risk on any number of occasions. When we reach Barcelona, you'll have to choose between staying on and fighting in our camp, or leaving, and doing what you please."

"My decision has been made. I will stay and fight with you. Something in my heart directs me to you. I'll learn to be strong. You are going to be proud of me."

"I have to admit I'm very happy you made this decision. I like you by my side."

Anna bent over and kissed David on his cheek. He liked it a lot. He began feeling maturity, of being a man. They continued silently for a while and then David suddenly exploded with many questions.

"Do you have other relatives in Barcelona? Aunts, uncles, cousins or grandparents?"

"I have two uncles and aunts and a number of cousins. They converted long before my father did. Due to circumstances with the Church and the Inquisition, my parents decided to keep away from our relatives. Each family lived like an island of its own. What a shame, for my parents died anyway and I have no knowledge of what happened to them."

"You see? This is precisely what we are fighting about. We want to abolish the brutal and murderous Inquisition. We want to change the opinion of the masses, which have been mislead and cheated by the Church, and above all, we want to restore decent living conditions for the Jews. People should learn that tolerance and respect for their fellow man is what God wants. We have a massive job on our hands, but we are committed. We will not rest until we have succeeded. I can see our actions as the retribution for our parent's death."

"You must know the Bible well," Anna said, changing the subject.

"Indeed I do. Since the age of four I've been attending the Hebrew school in our synagogue. Our Rabbi was a very interesting man. All of us loved him a great deal. He always taught us the Bible, interpreting it through vivid stories. As we grew up, the studies became more intense, but we didn't mind. He was a very colorful personality. My parents loved him, too. He was highly respected in the community and never had trouble getting an audience with Queen Isabella."

"Why was he beaten to death?" she asked.

David recounted his talk with his father and the Rabbi's visit with the queen. Again, he repeated his oath and determination to fight the Inquisition.

"You are absolutely right. Somehow these brutal people have to be stopped. Unfortunately, being a girl, I was left out. As you know, men don't think much of women. We cook, clean, give birth, attend to our husbands' needs, and what they tell us is the extent of our knowledge. I'm ignorant in these matters, but now that my parents are dead and you are painting the picture of our lives in this country, I'm beginning to see and understand better. I promise you again I will be at your side and help fight these monsters."

David was pleased with himself. He had recruited his first person. The sun had set, and his natural hunger reminded him his horse needed to be fed and watered. He stopped at the trading post, and Anna prepared supper. The horse was fed and watered, and placed in the barn for the night. He got a cheap room. There was nothing in the room except a thin mattress on the floor, a basin for washing and a huge candle on a pedestal. He went out and brought fresh water.

Anna washed her face and suddenly dropped her dress. David almost passed out. He had never seen the naked body of a woman. Anna continued to wash her body and when done walked over to David and kissed him on the mouth. David was shocked. He couldn't utter a single word.

"You are in total shock, poor David," she said. "I wish you could see your face. Would you like to touch me?" He was lost for words and couldn't take his eyes off her beautiful body. "You are beautiful," he finally mumbled. "You shouldn't have done this. I've never seen a naked woman before."

"Here, let me help you undress. You must wash, too." And having said that, she proceeded to undress him. He moved back a bit, but she paid no attention. A minute later he was nude. She washed him, and when done, came closer and kissed him on the mouth. She knew this was his first time and did not want to push him too hard. She helped him into a fresh garment she took out of his sack and suggested they go to sleep. David allowed her to guide him like a sheep. She lay next to him naked and soon they were cuddled as all lovers do. Sleep came easily as they were tired from the many hours of travel.

They awakened the next morning from a sound sleep. Anna caressed David's body from head to toe and kissed him again. David thought he had landed in paradise and discovered parts of his body he had not known before. Anna asked him to caress her, which he did after a slow start. Suddenly, there was a knock on the door and the innkeeper's voice announced that his horse was ready. They dressed quickly and left the room. After a hearty breakfast of bread, cheese, eggs and olives, they continued their journey.

It was late afternoon when they began descending the high ground towards Barcelona. The entire city could be seen from the road, which slowly wound its way to the coast. San Christopher Monastery was outside the city limits and easily distinguished by its size and structure. David decided to settle for the night in a small forest bordering the road. It wasn't too far from the monastery. He drove the wagon into the forest so it wouldn't be seen.

"My dilemma is how to communicate with Reuven," David said.

Anna suggested she go to the monastery, ring the front entrance bell and ask for Reuven. David rejected the idea.

"That's not a good idea," he said. "I know Reuven goes out for a walk every day after the midday meal when the monks take their siesta. We'll have to watch the grounds. Once he's out of the monastery, you can approach him and tell him that I'm here in the forest. He will join us at night. We must play it safe."

"Very well," Anna said. "Let's eat and rest our aching bones. I'm not used to sitting on a bouncing bench for hour after hour. At least Barcelona is in sight."

Anna took out the food and they ate in silence. David's mind was racing. He finally spoke. "I've been thinking a great deal about how we should start our operation, but I can't make any decisions without hearing Reuven and Zevulun. I want to hear their plans then we can reach some consensus. Reuven is going to be quite surprised when he hears what I've done. He hasn't touched a fly yet, while I killed about ten priests. I'm well ahead of him, and supposedly he is the leader. I'll admit, though, he is the spirit behind our movement. What happened to me was pure fate. I will let him lead the fight and take charge."

"What does it matter who leads the fight? The three of you should be working as a team. The best idea should be pursued. In my mind, it's that simple," Anna said.

"That makes a great deal of sense," David said. "I'll suggest it if it becomes necessary. I suppose there isn't much we can do now but relax." They stretched out on what remained of the hay and were sleeping soundly within minutes.

It was impossible to see sunlight through the thickness of the wood. When they awoke it was close to noon. They hadn't realized the time until they came to the edge of the forest and saw the road and the monastery. David cut a big slice of bread for himself and one for Anna. The cheese had gone sour. They sat on the ground and talked until Reuven's figure appeared in the distance.

"That's him," David shouted excitedly. "Pretend to be playing or collecting flowers when you reach him. Talk briefly and quickly run in my direction -- that will tell him where we are."

Anna ran off like a gazelle. She began collecting wild flowers and by the time she reached Reuven, she was holding a sizeable bunch.

"David is waiting for you in the forest. Watch the direction I'm running. We'll wait for you after dark next to the first tree." She ran off, jumping and skipping like a child at play.

"He'll be here tonight after dark," Anna said. "Let's go into the city and buy fresh food. We may have to stay here a day or two. We need to be properly supplied."

"Very good." David hitched the horse and off they went, making a mental note of the location they were to meet Reuven later that night. The ride to Barcelona took about an hour. They purchased food and Anna bought some clothing for David and a blanket. They returned to their forest before sunset. They ate and drank fresh juice, even the horse had a smile on its face, David thought.

David was very tense. He wanted Reuven to be there already. He kept looking at the field between the forest and the monastery, but couldn't see much. It was hours before Reuven appeared. Their reunion was overwhelming. They hugged and kissed each other for the longest time.

"I can't tell you how overjoyed my heart is by your arrival," Reuven spoke first. "I have been dreaming of this moment for months. Zevulun arrived recently and has settled in a house in the middle of the city. He found a house with a large shed, which is what we need."

David expressed his joy too, and introduced Anna.

"Oh! I'm sorry, Reuven, please meet Anna. Anna, this is my brother Reuven. We call each other brother because we believe we are as close to each other as brothers."

Anna rose and shook Reuven's hand.

"Anna has joined our team," David announced.

"Good. Now, what did you mean by 'What you have gone through'?" Reuven seemed concerned.

"Reuven, this will shock you. My parents were burned at the stake. I vowed revenge and killed every priest that participated in the ritual." He fell silent.

Reuven grasped his head with his hands. "This is terrible. Where were you when this took place?"

"I was in the cheering crowd. I screamed and yelled but couldn't do a thing." David recounted the horrific events of the night his parents died. "I killed all the priests. They deserved to die," he concluded.

"So that was the uproar I heard last night," Reuven said. "The news of the killing of many priests arrived yesterday. They said one of the priests went mad and killed the others."

"I assume we can meet with Zevulun immediately. What is his address?"

Reuven gave him the address and they decided to meet in Zevulun's house the next day.

"I convinced the prior to use me as a courier for the monastery. I was given the job. This enables me to get into the city almost daily. I have a carriage at my disposal. I deliver produce and do some shopping. I'll meet you two at Zevulun's house sometime tomorrow. I have to be back. I don't want to be missed at night." They shook hands warmly and Reuven left.

CHAPTER TWO

On Friday, the 28th of August, 1476, Reuven, David, Zevulun, and Anna held their first meeting. David and Anna arrived on the 27th. Zevulun, dressed in a priest's habit, was ecstatically happy to see David, as was his wife.

"I can't begin tell you how happy I am to see you," he said. "Reuven told me all about your ordeal. I know your father and mother died in the name of our God. Please don't hold it against them. I loved your parents. I will mourn them for years to come. I'm very proud of you. Oh! I have a letter for you from Lisbon."

"It's good to see you, Zevulun," David said. "From now on we'll see each other often."

"We'll have to because we're going to work together," Zevulun pointed out.

"David told me so much about you," Anna said, "I feel like I've known you all my life."

"I'm sorry about your parents. It seems you're in good company."

"Thank you for your hospitality. I'm delighted to be here." She avoided his comment.

"We'll start our meeting as soon as Reuven arrives."

A gentle knock on the door indicated his arrival. He looked funny in the monk's habit and way of walking.

"Welcome, monsignor," David smiled. "Please take off this ridiculous outfit while we hold our meeting."

"What if someone suddenly comes in -- it'll seem legitimate if Zevulun and I stay in our usual habits. Let's begin the meeting. I wish to point out before we start that I've waited a long time for this day. My commitment and determination have not wavered one bit. I'm willing to do anything to fight the Church and its Inquisition. When I developed the first thoughts about the need to stand up to their barbarous acts, I hadn't personally suffered except for my parents forced conversion and my baptism. The killing of David's parents brings another reason to our cause. Let's begin, and God be with us."

"I'll get straight to the point. I suggest we discuss the ways in which to attack the Inquisition," David said.

"Good idea," Zevulun agreed. "We should attack and destroy their places of operation, create internal confusion within their hierarchy, and help change public opinion."

"We also need to break the relationship between the Crown and Torquemada," David added. "This is an absolute necessity."

"And we need to recruit more people. We can't possibly do all of this by ourselves. If Inquisition buildings are attacked simultaneously throughout Castile and Aragon, the impact will be greater than one building at a time. It will send a message and create greater panic."

"While more operatives are recruited, I'd like to flood the priesthood with fabricated letters, which will start the confusion and develop suspicion among the clergy. For example, I write a letter addressed to Cardinal Pedro Gonzalez de Mendoza, signed by a leading priest, demanding a change in the behavior of the Inquisition. The priest will most probably be called in. He will deny having written the letter, and 'suspicion' is introduced. Similar letters should be sent from one clergy to another, from clergy to Crown, and from Crown to clergy. If every day three to five such letters circulate, I believe the confusion will be tremendous because no recipient will trust the other."

"This is formidable. I like it a lot," David said, "but remember, you need wax seals for each of the letters."

"That is were Anna could help. She could pretend to be a member of the cleaning staff and steal seals. It's very easy to enter any of the establishments, as all doors are open and unlocked. I also believe that anyone could enter in the early hours of the morning, just as you did in Toledo," Zevulun said.

"First order of the day is to develop a list of names and addresses of all the people we want to include in our fabricated letters. I would suggest that once the first letters have been written and delivered, a number of fires be set in select locations. The leaders of the Church, Torquemada in particular, will not know what to make of it, and would certainly start an investigation. Such a massive investigation will take their minds off the dealings with the Jews and Marranos and give many of our people a reprieve. And, while they're investigating, we send a new batch of letters advising Torquemada of a Christian underground fighting for change and the liquidation of the Inquisition," Reuven said.

"I've compiled a list of the major cities the Inquisition operates in. They are: Toledo, Barcelona, Zaragoza, Segovia, Tarragona, Valencia, Bilbao, Santander, Valladolid, La Coruna, Salamanca, Leon, and Alicante. I suggest we penetrate the offices of the Archbishop, as he surely will have the addresses. Stealing the mailing list should not be a problem. I'm sure we'll find it in the room used by his secretary or scribe. The Archbishop does not write his own letters, he just signs and seals them. Stealing the seal may be the problem," Zevulun said.

"As far as we know, no thefts of any kind have occurred in offices of the clerics, so the first time should be the easiest. I propose we steal the seals and addresses all at once, during the same night," Anna said.

"This is good thinking," Reuven agreed. "The only issue is that the key offices of the Archbishops, Cardinals and bishops are scattered in every one of the cities Zevulun outlined. We desperately need more people."

"I can recruit some of my friends in Barcelona," Anna stated. "How about you, Reuven, you should know people in this city."

"In fact, I do. I have three old time friends I haven't seen in a while. I'll look them up. I believe all of them are Conversos. I shouldn't have difficulty recruiting them," Reuven said.

"I suggest you start writing the letters," David said to Zevulun. By the time we come up with the seals and addresses, you'll be ready."

"Excellent idea," Zevulun said. "I plan to spend the rest of the day to canvass the holy offices in Barcelona while the two of you are recruiting. David can go on his own. Let's meet back here as soon as the sun has set. My wife -- that is my housekeeper -- will prepare supper."

"Before we leave, there is one issue we need to discuss. I have limited time to run errands in the city. I have to return to the monastery. The question is whether I should continue to stay there, or leave," Reuven said.

"I think you should continue to stay in the monastery until our operations begin. Your disappearance may cause undue attention," Zevulun said.

"Very well, so be it," Reuven agreed.

They left the house one by one so as not to draw attention. With a list of Churches and Holy Offices in hand, David proceeded to explore each and every one of them. Anna, who knew Barcelona well, advised him on the best route to save time. She went directly to homes of her friends. Reuven went about the monastery business, and Zevulun went to meet some of his new priest friends.

They returned by sunset. Zevulun learned there were two bishops in Barcelona and produced their names and addresses. Anna was very excited. "Four of my friends will join us. I arranged to meet them in San Miguel's Cathedral at 10 o'clock in the morning. There is a large garden in the back where we'll have absolute privacy. I suggest Zevulun and David interview them."

"This is good news. We'll meet them together at the Cathedral tomorrow morning," David said.

"I'm getting tremendous recognition as the priest who managed to flee Moorish territory. I've been offered all kinds of help. I told them I inherited some money, which I used to buy a house," Zevulun said. "I was offered a job, but I declined. I told them I was in very poor health and could not work."

"That was quick thinking on your part," David said.

"I had some time when I returned home, and here is a letter I wrote.

His Eminence,
Archbishop,
 Juan Capisato de Aruba,

It is with much remorse that I'm writing to you this morning. My heart and soul are very disturbed at the affairs of our Church. I pray you will accept these words coming from my heart and not misunderstand them.

I have come to realize that we have been interpreting the words of our fathers much too harshly. If Saint John said that those who do not abide by the words of God should wither, I don't think he meant that we should kill them. The entire approach to conversion of people from other faiths should be re-examined. There have to be better ways to convert people to Catholicism than through threats, blackmail, torture and force. Frankly, what are those people to think of us? It wouldn't surprise me at all if they considered us animals. Is this what we really want to achieve? All the forced Conversos are suddenly praying to a new God, and most probably curse him under their breath.

I sincerely believe we should examine our missionary work. We should be able to reach people in a friendly manner rather than by force. I'm very concerned that as the news of our behavior gets out to the world at large, people's perception of Catholicism will worsen.

I would suggest you discuss this matter and my ideas with the clerics in your Church areas and parishes, and respond to me in about a month.
Yours,
Bishop

"This is phenomenal," David said. "One of two things will happen. If the Archbishop has a soft spot in his heart, he will start the ball rolling as the Bishop suggested. If he is radical, he'll travel to the Bishop and argue his case. Either way the Bishop will deny having written the letter. The Archbishop will become suspicious and will go to higher authority. Who knows who will call whom, and the confusion we are talking about will start. People within the Church will begin questioning each other's loyalty, sincerity and belief."

"At first I thought to flood the country with fabricated letters, but now I'm of the opinion that such letters should not be mass produced. A letter here and a letter there from one authority to another will slowly find its way to the creation of the greatest disruption. Hopefully, one day some of the clerics will restart their thinking and come to the sensible conclusion that ways of conversion have to be modified," Zevulun said.

"And while these letters are surfacing in Castile and Aragon, we burn down a few of the Inquisitions' buildings, and kill some of the most radical priests," David said.

"What is it you wish my friends to do?" Anna asked. "I'm fascinated by this discussion."

"The first order of the day is to steal the wax seals from the Archbishops, Cardinals, Bishops, and the Crown in major cities. We have to make lists of the names and addresses of all clerics in each of them. If your friends join us we'll send each one to cover one or two cities. We'll meet back here, say in a month. Meanwhile Zevulun will prepare the letters, which will be sent to different clergy at different times. This task should not be too difficult as every Church or Holy Office I've been to was unguarded. I walked in after midnight and did what I pleased."

"I'm going to ask for an audience with the Queen's scribe," Zevulun said. "Getting her seal will be the most difficult, but try I will."

CHAPTER THREE

The meeting in the gardens of San Miguel Cathedral went well. Anna introduced four of her friends.

"It's indeed a great pleasure to meet you. I understand from Anna that every one of you has suffered a loss of family to the Inquisition. I'm deeply sorry about it. I lost both of my parents. They were burned to death because they refused to convert.

"It must be understood that by joining our group you'll have to detach yourselves from anything you do today. You'll have to devote full time to our movement. There will be a great deal of traveling through Aragon and Castile. You may have to sleep outdoors so as not to attract attention. You'll be required to steal certain items from Churches and Holy Offices. Do any of you have a problem with this?" David began.

The two boys and two girls nodded. "We'll do everything you ask us to do," said Juan, formerly Itzhak Ben David. "Anna explained the objectives of the movement very clearly, and the four of us would like nothing better than to break the Inquisition. My father was tortured for days before he agreed to convert. Since his torturing, he has remained an invalid. My mother has to work as a housekeeper to support the family. I was baptized and am attending a Catholic school, which I hate. Yossef, tell David of your ordeal."

Yossef, whose name was changed to Ferdinand, said, "My parents were arrested about two years ago. I haven't seen them since. I presume they are dead. When I went to inquire about them I was forcefully baptized and placed in a Catholic school. I share a room with three other boys. I'll gladly work with you and the movement."

"What about you?" David asked Maria, previously Elisheva.

"My mother is an exceptionally beautiful woman. One day, she was grabbed by two sentries while shopping in the Plaza and raped. My father went to the military authorities to complain. He was arrested and handed over to the Inquisition. I never saw him again. My mother is mentally ill. We are supported by my uncle who converted," Elisheva began crying. "I'll do anything to fight these animals."

"My parents were burned to death, too," Isabella, previously Yael, said. "I'll gladly sacrifice my life, if I have to. I'll fight the Inquisition until my dying breath. I was thinking about revolution many times, but what could I do on my own? I'm very happy this organization came into being. You will have my entire support."

"It saddens me to hear about the tragedy that afflicted your families. There isn't a family in Aragon and Castile that hadn't been vandalized, tortured and forced into conversion. We are committed to fight, and fight we will! We are preparing a war of attrition against the Inquisition. We will not stop until this beastly and inhuman office is closed down, and our people can practice Judaism freely and in the open," David stated. "The six of us will go in different directions tomorrow. We will travel in pairs. I'll designate two cities for each. I need you to list the churches, Holy Offices, and their addresses. I must have the names and addresses of Archbishops, Cardinals and Bishops, if any, and those of leading priests as well. In particular, I want those working for the Inquisition. Once you have completed these lists, you will steal their wax seals, and bring some samples of their writing. Make sure to note the name of the cleric each seal and writing sample belongs to. Once you have the seals and the information, you return to Barcelona."

David asked them to memorize Zevulun's address. He assigned Yossef and Elisheva to Toledo and Bilbao, Itzhak and Yael to Tarragona and Vallavolid, and for Anna and himself, Zaragoza and Segovia. It was later decided Zevulun would travel to Leon and Salamanca. He gave each couple two gold dukats and wished them well.

"Don't rush, do your job without raising suspicion, and avoid getting caught. Please don't take any undue risks. If questioned, you are brother and sister visiting relatives. Also, please wear simple clothing and appear to be plain people," David instructed. "I found out that tomorrow morning one of the freight ships is sailing for Constantinople. I suggest each of you leave a note to your guardians that you left on board the "Stambuli" for Constantinople. They will have no way of verifying your departure. This means that as of tomorrow you go underground. Please make the proper arrangements so that your message will be delivered tomorrow afternoon after the ship has departed.

"Take your clothing and any important items you cherish. Whatever you do not take with you when you leave on your mission, please leave at Zevulun's house for keeping. Are there any questions?"

"Everything is quite clear. I hope I can speak on behalf of all of us," Yossef said. "We're going to work with you all the way. We discussed the future among ourselves before this morning's meeting, and I want you to know we are committed to the cause. You can count on us in every way. We will not waver and we will not rest until the Inquisition has been terminated."

"Thank you for your words. I greatly appreciate it. I'm sure we'll make a great team," David said. They shook hands and Anna kissed them good-bye. The four youngsters left.

"We're on our way," Zevulun said, "God willing, we'll succeed."

"Amen," David agreed.

CHAPTER FOUR

David, Anna and Zevulun remained seated in the garden for a while. Zevulun expressed his satisfaction and sorrow at the tragedy that had hit every one of Anna's friends. He felt that only people who were badly hurt would truly fight for the cause. Anna said the reason she selected those four was precisely because of their suffering at the hand of the Inquisition.

"I'm convinced they'll be a great asset to us," Anna declared.

"How do you foresee the distribution of your letters?" David inquired.

"Thinking this issue through carefully, I quickly realized that mass distribution would indicate sabotage. Torquemada will automatically issue a communiqué to all concerned that someone was sabotaging the Church, and to disregard all correspondence. On the other hand, if letters are received one by one at different cities, it will start to create suspicion and confusion. When and if reported to Torquemada, it will open a can of worms. Suspicion will arise that some of the clergy oppose the brutality of the Inquisition and are out of line. If I'm not mistaken, the Church will exile or excommunicate them. The result will be the same – fewer priests working for the devil," Zevulun replied.

"This makes a great deal of sense. When letters questioning the role of the Inquisition and its methods circulate in every city at different times, there will be no connection to a countrywide scheme. At the same time I plan to liquidate any priest who participates in burning people to death. A note will be attached to every dead clergy, explaining why the priest was killed, and as these cases become known, priests will fear the vengeance of God," David said.

"I know it's a most difficult task to kill another human being, but I fully agree with you. A priest who can burn another human being to death does not deserve to live. It's the torturing and killing that is so beastly," Zevulun consented.

"I'm killing them with the same ease they killed my parents. I can't say I'm enjoying it, but I will admit to enjoying the vengeance part of it. Also, we want to break down the Inquisition. If we eliminate their trusted priests, we'll bring about the closure of the Inquisition sooner," David predicted.

"David, I'll be next to you and help you in any way I can," Anna said. "I'm convinced we'll succeed."

"I know Reuven has a list of the main Churches and Inquisition buildings in Barcelona. Through the monastery he has the information about the higher hierarchy of the clergy in this city. I'll be sure to take it from him. Let's get ready. I want to make a few more visits in Barcelona before leaving for Leon," Zevulun said.

They returned to Zevulun's house.

"I want to see Reuven before we leave," David said.

"I'm sure he would want to see you, too," Zevulun agreed. "He should be arriving sometime this afternoon."

*****

Reuven arrived later than expected. "I left the monastery later than usual. Bishop Alonso de Rocha, the city's lead Bishop, visited the monastery this morning. He was given a tour of the property. After midday prayers he had a long conference with the prior and some of the monks behind closed doors. Unfortunately, I couldn't listen in. The monk in charge of commerce attended that meeting, too. My wagon was loaded with boxes of apples for delivery to the city. I left without specific instructions."

"I hope you won't get in trouble," David said.

"Normally, I receive instructions every day. However, if he asks me why I left, I'll simply say the wagon was loaded and I didn't want to deliver the apples too late."

"It sounds reasonable, but will he react reasonably -- that is the question," David said.

"I'm sure I'll find out soon enough. Well, how did it go this morning?" Reuven asked.

David recounted the events of the morning. He expressed his satisfaction with the new recruits, and explained their routes.

"Very good. We need to decide whether I should continue in the monastery or disappear," Reuven said.

"I believe you should continue there," Zevulun said. "You can do whatever needs to be done in Barcelona under the best cover there is."

"What is the situation in Barcelona?" David inquired. "We've been busy getting started and didn't discuss Barcelona at all."

"The situation here is similar to every other city. The Inquisition is systematically going after Jews who haven't converted. The torture chambers are used to capacity. Four men were burned to death last week. The priest who gave me this information was speaking with such delight that I almost strangled him in the open," Zevulun said.

"I would like to deliver one letter to the Bishop of Segovia supposedly written by the Bishop of Barcelona. Perhaps you could postpone your departure by a day. I'm terribly interested to know what the reaction would be, and what steps the Church would take. Your sample letter should do."

"We need the Bishop's wax seal for the letter. I'll go to his house after midnight and seal the letter. This way the seal will be left in its place, and the suspicion may be bigger than we anticipated."

"There's no question it would sound better. However, we have no other choice but to steal the seals," David said.

Zevulun produced the letter he had prepared, and added the names. "I'll give it to you tomorrow morning."

"Is it possible the Bishop will spend the night in the monastery?" Anna asked.

"Why would he?" Reuven replied. "After all, he lives near by and probably would prefer his own bed to the hard mattresses used at the monastery."

"I hate to see you go, but I don't want you missed at the monastery, particularly since you left on your own," David said. "We'll be back in about three weeks. Upon our return we'll stop at the forest across the field from the monastery. When you see Anna running and collecting flowers during your noontime stroll, you'll know we've returned."

They hugged each other and Reuven left. "I surely love the two of you," Anna said. "But you, David, I love the most." She crossed over to him and kissed him on the cheek. David was dumbfounded, but said nothing. Zevulun had a big smile on his face.

"Don't forget your age, lovebirds."

After supper they lingered at the kitchen table. Zevulun's wife, whose voice was never heard, suddenly erupted.

"Such young boys and girls about to start a man's job! Why aren't older and experienced men mounting a fight against the Inquisition?"

"It's really difficult to answer your question. Perhaps it's that Jews have never been a fighting people, particularly since we were exiled from our homeland. We're spread in thousands of cities around the world and we're minorities in each one of them. Also, I believe our educational system is so pacifist and Bible oriented that to most of us fighting is too remote," Zevulun volunteered.

"Please let me know if there's anything I can do," she said. "I for one would certainly want to fight."

"I'm sure you'll get your chance," Zevulun said.

"There is another aspect to our dilemma," David said. "The Inquisition didn't start an all out attack on the Jews. It developed slowly and is still continuing. With time it became more aggressive and their methods more brutal. I believe the masses know very little about the Jews except for what the Church tells them. Therefore, I have to conclude that it's a minority of extreme religious Catholic fanatics that rule. It is this minority we have to eliminate."

"Do you mean "kill" when you say eliminate?" Anna asked.

"The answer is yes. They have no qualms about killing innocent men and women. Why should we?" David answered.

"Wouldn't killing their priests raise a new Satan in their eyes? The Church might fight fire with fire. Imagine what would happen if the Church suddenly informs the masses the Jews are killing their priests. Stupid, ignorant, and superstitious people that they are, they'll swallow any new statement made," she said.

"Anna has a point. We didn't think of such a possibility."

"It's true the Church or the Inquisition might announce that Jews are killing their priests. But superstition works both ways. Let me put it this way. Once we've eliminated a good number of priests and have caused enough confusion and mistrust among the clerics, we can announce our existence. Our announcement will denounce the methods of the Inquisition and explain the truth. I'm sure that not all the public will accept our word, but some will, and that is what we should count on. Just as we create a confusion among the clerics, we should create confusion in the general public. One way or the other we have to break the Inquisition and anything that supports it. In any fight or revolution there are bound to be casualties. We'll do the best we can, but whatever sacrifice is needed, we have to be prepared to expend it," David stated.

"You're right. There can't be a 'perfect' revolution. Some people are bound to get hurt, but the results of the fight will save hundreds of thousands of lives, not to mention torture, agony and disaster," Zevulun concurred.

"I agree. Your argument makes a great deal of sense."

"I can imagine the chaos that will be created when one Bishop writes to another questioning the ways of the Inquisition. I believe we can bank on human behavior. No matter what the Bishop says to defend himself, the suspicion will have been created in someone's mind. And as more letters circulate, there will be more talk, more denials, more suspicion, and an atmosphere of uncertainty will develop.

"We shouldn't forget letters to and from the Queen. Those letters will be the ultimate in confusion. I'd give anything to see Torquemada's face," David said.

"We're going to have a long day tomorrow. Let's go to bed," Anna said.

Sleep did not come easily to David. His mind was mulling over the work that needed to be done, the necessary killings, and the massive hunt they'd have to evade. Surely the Crown and the Church will be after them. After a while, unable to sleep, he got up. He couldn't stay in bed. He decided to sit on the front porch and wait for Zevulun. It felt like hours, but finally he was rewarded. Zevulun appeared, walking briskly. David hugged him. "I couldn't sleep knowing you're on a mission."

"I'm very happy you waited up for me. Here's the letter. The wax seal was on the Bishop's desk. His entire household was asleep. I found his study easily. The seal was on top of his desk. I was in and out in two minutes flat," Zevulun said.

This time, when he finally went back to bed, David fell asleep without any difficulty.

CHAPTER FIVE

Yossef and Elisheva met early on the morning of their departure. Each was carrying a heavy sack. They decided to drop unnecessary items at Zevulun's house. The two gold dukats David gave them was far more than they'd ever need. David and Anna were gone by the time they arrived. Only Zevulun's wife was there. She greeted them warmly and offered a hot drink. They accepted with pleasure since they hadn't had breakfast.

They left the house in mid afternoon and walked towards the city limit. Several wagons and coaches passed by. Finally, a large wagon let them mount on the rear empty platform. The driver said he'd take them as far as the village of Nabatia, a day and a half ride from Bilbao. They made themselves comfortable for the long trip.

"This is the first time I'm traveling like a pauper," Elisheva said. "In the past, when I traveled with my parents, we used one of my father's coaches. The seats were comfortable, but the long trips were boring. At least today I'm traveling with you and have a great reason."

"This is a first for me too. I suppose we'll get used to rough traveling conditions. We have to be careful, as there may be thieves and robbers on the way. I suggest you keep one dukat and I the other. I brought a lot of loose change from my savings, which I'll use first," Yossef declared.

"I have a few coins too. Do you think it'll be difficult to complete our mission?"

"I believe our mission is quite simple. We enter one Church after another and ask questions."

"What kind of questions?"

"Plain conversation – anything that comes to mind. Eventually, we ask pointed questions. We'll use the name of Carlos Ramirez."

"If we're asked who this Priest is, we can say he's an uncle of ours who escaped Cordoba, and we heard he was in Bilbao," Elisheva suggested.

"That's fine," Yossef said. "Did Anna tell you about her ordeal? Poor girl, she was sold to some man and served him as his housekeeper and maid. She met David by accident when he was traveling to Barcelona."

Elisheva ran a large comb through her hair. "I like David. He seems to be a fine young man. He's very talented, and I must say, extremely committed to the cause."

"He comes from a very wealthy family. I remember my father talking about the Abulafias. I wonder if he has the money his parents left before they were burned to death."

"It could very well be that the inquisitors took away their belongings before killing them." Elisheva kept combing her long hair, holding the ends while she worked on the tangles.

"That's possible, but knowing the caliber of this family, it wouldn't surprise me if they made special arrangements. Did you notice how casually he gave us the gold dukats?"

"Not particularly. It was kind of him to give us this much money."

"To mount an operation as big as this, we'll need a great deal of money. Many people will have to live underground without earning anything. All of us will have to be supported, as well as any families." Yossef said.

"I wonder why he wanted us to travel in pairs?" Elisheva wondered.

"I believe it's for safety reasons. Also, one can help the other when the necessity arises, and two are less suspicious than one. As he said, we can pretend to be brother and sister." Yossef was pleased with his response.

"Should we plan our own mission so that we follow a routine?" she asked.

They discussed various methods they could use to uncover the needed information, and agreed that David's idea to steal the wax seals during the last night in the city was excellent.

"Is the driver of this wagon planning to stop anywhere?" Elisheva wondered.

"I'm sure he will. I didn't ask him how far he was going. Let's try and rest. I don't know about you, but I'm tired."

"Very good. I'm sort of sleepy, too."

But sleep didn't come to either of them. The constant bouncing of the platform and the galloping horses made sleep impossible. They sat up against the rear wall and watched the scenery. The driver kept going until he could no longer see. He stopped the wagon on the side of the road. "We'll spend the night here. Do you have blankets?"

"Yes, we do." Yossef answered, "and some food. You may join us if you wish."

"I have a basket my wife prepared," he said. "Let's share the bounty of God." The three of them made themselves comfortable on the ground and had their supper. The driver offered Yossef and Elisheva a drink laced with wine. He had a few cups and was sound asleep before they settled. Yossef found his blankets and covered him. He put the rest of the food away and both lay on the flat floor of the platform. The wine took away the discomfort of the hard floor and they were soon in deep sleep.

A galloping cavalry unit woke them up. It was the first time they had noticed the wagon was parked next to a side road leading to a castle. The cavalry stopped and a handsomely decorated officer faced them. Armour covered his body, arms and legs. Even his head was partially covered with a steel helmet. "What are you doing here?"

Yossef looked around for the driver, who was nowhere to be seen. "We're on our way to Bilbao. The driver stopped here for the night because he couldn't see the road anymore."

"Where is this driver?"

"He slept right here on the ground. You can see his blankets." Suddenly a notion went through his mind. He quickly checked his pocket to find that his money was gone. "He stole my money."

"Mine, too," Elisheva said, and began to cry.

"I saw a man walking into the Castle early this morning," said a soldier.

"Let's find him," the officer said. "I am Juan Castelon, the son of the Landowner." Yossef and Elisheva introduced themselves.

"Why are you two youngsters going to Bilbao on your own?"

"Our parents left for Bilbao three weeks ago and haven't returned. We don't know what happened to them. They should have been back last week. We were worried and decided to go look for them," Yossef responded.

"Mount this horse and follow us," Juan said. "Leave your things on the wagon. I'll have one of the soldiers guard it while we ride into the castle."

Yossef had riding experience, but Elisheva did not. He mounted the horse with ease and pulled Elisheva up. She was terrified. It was a very short ride. As they entered, galloping over the open drawbridge, Juan made a sharp turn to the right and stopped almost immediately. "Wait here," he ordered and walked through a narrow doorway. A minute later he came out pulling a man with him. "Is this the driver of the wagon?"

"That's him!" Yossef exclaimed.

"Where is the money you stole from these youngsters?" the officer asked.

"I gave it to the tavern keeper," he answered.

"Bring the tavern keeper out here," he ordered one of his men.

"How much money did this man give you?" Juan asked the tavern keeper as he came through the door.

"He gave me two gold dukats. He owes me three," the tavern keeper responded firmly.

"Let me have the two dukats. As far as you are concerned, he still owes you the money. He cannot repay his debt with stolen money." He took the gold coins and gave them to Yossef. "Put this man in chains for one week in the cellar," he ordered a soldier. "Let's escort these youngsters back to the wagon."

They reached the wagon within minutes." Take the wagon and be on your way. I hope you find your parents."

"This wagon does not belong to us," Yossef protested.

"It does as of this moment. Stealing is rewarded with great punishment around here. Take the wagon. I'm giving it to you as a gift of the House of Castelon."

"Thank you, Sir, for your kindness. We shall never forget you." He helped Elisheva mount the wagon. They were back on the road and on their way to Bilbao.

"You didn't say a word," Yossef confronted Elisheva.

"I was terrified. I'm still in shock. I'm afraid I didn't handle myself very well."

"Don't worry over it. I'm glad I had the guts. Actually, I was mad when I discovered our money was gone. This should teach us a lesson. From now on, unless we're in a secure place, one of us will stay on guard while the other is sleeping."

"Where did you learn to ride?" she inquired.

"My father was a horse lover. He always took me with him when he visited horse farms. It's really quite simple. I'll show you when we stop at the next post."

At the next trading post they ate and had the horses fed and watered. Yossef made sure they had food and water for the horses and themselves as he had no idea where or when they would be stopping for the night. Two days later, they arrived in Bilbao.

CHAPTER SIX

When they got to Bilbao, they left the horses and wagon at a livery stable for safekeeping. Since neither had been to Bilbao before, they needed to determine where to stay and how to operate. With sacks over their shoulders they walked towards the center of the city. The streets were full of people. Many women were carrying empty bags, which indicated they were on the road to the market. Yossef decided to follow the stream of women and they soon found themselves in a central plaza where merchants were lined up in small booths selling their wares.

"Let's find a friendly face among the merchants and inquire about an inn."

"Here's a fine looking woman," Elisheva said. "She looks as though she doesn't belong here. She's dressed better than any other merchant I've seen." They approached the woman. She was standing behind a large table filled with memorabilia. One look at the items on the table and Elisheva pulled Yossef aside. "This woman must be Jewish. She's selling household items."

"Let's approach her cautiously."

"Nice things you have here," Elisheva opened the conversation.

"Unfortunately, I have to sell my possessions. My husband died and I was left without means of support," the woman spoke with teary eyes.

"When was that?" Elisheva queried.

"About two weeks ago. Are you going to buy something?" she asked.

"Some of the items you have here are Jewish," Elisheva stated.

"How would you know?" the woman asked.

"I'm a Converso," Elisheva said, "I was baptized two years ago."

"How old are you?" the woman asked. "I had a daughter your age."

"I'm sixteen. My brother is fifteen. Why did you say 'had'? Where is she?"

"She died last year from the black plague." The woman started crying. Elisheva walked around her table and embraced her.

"Don't cry," she said, "I'll be your daughter. I lost both my parents to the Inquisition." The woman's face lit up with delight. She held Elisheva in her arms and wouldn't let go. "Will you be my child? I couldn't find reason to live without my husband and daughter."

"We'll be the happiest children in the world," Elisheva promised, poking Yossef to say something.

"I would love it, too," Yossef finally uttered.

"Where did you come from? And what are you doing in Bilbao?" the woman asked.

"We just arrived from Barcelona and we're looking for a place to stay until our work is completed," Elisheva replied.

"Are you going to leave Bilbao when your work is done? And what will become of me?" she sobbed.

"We don't have a mother," Elisheva announced. "You're welcome to become ours. Would you like that?" It was obvious the stranger and Elisheva had taken an immediate liking to each other. She grabbed Elisheva and Yossef in her arms and kissed them. She smiled. "I have my children again, God, thank you," she said looking up to heaven.

"Let's go home. There's no need for you to sell your life's possessions. We have money. When we leave Bilbao, you come with us," Elisheva declared.

"Why leave Bilbao?" the woman asked; "I have a nice house here. We can certainly make a modest living selling anything in this market."

"We have a job to do in this city and we'll have to leave when we're done. " Yossef challenged.

"What kind of job?"

"It has something to do with the Inquisition," Yossef said.

"Then I don't want anything to do with you." She stepped back, her face turned away in dismay.

"Oh! No!" Elisheva said, "It's not what you think. We're working with a group trying to convince the Crown to liquidate the Inquisition."

"Are you serious? No one can dismantle the Inquisition, not even the Queen," the woman blurted.

"No one said it was going to be easy, but try we must. Please welcome us the way you did a few minutes ago, and be our mother. We need you as much as you need us," Elisheva said.

Once again she embraced them. "I'll help you with your silly dream. Let's go home."

Elisheva and Yossef helped her pack up and they left the market. It was a short walk to the woman's small but comfortable house. It consisted of two bedrooms, a decent size kitchen with a wooden burning stove and a small sitting room. Yossef and Elisheva settled in one of the bedrooms.

"What's your name? You never told us."

"My name is Rachel. I'm the daughter of David ben Yehoshua and I was married to Israel Mimon," the woman said. "What is it you have to do in Bilbao?"

"We need to compile a list of the main Churches, the names of their priests, and their addresses. Also the same for any of the Archbishops,

Cardinals, Bishops and houses of Inquisition in this city." He chose not to tell her that they would need to steal wax seals.

"That should be fairly easy," the woman said. "Why would you need this information?"

"I don't have an answer. This is what we were told to do."

"Who told you?" she was curious.

"It's better we don't answer that question for the time being. When the time comes you'll know."

"The day is still young. Can we go out and get started?" Elisheva asked. "I'm sure we'll have a great deal of ground to cover in the next few days, and we need to know our way around the city."

For the next four hours, Rachel took them around the city's center. Yossef kept notes. She pointed out the three Inquisition buildings as they passed by, as well as Cardinal Jose Cardenaz's residence. The house belonging to Bishop Emanuel Armand was just down the same street. Yossef took special notice of those two houses and looked into their main entrances. He didn't see anything unusual in either.

Rachel prepared a simple supper, after which they remained talking for quite some time. She told them all about her husband and daughter. She also had a son who was born dead. The tragedy of losing her daughter wasn't going to be forgotten any time soon. Elisheva told her about the loss of her parents. Yossef kept quiet most of the evening. The single candle was about to end its life when Rachel declared it was time to retire. They were tired, and sleep came easily.

Rachel was already up and about when Yossef left his bedroom the next morning. He washed his face and combed his thick hair. Elisheva emerged soon after and followed suit. They helped Rachel set up her table in the marketplace and went about their business. The story about seeking Father Carlos Ramirez, their uncle, worked well. Not one priest had heard of him, and before they left, they had the names of priests in other Churches. By the end of the third day, all major Churches and Cathedrals in Bilbao had been covered. They sat on a bench inside one of the Cathedrals and discussed ways to penetrate Inquisition buildings.

"Finding the names of the Churches, priests and addresses was simple enough. How do we approach the Inquisition?"

"I have an idea," Elisheva smiled. "We approach the first priest we meet and tell him we've been through every Church in Bilbao, but haven't been able to locate our uncle. Then, ask him if he would introduce us to the priest in charge of the Inquisition building."

"I wouldn't do that," Yossef stated. "It's too dangerous. I have a better idea."

"What's that?"

"Let's wait on the street about a block away from the Inquisition building and approach a priest who comes out. I'll simply tell him that we're looking for our uncle and haven't found him in any of the Churches. Could he direct us to the priest in charge of the Inquisition building so that we could ask him? We'll get the name of the priest, and we'll pretend to be going there."

"That's perfect," she agreed. "Let's go."

Off they went towards the first house occupied by the Inquisition. Yossef's plan worked like a charm. The name of the priest in charge was given without hesitation. They repeated the same maneuver at each of the other locations. The first phase of their mission was completed.

"David wants us to steal the wax seals during our last night in the city. I don't believe we'll be able to cover so many Churches, Inquisition buildings and the offices of the Cardinal and Bishop during the few hours in one night," Yossef said.

"What bothers me is that if so many seals disappear all at once, it may raise an alarm," Elisheva said. "Let's get the seals from at least two of the Inquisition's offices, the Cardinal, the Bishop and as many Churches as we can until about an hour before dawn."

"This sounds right. I can't see sending letters to every Church in the city. Unfortunately, we didn't have enough time to thoroughly discuss our mission and its objectives before we left."

"I agree. A very select group of letters should do. Since we have all the names and addresses, when should we make our final move?" Elisheva asked.

"We need to talk this over with Rachel so that she has enough time to liquidate her affairs," Yossef suggested.

"Good thinking," Elisheva said.

That evening, after supper, Yossef opened the conversation. "Rachel, we have completed the first phase of our work in Bilbao. We're now ready for the final act, which requires that we leave immediately at dawn. You are more than welcome to join us if you still want to."

"I'm ready any time. While you were running around the city, I managed to sell most of my belongings. This house is sold, too. All I have to do is tell the buyer when I'm leaving. I gave away the house at a great loss, but it's more important for me to be with the two of you. I fell in love with you the first time I saw you. You are my children now. I want to be with you and live with you. Obviously, you are on a holy mission. I want to help you achieve your goal. You have brought me back to life and given me the desire to live. I'll love you as if you were my own," Rachel declared.

Elisheva and Yossef were touched by her sentimental statement. They walked over to her side of the table and kissed her. She got up and the three of them hugged with much love and inner satisfaction.

"Very well, then," Yossef said. "Tomorrow night we complete our last task and depart Bilbao before dawn."

"Good! This will give us a chance to rest all day," Elisheva said.

The final task, as Yossef called it, went better than expected. They moved rapidly from residence to residence, cathedrals and churches. By dawn they were in possession of the wax seals they were after.

Shortly before dawn they picked up their wagon and horses. Yossef paid the keeper and left. Rachel was ready. They loaded a number of sacks and departed. The front driver's bench was wide enough for all three of them. Yossef calculated that their food supply would last at least two days. He planned to ride late into the night in order to be as far as possible from Bilbao. He had no idea how far Toledo was, nor did he care.

It took them four days to reach Toledo. When the city walls came into view, Yossef decided to spend the night in the country.

"I want to enter the city during the rush hour together with other wagons carrying fresh vegetables and fruit from the farms. It will make us less conspicuous." They entered the city the next morning and left the wagon in a livery stable. They checked into a small inn, away from the center of the city, and decided to rest before embarking on their mission.

CHAPTER SEVEN

After a light supper provided by the innkeeper, they went out for a stroll. The weather couldn't have been nicer. A warm, and light breeze was blowing. The sky was clear, and the moon was shining in all its majesty. The innkeeper told them the weather was exceptionally pleasant that year. A huge cathedral stood at the corner of the first intersection they passed. They decided to enter. Hundreds of candles provided light. A few worshipers were kneeling in the pews. They crossed themselves as they walked in and sat on one of the benches. Pretending to be praying, Yossef looked around and examined the ground floor. There were a number of chapels along both sides. Each chapel had its own door, which provided total privacy to its occupants.

A few minutes later they walked out and continued their stroll. "This is a beautiful city," Elisheva remarked.

"Indeed, it is," Rachel confirmed. "I couldn't help notice it as soon as we drove in."

"Perhaps it's a better cared for city because the Crown makes its home here," Yossef said.

"What do we know about Queen Isabella?" Elisheva asked.

"I've never seen her. They say she's a beautiful woman and blond, which is rare in Castile. Also, that she is very religious."

"David told me that a high priest named Tomas de Torquemada is her private confessor. He is also the Chief Inquisitor and the voice of the Inquisition," Yossef said.

They returned to the inn and retired for the night.

After breakfast Rachel and Elisheva went in one direction and Yossef in another. They decided that Yossef would seek out and survey the houses of the Archbishops, Cardinals and Bishops while the women will deal with the Churches and Cathedrals.

Yossef walked into one of the largest Cathedrals he had ever seen. As soon as Mass was over, he addressed the priest.

"I'm in Toledo with my family on a short visit. I'm in the midst of writing a thesis about the importance and functions of the Inquisition. Could you tell me about the Catholic hierarchy in Toledo? I would like to visit with each of their offices."

"Where are you from, son?" the priest asked.

"I come from Barcelona. I am attending the Central Catholic School and am considered at the top of my class in religious studies," Yossef stated emphatically.

"I am Father Juan Castro de Medina. What is your name, son?"

"My name is Alvaro Lunas de Leon. I liked your sermon very much. It touched my heart and feelings." The priest enjoyed receiving a compliment and provided Yossef with the information he sought.

"Being the capital city of Castile, we have in this city one Archbishop. His name is Alfonso Carrillo de Acurra. I consider him to be the most eminent Catholic cleric in Castile. Tomas de Torquemada, the chief Inquisitor, was his student," the priest said.

"Where can I find the Archbishop? I would very much like to talk to him. My school will be very proud of me if I succeeded in interviewing him."

"Actually, he lives near this Cathedral. He likes to pray here. He believes that Saint Rafael stood on the very grounds this Cathedral was built on and prayed to Jesus for rain. That was the year of the great famine," the priest volunteered.

"Would you please direct me to his house?"

"It's the fourth house from that corner on the left side," the priest said pointing. "Would you like me to give you a letter of introduction?"

"That would be very gracious of you." The priest maneuvered Yossef into a small study at the rear of the Cathedral.

"Please sit down while I write."

Yossef took note of the drawer from which the priest retrieved his seal. He was happy the drawer didn't have a lock. The one page letter was written quickly and Yossef thanked the priest profusely.

"I will remember your goodwill and will mention your name to my priest and teacher in Barcelona. Thank you for your kind courtesies." Yossef left the Cathedral and walked over to the Archbishop's house. In fact, he was shivering a little from fear, but decided he'd better take control of himself. *"Consider this to be a military exercise,"* he thought. *"You must act firmly, with courage and conviction."*

A few minutes later he entered the Archbishop's house. The front door was wide open. However, the second door, the one that led into the front hallway, was shut. He tried the knob. The door opened. He decided to ring the doorbell so as not to appear audacious. The door was opened a few minutes later by a manservant.

"What can I do for you, young man?"

"I'm a student from the Central Catholic School in Barcelona and I'm writing a thesis about the importance of the Inquisition. I was wondering if His Eminence, the Archbishop of Toledo, could give me a few minutes of his valuable time." He decided not to use the priest's letter as it could serve as a sample of his writing.

"What is your name, son?" the servant asked.

"My name is Alvaro Lunas de Leon. It will be a great honor for me."

"Please sit here while I ask His Eminence." The servant pointed to a chair.

Yossef began to shake. His nerves and fear increased by the minute. He tried hard to control himself. This was the first time in his life he had undertaken a deceitful role. *"What if I'm caught in this lie?"* he thought. Instinctively, he realized he must calm down. He bent over, took a deep breath, and released it slowly as he rose. The manservant returned.

"His Eminence will see you, but only for a few minutes. He is expecting Bishop Garcia any time now. Follow me. I'll show you in." He led the way to the second floor. The Archbishop's study was on the left side of the landing.

"Come in, my son, and sit in front of me. My eyesight is not as good as it used to be," Archbishop Carrillo said. "My manservant tells me you are here on a visit from Barcelona."

"Yes, Your Eminence. I'm a student at the Central Catholic School and am writing a paper on the importance of the Inquisition," Yossef said.

"This is remarkable. I didn't realize they teach you in school about the Inquisition," the Archbishop seemed surprised.

"During the past two months we've been told quite a bit. In fact, our priest thinks I should consider priesthood because I'm the most knowledgeable student in the scriptures," he claimed hoping this would help him in his quest.

"What is it you wish to know?" the Archbishop asked. But before Yossef could respond, Bishop Garcia walked in.

"We have an interesting visitor." The Archbishop explained Yossef's reason for the visit. "This young man is a distinguished student in the Central Catholic School in Barcelona. He was about to tell me what he wished to know."

"Our priest, Father Eugenio, was questioning the class on whether we thought that torturing people of other faiths was the right way to obtain acceptance for conversion." Yossef opened. "The class was divided. Some students thought it was the right way, but many thought it was not. I'm having a difficult time making a decision. Sometimes I feel all for it, but on occasion I feel differently. Since I'm writing a thesis on the subject of the Inquisition, I would very much appreciate clarification."

"What did your priest, father Eugenio, say?" the Archbishop asked.

"I'm not sure he was entirely for torturing innocent people whose only crime was being of other faiths," Yossef said.

"And on what do you base this assumption?" Bishop Garcia asked.

"I'm basing it on a variety of small statements he made," Yossef replied.

"Such as?" the Bishop interrogated.

"Well, he used the phrase once 'the poor souls' when talking about punishment. I believe they are sinners, therefore, they are not poor souls," Yossef stated emphatically.

"Anything else he said?" the Archbishop asked.

"Yes, he said that he could not watch those people burn to death. He even stated that you cannot burn the Devil," Yossef added.

"The opinion of the Church is that no other faith exists in our world worthy of our Lord. Anyone who practices another religion is not only a sinner, but also the Devil himself. There is no other Lord but our Catholic Lord. When this young man leaves, I would like to speak to you about this priest Eugenio." The Bishop looked at the Archbishop.

"Barcelona is in Aragon. There isn't much we can do there. You'll have to channel your complaint through Rome," the Archbishop said. "It will be very wise of you not to say anything about this comment."

"I will keep my mouth shut, I promise. But Your Eminence, what is the right answer?" Yossef persisted.

"The right answer is that any person who refuses to convert should be made to do so or face any pain and suffering. It is our religious duty to be missionaries for Jesus Christ. He would want us to continue his work," the Archbishop said.

"While our Lord Jesus brought many people under his wings, I do not recall anywhere in the New Testament that he used force to achieve his life's mission," Yossef said, "Why do we?" Yossef knew he was treading on thin ice, but felt the time was right for such a question.

"Jesus died for all of mankind's sins. His disciples wrote up Christianity after him. There is no other religion but our Catholic belief. Even the Pope sanctions the actions of the Inquisition."

"If that is the case, it's good enough for me. Your opinion, Your Eminence, and the Pope's are more of value and importance to me. I personally will comply with all my heart," Yossef stated. "Could you write to my priest? I will gladly deliver your letter to him."

"This is an excellent idea, but better than that, I'll write to the Bishop of Barcelona, Alonso de Rocha, as well as your priest," the Archbishop said. "Since we cannot reach into Aragon, letters might do the job."

"I'll be happy to pick up your letters after mass tomorrow morning," Yossef said.

"You are a remarkable young man," the Archbishop admitted. "Please come see me when you complete your schooling. You will make an excellent investigator in our Inquisition. Stop here tomorrow. I'll have the letters ready. Now let me conduct my business with our Bishop."

Yossef got up, shook the Archbishop's hand, kissed it and left in a hurry. *"What an unbelievable accomplishment,"* he thought. *"David will have a field day with these two letters."*

From the Archbishop's house he decided to look into the possibility of entering the Queen's Castle. It was located on the outskirts of Toledo and connected by a road lined with beautiful trees. No one stopped him as he neared the main gate even though he passed by many sentries. A few carriages passed by, as well as wagons. At the gate he encountered four sentries, two on each side.

"Are visitors from out of town allowed in the Castle?" he asked politely.

"The Queen permits out of town visitors to tour the Castle once a week on Friday mornings from 10 to 12 only, when she is with her confessor." One of the sentries answered.

"Is there a guide available?" Yossef asked.

"There is. All visitors wait here by the gate." The sentry pointed to a small enclave.

"Thank you kindly, Sir," Yossef said, "I will come with my mother and sister on Friday."

"Yossef left the Castle's gate. A carriage driver stopped and offered him a lift.

"This is very kind of you."

"Why not help someone when I can," the carriage driver said. "At Church they preach us to be nice to each other, but so few people are. Last night a mob attacked the old Jewish quarter and destroyed what was left of it. I saw my priest and other clerics lead the mob. The Jews didn't harm anybody, now most of them have gone to other cities and business is dying in Toledo."

"I don't know a thing about this. Why are the Jews harassed by the Church?" Yossef professed ignorance.

"The Church wants everybody to be Catholic. I remember when the Moors were here -- they didn't bother us. They didn't force us to convert to Islamic beliefs. Life was quieter and more peaceful. Every citizen went about his business and all the people of Toledo benefited from it. Now, thousands of people are without work and looting has become fashionable," the driver vented.

"Have you tried complaining to people of importance?" Yossef asked.

"I don't know any important people. Those who ride in my carriage will not speak to me. It would be beneath them. By the way, what where you doing at the Castle?" he asked.

"My family is visiting Toledo. We are Barcelonians. I thought it would be nice to visit Queen Isabella's Castle. I was told that visitors are allowed on Fridays. Could you drive us to the Castle on Friday?"

"Of course, where are you staying?"

"We're staying at the Ismeralda Inn. Do you know where it is?"

"Very good, I'll pick you up at nine o'clock in the morning."

Yossef gave the driver a few pennies when he was dropped off in the center plaza. He was very excited at his successful morning. He came to the conclusion that being deceitful, telling lies and acting was not so difficult after all. *"The masses are dumb and ignorant, they'll do anything you tell them to for salvation in heaven,"* Yossef said to himself. He returned to the inn and waited for Rachel and Elisheva. He lay on the bed and fell asleep.

It was late afternoon when Rachel and Elisheva returned. They too were excited.

"Yossef, we have the names and addresses of six Cathedrals, fourteen Churches and three main Catholic schools in Toledo. We think the priests who head the schools would be excellent targets for the letters."

"That's good news. I've been successful too." He went on to describe his various meetings and the plan to visit the castle on Friday. "We heard that last night a large mob attacked the Jewish quarter. Since it's on the other side of the city, we didn't know about it. Apparently fights broke out between the looters who were stealing everything they could lift. The Queen's guards had to break up the fights and her emissaries confiscated most of the goods. It's said that all items will be auctioned at a later date," Rachel said.

"I'm very hungry," Yossef said. "Let's talk after supper." Rachel and Elisheva agreed. The innkeeper was asked to serve supper in their room. Even though Yossef wanted to concentrate on his food, he wasn't allowed to. Rachel hammered, "You must tell us again about your meeting with the Archbishop. I want to know every detail."

Yossef repeated his adventure once more – this time he didn't leave out a single detail. "I'll pick up his letters tomorrow morning. On Friday we'll tour the Queen's Castle, and if we are lucky, we'll be able to find the seal and steal it. I cannot see another way to penetrate Isabella's fortress," Yossef concluded.

"We have the names and addresses of most major Churches and their priests. We found out that Toledo has one Archbishop, two Cardinals and two Bishops. Let's concentrate on these four," Elisheva suggested.

"You only have one Bishop to look up because I met one of the two at the Archbishop's house. We only need his address, and I'll get it tomorrow with the excuse that I want to send him a thankyou note," Yossef said.

"The weather is extremely pleasant here. Let's take a stroll in the park before we retire," Rachel suggested.

They strolled for a while and enjoyed the warm breeze. The moon was full and the stars dusted the sky from one side to the other. It was a most delightful evening.

CHAPTER EIGHT

Next morning, the carriage arrived at the inn a few minutes after nine. Yossef and Elisheva enjoyed the ride a lot. Rachel was rather quiet. "I'm concerned about my future," she said in a low voice. "I understand what you youngsters are doing, and that's remarkable. But what will happen to me?"

"Why think so far ahead?" Yossef asked. "We have major work ahead of us and we're committed to it."

"Why are you worried? From now on you are our mother and we're your children. We'll look out for you no matter what. I have come to love you, and I'm sure Yossef loves you, too."

"I do," Yossef said. "Please stop worrying. As soon as we return to Barcelona, you'll have a nice home and you'll be happy again."

"We're entering the most beautifully landscaped road in Castile," the driver tried to draw their attention. They admired the view and its landscape. The trees were dressed with beautiful large leaves and colorful flowers were growing between them. Minutes later they arrived at the Castle's gate.

"Please wait for us. At the end of the tour we'd like to return to the inn," Yossef said. They walked over to the enclave and waited with the others.

"My name is Miguel Arosso de la Madrid, I wll be your guide this morning. I'm the assistant secretary to Queen Isabella's scriptwriter. Please follow me. If you have any questions, don't hesitate to ask."

The tour began by entering the Castle's main building. The gate was the most imposing structure they had ever seen. Apart from its size, they were mesmerized by the magnificent carved wood and artistic design. Once they passed through they entered a lobby the size of an entire city block. The floors were white stone and its walls were whitewashed. There were several doors on either side of the lobby. One door led to a ballroom with a white marble floor and the walls also paneled with dark stained wood. Another door led to a dining room, also wood paneled. The large table could seat thirty-six people. Many questions were asked, and the guide seemed to enjoy responding to each one with a lengthy answer. Yossef's mind was elsewhere. He was anxious to get to the scribe's room. He didn't know whether he would be able to see or find the wax seal, but his mind was set on it.

The guide took them through the Queen's throne room and reception hall in which she received foreign dignitaries and noblemen. Then he rushed them through her music and smoking room. Finally, the tour passed through a series of private offices and the Queen's chapel. The scribes' quarters were next to the chapel. "Four of the Queen's scribes work out of this room. The Queen dictates her letters, which the scribes write on her special papyrus and later bring to her for signature," the guide said.

As they passed, Yossef noticed the wax seal on one of the desks. He quickly whispered something in Rachel's ear. She was quick to comply, and with a terrible sounding groan fell to the floor. The guide as well as the others rushed to her, and at that moment Yossef grabbed the seal and pocketed it. Elisheva, not knowing what had happened, fell to the floor besides Rachel and tried to revive her.

"Would someone please bring some water quickly," Yossef yelled. "She must have water immediately." The guide rushed out and shouted an order. One of the footmen brought water in a metal cup.

"Please move away," Yossef commanded, "give her air to breathe." When Rachel saw Yossef by her side, she came out of her fainting spell. He helped her sit up. "My mother is very weak," he stated. "Her life-dream was to see Queen Isabella's Castle before she died. She really shouldn't be walking this much."

"We better take her to the inn," Elisheva said.

"Would you be kind enough to assist us to the front gate? Our carriage is waiting there," Yossef asked the guide.

Two sentries helped them out. The Carriage was waiting where they had left it. They thanked the sentries and left the Castle. However, as soon as they reached the inn, Yossef picked up all the notes, letters, and anything that had to do with their mission, and walked briskly to the barn where the wagon and horses were kept. Before leaving he instructed, "Rachel, you performed well. Please stay in bed and pretend to be resting. If anyone should come asking for anything, you don't know, you have seen nothing and know nothing. You have an illness which causes fainting and the disease has no cure. I'll be back as soon as possible." He ran out.

Yossef told the barn keeper that he wanted to take some clothing out of his wagon and was shown to the storage area. He looked around. No one was in sight. He quickly dug a hole in the ground underneath the wagon and placed in it the letters, the lists and the seals. He then covered the hole with dirt and pressed it down as hard as he could. "I couldn't find the scarf my mother wanted," he told the barn keeper on his way out. "We'll be leaving the day after tomorrow."

As he entered their rooms, he found Rachel in bed and Elisheva sitting next to her. "I hid all our notes, letters and seals just in case anyone comes here. You were wonderful. Because of the momentary panic nobody noticed that I snatched the seal. I hope they won't miss it too quickly."

"Why don't we leave immediately?" Rachel asked.

"That would sound the alarm. If we leave now they'll surely come after us. I told the barn keeper that we'd be leaving the day after tomorrow."

"Since we have everything we need from this city, we can just relax and rest before our long journey to Barcelona."

"Everything happened so fast," Elisheva said. "When you fainted, I thought is was for real."

"It almost was real," Rachel said. "I'm glad I responded quickly. Normally, my reflexes are much slower. I had a funny feeling when I saw the seal on the desk. I knew Yossef had seen it, too. When he told me what to do, I did it instantaneously."

"This is a major breakthrough. To get the Queen's seal and not be caught is a great accomplishment," Rachel said. "I hope it will be worth the risk."

Evening supper at the inn was very pleasant as usual. The owner did his utmost to please his guests. The roasted lamb was well cooked and very tasty. The accompanying potatoes and vegetables were a delight. The wine was even better. Rachel enjoyed it immensely. As they were finishing up an army officer accompanied by six well dressed soldiers walked into the dining area and began questioning the guests.

"Were you at the Castle this morning?" the officer addressed Rachel.

"Yes, I was accompanied by my son and daughter. Why do you ask?"

"Something is missing from the scribe's room," he responded.

"Did any of you take anything?" the officer looked sharply at every one of them.

"This is ridiculous," Rachel said. "In fact, I was feeling rather dizzy and fainted while the guide was showing us the scribe's room. My children helped me up and we were escorted by two sentries to our carriage."

"I'd like to search your rooms," the officer said, and instructed his men to so do. "I'm sorry, but I must follow orders."

"This is preposterous," Rachel said. "All my life I wanted to see the magnificent Castle you have in Toledo. This has been my life's dream. And finally, after all the years of hard work when I can finally do so, I find myself being insulted and accused of stealing."

"No one is accusing you of anything, Senora," the officer said. "If nothing is found in your room, we'll leave, and you can forget all about this visit."

He left their table, went over to others and began questioning them. Only one other couple having dinner had been at the Castle earlier that day. The officer sent his men to their room, too. A few minutes later a soldier came running. "Your Lordship," he said, "I found this wax boxlet in their suitcase. It is the Queen's property."

"Arrest this couple," the officer shouted. Protesting their innocence, the couple was arrested and taken away. Rachel breathed a sigh of relief. "Thank God," she whispered. Yossef and Elisheva said the same.

"You didn't fabricate that event, too? Or did you?" She looked at Yossef.

"What if I did? It'll get us off the hook."

"But those innocent people!" Rachel said. "They'll surely be tortured until they confess they stole the seal as well."

"The wax boxlet and the seal are part and parcel of the same thing. I'm not sorry at all about their being tortured. What about the thousands of Jews who were tortured? Does anybody cry for them?" Yossef said. "We are committed to fight the Inquisition, and that's all I have to say. Let's change the subject."

Elisheva, who had been very quiet, suddenly spoke, "Rachel, Yossef is right. We have a job to do. Someone has to stand up to the Inquisition and fight it. There are bound to be some casualties, and I hope such casualties are among them and not us."

The innkeeper came to their table and apologized for the inconvenience. "They always come here looking for trouble. They're so stupid they can't distinguish between decent people and crooks. Can I get you some more wine?" he asked. "It's on the house."

"You know, all my life I dreamed of visiting the Castle of kings and now that I made it I'm being accused of stealing, and my things are searched. I wll never forget this insult for the rest of my life," Rachel said somberly.

"I'm very sorry, Senora," he said. "Please enjoy the balance of your stay. The weather is exceptionally good. Let me know if there's anything I can do for you."

"Thank you very much, you are very kind," Rachel said. "Come on children, let's go to bed. Tomorrow is our last day in Toledo. We must be rested."

They spent most of the following day in the beautiful park. They spread a blanket on the ground next to the small man made lake, had the lunch they brought with them, and relaxed. "I didn't want to press the question last night, but tell me," Rachel addressed Yossef, "what made you hide all our valuables yesterday?"

"I had a feeling we might get a visit. We had our own carriage. The stolen item came from the room you fainted in. It just made sense that when the disappearance of the seal was discovered, they'd suspect one of the visitors."

"How did the wax boxlet get into the man's suitcase?" Elisheva asked.

"That I couldn't tell you. I put it in his pocket on our way out. He must have discovered it when he returned to the inn and didn't think much of it. After all, it's a common item," Yossef answered.

"It certainly took the heat away from us," Rachel said. "God knows what they'll do to him."

They returned to the inn, had supper and retired. Yossef didn't go to bed. He sat next to the lit candle and planned his midnight seal-chasing route. He waited until the inn was totally quiet before sneaking out. He walked straight to the Archbishop's house. The front door was locked. He walked around the house and found a basement door, which he managed to pry open. He moved quietly touching the walls until he reached another door. This one opened without any trouble and he found himself in the kitchen. He climbed the stairs to the second floor and entered the Archbishop's office. The seal was in one of the top drawers.

"Who's there?" he heard a sudden cry. It was a voice he didn't recognize. He crouched to the floor and waited. Someone walked out of the room. His eyes, having adjusted to the darkness, saw no one. He quickly ran out through the door and down the stairs into the kitchen. The door to the basement was still open, the way he'd left it. He shut the door behind him and descended. He looked out, but saw no one. He walked behind the house and returned to the street after the fourth house.

His next target was the Cardinal's house. He found an unlocked front door and entered. It took a while to find the Cardinal's office, but finally he did. The seal was on the desk. There was also an unfinished letter. Yossef took that, too.

His next stop was the Inquisition building. He had never been inside it. The search from room to room took longer than expected. He had to have a seal from at least one of the Inquisition's buildings. When he finally opened the door to the office he saw a flickering light. He peeked through the crack and saw a priest writing at one of the desks. The priest was deeply involved in his writing and didn't hear the door open. Yossef entered one of the bedrooms, picked up a priest's habit, and put it on. A minute later he entered the office.

"Is that you, Father Miguel?" Yossef asked, surprising the priest. The priest lifted his head, but his eyesight had not adjusted and couldn't tell who walked in.

"Is that you Father Carlos?" he asked. By that time Yossef was next to the priest and hit him on the head with his hand, using all his strength. The priest fell to the floor unconscious. A minute later the seal was in Yossef's pocket.

As he left the room, he thought he heard moaning, and decided to explore. There was a staircase near the office leading to a basement. He quickly descended. The moans were getting louder. He opened the first door and was horrified at what he saw. At least a dozen men were tied to a variety of torturing machines. All men but one were unconscious. Huge candles were burning and the horror chamber fell into focus. Yossef walked over to the moaning man and released him from the chains. "Can you walk?"

"If you help me," the feeble voice replied. Yossef helped the man and pulled him up the stairs with all his strength. They exited the building and Yossef carried him to the inn over his shoulder. He laid the man on the floor next to the entrance and checked the lobby. No one was there. He lifted the man, carried him to his second floor room, and laid him on his bed. He woke up Elisheva, who was sound asleep, and entered Rachel's room waking her too. "I saved a man from the Inquisition's torture basement. He is in my bed. Please help me."

They washed the unknown man, cleaned him up, and gave him food and water. "Let him rest a while. I'll fetch a carriage after breakfast, then we can leave," Yossef said.

"How did you find him?" Rachel asked.

Yossef told them.

"I'll get dressed and sit next to him," Rachel said. "Elisheva, please get dressed, too. We better get ready. We must leave in a hurry."

"I suggest we don't wait for breakfast," Elisheva said. "Go find a carriage. Let's take this man down so no one sees him in the inn."

"Good thinking," Rachel said. "Come on, Yossef, please help."

Rachel and Yossef, one on each side of the unknown man, maneuvered him down the stairs and out onto the street. They sat him on the edge of a large stone bench, and Rachel remained sitting next to him. Elisheva packed their valises while Yossef went looking for a carriage. The first signs of day appeared and Yossef grabbed the first carriage that came into view. He paid the innkeeper. "Thank you for your hospitality. We decided to get an early start as we have a long way to Bilbao."

"Please wait just a moment. I'd like to give you some food for the journey." the proprietor said and ran off. He returned a minute later with a basket full of bread, cheese, olives and fruit.

Rachel and the stranger were dropped off a few blocks before the barn. Yossef decided it would be better if the barn keeper did not see the man. He paid for his services, hitched the horses, and dug up the buried materials. After picking up Rachel and the man, they started their journey to Barcelona.

CHAPTER NINE

David and Anna left Barcelona enroute to Segovia, the capital city of Aragon. David decided to buy an additional horse to increase his riding power. It took them two days to reach Segovia. They were amazed at the number of castles in the cosmopolitan area. While Segovia was fairly high up the mountains, the large valleys provided excellent ground for fruitful agriculture. The entire area surrounding the city was dotted with small peasant houses. The land was green with hundreds of vegetable and fruit patches. They stopped the wagon at one point on the road and observed the incredibly beautiful scenery. One valley after another lay in front of them, as if arranged by some magic hand.

They toured the city looking for a place to park.

It didn't take long before they came across a large orchard located behind one of the Church buildings next to a cemetery. David parked the wagon deep inside the orchard. They walked back to the street they'd come from and bought food, fresh fruit and refilled their water container. David decided to relax that evening and begin his search the following day. They stretched out in the back of the wagon on their backs, using the hay as a mattress.

"I wonder how Yossef, Elisheva, and Itzhak and Yael are doing. I've gained a lot of experience since the death of my parents, but for them this is all new."

"I don't think you need worry about Itzhak and Yossef, they're very good boys. I've known them for years. They are serious and good family people. I'm sure they'll do exactly as they were told," Anna said.

"I sure hope so."

"Also both of them are pretty sharp. They'll be able to think fast and deal with whatever comes up."

"I'm glad. All of us need our wits about us in dealing with unexpected surprises."

"You mean situations that come up?

"That's right. I'm sure Torquemada isn't going to take our revolt lying down. He'll surely force the Queen into action. We'll be hunted, but I doubt they will ever find us. For one thing, they haven't got a clue as to who we are."

"I can hardly wait for that day."

"Neither can I."

Anna lifted herself, leaned over, and kissed him. At first David was surprised and somewhat shocked. He had never had anything to do with the opposite sex. Her kiss electrified him, and a sensation of unfamiliar magnitude went through his body. He suddenly realized he liked that sensation a great deal, and as he balanced his thoughts and feelings, he returned her kiss with passion.

"This is totally new to me, but I must say that this odd new feeling going through my body is wonderful."

"You really don't know a thing about love, do you," Anna said.

"I loved my parents, but this is certainly different."

"You're right. The love for a parent is a natural kind of love. The love for a woman you want to spend the rest of your life with is real love."

"There's a feeling running through me I'm not familiar with," David admitted.

"I love you, David Abulafia," Anna declared. "I've never felt like this before, nor did I want anyone before. I do want you, and I want to spend the rest of my life with you."

"I think I'm beginning to feel the same, but please give me time. My emotions are all mixed up," he pleaded.

Anna moved closer to him and cuddled against his body. They held each other with passion. David suddenly touched her breasts and she moaned with pleasure. She touched him, and he felt his senses leap. He had no idea what to do next; no one had ever discussed man-woman relations with him. "Please forgive my ignorance. I don't know a thing about the relationship between men and women. All I know is I enjoy your company more than anything else. Particularly, I feel so good holding you and you holding me," David confessed.

"That's all right, don't let it bother you. Girls know more about this because of the monthly visitor we have," she said.

"Monthly visitor? What do you mean?"

"Girls get bloody down here once a month. It's part of the female body, which has to do with reproduction. Mothers explain this to their daughters so they don't get shocked when blood first arrives," Anna said.

"All this is too confusing for me. Let's talk about it another time."

"Do you love me?" she persisted.

"I think so," David said, "My feeling for you is very strong and it must mean love."

"You know, the fact that we found each other in the most unusual circumstances has fate on our side. It was meant to be."

"If fate meant for our meeting to happen, then it did."

This time, he raised himself and kissed her. He felt that he wanted to kiss her, to hold her tight and develop the love she was talking about. They fell asleep in each other's arms.

They woke up to a most beautiful day. The weather was perfect. Because they were hidden in the orchard and sleeping inside the wagon, they didn't realize how late it was. Since they were in the immediate vicinity of a church, they walked in. A priest was cleaning the floor.

"Good morning, Father," David greeted.

"It is afternoon, my son," the priest said laughingly. "What can I do for you?"

"I was wondering if you could give me the name of our Cardinal in Segovia?" David asked.

"What is it you want with the Cardinal?" he inquired.

"As a child I heard my parents say the Cardinal in Segovia was a relative of my mother, and now that both my parents are dead, I thought I'd look him up."

"Do you live in Segovia?"

"No, Father, I live in Barcelona. This is my sister Anna. We have no family in Barcelona, and that's why we wish to look up the Cardinal."

"I'm sorry about your parents. When did they die?"

"About three weeks ago."

"I can understand your desire to find the Cardinal. His name is Ferdinand Avila de Rimor," the priest finally revealed, and gave them directions to his house.

"Thank you, Father. By the way, what is your name? I would like to mention your kindness to the Cardinal," David said.

"My name is Jose Alonso de Aguiles of the Church of Santa Maria," he said.

"You are very kind," David said. They left in a hurry.

"We didn't feed the horses this morning," David suddenly remembered; "Let's go back." They returned to their wagon. The horses were restless. David gave them water and they calmed down. He threw plenty of hay on the ground and the horses dug in.

"Now, let's find the Cardinal," he stated.

"What are you going to tell him?"

"I'll tell him the same story I told the priest, just to get us in, and somehow I'll change the subject."

"Could we stop for something to eat before we go looking for the Cardinal? I'm starved."

"I'm sorry," David said, "meeting the priest and getting the Cardinal's name and address so easily made me forget. Here's a store."

They bought cakes stuffed with cheese and spinach and a jug of a sweet drink they'd never had before. They sat on the ledge of a nearby fountain and had their meal. Satisfied, they continued on their way.

The Cardinal's house was enormous. In fact, it frightened them. "Why would the Cardinal have such a huge house?" Anna questioned. "A hundred people could easily live in it."

"We'll soon find out," David said. "Gather your nerves, we're going in."

"This is no place for children," they heard a voice say. "What do you want?"

"We wish to see Cardinal Avila," David said.

"The Cardinal does not see children," the voice replied.

The hall was dark, and only after their eyes adjusted did they realize they were talking to an invalid seated on a low chair.

"Who are you? David asked.

"I'm the door keeper. I can scream if necessary," the invalid warned.

"Why would you want to scream?" Anna asked, "We only want to see the Cardinal because he's related to my deceased mother."

"In that case, you may go up the staircase. Be sure to go up, not down. Our House of Inquisition is down there. You'll find Father Carlos in the first room on the left. He'll direct you."

They climbed the stairs in silence. David observed the entrance hall from the stairs as they turned. He knocked on the first door to the left and opened it. The room was empty.

"Anna, stay at the door and warn me if anybody comes," he said, and dashed into the room. He opened one drawer after another. The wax seal was in the middle drawer. He pocketed it.

"There's no one in the hall," Anna whispered.

"Let's get out of here."

"The Cardinal is not available," David told the invalid. "We'll come back tomorrow."

They toured the city, took down the names of the various churches, looked up the priests, and compiled their list.

"I'm surprised at the number of churches in this city. It looks as if you have a church for every ten persons."

"Look, David, the building at the end of this plaza looks like a Cathedral. Let's check it out."

They walked towards the Cathedral, passing the center of the large plaza. A large water fountain was in the center, and nearby a number of vendors selling vegetables and fruit. As they neared the Cathedral, they noticed a crowd of beggars standing by its main entrance. One distraught woman caught Anna's eye.

"David, this woman is wearing a Magen David charm on her necklace."

"Should we single her out?" he asked.

"Give the others some money and tell them to go buy bread. All of them seem to be starving." David gave each of the beggars a few pennies and sent them off. Anna approached the woman and took her by the arm. The strange looking woman didn't say a word and allowed Anna to take her off. David followed them. Anna sat the woman next to the water fountain and gave her a drink of water.

"Get her something to eat," Anna commanded. David ran off and returned with a number of small bread loaves and fresh cheese. Anna fed the woman as though she was a baby. She devoured the food and drank more water. Finally she looked up at Anna and David.

"Thank you," she said in a feeble voice. "Where am I? Did you see Ya'acov? Where is he?" With those last words she passed out. David managed to catch her and saved her from crashing on the stone floor.

"Let's take her to the wagon," David said. "It's obvious she's a Jew."

"I suppose the beasts let her go because she was distraught and they thought her mad," Anna said. "With good care we'll revive her."

"Only God knows what she's been through. I'm going to take revenge!" He had that awful look on his face, which frightened Anna.

"I'll kill every one of them, the beasts! How can they torture a woman until she loses her senses? What kind of animals are they? I'm going into this Inquisition building tonight and kill them all," he declared.

"You frighten me," Anna said.

"I'm burning with vengeance. I can't help it. I cannot see human beings brutalized like this. We have to bring it to an end. People who do these sort of things should not be permitted to live."

They arrived at their wagon and helped the woman onto it. Anna washed her face and body and dressed her in one of her dresses.
"This woman must be about thirty-five years old, but she looks as old as my grandmother. She's so thin she can fit into my size dress!" Anna exclaimed. She gave the woman some more water and laid her on the hay. The woman fell asleep and Anna joined David sitting on the ground.

"I'll stay here with her. You go and make more inquiries. When you return, bring back roasted meat and some wine. We must give this poor soul some strength."

"Very well, I'll be back by sundown." David left.

He was furious. He kept seeing the woman's distraught face and his anger kept mounting. He decided to walk in a different direction and came to a stop in front of a big Church. He walked in. People were praying. He crossed himself and walked down the center aisle. He stopped at the alter. A Bible was open. He looked at the open page and began to read: "And Moses spoke to the children of Israel……….."

"Is there anything I can do for you, son?" A priest interrupted him.

"Good day, Father," David said, "I'm looking for an uncle of mine who is a priest, but I lost his address."

"What's his name, son," the priest asked.

"Carlos Ramirez de Segon."

"I never heard of him. You might try the Bishop's office. He surely would have a list of all priests in Segovia," the priest said.

"Thank you, Father. Could you direct me to the Bishop's house?"

"The Bishop of Segovia is Alfredo Molina de Russo. His house and office is on the outskirts of the city, near the Church of Santa Maria. You can't miss it."

"Thank you, Father." David left. *"The Bishop is very kind to have placed himself so conveniently close to my wagon,"* David thought. He bought the roasted meat that Anna asked for and some fruit, and returned to the orchard.

"Has the woman awakened?"

"She's still sleeping. The food and drink must have relaxed her. I'll let her sleep. It'll do her good," Anna said.

"I'm going to the Bishop's house. He lives on the other side of the Church. I won't be long."

David wondered how to get an audience with the Bishop and an idea struck him. He took a single gold dukat from his money belt and held it in the palm of his hand. He entered the Bishop's house without hesitation.

No one was by the front entrance. He knocked on the first door he saw, and walked in. A priest sat at a desk, writing. He looked up. "What can I do for you?"

"I'd like to see Bishop Molina," David said.

"You cannot see him. His Holiness is sick and in bed upstairs."

"I have a contribution for him."

"I'll take it."

"I have to give it to him personally," David said. "It is my mother's legacy."

"What do you have for the Bishop?"

"One gold dukat," David responded.

"I'll give it to him. Do not fear," the priest said.

"Before my mother died, she gave me this coin and told me to give it to the Bishop. I must give it to him personally with her message," David said.

"He is resting now, that's why I'm here. Come back after supper when the Bishop will be sitting in bed praying," the priest said.

"Very well, I'll return after supper." David walked out. He returned to the orchard and found Anna very excited. She ran towards him.

"The woman woke up. Her name is Miriam Matalonus. She ate some fruit and is resting."

"Did she say what happened to her?"

"I didn't want to push her, she is very weak," Anna said. "I believe by tomorrow morning she'll feel better. I washed her again and that helped relax her further. Let's eat. I'm very hungry. They sat on a blanket Anna spread on the ground, and ate heartily. David gave Anna some wine; he wanted her to sleep soundly. She didn't notice, but he had her drink a little with each bite of the meat. It didn't take long before Anna was asleep next to the woman.

David took the carving knife from its hiding place underneath the driver's bench, stuck it in his belt, and walked towards the Bishop's house. It was dark by the time he reached it. No one was on the ground floor. He walked into the room where he had encountered the priest earlier and checked the desk. In the center drawer he found the wax boxlet and the seal. He also took a sample of writing and pocketed his loot. He left the room and walked up the staircase. He followed the sound of voices, opened the door a crack and looked in. The Bishop was sitting in bed resting on a large pillow. The priest he had met earlier was sitting on a chair next to the bed praying. David walked into the room and stood behind the priest. The Bishop suddenly noticed him.

"What do you want, son?"

The priest turned around and saw David. He tried to get up, but David pushed him back into his seat.

"There's no need for you to get up," he said. "You can hear me from there just as well."

"You are interrupting our prayer, son. Please wait till we finish," the Bishop said.

"What I have to say is more important than your prayer." David's anger was on the rise. The priest began to turn again, but David held the knife against his back.

"If you move, this knife will sink in your back." The priest became motionless. The Bishop hadn't seen David's knife and seemed bewildered at his statement.

"What knife? What are you talking about? What do you want?"

"I want to ask you one question," David said. "Do you condone the 'Auto-de-Fe'?"

"Of course I condone it. These stubborn idiots who refuse to convert and curse Catholicism deserve nothing better than dying in the fire of God," the Bishop said defiantly.

"And you," David asked the priest poking his back, "do you agree?"

"Of course, I agree," he answered. The knife found its way into the priest's heart. As he fell to the floor, David pulled the knife out of his back and took two steps forward towards the Bishop.

"What do you want?" The Bishop tried to raise his voice, but couldn't. "I'll tell you what I want," David said, sticking the knife to his throat, "I want to kill you for all the poor souls you murdered in the name of your religion."

"You fool," the Bishop uttered, "you'll burn in hell."

"Together with you..." David plunged the knife through. The Bishop fell backward, dead. David wiped the knife and left the room. He entered the kitchen, found a jar of oil, poured it on the floor, and set it afire. From the Bishop's house he walked briskly to the Cardinal's house, which was also the residence of the Inquisition.

He noticed candlelight flickering in a few of the rooms. He stood in a nearby alley and watched the building until the last light went out.

It was well over two hours since the last person had passed by, he looked left right, saw no one, and quickly crossed the street and headed directly to the main entrance. The front door was unlocked. He took the knife out, held it close to his body, and entered. He stood quietly for a moment adjusting his eyes to the darkness. The invalid was sound asleep in his seat. David could hear his heavy breathing and light snore. He entered one room after another on the ground floor, but found no one. He took the stairs down to the basement and was shocked at what he saw. All the candles were out but one. The little light it gave was enough for him to see human debris. Men and women were tied to a variety of torturing machines – not one of them was conscious. Men's faces were deformed, beaten, and they may have been dead. Women were violated beyond his wildest imagination. He dare not touch any of them, for disgust and horror engulfed him.

He suddenly heard something stir behind him and discovered a priest sleeping on a large bench. David walked over and stabbed him through the heart. He left the basement and walked upstairs. The invalid was still breathing heavily. He continued his climb to the second floor and entered one room after another. A number of rooms housed what looked like a school seminary; others were dormitories, with six beds in each. He sneaked up to the beds and stabbed each occupant's throat. Not a sound was heard except for the silent flow of blood.

He then proceeded to the third floor. The Cardinal occupied the first room, a large bed-sitting room combination. The Cardinal was sleeping comfortably in a huge bed. David rolled him over to expose his chest. The Cardinal woke up from a deep sleep and was mumbling something when the knife went through his heart. *"I hope you spend the rest of your eternity in hell,"* David said, wiping the knife on his blanket. In the next rooms he found the Cardinal's assistant and two other priests. He cut their throats, put on a priest's habit hanging on a wall by the bed, descended, and left the building. The invalid was still asleep.

He walked briskly to the orchard. Anna was sleeping, and so was the woman. He drank some water, ate some fruit and sat down on the ground, leaning against a wagon wheel. He deliberately didn't want to be too comfortable as he planned to depart early in the morning. Long before dawn, he got up and woke Anna.

"We have to leave Segovia immediately."

"Why? What's the matter? Why are you wearing a priest's habit?"

"Please don't ask any questions. Help me hitch the horses, let's pack and leave," David ordered. Anna obeyed without further question. She knew there was a reason for this sudden departure, and was certain David would tell her in due course. Miriam also woke up.

"Who are you?" Obviously she didn't remember a thing.

"David and I saved your life yesterday. We washed you, fed you and put you to sleep. We have to leave now. We'll have plenty of time to talk."

"Where are we going?" the woman asked.

"We're going to Zaragoza," Anna replied. The woman fell back. She was still weak and couldn't hold herself.

"Please don't worry, we'll take good care of you."

David gave the horses water before leaving. He drove the wagon slowly and carefully through the orchard until it was out and followed the dirt road southward. Soon the sun came up, and another day came into being. Anna sat next to him, her arm through his.

"David, what happened that we had to leave in such a rush?"

"The Bishop and his priest are dead. I burned his house. The Cardinal and his entire crew of priests are dead, too. In the basement of his house I found men and women tied like beasts to all kinds of torturing machines. Not one person was conscious. People's faces were bashed; eye sockets turned inside out, and beaten beyond description. Women's bodies were exposed; breasts cut off and wood rods sticking out of their abdomens. And blood everywhere! It was sickening beyond imagination." David said hysterically.

"You had better take the priest's habit off," Anna said, "You look ridiculous in it."

"I'll keep it on for a while," he disagreed. "If we come across another wagon, you better sit a little more to the right."

"As you wish, my dear," Anna said. It was the first time she had called him 'My dear', he thought. David pushed the horses as hard as he could. He wanted to get away from the city of sin, the city that tortured and killed innocent people. He also didn't want to be caught. Suddenly he stopped the wagon on the side of the road and jumped off. He looked around and seeing no one, took the knife from his belt, removed the priest's habit, and buried everything in the ground.

It occurred to David that Segovia was the capital city of Aragon and the discovery of the slain clerics might send an army to look for the killers. His intuition was right; an hour later, a cavalry regiment was galloping behind them. David's wagon was stopped.

"Who are you and where are you going?" an officer asked him. "We came to Segovia looking for our mother, who is insane. We found her on the streets begging for food. We are taking her home," David replied.

"Search the wagon," the officer ordered one of his deputies. "You two, get off the wagon."

His deputy climbed on the wagon and sudden screams were heard. Seeing the soldier, Miriam had panicked. The soldier soon jumped off.

"There's nothing in the wagon except hay, water, and some food. The woman in there is crazy," he said.

"Where were you last night?" the officer asked.

"We found our mother late in the afternoon begging near one of the churches, and decided it was too late to get started. We spent the night on the side of the road by a small group of pine trees. We left this morning as the sun came up."

"This is a young boy, Sir, he couldn't have killed so many people," the deputy said to his superior.

"You're right, Miguel," the officer agreed, "but I have to check everyone."

"I'm sorry I disturbed you. Continue your journey home."

David maneuvered Anna, who was paralyzed, onto the wagon and departed.

"Well, we're in the clear," David stated.

"I lost ten years of my life," Anna said. "Miriam surely knew when to scream."

"She must have been terrified when she saw the soldier. Who knows what she went through," David said.

After a while he stopped the wagon on the side of the road and fed and watered the horses. He thought he saw gratitude in one horse's eyes.

The road began to zigzag as the terrain became more mountainous. It got colder, too. Anna pulled out their blankets and wrapped them around themselves. She also made sure Miriam was properly covered. They stopped at a trading post in a small village. Miriam suddenly appeared at the front of the wagon.

"Please tell me who you are, and where are we going," she said calmly.

"I'm very happy to see you better. You were very sick. My name is Anna and this is David. We saw the Magen David charm on your necklace and took it that you are a Jew. You were completely distraught and were begging for food near one of the churches in Segovia. We decided to pick you up and save you," Anna said.

"Are you Jews?" she asked.

"Yes, we are," David responded. "Do you feel better? Can you talk?"

"I feel much better. I still have a headache, but I feel that my senses have returned."

"You told us your name is Miriam Matalonus. Is that correct?"

"I told you that? When? I don't remember talking to you or anyone," she said. "Yes, my name is Miriam Matalonus and I'm from Toledo."

"How did you get to Segovia?" Anna asked.

"I'm ashamed to say, but I gave myself to one of the soldiers who rescued me from the Inquisitors. I couldn't bear the torture chambers." Her face saddened.

"You are a beautiful woman," Anna said. "I have not seen a torture chamber, but David has. I can well understand your predicament."

"How did you become a beggar if the soldier harbored you?" David was curious.

"Someone reported him for saving me. He was sentenced to six months of hard labor. I was flogged, my clothes were torn off, and I was thrown into the street," she answered.

"There is no end in sight to horror stories," David said. "I'm happy we found you. Are you married? Do you have children?"

"I was married, but I don't know where my husband is. He disappeared about a year ago. I don't have children."

"Was he taken by the Inquisitors?"

"Possibly. Many others have been."

"Was he a religious Jew?"

"He was not a Jew. He was Muslim."

"What about your parents?"

"My parents were burned to death by the Inquisition about that time. My father would not convert."

"Have you heard of the Abulafia family?"

"Yes. My father used to speak often of this magnificent family."

"I am the son of Abulafia. The Inquisition also burned my parents to death. My father would not convert under any circumstances. I managed to escape."

"Let's buy provisions and continue our journey," Anna interrupted. "We'll have plenty of time to talk on the way to Zaragoza."

"Where do you two live now?" Miriam asked.

"We live in Barcelona, but we're on a mission to Segovia and Zaragoza. Our work was completed in Segovia. From Zaragoza we'll return to Barcelona."

They got off the wagon. David purchased food and drink. He also asked Anna to buy clothing for Miriam, as she had none. They had their meal by the side of the road. The horses got their share, too. The sun had begun to set when they continued toward Zaragoza.

David was very pensive during the next few hours. The vision of the chamber of torture kept creeping up. He kept asking himself, over and over, how men of the cloth could be so cruel. Anna understood his solitude and kept silent, too.

The first night was spent near another trading post. This one was larger and offered a greater variety of food. The smell of freshly roasted beef drove them to buy a huge chunk, which they split amongst them. To cut the beef, David bought a brand new carving knife. He made sure it was big enough, as he knew he was going to use it for another purpose.

After supper Miriam became very talkative. David's mood had not changed. He was certain the horrors he witnessed and Miriam's story brought home once again the pain and suffering of the Jews. His parents also came into his thoughts and his heart hurt. How he missed them! He didn't notice, but he began to cry.

"What is it, David?" Anna asked. "Why are you crying?"

"I'm sorry," he said. "My parent's suffering and their horrible death suddenly came into my mind. Also, the sight of the tortured people in the Inquisition establishment is enough to destroy any normal person's feelings. It hurts very much -- the killings, the vengeance, and the ease with which I executed the priests. It's a heavy mental burden I will have to live with."

"What are you talking about?" Miriam inquired.

"David saw his parents burn at the stake. That night he went into the Inquisition building and killed every priest who was involved," Anna said.

"Serves them right," Miriam concurred. "If I were you I wouldn't shed one tear about having killed them. In fact, I wish I had the guts. I'm proud of you."

"How did you come to marry a Muslim?" Anna asked.

"They were neighbors of my parents. Their son was about my age and we used to play together almost every day. As we grew up, we felt we were the best of friends and decided to live the rest of our lives together. We got married with false papers. Somehow the Inquisition found out about us and we were arrested. I was too weak to surrender to torture... Well, I told you my part. As to my husband, he disappeared. I assume he died at the hands of these beasts. Those who die inside the Inquisition are buried in mass graves and no one knows a thing about them. The priests say that non-Catholics don't deserve to have a decent burial since they're going to hell anyhow," Miriam said.

"Let's call it a night. David needs a good night's sleep. Have some wine, it'll help." Anna brought David a cup and filled it with wine. And it did help. Despite the fact that his mind was preoccupied, he fell asleep and slept until the sun woke him.

CHAPTER TEN

It was almost dark when they reached Zaragoza. David didn't want to stop. He replaced the horses at one of the trading posts and worked them hard to gain time. He wanted to complete his mission and return to Barcelona. He wanted action to begin. He knew that the killings in Toledo and Segovia would cause much concern in the Church and the Inquisition. Since he left each city immediately after the killing he had no way in which to assess the Church's reaction. Perhaps Reuven would know more from messages the monastery might have received.

He parked the wagon in the first barn he saw and unharnessed the horses. There were very few wagons in storage and because of the late hour, they decided to eat and stay put.

"I'm delighted to see you feeling better," David said. "Color has returned to your face. You look human again."

"I'm very happy for you," Anna added.

"I will never be able to repay you for your kindness," Miriam said. "You're right, I do feel better. Living on the street stealing food to survive drove me to madness. I knew I was losing my life piece by piece, but there wasn't a thing I could do. I began roaming the streets with bands of beggars, criminals and gypsies."

"I know it's difficult to forget the past, but you must try. From now on your life will return to normal. We'll take care of you," David declared. "You can be my mother if you wish. I need a mother."

"And mine, too," Anna said.

Miriam bent over and kissed them warmly. "The two of you are simply magnificent people. I'll be your mother for as long as I live."

"You don't have to cry," Anna said, her own eyes teary.

"I'm crying from happiness," she said.

"I can't imagine why the Church doesn't provide any help to homeless people." David questioned.

"Let's forget the past. We must think of the future. We have a great many things to do," Anna stated.

The single candle they used for light spluttered. It signaled the end of a long traveling day. Miriam and Anna slept inside the wagon while David tried to make himself comfortable on the ground. However, as tired as he was, sleep did not share the night with him, not yet. His mind was racing with past events and plans for the future. He was very anxious to return to Barcelona and join Reuven and Zevulun. Finally, sleep conquered him, too.

"Wake up, David, it must be late," Anna shook him.

"Where am I?" David mumbled. "You stopped a dream where I was flying from church to church delivering letters." Anna kissed him.

"Miriam went out to search for fresh food. She should be back soon. Wash up," she ordered.

Miriam returned with a big basket. They ate and drank while the barn keeper fed the horses. They decided to tour the city driving the wagon. David waited until the horses finished their breakfast and hitched them up. The three of them sat tightly together on the driver's bench and off they went into Zaragoza. It took them about three hours to complete their sightseeing. Zaragoza wasn't as large as Segovia. In the city's square peasants were selling their produce and merchants were selling anything from pots and pans to woven socks. Facing the square was a Cathedral, but not as big as others they've seen. David left the women wandering around the square and walked into the Cathedral.

Midday Mass was over for some time and a priest was dusting the Alter. David approached him. "Father, I'm visiting Zaragoza with my mother and sister for the first time. May we pray here?"

"Of course, my son," the priest answered. "This house of prayer is open to the public at all times."

"Do you have a midnight mass in this Cathedral?"

"Why do you ask? You should be sleeping at that hour," the priest said.

"I go to midnight mass every night. It's only at midnight that the Lord reveals himself to me in all his glory," David acted.

"The Lord reveals himself to you!" the priest repeated.

"Oh! Yes, Father, in all his glory. I can hear him talk to me."

"What does He tell you?" the priest asked.

"He tells me that the killings must stop."

"What killings, my son?"

"The killings made by the Inquisition."

"These are not killings. We send sinners to hell. In fact, tomorrow night you can witness the delivery of two sinners to hell."

"What *is* their sin?"

"They refuse to convert. They said that their God is merciful and that ours was a murderer," the priest said disgustedly. "Our God is the true and only God."

"Have you ever thought what will happen to you when you die?"

"I'll be rewarded for devoting my life to Jesus Christ."

"Do you believe that Jesus wants you to kill people for him?"

"If they don't want to believe in him, they have no place in heaven. They belong in hell."

"Do you feel that you, as a mortal, have the right to take another human being's life just because he doesn't want to become Catholic?"

"You are telling me that you go to mass every midnight, which means you're a true Catholic, yet you speak the language of the Devil!"

"Why do you think I speak the language of the Devil, just because I question the right of one human being to take the life of another?"

"Wait here. I'm going to call one of the investigators to talk some sense into you. He might even take you to the Inquisition." The priest left through the rear door. David left the Cathedral in a hurry and mixed with the many shoppers crowding the square. He found Miriam and Anna and asked them to find the name of the priest in the Cathedral and the Zaragoza Bishop. "I'll wait for you at the barn."

"David, the name of the Bishop is Nicolas Obispo de Iglesias and the priest is Juan Pedro de Vega. Juan Pedro is the Bishop's nephew and they live in a small house behind the Cathedral," Anna reported as soon as she saw him.

"How did you find out so quickly?" David asked.

"It was simple. I told the priest my grandmother wanted to leave some money for the Cathedral and needed the names. He gave it immediately."

"I like to leave this city tomorrow," David said. "I don't like it here. I have a bad feeling about this place. Tonight I'll steal the seals and we'll leave at dawn."

"Whatever you say. We'll be ready," Miriam said.

"I'll pay the barn keeper this evening and tell him we plan to continue our journey early in the morning."

After supper they went out for a stroll. The weather was still pleasant. Many people were out enjoying the unusual evening warmth. When they returned to the barn, David told Miriam and Anna to call it a night. He took off for the city. As it was too early for midnight mass, he decided to spy on the Bishop's house behind the Cathedral. He saw a large oak tree behind the Cathedral and climbed it. He must have dozed off because suddenly he was awakened by voices beneath him.

As soon as the men passed and entered the Cathedral, David ran to the Bishop's house. The front door was unlocked, and no one was in sight. He quickly went through the house looking for the Bishop's office. He found it on the second floor. The seal and wax boxlet were on the desk. He took it along with various letters he found in a drawer and left the house. He walked in the opposite direction for a while, circled the neighborhood and found his way to the barn. Miriam and Anna were sound asleep. He hid his take with the others and sat leaning against the wagon wheel. He didn't want to sleep since he planned to leave at the crack of dawn.

David got up when he saw the first reddening on the horizon.

"Anna, please wake up. We need to leave immediately," he said. Anna woke Miriam and got ready. David hitched the horses and off they went. They rode in semi-darkness for at least an hour, and finally the sun came up. "We're going to have another beautiful day," Miriam said. "The weather has been extremely good lately."

"Why are we rushing?" Anna asked.

"I want to be back in Barcelona as soon as possible. I want our little organization to really get started," he said. "If Yossef and Elisheva, Itzhak and Yael bring in their loot, together with ours we would have the ammunition to start our campaign. I'm terribly curious to know how the others are doing."

"You will soon find out. Zaragoza is not far from Barcelona. If we ride without stopping, we should get there by tomorrow evening," Anna said.

CHAPTER ELEVEN

I tzhak and Yael decided on a different method of transportation. They joined four other passengers on a six-horse coach to Valladolid. Their luggage was placed in a compartment on the rear of the coach. The coachman told his passengers he would make brief stops every four hours until nightfall, and start early in the morning.

Itzhak was amazed when he realized that trading posts, inns and horse-barns were built at specific distances to accommodate the endurance of a horse.

The first day of travel passed quickly. However, as the days progressed, the journey seemed to be endless and boring. On occasion their traveling companions, one of whom was a priest, burst into conversation.

Before mounting the coach, Itzhak told Yael that if asked they should say they were brother and sister visiting their uncle in Valladolid. At first the passengers were engrossed with the scenery, but soon they abandoned the beauty of the landscape as it repeated over and over. Conversation followed, which didn't make Itzhak too happy. *"Why are people so inquisitive about others,"* he thought. *"I don't have the slightest interest in any of you, who you are, what you are, where you are coming from or going to. Why is it that you need to know everything about us?"*

"I don't wish to appear impolite," Itzhak said, "but you are asking us many personal questions. We are visiting our uncle in Valladolid."

"There isn't a thing to do on this long trip and I'm curious about the two of you," one of the passengers said.

"There is nothing to be curious about." Itzhak forced himself to be calm. "Our parents couldn't make the trip and sent us, and that's all there is to it."

"Shouldn't you be in school?" the priest asked.

"I am attending the Central Catholic School in Barcelona," Itzhak responded. "My parents obtained permission for my leave from the High Priest due to family circumstances."

"And what are those? Perhaps I can be of help," the priest said.

"That's very kind of you. When we arrive in Valladolid and meet with our uncle, I'll know whether he needs help."

"Why are you so prickly?" the only other woman in the coach asked.

"Because everybody wants to know all about us and I don't frankly see that it's any of your business. Am I asking any of you personal questions?"

"The young man has a point," the woman said. "All of us are questioning him endlessly. It's not right."

"Have you traveled by coach before?" the woman turned to Yael.

"No. This is my first trip," she responded.

"I've traveled many times. It does get boring sitting like this for days and days. I don't knit or crochet like other women do."

"I can crochet, but I didn't think of it. I was too excited about this journey. Next time I'll bring my crocheting with me," Yael said.

The priest took a big batch of papers out of his briefcase, which he'd placed under his seat, and began reading. Suddenly he made a peculiar sound. "Can you imagine, someone murdered all the priests in Toledo's Inquisition building and then burned over a dozen houses in the old Jewish quarter. I wonder what kind of a man would commit such an atrocity."

"It must be one of the Jews," one of the men said. "Our priest told us they're associated with the Devil."

"Forgive me, for I'm very young and a student of the Catholic School, but I can't see how any human being can be associated with the devil, Jew or not," Itzhak said.

"Is that what they teach you in Barcelona?" the priest asked.

"That is not what they teach us. I'm questioning it. Let's say you and I want to be associated with the devil. What do we have to do to reach such an association?" Itzhak asked.

"You don't have the right to ask such questions," the priest said. "You are to believe with all your heart what you are told. The Pope in Rome, our Archbishops, Cardinals and all men of the cloth do not question Torquemada. He is the authority. He knows the truth," the priest announced.

"I happen to be a devout Catholic," Itzhak said, "however, the Lord has given us a brain with which to think. I cannot for the life of me, accept anything without evaluating it in my own mind. Our beloved Jesus did a great deal of thinking. Otherwise he wouldn't have accomplished anything. A man needs to think in order to advance."

"You are pretty sharp," the priest said, "but you're impudent. If you are told that Jews are the devil, you should accept that as fact."

"I don't like this conversation," Yael interjected for the first time.

"Your sister is right," the priest said. "There is nothing to talk about. The Church is our guide and nothing else."

"I find such a statement disappointing," Itzhak persisted, "The Lord gave us a brain the way he has given us limbs. If your legs can walk and your hands can work, so should your brain. What is wrong with using your brain to think? What is wrong with making your own decisions and coming to your own conclusions? I will go further than that. If a man should accept everything without thinking, how could he be generous unto others? On any given day, man has to make endless decisions, and in order to make them, he needs to think."

"For a student in a Catholic School, I'm disappointed in you," the priest repeated.

"Can you tell me in what way you see the Jews as blasphemous people?" Itzhak persisted.

"Because they do not believe in Jesus."

"Let's say they do not believe in Jesus, what difference is it to you?" Itzhak asked

"We want a pure Catholic society, a society which lives by the Bible, a society which is pure Christian, a society which is not associated with the devil," the priest said.

"It seems to me, from what I know of the Jews, is that they do live by the Bible. Isn't it a fact the jails are full of Catholic citizens, murderers, thieves, and crooks of every kind? How many Jews are there in jail? As far as I know, none!" Itzhak said defiantly.

"You speak like a Jew," the priest said.

"I speak like a person who uses his brain. I'll give you another example. Who made Torquemada the ultimate authority on thinking in this country? And who says that only his thinking and his knowledge is superior to the rest of mankind? You lead me, just as my teacher priests do, to believe that Torquemada is the Son of God."

"I'll have to report you to the Inquisition when I get to Valladolid," the priest said. "You are a disgrace to Catholicism."

"I was hoping you were an intelligent man of the cloth," Itzhak said, "but you are no better than the stupid, superstitious masses whose lives you try to run by fear and intimidation."

"Young man, your days are numbered. You better keep your mouth shut." The priest turned his head, signaling the end of the conversation.

The coach reached the trading post and stopped. The passengers descended and entered the post. Yael pulled Itzhak aside, "What was the point of this whole conversation? You are increasing our risk."

"May be I am, but I needed to test matters in my own way. I can see how important it is to fight the Church and the Inquisition. These people are blind followers without a heart, brain, or self-respect. Their beliefs drive them into missions which are creating inhuman behavior. The masses of the people are illiterate, ignorant, and superstitious. Their doctrine is to intimidate people, put fear into their hearts instead of love and care. Just think for one moment if they would make an effort to educate the people instead of directing them to hate all others. If a Catholic steals from a fellow Catholic and is caught, he is sentenced to jail. However, if he steals from a Jew or a Muslim, that is not a crime!"

"The Church is surely hypocritical," Yael agreed. "I'm entirely with your line of thinking, but all I'm saying is that we are on a mission, and we shouldn't expose ourselves to undue risks."

"You're right, of course, but I couldn't help myself," Itzhak responded.

"Who knows what this priest will do. If he comes across other priests on this trip, we might be arrested and taken away before we reach Valladolid."

"You are absolutely right. Let's see if we can get out of here," Itzhak said.

The coachman called the passengers back; he had replaced the horses with a fresh team. They mounted the coach and it departed promptly. The next four hours were silent. The priest kept looking the other way, as he had no intention of speaking again to Itzhak. The other three passengers were quiet, too.

Itzhak decided to play a game with the priest even though it would be without his participation. He turned his head to Yael. "Our Uncle the Cardinal of Tarragona always says that a good Catholic is one who is charitable unto others. He never said that 'others' means Catholics only. In fact, the Old Testament directs in various places that you should be charitable to 'the strangers among you'."

"I'd like to sleep," Yael signaled her displeasure of any conversation. She slumped in her seat and closed her eyes.

"Your uncle is the Cardinal of Tarragona?" The priest was bewildered.

"Yes, and he is the one who encourages me to think, use logic and respect the other man for what he is. Never did he distinguish a Catholic from anyone else," Itzhak said.

The priest became silent and didn't say another word until they reached the next trading post. The passengers were told that they'd spend the night at that location.

"Yael," Itzhak said when they were alone in the room, "the priest is following us from a distance. It seems to me he wants to know the room we're staying in."

"Do you suspect anything?" she asked.

"I certainly do," Itzhak responded. "I probably drove the 'thinking subject' too hard. He did say he would report me to the Inquisition. He might decide to take action on his own. I'm going to buy a knife. I'd like you to look around while I'm buying it. I don't want him to know about my purchase."

"Do you think he may want to kill us?" Fright was taking hold of her.

"You never know how these people react. I want to be ready. When we go to sleep one of us has to stay awake. We'll take turns sleeping." He propelled her towards the trading area. The priest was nowhere to be seen when Itzhak made his purchase. He bought a long carving knife and a rope. They hurried back to their room. Itzhak went to sleep and Yael sat next to him. When her eyes began to close on her, she awakened him and they changed places. Yael was sound asleep before she hit the mattress. It must have been a full moon night because some light came in through the open window. Itzhak adjusted his eyes to the semi-darkness and waited. His gut feeling told him that something was about to happen. It must have been well past midnight when he heard the door to their room open. He quickly lay on the floor next to Yael and pretended to be sleeping on his back. He held a firm grip on the knife, which was next to him.

He wasn't surprised when he saw the priest enter the room. The priest held a knife similar to the one he'd bought. He tiptoed towards them. Itzhak made the sound of gentle snoring and watched the priest through slightly open eyelids. When the priest was convinced that Itzhak was sleeping, he changed his hold on the knife, lifted it up and swung down with force. At that instant, Itzhak leaped to the side. The priest's knife penetrated the mattress, and at that very moment Itzhak's knife stabbed the priest from the side. It entered his heart. The priest fell over his knife with its handle penetrating his stomach.

Itzhak woke Yael. "The priest came in here and tried to kill me. My intuition was right. I let him think I was asleep. He swung his knife, hoping to stab me in the chest, but I leaped to the side, and while his knife was descending I stabbed him. I believe he is dead."

"I'm frightened," Yael said.

"He wanted me dead. Now he's dead. Let's get out of here."

"What will happen when they find him? Someone is bound to chase us. We better do something about his body."

"Let me look out the window." He leaned out. "No one is out there at this hour of the night. I'm jumping out to check the territory." Itzhak jumped out and returned a few moments later.

"There's a well on the side of the building marked for horses only. Let's drop his body in there."

With great effort they lifted the priest's limp body and threw him out the window. Itzhak checked his pockets carefully and took a variety of papers and two letters. They kept looking around and were very happy that no one was in sight. They dragged the body, lifted it and dropped into the well. Instead of a big splash, they heard a heavy thud.

"There's no water in this well. This is our lucky day."

They returned to their room the way they'd gotten out and lit a candle. There was very little blood on the mattress. Itzhak turned the mattress over and hid his knife inside his clothing bundle. They waited in their room until dawn and came out when they heard the coachman's call for the continuation of the trip.

When the priest didn't show up, the coachman went into the trading post building looking for him. He returned a few minutes later.

"I can't find the priest," he said.

"I saw him earlier this morning walking toward the apple orchard," Yael said demurely.

The coachman called him numerous times and finally gave up.

"I can't wait any longer. I have a schedule to keep. Let's go." The coach left without the priest. Itzhak and Yael looked at each other. Their eyes spoke.

"I wonder what happened to the priest?" The woman passenger asked.

"Obviously he went for a walk early this morning since he wasn't in his room nor in the trading post store. Perhaps he was attacked by a wild animal" one of the other men suggested.

"My father always warned me not to wonder too far when we went horseback riding," Itzhak said.

"The priest was quite upset yesterday with you," the man said.

"That's his problem. I firmly believe that we were given brains to think. I don't believe that God intended us not to use them."

"You certainly have a valid point," the man said. "I tend to think that the Church is going too far. In every sermon the priests tell us what we should not do. They rarely tell us what we may do. I'll admit that on many occasions I felt uncomfortable. However, I didn't want to intervene during your conversation yesterday because I don't need to waste my time in the Inquisition."

"I'm attending the largest Catholic School in Barcelona." Itzhak said. "Some of the students in my class are Conversos, yet the teacher-priests treat them differently than us. The priests say that their souls are tainted. If they were baptized, accepted Jesus and the Catholic religion, what more does the Church want of them?"

"You're right. It's quite confusing. Every week I have to go to confession. Most of the time I live my normal life. I go to work every morning, I work diligently, I provide for my family, and sleep at night. The priest tells me I must confess, but the problem is I have nothing to confess. On occasion I think I should commit a small crime so I'd have something to talk about," the man said.

"We're not equal in our relationship with religion," the woman said. "Some of us are more religious than others."

"I fully agree with you."

"Do you believe that Jews and Muslims must be forced to convert to Catholicism?"

"I don't see why," the man said. "After all, the Jewish religion is much older than ours. The Jews in Aragon and Castile do no harm to anyone. I can't understand why the Church is so obsessive about conversion."

"I'll say what the priest had said to me -- 'you sound Jewish'," Itzhak smiled.

"I'm a good Catholic," the man said, "I just don't care what faith anyone else has. As long as people behave well, have good morals, and respect their fellow men, who cares what they pray to."

"You are quite unusual," Itzhak said. "It seems the Church is able to mobilize the masses which understand religion by route of ignorance."

"I'm an educated businessman. I've traveled a great deal and appreciate people for what they are and not the religion they embrace."

"I wish you would have said something to this effect to the priest," Itzhak said.

"I told you before, I don't wish to be involved with the Inquisition, that's why I kept my mouth shut."

"I'm glad someone else thinks as I do," Itzhak said.

"I'm sure many thousands think like you and me, but fear the long arm of torture," the man said.

"Do you think that Aragon and Castile will unite under Ferdinand and Isabella?" Itzhak changed the subject.

"I believe so. We all speak the same language, have the same heritage, and believe in the same God -- it would only make sense that the countries unite."

"I'm told that Queen Isabella is extremely religious and greatly influenced by this priest, Tomas de Torquemada," Itzhak said. "Who is he anyhow? Where did he come from? And how did he become the Chief Inquisitor of the Inquisition?"

"Torquemada was born in Valladolid in 1420. He's said to be the nephew of Cardinal Juan de Torquemada. He spent many years in a monastery in Valladolid and eventually was transferred to the monastery of Santa Cruz, in Segovia, where he became prior. Queen Isabella chose him as her confessor while in Segovia and made him her trusted counselor as well. Perhaps due to his position with the Queen, he was also appointed to be the Chief Inquisitor," the man said.

Itzhak was only too happy when nightfall arrived. While he enjoyed talking to the unknown passenger, he felt a certain discomfort with his statements. *"How come he is so open with me when every Aragonian and Castilian are afraid to open their mouths in public,"* Itzhak thought. After a small meal they were assigned their rooms. Itzhak lit two candles, took the papers and letters he had removed from the dead priest and laid them on the floor. He asked Yael to shut the heavy curtains so that no one could look in. One of the letters was addressed to Archbishop Carlos Nujes de Miranda and the other to Bishop Joackim Nujes de Miranda. The papers articulated the words exchanged between the priest and Itzhak the previous day. "The priest recorded everything I said yesterday," he stated.

"This is rather odd," she said. "Why did he do that?"

"I don't know. He must have written it in his room last night before he set out to kill me."

"You have his handwriting now. Are you going to open the letters?"

"Absolutely." He opened the one addressed to the Archbishop.

"His Holy Eminence Archbishop Nujes,

It is with much sorrow and pain that I write to you with such news. Every priest in the Inquisition building in Toledo has been killed. I suspect it is the work of a fanatic Jew. During the same night all houses belonging to Jews who refused to convert were set afire. The Devil himself is at work and as you very well know the Devil is lodged in the heart of every Jewish person. Please take the necessary steps to guard our institutions.

In a conference I held with King Ferdinand and Queen Isabella, I was promised sentries for each one of our Inquisition buildings throughout both kingdoms. The commander of the Crown's guard will be visiting with you in the near future to coordinate all security matters. May the Lord be with you.

Inquisitor General
(-) Tomas de Torquemada"

"I'm going to reseal this envelope and use it as a pretext to visit the Archbishop," Itzhak said. "We'll go together. I have an idea now that we know the name of the priest I killed."

"When do you think they'll discover the priest's body?" she asked.

"Since the well is dry they'll never find him."

"Time is certainly on our side. Tell me, how do you feel about having killed a man?" Yael queried.

"I have no remorse whatsoever. This man tried to kill me. Had I not been suspicious of him, and had I not been alert, I would be dead."

"Are you going to open the second letter?"

"I don't think so. The seal on the envelope is the same, which leads me to believe that Torquemada wrote the same letter to all Archbishops, Cardinals, and Bishops cautioning them about the killings and the need for security."

"Do you think the new security measures might hamper our group's operations?"

"I doubt it very much. There are many ways we can carry out our mission. Now that we have Torquemada's letter, I'm very anxious to return to Barcelona."

"Let's get the seals from the key people and leave. Barcelona is quite close to Tarragona. It shouldn't take us more than two day's travel."

They were surprised the next day when one of the men and the woman took a coach which went in a different direction. The man Itzhak had held a lengthy conversation with was still there. This time, however, he avoided conversation, which Itzhak was very happy about. He closed his eyes for the longest while, but his mind was not idle at all. He tried to figure out how to handle the Archbishop.

Finally, the coach arrived in Tarragona and the owner of the trading post directed them to a centrally located inn. With clothing sacks over their shoulders, they walked to the inn. The proprietor gave them a room and Itzhak inquired about the Archbishop's address. "Would you have Archbishop Nujes address?"

"Of course." He gave it to him. "Why do you wish to see the Archbishop?"

"I have a letter for him," Itzhak answered.

"Aren't you a little too young for a courier?"

"The regular courier fell sick at the last moment and I was asked to take his place."

"Show me the letter. I'll take it to him," the proprietor offered.

"I regret to tell you but I was specifically warned about having others carry this letter. I am obligated to deliver it personally to the Archbishop."

The proprietor kept persisting but Itzhak turned him down. They had a late supper and retired to their room. Before he went to bed, however, Itzhak pushed the large chest of drawers to the door so that no one would be able to enter their room. Satisfied they were secure, he went to bed. Yael was already sleeping.

The Archbishop's house was conveniently located and they found it easily. The city's main plaza was two blocks away. Itzhak pulled on the doorbell and an old housekeeper opened the front door.

"I have a letter for His Eminence," Itzhak announced.

"I'll take it," she said.

"I'm obligated to deliver this letter personally. It is from the Chief Inquisitor, Tomas de Torquemada."

"I'm too old to climb the stairs so many times a day. Run up, his office is on the second floor, third door to the left," she said.

Itzhak was in no hurry. He carefully examined the ground floor on the way to the staircase, which was to the left of the large lobby wall.

"Is that room the dining room?" Itzhak asked.

"Why do you want to know?" she asked suspiciously.

"I love old houses. Would you say this house is a hundred years old?"

"It's certainly older than me. I was born here. My mother was the housekeeper to the two previous Eminences," she answered.

"Thank you," Itzhak said, and guided Yael up the stairs. Once on the upper landing Itzhak opened the first door to the left. It was a narrow broom closet. The second door opened on a library. The walls were covered with shelves and hundreds of books and manuscripts were piled up without any specific order. In the center of the room was a large table and four chairs. On the right hand side a door was open.

"This door adjoins the Archbishop's office," Itzhak whispered. "Let's take a quick look." They advanced slowly towards the open door. The Archbishop was sitting at his desk reading a large book. His head was no more than a few inches above the paper.

"His eyesight is poor," Itzhak whispered again. "I'd guess he's well over eighty."

"What's our next step?" Yael asked.

"We knock on the door and walk in." They reentered the corridor, knocked on the third door, and walked in.

"Good morning, Your Eminence," Itzhak said, "I have a letter for you from Tomas de Torquemada."

"Who are you? Your voice is unfamiliar to me," the Archbishop said.

"My name is Juan. The priest who was supposed to deliver this letter died enroute to Tarragona. He was very ill. Before his death he asked me to bring this letter to you as it is of primary importance. This is my sister Maria."

"Please open the letter and read it to me. My eyesight is mostly gone. I can barely see you." Itzhak opened the envelope and read the letter very slowly. The old Archbishop gasped.

"Your Eminence," Itzhak opened the conversation, "Do you believe that Jews should be burned to death if they refuse to convert?"

"Who are you to ask me such a question," the old man blurted. "You delivered the letter, be on your way." As the Archbishop completed his instruction, the man who had engaged Itzhak in conversation on the coach walked in. Itzhak and Yael were shocked.

"What are you two doing here?" he asked.

"We delivered a letter to his Eminence," Itzhak gathered his strength. He grabbed the letter off the desk and read it.

"You couldn't possibly have been the messengers of such a letter," he announced. "The priest on the coach, what have you done to him?"

"I don't know what you're talking about," Itzhak said. "It was the priest who asked me to deliver this letter. He was a dying man."

"You are a liar. The priest was healthy as a horse," the man said, advancing toward Itzhak and grabbing his arm firmly. "I will personally deliver the two of you to the Inquisition. They will get the truth out of you."

Yael leaped towards the man and kicked him in his groin with all her strength. He released Itzhak and fell to the floor, screaming with pain. Yael grabbed Itzhak's arm and pulled him out of the room. His senses returned as they ran out. He propelled Yael into the small closet next to the staircase, and left the door slightly ajar. A few minutes later the unknown man came rushing out of the room, and as soon as he neared the staircase, Itzhak jumped out and propelled him down the stairs. He rolled several times and knocked his head against the wall at the bottom. He didn't move. "Watch him," Itzhak ordered, "I'll be right back." He ran into the Archbishop's office and emerged a few minutes later with the seal and wax boxlet. The housekeeper came out of her room.

"What is this noise?"

"This man fell down the stairs," Itzhak said. "We're going to call for help."

They ran out of the Archbishop's house towards the plaza.

"Let's go to the Bishop's house now, and then leave this city," Yael said.

"You're right. Let's get the Bishop's address from the priest in the Church at the far end of the plaza." The priest was quick to oblige upon hearing whose letter they carried.

"How will you gain an audience with the Bishop?" Yael asked.

"Simple. I'll tell him the Archbishop wants him in his office with great urgency due to a letter he received from Torquemada. The Bishop will surely comply, and that will give me the opportunity to get his seal."

They walked briskly towards the Bishop's house and knocked on the front door. A young priest opened the door.

"What do you two youngsters want?"

"We have a message from the Archbishop."

"The Archbishop never sent children before. Who are you? Answer truthfully," the priest said.

"The Archbishop received an urgent letter from Torquemada, and wants to see the Bishop immediately." Itzhak replied.

"Come in," the young priest said. "Follow me."

The Bishop's office was on the ground floor towards the rear of the house.

"Wait here. I'll be right back." He knocked on the door and walked in. Itzhak looked around and noticed a door and a window facing the rear of the house. He had no more time to study the premises as the priest came out and motioned them in.

"What message do you have for me?" the Bishop asked.

"His Eminence Archbishop Nujes wants you and your assistant to meet with him immediately. He said to come right away. It is a matter of great urgency."

"Where is Cordilla? Why did he send you? I don't like it," the Bishop said.

"Cordilla fell down the stairs and broke his neck. I delivered the letter to His Eminence. A priest gave it to me enroute to Tarragona. The priest was dying from some disease and knew he wouldn't make it. He gave me the letter and instructed me to deliver it to the Archbishop, which I did."

"Do you know what's in the letter?" the Bishop asked.

"I do not. Cordilla read the letter to the Archbishop in privacy. When Cordilla escorted us out of the house he slipped and fell down the stairs. My mission is over. I came to visit my family and I have wasted a great deal of time. Whether you go to the Archbishop or not is not my problem. Good day," Itzhak said and pulled Yael out with him.

They left the Bishop's house and walked across the street. A large wagon was parked between two houses. They hid behind it. A few minutes later the Bishop and his young assistant came rushing out of the house and walked away.

"They're on their way to the Archbishop. Let's get his seal."

As soon as the Bishop was out of sight they ran across. The front door was locked. Itzhak guided Yael around the house to the back. The rear door was also locked. The only way in was through the window, but Itzhak couldn't open it. He found an old piece of furniture lying around and smashed the window with it.

"Stand out here and watch," he instructed. "It'll only take a minute." He jumped in, entered the Bishop's office, and retrieved the seal. In his haste he overturned a candle and the papers on the desk caught fire. He made a fast decision. It would take a few minutes before the flames would be noticed and within those few minutes they would be blocks away. He jumped out, and grabbed Yael's hand.

"Run! I'll explain later." They ran behind the house, jumped a couple of fences and soon found themselves on a narrow road. They strolled casually so as not to attract attention and finally reached the main plaza.

"We have to leave this city immediately," Itzhak said.

"What happened? You didn't say a word."

"First, the Bishop was suspicious, but more importantly, when I took the seal, I accidentally overturned a burning candle and some papers caught fire. I couldn't put out the fire. By now the fire must have burned the entire office and more. The Bishop will most certainly suspect us, and that's why we must leave this moment."

"Should we get our clothes from the inn?" Yael asked.

"No," Itzhak said. "If the sentries will check the inns, they are bound to find our belongings and will think we are somewhere in the area. On the other hand, if we take our things and leave in a rush, the innkeeper will become suspicious and sentries might look for us. This way we gain time."

"You're right. Are we walking toward the road leading out of the city?" she asked.

"Yes, we are. We should reach the Barcelona road in a few minutes. By the way, can you ride a horse?" Itzhak asked.

"I've never ridden a horse in my life," Yael responded.

"A large cargo wagon is approaching from the right. Let's run! Perhaps he will take us with him." They ran towards the wagon, which had turned into the road leading to Barcelona. The wagon driver was extremely happy to provide transportation for twenty pennies and invited them to settle between the big bundles he was carrying.

"How much longer before the sun sets?" Yael asked.

"I'd say three to four hours."

It was dark when the wagon stopped in a small village.

"You can sleep in this barn," the driver said, "we'll continue at daybreak tomorrow morning. I'll bring you some bread and water."

"This is very kind of you," Itzhak said. "My sister and I greatly appreciate it."

The wagon driver brought them bread and an assortment of fruit. Itzhak placed the knife by his side and hoped the day's events and the tension would not disturb his sleep. Nothing did. He fell asleep almost immediately, and so did Yael.

The wagon driver woke them from a deep sleep and urged them to hurry. He wanted to reach Barcelona by nighttime. So did Itzhak and Yael. Riding in the back of the wagon was not as comfortable as the coach, but they had no alternative.

CHAPTER TWELVE

The sight of Barcelona in the distance was most gratifying. Itzhak kept pointing at different castles and landscapes as they appeared. "I'm very happy to be back. I don't know about you, but I'm tired of traveling and looking forward to the beginning of our fight against the Inquisition and the Church."

"Traveling the way we did is certainly tiring. I too am looking forward to an exciting future," Yael said. "However, I can sense great danger for all of us. I can't imagine the Church giving up easily."

"Every revolution is painful and dangerous. We'll need to take a great deal of precaution as we proceed. David and Reuven are right in saying that someone has to fight the cruelty and brutality of the Inquisition and its doctrines. I can tell you, I feel completely committed to the cause."

"Me too," Yael declared. "I'm glad Anna recruited us."

"We'll probably need to recruit many more youngsters in all the major cities. We'll have to wage a long and fierce war against the Inquisition."

The wagon finally arrived at its destination. Itzhak and Yael thanked the driver and walked in the direction of Zevulun's house. It was dark when they got there. Zevulun and his wife hugged and kissed them.

"Come on in. You must be exhausted."

"Yes, we are," Itzhak said. "We need to wash up. We're as dirty as a couple of pigs in the mud."

"Am I happy to see you," Yael declared. "Is everything all right here?"

"Everything is fine. Yossef and Elisheva arrived yesterday and brought with them an interesting woman and a very sick man. They actually saved this man from the Inquisition. I expect David and Anna any day, perhaps tomorrow," Zevulun said.

Itzhak handed the seals he had collected along with lists of names and addresses. Due to the late hour accommodations had not been prepared for the new arrivals. Itzhak, however, would not retire. He was wound up. Zevulun listened attentively as Itzhak recounted the ordeals he and Yael experienced.

"You did well. Don't let the killing bother you. The priest deserved to die. I suspect we'll have to kill many more priests before our fight is won."

"I'm ready," Itzhak said. "I'll gladly kill anyone who tortures and murders innocent people."

"You better go to bed. It's late. Tomorrow I'll start the letter campaign," Zevulun said.

"I can help you write," Itzhak said, "I'm an excellent writer."

"Very good," Zevulun said, "I'll look forward to working with you. Now, go sleep and forget the dead priest."

CHAPTER THIRTEEN

It was early morning when David and Anna arrived. They parked their wagon in Zevulun's barn and unhitched the horses. The reunion of all members brought excitement to a peak with Reuven's arrival from the monastery. They spent the next few hours telling each other about their travels and ordeals. The unknown man was still lying in bed and Devorah, Zevulun's wife, was at his side.

"He's still sleeping. I heard him mumble a few words. I hope that with rest and care he'll recuperate."

"Do we know who he is?" Itzhak asked.

"Let me look at him," David said, and no sooner than he took his first glimpse he shuddered. "My God, this is Nechemia Shomroni. He was the Director of the Toledo synagogue before he disappeared many months ago."

"Will he recover?" Yael asked.

"I hope so," Zevulun answered. "I checked his body carefully. He was beaten, flogged with all kinds of instruments, and stretched. His head must have been hit, too. He is semi-conscious. In my opinion, he shouldn't move until his head injuries heal."

"We shouldn't crowd him. He should really have a room by himself," Rachel suggested.

"He should, but we don't have room for so many people."

"Devorah is right, we need to discuss our housing because none of us can return to our old homes," David stated. "Leave me alone with this man for a while, perhaps he'll remember me."

They filed out and David took a seat next to his bed. He touched the man's hand. "Nechemia, can you hear me?" There was no answer. Again, "Nechemia, can you hear me? I'm David Abulafia from Toledo." The man stirred and gradually opened his eyes. "I know your father well," he whispered and tried to move.

"Please don't move," David said. "You must rest until your head injuries have healed. It's very important you stay still. Our friends will take good care of you."

"Where am I?"

"You're in Barcelona. Yossef and Elisheva saved you from the Inquisition. You're a lucky man."

"My entire body feels on fire and my head hurts," he whispered.

"Please stay still and don't try to move. You'll be given all the care in the world. You'll get better, I'm sure."

"Thank you." he closed his eyes. David walked out of the room. "We have new members. This is wonderful."

"We need to discuss housing before anything else. This many people cannot live in here. We also don't want to draw attention to this place."

"We'll have to buy or lease a farmhouse with a large barn along with a good size tract of land from one of the landowners and pretend to be farmers. We can hire a few peasants who would teach and work with us."

"This is an excellent idea," Zevulun said.

"Leave this matter to Zevulun. I'd like to express my thoughts about future activity," David declared.

"Go ahead," Reuven said.

"There are nine major cities in Aragon and Castile. We need to have presence in each one of them. I therefore suggest that the new farmhouse we purchase or lease becomes our headquarters and that we set up regional operating branches in central locations among these cities. For example, Leon and Bilbao would become one region, Valladolid and Salamanca, another, Zaragoza and Tarragona, another, and Toledo and Segovia another. The city of Barcelona will be handled from here. Furthermore, once we assign one of us to head each region, the primary function of this person would be to recruit more operatives as needed for his region. The letter writing and distribution should commence immediately."

"This is a grand plan, but if all of us are to remain underground, and we need to buy or lease farmhouses, where is the money coming from?" Rachel asked.

"We have plenty of money. In fact, we have money to last us twenty or more years," David stated.

"Where is it?"

"There's no reason for any of you to know. There are three people who have that information, and for safety's sake it should remain that way," David said firmly.

"This plan makes a lot of sense. Let's refine it further. It's imperative that we all wear cheap peasant clothing, and when we travel, men should wear monk habits. No one ever accosts monks," Reuven said.

"Are you going to stay in the monastery?" David asked.

"I've been thinking a great deal about this. If I stay at the monastery, I'll only be partially active, and any such activity will have to be in Barcelona. However, if I drop out, I could become active full time, which is really what I want to do," Reuven said.

"Despite your wish to be active full time, none of us will. There is a time element we have to live with. Once letters have gone out, we have to wait for results," David opined.

"Perhaps we should declare an all out war on the Inquisition." Reuven asked.

"Please don't get carried away," Zevulun said. "I know all of you want to start and finish this war as quickly as possible, but it won't work that way. Think about this for a moment. If we start an all out war, the Crown with its Queen and King, who are deeply religious Catholics, have the armies to fight back, and they will. We said from the start we would need to soften opinions first. By sending the letters, we will start an internal revolution within the Church and the Crown. One authority will question the other. Each will deny having written letters, and suspicion enters the play. Torquemada, the chief Inquisitor, the most fanatic clergyman, will excommunicate those he suspects the most, and some may even be exiled. Those clergy whose honor and integrity have been destroyed will fight back in one form or another. This will create the confusion we are seeking. Once we have reached that goal, we can surface and fight. The Crown or the Church will think of us as new comers into the picture and will have to listen to us."

"This makes a great deal of sense," Miriam said. "It is the mature and sensible way of attacking the problem. The Church and the Inquisition are extremely powerful. They will not easily change their attitude or behavior."

"What about assassinations?" Yossef asked.

"We should have a few; one or two in each city, just enough to frighten the clergymen who will have to deal with the letters," Zevulun said.

"Let me sum this up before we proceed," Reuven said.

Everyone nodded in agreement.

"Just one moment. I have an idea we should consider," David said. "It would make a great deal of sense if the Archbishop of, say Tarragona, wrote a letter denouncing the Church and its doctrines and then committed suicide."

"Excellent thinking," Zevulun proclaimed. "We'll discuss this phase when we get to the letters. Reuven, please continue."

"Barcelona will be the headquarters, run by Zevulun. David and I will visit Barcelona periodically to confer with him. Decisions coming out of our headquarters will be sent by Miriam and Devorah, who'll become our couriers. Both Miriam and Devorah will dress as nuns when they travel and will be known as Sister Maria and Sister Teresa. The four regions are: Leon-Bilbao, manned by Itzhak and Yael, Valladolid-Salamanca, manned by Rachel and me, Toledo-Segovia, manned by David and Anna, and Zaragoza-Tarragona, manned by Yossef and Elisheva. Each region head will receive 5 gold dukats, enough to buy or lease a sizeable farmhouse, as well as peasant help and supplies for a few months. Each region should develop a productive farm and sell produce on the market. The women can help with that work and other operations that will develop. Before we depart to our respective locations, Sisters Maria and Teresa will deliver the letters at each destination. I suggest that everyone begins to attend mass on Sundays in Churches closest to you and befriend the priests in order to find out what's going on. Usually, contributions to the church will spark the priest's interest in you. Use it to our benefit. Our letters are certain to create panic, debate, mistrust, confusion, and who knows what else. We are counting on it. Based on developments, we'll decide on future steps and timing."

"This sounds good for a start. I'm excited," Elisheva said.

"I think some killings must accompany the letters. It will throw the leaders of the Church into two different directions. They may begin to think the killings are inspired and connected to a defecting priest or priests," David said.

"It's interesting. The more we discuss our thoughts, we come up with better ideas and strategy," Zevulun said. "How do the women among us think about these plans so far?"

"I think we're on the right track. Confuse them, create distrust within their institutions, create a few suicides and a few murders, and then strike if we see no results," Rachel said.

"I agree with that," Yael said. "I would have three Cardinals commit suicide on the same night and made sure each left a note to Torquemada stating the same reason. Once these notes have reached him, he'll have a lot of thinking to do."

"We're getting better as we talk," Reuven said. "Let's plan it that way."

"Three dead Cardinals on the same day will have to weigh heavily on Torquemada and the Pope. Don't forget the pope because it's the Vatican that elects and appoints Cardinals," Elisheva said. "I'm in full agreement with the plan. I'd like to also add that I'll be ready to kill any one you designate. I have no feelings for this common enemy of ours."

"Let's go over the names of the Cardinals. We have Jose Cardonaz de Madrid in Barcelona, Pedro Gonzalez de Mendoza in Toledo and Ferdinand Avila de Rimor in Segovia. This means that Zevulun will kill Cardonaz, David will kill Gonzalez, and Elisheva will kill Avila in Segovia, as David cannot be in two places on the same night," Reuven said.

"Are there any questions?" Zevulun asked, "I don't have any."

"I do," Devorah said. "What about the sick man in the next room?"

"I hope that by the time we have prepared all the letters, he will have recovered, or at least enough to hold a conversation," David said.

"What if he doesn't want to join us?" Miriam asked.

"Then we are faced with a major problem," Zevulun said.

"Not necessarily," Reuven said. "As of now he knows nothing. By the end of the week, Zevulun should find a farm to purchase or lease. We should take special care not to divulge its location. He is not to know a thing about the letters and the suicides, nor about the four branches in the regions."

"I have a feeling he will join us wholeheartedly out of sheer vengeance for the Inquisition," David said.

"We'll find out soon enough," Reuven said.

"He was a prominent man in the Toledo Jewish community. I'm certain he'll join us," David said. He wondered why Anna hadn't said a word. "Dearest, you didn't say a thing today. Is something bothering you?"

"I've been listening attentively to the conversation and am with you, body and soul. My mind has been preoccupied with the recruitment issue about which little was said."

"You're absolutely right," David responded. "We have to address this matter."

"I propose the women attend to this matter. I know I'm going to check every candidate very thoroughly. We cannot afford to make a single mistake," Anna said.

"I think we should postpone recruitment until phase one is complete," Reuven said. "Perhaps, with God's help, we won't need to recruit anyone and our plan will work on its own."

"I'll be the first to agree. However, I cannot imagine Torquemada would give up so easily. I'm sure he'll pass the dead Cardinals as martyrs for the cause of Catholic cleansing," David remarked.

"I agree with David," Itzhak said, "I doubt Torquemada will bend so quickly, if at all."

"If he doesn't change, what stops us from killing him?" Yossef asked. "I'll be happy to give up my life for his."

"What about me?" Yael asked. "Don't give up your life so quickly, please."

"If killing Torquemada becomes necessary, I'm sure we'll find a way," Zevulun said. "After all, he has to sleep somewhere, too."

"Then we're in agreement. Recruitment will be postponed until further notice." Anna stated.

"I suggest that meanwhile we develop a list of candidates and befriend them without divulging our activities. Actually, this method will give us time to get to know those people, and we'll be making less mistakes," Reuven said.

"It appears that you won't return to the monastery," David interposed.

"You're right. According to our plans I'll have the Valladolid-Salamanca region. I'll be far away from the monastery. I'll return tonight and bring back monk habits for all of us," Reuven said.

"I'm anxious to start writing letters, but before I do, I'd like to prepare a list of all the names and addresses so that we have a central file," Itzhak said.

"Very good," Zevulun agreed. "Let me help you."

The meeting broke up. Reuven left and Miriam and Rachel went to look after the sick man. "I'm very pleased with our first meeting, and the decisions we took. I know my father is very proud of me. I can sense his presence," David stated.

CHAPTER FOURTEEN

*His Eminence the Inquisitor General
And Counselor to Queen Isabella
Tomas de Torquemada,*

During the past week I've observed for the first time an actual ritual of Auto- de-Fe and my heart shuddered. What are we doing burning people to death? Is there no other way to reach them? Are people who do not believe in Jesus sinners under their own religious laws and traditions? The world has existed thousands of years before Jesus and I suspect will exist thousands of years after him.

Since this week I've began to ask myself whether Jesus wants us to burn to death any human being no matter what the cause is. I'm beginning to feel we are making a very serious mistake. Punishment by fire is getting us nowhere except on a one way path to hell. Jesus convinced his disciples by plain soft talk and deeds. We are trying to convince the people who brought us Jesus by torture, by blackmail, by vandalizing their lives and property, by intimidation, and by fear. I believe that Jesus, up there in heaven, is wondering what kind of animals we turned into.

I, for one, who was appointed by the Pope to be the Cardinal in this area, cannot live with myself under the present rules that you instituted. Therefore, I've decided to take my life as self-inflicted punishment for the sins I have committed against any fellowman. I don't believe that going to a confessor will clear my sins – they are too deep. I hope and pray it won't be too late for Saint Paul to accept me in heaven. I will fully understand if I am sent to hell. In actuality, that is where I belong.

When you receive this note, I shall be dead. I beg of you, rethink your policies and become a real saint for the cause of Catholicism.

*Obediently yours,
Pedro Gonzalez de Mendoza
Cardinal of Toledo*

"This letter is incredible," David burst. "Are the other two going to be the same?"

"No. I don't think the letters should be the same. They should follow the same theme, but with different words," Itzhak said. "When Torquemada receives three letters from Cardinals who committed suicide, he'll be shocked, as I'm sure the Queen will be. I'm now going to compose letters addressed to the Queen from the same Cardinals."

The Great Majesty
My Honorable Queen Isabella
Of Castile,

The attached copy of a letter, which I've written to the General Inquisitor, Tomas de Torquemada, is self-explanatory. However, I felt that I owe you an explanation as well, since you are the Queen ruler of this land, a true Catholic and firm believer in Jesus.

There is nothing wrong with believing that Catholicism is the only pure and holy Christian faith. However, to kill innocent people whose only crime is belief in another God is not what Jesus wanted or wants us to do. I believe that all of us were carried away with misplaced zealousness.

Forgive me for not consulting with you before taking my own life, but I cannot live with myself. I have sinned, and I deserve the same fate the poor dead people had. I hope Jesus will forgive me, as I'm sure you will.

Your Obedient Cardinal
Pedro Gonzalez de Mendoza

"I'm fascinated with your ability to write so clearly and majestically," David admitted. "Surely Queen Isabella will call Torquemada to a meeting."

"Don't forget other letters, those without suicides; letters from priests to priests and from Archbishops to Bishops and so on," Itzhak said.

"I'm composing these letters right now," Zevulun said.

Zevulun felt that young Itzhak outdid him and decided to revise his first letter. Suddenly he lifted his head from the paper. "I'll admit that you write better than me. I'll follow your way of writing. It makes sense."

"Don't underestimate yourself. I'm sure you're an excellent writer too," Itzhak replied.

His Eminence Bishop
Marcos Garcia de Colon
Toledo, Castile.

A young boy came to see me yesterday. His name is Juan Medina de Odilon. My guess is he's fifteen years old. He is a student at one of the local Catholic schools in Bilbao. He told me his parent's neighbors, a Jewish family, converted about a year ago. He said that he and his brother and sisters used to play with the neighboring Jewish children since early childhood and have become good friends. He said that as far as he can remember, the Jewish family treated the Medina children with care and love and always welcomed them warmly into their household. On occasion, when his parents were traveling, all four of them would stay with their neighbors.

"My parents also thought highly of their Jewish neighbors and could not understand the hateful sermons they were hearing about Jews in church every Sunday. One day the Jewish neighbor came to visit my father and I overheard him say that two inquisitors came to see him and told him unless he and his family convert, all of them would be taken to the Inquisition building for interrogation. My father suggested they convert as it would be impossible to fight the Church, and they did.

It has been a little over a year since they converted, and now they are called Conversos. Last week this man was told the government could no longer employ him because he is a Converso and impure Jewish blood runs in his veins." These were what the young boy said word for word.

This is not the first time I'm hearing about discrimination against Conversos. In fact, in a recent meeting of priests with Bishop Juan Martinez de Aculla we were told not to accept Conversos as true Christians, but to consider them as New Christians.

I'm at a loss to understand why the Church decided to differentiate between Old and New Christians. In my simple mind, if a man is baptized, he has converted. If he goes to Church every Sunday, follows the Catholic doctrine and believes in Jesus, he is a Christian like any of us.

Just like Juan's family, there must be hundreds of families, if not thousands, who are neighbors to Conversos. How do we explain to these Old Christian children the reality which the Church has imposed upon us?

I find it difficult to be a true and devout priest under deceitful conditions. I wish the Church would revise its thinking on the subject of Conversos.

Obediently yours,
Juan Carlos de Medina
Church of the Resurrection
Toledo, Castile

"What do you think of this letter?" Zevulun asked.

"I think it's fine," Itzhak said. "I suppose in each such letter you'll be changing the text."

The Honorable
Joackim Nujes de Miranda
Bishop for Tarragona,

As Bishop Alfredo Molina de Russo was found dead some time ago, I decided to write to you since you are the closest to Segovia.

Recently, a Church directed mob attacked the old Jewish neighborhood, known as Barrio Israelita, where all Conversos live. There are no more Jews in that section of our city.

I was instructed by the Segovia Chief Inquisitor to take my flock and march on that neighborhood. The Inquisition sent hundreds of peasants to join my parishioners in the demonstration march. As soon as we got to the old Barrio Israelita, someone unknown to me gave a signal and the mob attacked the houses of the Conversos. Within minutes dozens of houses were vandalized and peasants walked away with all kinds of loot.

My questions to you, as Bishop in this city, are: When are we going to accept the Conversos as Christians? If we got them to convert, why are we destroying their property and morale? How do we expect them to go to church next Sunday and pray to the Jesus who sent mobs to ruin them? Aren't we defeating our own intentions by deeds of violence? Aren't we contradicting the ways of life of our Savior?

Unless the Catholic Church changes its stance on the Converso matter I shall resign my position as head priest for the Church of St. Mary and return to civilian life.

Your Highness, please forgive this outburst of mine, but I cannot continue to preach Christian values under false and deceitful methods. In my next sermon I shall so tell my flock.

> *Jose Alonso de Aguiles*
> *Church of Santa Maria*
> *Segovia*

It took about a week before all letters were written. David, Reuven, Zevulun and Itzhak sat down around the dining room table and discussed dates. It was decided to have the three Cardinals commit "suicide" on the night of Saturday, 3rd day of November, 1476. All other letters, one for each region, were dated for the following week.

CHAPTER FIFTEEN

Nechemia Shomroni's condition improved with every passing day. Miriam, Rachel and Devorah took turns and nursed him around the clock. A week after he was brought to Barcelona, Nechemia became very talkative. His pain subsided and he was allowed short walks around the house. By the time the letters were readied and preparations for departure commenced, Nechemia appeared to be a new man.

"I don't know how I'll ever be able to repay you for your kindness," he kept saying. Everyone assured him there was no need for repayment.

"What am I going to do?" he asked. "Where am I to go? I feel so fatigued. I have no idea what became of my wife and two sons."

"What is your wife's name?" Zevulun asked.

"Her name is............Oh! My God! I can't remember. I have a mental block," he began to cry. "I know I have two sons, the older one is Michael and the younger is Avraham. I can't remember their ages or what they look like. My memory is shattered."

"How do you feel physically?" Zevulun asked.

"I feel much better. My headaches are gone, and so most of the pain. My body is beginning to function normally. It's my memory that bothers me. There are things I remember and things I don't."

"I wouldn't worry about it. With time your memory will come back, I'm sure. The trauma you've been through will slowly disappear, and as your body heals so will your mind."

"I wish I were as confident as you," he said.

"I'll be going out to look for a farmhouse. Come with me, the cool autumn air will do you good," Zevulun offered.

"Are you a priest?" Nechemia asked.

"Sometimes, when I feel like it," he smiled.

"You're making fun of me. From the little I've heard in your house all of you are Jews," he said. "I'm a Jew and proud of it."

"Let's put it this way -- today I'm a priest. This leads me to ask you a question. If, and I say if, there was an organization determined to fight the Inquisition and bring it down, would you join it and fight?"

"If God has given me my life again and I return to normal, and if there were such an organization, I would fight the Inquisition until the last drop of my blood. I've gone through unimaginable torture. If I can be instrumental, in any way, in bringing down the Inquisition, I'll gladly sacrifice everything I have, including my life."

"We'll be arriving shortly at the offices of a landowner named Carlos Madeira de la Curzon. Don't say anything. If asked I'll tell them you're a mentally retarded relative. Just listen. Be sure not to talk," Zevulun ordered.

The conversation was brief. Zevulun explained to the land manager that he was a priest who wished to rehabilitate several ill persons and was using the money given him by a wealthy donor to lease a farmhouse, barn and a suitable tract of land. He further explained he would be hiring experienced hands to assist him in making the lives of these ill people productive in agriculture. The land manager took them in a horse drawn coach to view a farmhouse that was available. The farmhouse was in fairly good condition, with a large barn next to it, and the land manager explained that the tract of fertile land that came with this farmhouse was about twenty-five dunam in size. The price of two gold dukats was acceptable and would cover the first year's lease. Thereafter, the annual fee to the landowner would be one gold dukat. Zevulun paid the two dukats, received a receipt and left. He was very pleased as the farmhouse was not too far from the city and a small tributary of the Tago River passed through the grounds.

"I thought it would take days to find a good farmhouse. I was lucky. The first landowner we visited had what I was looking for," he said as he walked into the house.

"What are you planning to do with this house?" David asked.

" I'll keep it," he said, "you never know when we might need it."

"You'll have to show up here from time to time so people know its being lived in," David said.

"I have to tell you, David, I'm very impressed with your maturity. I know your parents would be very proud of you. You have become a man at a young and tender age," Zevulun said. "I miss your father very much. I always loved him, a man of great integrity and character."

"Thank you for these kind words. I loved him, too, and my mother," David said. "I miss them more than you'll ever know."

Nechemia walked into his bedroom and Zevulun found the right moment to tell David of his conversation with him.

"Nechemia could become an active member of our organization. He is full of venom. Unfortunately, his memory has not returned to normal yet. There are things he remembers and things he cannot. I would have liked him to go with you, but Toledo is not the place for him. I think I'll have to keep him in the farmhouse until he is completely recovered. Meanwhile, when you're in Toledo try to find out the whereabouts of his two sons. He has no recollection of his wife. He couldn't even remember her name. It could well be she was tortured to death in front of him and he has created a mental block about it. One day we'll know the truth."

"He was well known in Toledo's Jewish community. He was the Director of our synagogue, but I was too young to pay attention," David said.

"Did I hear you say 'synagogue?'" Nechemia asked as he entered the hall.

"Yes, I said that you were the Director of the Toledo synagogue," David answered.

"Do I know you?" he asked.

"You knew my father, Moise Abulafia."

"Of course, now I remember. Abulafia, the big trading company. Yes, I know your father well," he said.

"My father and mother are dead. They were burned by the Inquisition because they refused to convert."

"The Inquisition? The Inquisition?" he echoed. "That's where they took me. It's coming back. I was torturing myself with so many questions. Yes.... the Inquisition.... They beat me with sticks and put me through so many torture machines I lost consciousness. Their faces are coming back to me now, those murdering priests! Animals in the desert treat you better."

"Please calm down," Zevulun said. "You are regaining your memory, but it's not healthy for you to get this excited. Let's have a hot drink in the kitchen."

Zevulun took his arm and led him into the kitchen.

"Please sit here. I'll prepare the drink for the three of us."

Yossef and Itzhak entered the kitchen.

"What are you three up to?"

"The first piece of good news is that Nechemia is regaining his memory, and second, I leased a farmhouse, barn and a beautiful piece of land nearby Barcelona. The previous tenant passed away recently and his farm was up for leasing. I came at the right time. I'll keep this house, too. It's not costing us much, and who knows, we might need it one day."

"This is excellent news," Itzhak said.

"Pull up chairs. We'll continue our chat here."

"The picture is suddenly clearing up." Nechemia was joyful. "I couldn't remember my wife's name. It's Esther, daughter of Nahum and Bat Sheva Eliashar. Esther died on one of the beast's machines. I couldn't bear watching her. They flogged me and made me watch her suffering. I'll kill them with my bare hands," he screamed.

"Calm down," Zevulun instructed. "You mustn't excite yourself like this."

"I can't bear it." He burst into tears. Zevulun handed him a cup of tea. "Drink some tea. You must rest." He called his wife and asked her to take Nechemia to his room.

"Make sure he rests. His memory is returning, and it hurts him a great deal."

Devorah took Nechemia's arm and maneuvered him away. "Next time I kill some of these bastards, I'll call his wife's name, too,"

David said. "How many lives were destroyed in the name of Catholicism and for what?"

"When Reuven arrives from the monastery, let's have a final meeting before we depart to our various destinations," David suggested.

"I believe Nechemia will be a great asset to our organization. First and foremost, he's full of vengeance, and secondly, he is a wise man. His memory seems to be returning. I feel he'll regain full capacity soon. The shock is over. We can tell him who we are and what we're doing."

"I believe you're right. I'll be alone in Barcelona and he can certainly help. Furthermore, no one knows him in this city," Zevulun said.

"Reuven is arriving in his wagon," Miriam announced from the kitchen door.

"Let's greet him," Yossef said.

"No," Zevulun said firmly. "I don't want the neighbors to see this many people here. We should be more careful. I'll step outside since I'm wearing a priest's habit and Reuven is for sure in a monk's habit."

A few minutes later Reuven walked in carrying a large sack over his shoulder.

"Here are your new clothes, gentlemen," he announced and handed out monk's habit to each of the men. He had a large smile on his face.

"I'm not returning to the monastery. Tomorrow I leave for my new destination as you will, too."

Zevulun gave each of the men five gold dukats. David suddenly propelled Zevulun out of the room.

"We need to get the money out of the broken wagon in the house you rented in Toledo," David whispered. "I don't think it's safe there."

"You're right. When you're in Toledo, take it out and put it in a safe place in the new farm you'll be leasing," Zevulun said. They returned to the room. Suppertime was nearing and everyone was ready.

Somehow they all squeezed around the dining table. Devorah opened a bottle of wine and poured some in each glass.

"I want to make a toast," Zevulun announced. "Our campaign will kick off tomorrow morning. Nechemia doesn't know what I'm talking about, but I would like to say to you, Nechemia, welcome into our fold." They raised their glasses with a unanimous 'LeChaim'. "To Life, to success!"

"Perhaps you'll be kind enough to tell me what campaign you're talking about?" Nechemia asked.

"We decided that in the event you qualify you'd be able to join our organization. Happily, you more than qualify. Every one of us has suffered major personal losses to the Inquisition, and the fourteen of us, and that includes you, Nechemia, have vowed to mount a battle against the Inquisition. The battle actually began when David, single handedly, killed all the priests in the Inquisition house responsible for burning his parents to death. A few others have been killed elsewhere, and I'm sure more will die in the future.

"Tomorrow morning, every one of us will depart to our designated destinations and carry out our work. Saturday night, the third day of

November, 1476 will be the night the three Cardinals will commit suicide. Letters that Anna will deliver to Tomas de Torquemada will follow. These letters should be delivered over a period of seven to ten days so that each one appears to be authentic. During that week a number of other letters will be delivered to different Bishops and priests. Each of you will receive letters you'll have to deliver in due course. The envelopes are clearly marked with names and addresses.

"Before I bring my little speech to a close, I want you to know that Reuven is the original mastermind of this campaign and David, his cousin, actually started the fight. We decided to mount a psychological battle first in order to create chaos within the Church, the Crown, and the Inquisition. Based on the results of our soft offensive, we'll decide on future steps. In the meantime, lease or buy if you can, farmhouses as we planned, and build a decent farming organization in each location. Hire the help you need and let the world know you're first-class farmers. Also, don't neglect going to mass every Sunday. Befriend your neighbors and let them know you are devout Catholics. Our next meeting will take place in the Toledo region, which is central to all of us. This meeting will be held on the thirty-first day of January, 1477," Zevulun spoke. "Reuven, I didn't mean to steal your thunder, but as the oldest one here, I thought I should make this speech."

"That's fine," Reuven said, "but I'd like to add one more item. Be sure to advise David or myself when you run out of money. You have enough to carry you for many months."

"I'm absolutely baffled," Nechemia said. "It's high time that someone took action against this brutal and inhuman Church. I know my wife is dead because I watched them while they tortured her to death. I don't know the fate of my two sons. I believe they were baptized and are attending a Catholic school in Toledo. If you can find them, I shall be ever grateful. Also, rest assured that I'm ready to fight on your side and defeat this monster. Thank you for having confidence in me."

"I'll be in the Toledo area. I know many of the Conversos boys and will make inquiries about your sons," David promised.

"Zevulun, I have a list of most of the Conversos boys my age. When recruitment time comes, you can use it." Reuven handed over his list.

"I'd like to add one more thing. Since we'll be leasing farmhouses and will spend money in developing our farms, make sure that if asked the funds were inheritance monies. Also, wear the oldest and most rugged clothing. Always appear to be poor, hard working workers. Once the farms start producing, the women can become salesladies in the central markets. It is of vital importance that we are thoroughly camouflaged."

"I'm very excited," Rachel said. "Only a short few weeks ago I was on the verge of killing myself, and thanks to these wonderful young people, my life has been restored. I shall devote my entire body and soul to this organization."

"I share the same opinion. I too was almost dead. Thank you all for what you've done for me. I shall work with you to my last day."

"I must repeat," Nechemia said. "I'm overwhelmed by everything I heard. Thank God for our new Moses. May he eliminate Pharaoh. As to my participation, you may count on me for anything you want. If you want me to kill any of these killer-priests, just say the word. There isn't a thing in this world that would give me more pleasure." "You shouldn't get excited," Anna chided. "You just came out of a major trauma. Please try and stay as calm as possible."

"As suggested, I'll stay with Zevulun for the time being. When I'm fully recovered, you can count on me for any job you want," Nechemia stated.

"My dream has come true," Reuven sighed.

CHAPTER SIXTEEN

Fter midnight, on Saturday the 3rd day of November, 1476, Itzhak approached the house in which Cardinal Jose Cardenaz de la Madrid lived. He checked the neighborhood carefully. All the houses in the area were dark except for one where the flickering light of a single candle could be seen at a window. He moved slowly keeping close to the walls. He wore a black priest's habit and blended into the landscape. The front door was locked. He walked around the house and managed to lift one of the windows and jumped in. He waited a moment and tried to adjust his eyes to the darkness, but to no avail. He lit a match and found a candle near a narrow staircase. He realized he was in the basement. He climbed the stairs slowly, testing each step in case it creaked. The door at the top of the staircase opened easily without any noise. He held the candle in his left hand and the knife in the right. The household was sound asleep. He decided that the bedrooms were on the second floor and walked up. *"The Cardinal's bedroom has to be the last one at the end of the hall,"* he thought. He opened the door slightly, and indeed, a large bed came into focus. He walked in, closed the door, put the candle down on top of a chest, and approached the bed. He heard a gentle snore. He walked around the bed as the Cardinal was facing the other side. The knife in his right hand was poised. He poked the Cardinal gently.

"Are you Cardinal Cardenaz?"

"Is that you Julio?" the voice asked.

"I'm not Julio," Itzhak said softly. "Are you Cardinal Cardenaz?"

"Yes, what is it? Why are you waking me in the middle of the night?"

"Because you are committing suicide." Itzhak pushed the knife through his heart. He then took the Cardinal's right hand, wrapped his fingers around the knife's handle, lifted and turned his limp body over the knife so it would appear he had fallen on it. Satisfied that his job was completed, Itzhak left the house the way he entered it. He walked toward the small wood where he'd left his horse and rode back to his farmhouse.

⊗⊗⊗

At about the same time, in Toledo, David found his way to Cardinal Pedro Gonzalez de Mendoza's house. The entire area was dark; however, light could be seen in two windows of the Cardinal's house. David waited until one of the lights went out and then proceeded. To his surprise, the front door was unlocked, however, a sentry was sitting in the foyer, leaning against the wall, sound asleep. David walked around him, took his sword, and climbed the staircase. The third door yielded the Cardinal's bedroom. A candle was nearing the end of its life on the end table next to the bed. The Cardinal must have fallen asleep while reading; he was half sitting, half lying. A handwritten Bible was on his lap. David moved gently toward the bed and stuck the sentry's sword into his heart. The Cardinal gasped once and was silent. David pulled his body off the bed and leaned the Cardinal over the sword, which he stuck between two chairs. *"The person who'll find the Cardinal in the morning will surely testify he committed suicide,"* David thought. He tiptoed out, descended the stairs, and walked out. The sentry never knew anyone had entered and left the building.

⊗⊗⊗

In Segovia, Elisheva, wearing a monk's habit, walked slowly towards Cardinal Ferdinand Avila de Aguiles's house. Her head was completely covered with the hood. Her right hand held a dagger; she was ready. She found the front door locked and walked around the house. The rear door was also locked, as were the windows. She descended some steps leading to a basement door. It was locked, too. Next to the door was a small window. She smashed it with the butt of her dagger. She entered the basement after clearing the glass and found her way to a staircase. The door at the top of the staircase was locked. She pushed the door with her body and after several tries managed to open it. She quickly walked into the hall and crouched against the staircase wall. The noise had aroused somebody on the second floor, and soon enough she heard footsteps. The light of a candle suddenly appeared as its holder was descending the stairs. A young man in his nightgown looked at the broken door, and as he turned around, Elisheva's dagger entered his chest. He fell to the ground without uttering a word. She extinguished his candle, which fell to the floor and quickly ran up the stairs. She opened one door after another. *"How many rooms are up here?"* she thought. Her eyes slowly adjusted to the darkness. The last door yielded the Cardinal's bedroom. She held the dagger close to her right thigh and woke the Cardinal.

"Your Eminence, please come down immediately, your manservant passed out on the floor."

"Who are you?" the Cardinal asked, half asleep.

"I have a letter for you from Prior Carlos, but your man fell on the floor after opening the door for me. I think he fainted," Elisheva said. The Cardinal got out of bed and walked down the staircase. He bent down over his manservant's body and a moment later declared, "He is dead." As he turned around Elisheva stabbed his chest. The dagger plunged easily into the Cardinal's heart. He fell down. Elisheva left the dagger in his heart, walked around the fallen manservant and pushed his body towards the Cardinal's. With great effort she lifted the man, got his right hand to clutch the dagger's handle, and placed him over the Cardinal's body. Satisfied with the scene she created, she left the house through the front door.

⊗⊗⊗

During the week of the fourth of November, 1476, three letters addressed to Tomas de Torquemada, Inquisitor General, were delivered to the sentry guarding the Inquisition's front entrance. Anna, wearing a monk's habit, head covered with a hood, delivered the first letter. Two days later; David, in a priest's habit, handed the second letter, and an innocent woman who received two pennies for doing the favor delivered the third letter. David stood at a distance watching the woman.

The letters addressed to Queen Isabella were delivered in the same fashion, two days apart.

CHAPTER SEVENTEEN

"You called for me, my Queen?" Torquemada walked into Isabella's private chambers.

"Yes, I did. What do you make of these letters? Three Cardinals commit suicide on the same night. I've never heard of such a conspiracy in my life," Queen Isabella stated.

"I don't know what to make of it either," Torquemada said.

"I want you to investigate this matter immediately. You must get to the bottom of this."

"Your Majesty, I received three letters over the course of the week just as you have. When I received the first letter, I thought that Cardinal Cardenaz had simply gone insane. He was one of the most vigorous fighters for pure Catholicism. It was he who inspired so many of us. I was at a total loss to understand his suicide. The first thing I did was to check his papal seal. My expert scribe certified that the seal was genuine. But when I got the second letter, two days later, I was bewildered. That seal, too, was authentic. The third letter arrived by the end of the week, which put me in complete shock," Torquemada admitted.

"Why didn't you draw this matter to my attention when you received the first letter?" the Queen asked.

"The Church is not immune from suicides, Your Majesty. Of course, the letter was shocking news, and it wouldn't be the first time a person who committed suicide writes a nonsense message," Torquemada responded.

"But when you received the second letter, which uses different words to the same effect, why didn't you come to see me?" she asked.

"Your Majesty, I can't always bother you with matters of Church," Torquemada said.

"This is not a matter of Church. When two Cardinals appointed by the Pope commit suicide in unison, it becomes a matter of State, and when you received the third letter, you still stayed away from the Crown," Isabella said. "I'm very disappointed."

"Your Majesty, my reasons for not coming forward immediately are not nearly as important as the reasons for these suicides," Torquemada said. "I sent three of my best Inquisitors to the Cardinal's residences to investigate their deaths. I should have their reports within a few weeks."

"I'm very bothered that you didn't come forward and advise me of these occurrences. Had I not received copies of the letters, I probably wouldn't have known the true facts for months," she said. "I'm deeply disappointed in you."

"It hurts me to think I disappointed you," Torquemada said apologetically. "I shall pray hard and diligently for forgiveness. In the meanwhile, I wish to state that I find the feelings of these Cardinals extremely out of the parameters set by the Pope. At meetings of the highest level held in the Vatican, it was decided unanimously that Jews harbor the Devil. It is a known fact that the Jews steal Christian babies and use their blood in traditional rituals. It is a known fact that the Jews killed Jesus. It is a known fact that there isn't one Jew in heaven. All of them are found in hell."

"The three Cardinals didn't seem to share your views," the Queen said.

"I'm sure they shared my beliefs, otherwise they wouldn't have attained their positions. They question the methods by which we reach our goals," Torquemada said.

"I'm as devout a Catholic as you can find," the Queen stated, "and I am the one who questioned many times the methods of the Inquisition. If you recall, I objected to taking many Jews away because they were hard working business people. They brought into our country much needed merchandise and equipment, and, they were the best taxpayers. Where did you think we got the funds to arm our armies to fight and expel the Moors?"

"You are not going to change my mind about the Jews. They do not deserve your sympathy. Thanks to our efforts, tens of thousands of Jews have converted to Catholicism," Torquemada declared.

"And tens of thousands of converted Jews, the people you call Conversos, are practicing Judaism in secret," Queen Isabella said in anger.

"We are taking steps to prosecute these Conversos," Torquemada said.

"I hear plenty about the torturing that takes place in the Inquisition," she said. "But let's get back to the Cardinals. Have you notified the Pope?"

"Not yet. I find myself at a loss how to explain it. I shall submit my report when the investigators have returned."

"The main theme in the three letters is the same. The Cardinals could not reconcile themselves with torture, brutal treatment of fellow human beings, deceit, and above all, burning people to death," the Queen said.

"Even the Old Testament tells you that stoning to death is a sound punishment for a crime," Torquemada declared.

"There is a great difference between stoning to death and setting a person on fire," the Queen said. "However, you are the authority on Godly matters and if you are convinced that the Inquisition is justified in its methods, so be it."

"Thank you, your Majesty, I knew you'd see my side of it," Torquemada said. "I shall post guards in every one of our buildings as well as the homes of our elite clergy."

"I have one more question for you. It has come to my attention that a few weeks ago, all the priests living in the Inquisition's house in Toledo were killed. I was waiting for you to inform me about it, but you obviously chose not to."

"At first I thought one of the Jews killed my priests, but I have come to learn that a deranged priest did the killings," Torquemada lied. "That priest committed suicide. Anyhow, those employed in God's work do not fear death. They return to Jesus. There isn't a better place for any of us."

"As Queen of Castile, I have to be concerned with many issues -- not only the Church. While it is the Church's belief that Jews are the cause of all evil, I can't ignore the fact that most Jews are hard working people. They've been honest in their dealings with the Crown, and those employed by us have done outstanding work. If not for the Jewish Tax Collectors, the coffers of the Crown would have been empty. Now that a great number of Jews have been converted, your Conversos are also attacked and humiliated as the Jews were. The Church needs to decide what is right and what is wrong."

"The Church decided a long time ago that Jews have to be punished forever for having killed Jesus. There isn't a shred of doubt about the Jews harboring the Devil. My investigators found missing Christian children in Jewish homes, with their throats cut. The children's blood was used for religious rituals and to make soap. The Jew is always the merchant, the trader, and the moneylender. It is the Jew who develops the criminal element in our society," Torquemada made his case.

"Someone has to be the merchant and the trader, as you put it. Does anyone stop the Christians from being merchants?" the Queen asked.

"No one stops anybody from doing what they want except that I will stop anyone from being of another faith than the Catholic. We are obligated to purify all Catholics. All of us must live by Catholic doctrine -- there is no other." Torquemada was steaming.

"We are not discussing or questioning Catholic doctrines. We have a serious issue with the way you plan to achieve your goal. It is obvious that even your faithful Cardinals had a major issue with your methods. You must admit to it and recognize it," the Queen said.

"I will not recognize anything but the conscience of Catholicism. If some fools decided to kill themselves, and I'm not yet sure about it, that's their problem! It is their weakness! I will pursue the investigation of their death vigorously. I would not be surprised if there is a Jewish hand in these deaths," Torquemada said.

"You are a very stubborn man. You don't even have authority from the Pope to do what you are doing."

"I'm in the midst of obtaining His Holiness' permission."

"Let me know the results of your investigation as soon as possible. Don't keep me in the dark. What happens in this country is my concern and not yours." Queen Isabella walked out of her chambers.

Torquemada left the Palace with a bad taste in his mouth. As soon as he arrived at his office, he summoned Miguel Rosario de Ocuna, his most trusted assistant.

"Father Rosario," Torquemada said, "I've just returned from an audience with the Queen. We must prove that the deaths of the Cardinals was fabricated by the Jews."

"That's easy, Your Eminence, I will obtain a confession in no time at all. Let me find the right candidate. Give me a few days."

"I'll teach that Queen who she's dealing with," he thought. *"She is not going to humiliate me again."*

CHAPTER EIGHTEEN

"Bishop Marcos Garcia de Colon is seeking to see you as soon as possible. He is waiting in the foyer," one of the priests said to Torquemada, who was writing at his desk.

"Show him in."

"Your Honorable Inquisitor General," Bishop Garcia opened, "I've received this letter early today and I'm baffled. I immediately went to see Juan Carlos de Medina at his church and he denied having written this letter."

"What about the seal? Was it authentic?" Torquemada asked.

"That was my first question. Juan Carlos examined the seal and said it was his. However, he said that one of his seals was missing," the Bishop said.

"What do you make of it?" Torquemada asked.

"I don't know what to say. Since Cardinal Gonzalez committed suicide, many people are shaky."

"Who said he committed suicide?" Torquemada shouted. "As far as I'm concerned, the Jews killed him!"

"Do you have proof?"

"I don't need proof. Who else would want him dead?" Torquemada asked.

"This community in Toledo never had a Jew accused of murder. We have said many things about the Jews, but never associated them with murder."

"I want to see this priest, this Juan Carlos de Medina," Torquemada spoke loudly. "Have him brought to me immediately."

The Bishop walked out bewildered. He'd never seen Torquemada this upset. *"Something is seriously wrong, but what is it?"* he spoke to himself. He walked as fast as he could and entered the Church.

"Where is Father Carlos?" he asked one of the boys cleaning the hall.

"Father Carlos is in his private chamber," the boy answered. Bishop Garcia was almost running and entered the priest's chamber without knocking.

"Tomas de Torquemada wishes to see you immediately. Please go to his office now," the Bishop commanded.

"What's going on?" the priest asked. "First you accuse me of having written a letter to you, and now you want me to visit with Torquemada. What is it?"

"You better go immediately without asking any questions. Torquemada is very upset," the Bishop said. Father Garcia put on a cloak and walked out. "Are you coming with me?"

"No, Torquemada wants to see you alone."

The priest rushed through the streets. He was breathless by the time he arrived at the Inquisition building.

"Come in," Torquemada screamed when he heard the knocking on the door. "Who are you?"

"I'm Father Juan Carlos de Medina. You wish to see me?"

"Why did you write this letter to Bishop Garcia?"

"I didn't write this or any letter to the Bishop. I don't know what you are talking about," the priest stated firmly.

"You are a liar," Torquemada beamed.

"I'm not a liar. I never wrote this or any other letter to the Bishop."

"Your private seal was firmly placed on the envelope," Torquemada said.

"One of my seals has been missing for some time."

"How dare you lie to me? You know who I am. I can make you talk," Torquemada screamed.

"I've been telling you the truth. I did not write this letter or any other letter to the Bishop," the priest shouted. "Why would I lie to you? I have no reason to lie."

"You are excommunicated. You are no longer a priest. Go downstairs and report to Father Miguel Rosario," Torquemada commanded.

"I will not go downstairs to see anybody. You cannot excommunicate me. You have no proof whatsoever, and you are not going to treat me like you treat the Jews," the priest screamed.

"If you do not report to Father Miguel Rosario this instant I shall have you arrested," Torquemada yelled.

"We'll see about that," the priest flung, and left the room. He walked downstairs, but Father Rosario was not on the premises.

"Where is Father Rosario's office?" he asked one of the priests.

"He has no private office. Haven't I seen you before?"

"You may have. I'm Father Juan Carlos de Medina of the Church of Resurrection in Toledo," he answered angrily.

"What do you want with Father Rosario? Maybe I can help," he offered.

"You won't believe this, but Torquemada wants me arrested. He's accusing me of having written a letter to the Bishop. I don't even know what's in that letter, and he wouldn't believe me when I said I did not write such a letter at all," Father Carlos said.

"I suggest you wait for Father Rosario," the priest said. "If you don't, Torquemada will hunt you like a dog."

"All of this is insane. I'm at a total loss. I don't even know the Bishop I supposedly wrote to. I did not write the letter, and I have no idea how to prove my innocence," Father Carlos said.

"Why don't you go into the chapel and pray. The solution might appear by itself," the priest suggested.

Juan Carlos de Medina entered the little chapel, crossed himself, and kneeled in front of the tiny Alter.

"Dear Lord, why have you smitten me with such accusations? Not only have I not written any letter, I don't even know what's in it. I have been a devout priest since I was ordained. I've never stirred from your commandments. The only time I doubted the Church was when I was told that Jews steal Christian babies and slaughter them for their blood. The truth is, I've never heard of missing Christian babies. I've never spoken to anyone about this. I love Jesus more than life itself. Please help me with Torquemada."

"I was told that you were in the chapel," Torquemada said. "One of the priests told me that you couldn't find Rosario. What is this about your having doubts? You call yourself a devout Catholic and you dare have doubts? Are you questioning the authority of the Church or its integrity?"

"I'll admit here and now, that with all due respect, I cannot accept the that Jews slaughter Christian babies for their blood. I cannot accept such a story of any people because I cannot see any human being killing babies. Furthermore, I've never heard of missing babies. A few years ago I was sent to preach to prisoners in the central jail outside of Toledo and to tell you the truth, I didn't find one Jew among hundreds of prisoners," the priest said.

"I told you in my office that you are excommunicated and I shall repeat myself again. You, Father Juan Carlos de Medina, are excommunicated! You are not fit to be a priest. Wait here until Father Rosario returns. You are under arrest." Torquemada spoke firmly and left the chapel.

Father Juan Carlos turned to the statue of Jesus, "Oh Devine One, I came to you for help, and you are placing me under arrest for something I have not done." He fell to the floor, passed out.

CHAPTER NINETEEN

27th of October 1476
His Eminence Bishop
Nicolas Obispo de Iglesias
Zaragoza

My Bishop, the Eminent Alfredo Molina de Russo is dead and I have no one to communicate my thoughts to. Please forgive this intrusion on your time.

Before Bishop Molina passed on, he stopped at my Church one day and asked me some very strange questions. I wouldn't have thought much about his visit except that this morning the news of the killing of so many priests in Toledo came to my attention. It later occurred to me that there might be some connection between the killings and the methods by which we attempt to convert Jews to Catholicism.

Before he died mysteriously, Bishop Molina asked me what my opinion was about the ultimate punishment of Jews who refuse to be baptized should be. At first I didn't grasp the meaning of his question, and he proceeded to explain the 'auto-de-Fe' method of punishment. Frankly, I told him that burning people to death was not exactly my way to punish people, not even Jews. He then asked me how would I punish sinners like Jews, and I told him I would put them in jail and let them rot.

His next question was even more out of line with the instructions we received from the Inquisitor General. He asked me whether Jews or Conversos should be tortured until they convert or tell the truth? My answer was that forcing people to change religions would never work. People are brought up to believe in one God or another. In most cases the tradition of a religion, such as the Jews, dates back thousands of years. I felt that my Bishop was at some sort of crossroads in his thinking, and it did leave me with a great deal of confusion.

Since your office is the closest to Segovia I will appreciate your advice.

Yours Obediently,
Jose Alonso de Aguiles
Church of Santa Maria, Segovia

9th of November 1476

Father Jose Alonso de Aguiles,
Church of Santa Maria
Segovia

When I received your letter of 27th of October, I was wondering why you didn't consult with Cardinal Avila in Segovia. In the meantime, it has come to my attention that he committed suicide. Needless to say, I was shocked. Your city is now left without its Cardinal and Bishop.

As to the conversation you had with Bishop Molina I find it very difficult to believe he had any doubts about the Jews or the methods of the Inquisition. Tomas de Torquemada is one of the most knowledgeable men in the Catholic Church. Sometimes I feel that his knowledge is far superior to that of his counterparts in Rome. I respect Torquemada with all my heart and truly believe that he leads our Holy Church in the right direction. If Bishop Molina caused any doubts in your mind, I suggest you erase them. In fact, if I were you I would go to my confessor and ask for punishment.

As result of your letter and other reasons, I plan to travel to Toledo and meet with Torquemada to discuss this issue. I will advise you in due course. It could also be that by the time I return, a Bishop and Cardinal will be installed in Segovia.

Yours,
Nicolas Obispo de Iglesias
Bishop of Zaragoza

19th of November 1476
The Honorable Inquisitor General
Tomas de Torquemada
Toledo

I've been meaning to communicate with you sooner; however, the suicide followed by the funeral of Cardinal Pedro Gonzalez de Mendoza weighed heavily on my mind. I wanted very much to visit with you, but was informed of the other suicides and death of a number of priests in the Inquisition, and decided to wait.

I hope you can find the time to see me as I have matters of great importance to discuss with you. Awaiting your early reply,

Yours,
Cardinal Alejandro de
Parejas
Toledo

17th of November 1476
Her Highness, Her Majesty
Queen Isabella
Toledo

    A few days after Cardinal Pedro Gonzalez de Mendoza took his own life, I received a letter from him dated on the day of his death, 3rd of November, 1476. Needless to say I was shocked at the news and more so when I received his letter.

    In his letter he shared with me a number of conversations he had with Tomas de Torquemada, the Inquisitor General. The basics of his arguments were about the methods used by the Inquisition to convert Jews, the treatment of Conversos, and the general ill feelings among many priests.

    I feel the Catholic Church is going in a destructive direction and I hereby request an audience with Her Majesty at your convenience. Waiting anxiously for your reply.

Alejandro de Parejas
Cardinal - Toledo

    Queen Isabella, upon receiving the Cardinal's letter sent a messenger advising the granting of an audience. The Cardinal was shocked. He had not requested an audience, and could not understand the granting of the audience at his request. The messenger had been very clear. By midafternoon Cardinal Parejas was waiting in the Queen's waiting room.

    A large door on the left side of the room opened and a sentry announced: "Cardinal Parejas, you may step in." The Cardinal walked slowly and entered the Queen's private reception room nervously. He approached her large armchair and kissed her hand.

    "I'm delighted to be here, Your Majesty. You look well."

    "I'm glad to see you, my Cardinal. Perhaps you will be kind enough to explain your letter. I was baffled when I received it," the Queen said.

    "Your Majesty, I did not write you any letters," the Cardinal stated in great bewilderment.

    "What do you mean? I have your letter, clearly sealed with your seal, in my chambers," Queen Isabella stated.

    "I beg forgiveness, Your Majesty, but what did I write in this letter?" Cardinal Parejas asked.

    "How dare you speak to me like this and question me!" she demanded. "You send me a letter with all kinds of accusations, and now you tell me you didn't write it."

    Queen Isabella rose from her armchair, "Stay here. I'll be right back."

She walked out of her private reception room and returned a few minutes later with an envelope.

"Look at the seal carefully and tell me if it's yours."

"Yes, Your Majesty, this is my seal, but I did not write any letter to you. The Pope appointed me as Cardinal. He never had a doubt about me, and you shouldn't either."

"I will not tolerate such language from you or anybody else, for that matter!" she roared. "I am surrounded these days by liars. Get out of my sight."

Cardinal Parejas left the Queen's reception room in absolute shock. He entered the small foyer leading to the outer hall and collapsed into a chair. He didn't know how long he sat there. Someone poked his shoulder gently.

"Your Eminence, it's getting late, and we're about to close down the palace. Shall I call your coach?" a voice asked.

"Yes, please." The Cardinal woke up from his dream. He walked out and mounted his coach. "Take me to the Inquisition building."

The Inquisition building was full of activity. Priests were running in from every direction. The Cardinal stopped one. "What's going on? What's all the noise about?"

"A large number of Conversos were brought in a few minutes ago and more priests are needed to attend to them."

"Are all of them in the basement?" the Cardinal asked.

"Yes, Your Eminence. May I be excused?"

"Of course." The Cardinal looked for Torquemada, but couldn't find him on the ground floor. As he began climbing the stairs, Torquemada came running down. "What are you doing here?" he asked the Cardinal.

"I have to speak to you immediately about a matter of great importance."

"I can't see you now. My investigators brought in a large number of Conversos who have sinned. Come back tomorrow." Torquemada ran off.

The Cardinal decided to follow Torquemada and took the stairs to the basement. All the doors were shut. He opened the first door and walked in. About twenty men were standing in line and six priests were guarding them. At the far end of the room two priests sat at a desk, and one man was standing a few feet away facing them.

"What is your name?" one of the priests asked.

"Why have you brought me here? Where is my wife?" he asked in an irate voice.

"You are not here to ask questions. It is I who will ask the questions, and you had better answer," the priest shot at him.

"We haven't done a thing, and I demand to know why we were brought here for questioning," the man insisted.

"Juan," the priest called another priest sitting by the second door to the room, "twenty-four floggings on bare skin," he ordered. The priest walked over and took the Converso by his arm. The man resisted and pushed the priest away. "You cannot treat me like this. I'm not an animal. You wanted me to convert and I did. What more do you want?" he shouted.

"Take him away and flog him," the order was repeated. A number of priests suddenly showed up, got hold of the man and pulled him into the next room. The Cardinal followed them. One of the priests recognized him and said, "Your Eminence, this isn't a place for you to be."

"Don't tell me where I can or cannot be, go on with your work," Cardinal Parejas said.

The man's jacket and shirt were torn off as he kept resisting. Both hands were tied to iron hooks on the wall and two priests took turns flogging him with leather whips. After twenty-four strokes, one of the priests asked, "Will you now answer the investigator's questions?"

The man did not respond. Another set of flogging was ordered. Blood was flowing from the man's back. "Will you answer our questions?"

"You can kill me right here," the man shouted, "I will not answer questions or speak to you." A new order was given, "Take him to the table." The man was taken off the hooks and carried to a table on the other side of the room. He was placed on his back and his hands and feet were tied with thin metal wire. One of the priests took some nails and a hammer and hammered one nail into each of his toes. The man screamed.

The Cardinal left the room and returned to the first one. The screams could be clearly heard as the door between the two rooms was deliberately left open. "Do you want to be screaming like that man?" the priest behind the desk asked the line in front of him. "Answer our questions, that is all we ask of you." He continued, "What is your name?"

"Chaim Matalon," was the answer.

"I'm told that last Saturday morning you covered yourself with a Talit and prayed to your God in the darkness of your bedroom. Is that true?"

"No, that is not true. I do not have a talit. I threw it out when I was baptized."

"But you did pray in your bedroom!"

"No, I did not. The only place I pray in is the Church at Sunday mass."

"You are a liar. I have witnesses who saw you pray."

"I did not pray in my bedroom and your witnesses are liars," the man insisted at the top of his lungs.

"Take him to the table," the priest ordered.

Cardinal Parejas could watch no more. As he approached the exit door he asked one of the priests, "Where are the women?"

"On the other side of the hallway, Your Eminence." The Cardinal walked over, opened one of the doors, and walked in. He was shocked at what he saw. All the women were tied to one object or another. Their clothing was torn off and parts of their bodies were exposed. There was blood everywhere. Since there wasn't one priest in that room, he walked over to the first door on the right and opened it. The sight in the room horrified him. Two naked women were tied together, face to face, with thin metal wire. From both sides priests were sticking wooden rods into their abdomens. The women were screaming as the rods tore their skin and penetrated their stomachs.

At this sight Cardinal Parejas lost his senses and shouted, "Stop this beastly torture!" and ran to the large table. The priests stopped their work and moved back. "Get the hell out of this room," the Cardinal shouted. They left the room running.

The Cardinal took the rods out of the abdomens and threw them away in anger. He undid the metal wires. One of the women was dead. The other was moaning from pain. He looked around and found the torn pieces of the women's clothing and covered the dead woman's body. He picked up the wounded woman and carried her out of the room. He slowly walked up the staircase and entered Torquemada's office. Torquemada, seeing what the Cardinal was carrying, shouted, "What do you think you're doing?" The Cardinal dropped the naked woman on Torquemada's desk and said in a calm voice, "Why don't you rape her, she is ready for you." He turned around and left the room.

It was completely dark by the time the Cardinal emerged from the building. His coach was waiting at the curb. He climbed in and yelled, "Take me to the Queen's palace."

"Your Eminence," the driver said, "The palace is closed for the night. The sentries will not let you in."

"We'll see about that," he shouted. "Be on your way." The coachman hurried his horse as much as he could. They were stopped at the palace entrance.

"I am Cardinal Alejandro de Parejas and I have an urgent matter to discuss with the Queen. Please send someone into the palace. I need to see her immediately," he told one of the sentries.

"Your Eminence, I doubt the Queen will see you at this hour. She is probably having her supper. Also, King Ferdinand is in the palace tonight. They may be dining together," the sentry said.

"I don't care what the King and Queen are doing. I have a grave matter to discuss with her of the utmost urgency. Please send someone in with this message," the Cardinal spoke.

"Very well, Your Eminence. Please wait here on the side so as not to block the passageway." The coachman moved his coach. The Cardinal waited impatiently. It took quite a while for the sentry to return.

"The King and Queen will see you in their drawing room, Your Eminence," he announced. The gate was opened and the coach drove in. Another sentry at the main entrance to the palace escorted the Cardinal to the royal drawing room.

"What brings upon us this unusual visit?" King Ferdinand asked as Cardinal Parejas entered the room.

"Your Majesties, please forgive this intrusion. I have a matter of great importance to bring to your attention."

"You seem extremely upset," the King said.

"Your Majesty, earlier today I had a very unpleasant audience with the Queen. She accused me of having written a letter. I will swear to you on the Cross that I have not written her a letter. Because of earlier events of the day in the palace, I went directly to the Inquisition's building and sought a meeting with the Queen's confessor and counselor, Tomas de Torquemada. Since he could not see me, I followed one of the priests to the basement as everybody seemed to be rushing downstairs. In the basement I found that Conversos women were being tortured in the most inhuman way. Forgive the crude description, but I think you should be aware of the extent and methods our priests employ in carrying out their duties." The Cardinal described in detail what he had seen. "Torturing women in this despicable fashion must stop. I can assure you that our Lord Jesus is crying in heaven at the sight of such torture." He collapsed in his chair.

"I cannot imagine anyone doing this sort of thing," Queen Isabella said.

"Your Majesty," Cardinal Parejas said softly, "are you doubting my words again? I have no reason to lie to you or anyone. Furthermore, as a Cardinal and an appointee of Rome, I am not used to lying. The truth is my guide in life."

"The truth is that I received a letter with your signature, your envelope sealed with your wax seal, a messenger who told the palace sentry that you sent him with the urgent letter, and you expect me to believe that all this was a hoax?"

"My word should have more value than anything or anyone else, Your Majesty," the Cardinal said. "I am declaring again, I did not write any letters to you, nor have I sent any by messenger or otherwise."

"We have a most unusual case here," King Ferdinand interceded. "I tend to believe the Cardinal. I think we should have this matter investigated properly. I will talk with the chief of guards about it in the morning. However, the matter of torturing women the way you described it is another issue, which I'm going to discuss with Torquemada."

"Torquemada knows what he's doing," Queen Isabella said. "If not for Torquemada, I would not be alive today. He is my guide and mentor. He is the one who helps me embrace Christ with all my heart. He is the one who supports my deep conviction in Catholicism. There isn't a thing I can do or say. I believe that Torquemada was godsent to our Kingdoms. I will not challenge his authority and methods."

"Your Majesty, how can you, a woman, permit this inhuman treatment of women? After all, it is men who rule the house," the Cardinal said.

"No man runs this house," the Queen said. "I am the man of this house. My husband has his house in Aragon."

"I plead with you, My Queen, please stop this butchery."

"Torquemada is closer to Jesus than me. I leave his work to him. I shall not interfere."

"Very well, Your Majesty, may I take my leave?"

"You may."

"Thank you, your Majesties." Cardinal Parejas left the room slowly to his waiting coach. He was disappointed and sad about the turn of events. *"If the Crown will fail to stop the beastly torturing of women, I will take the matter up with the Pope,"* he said to himself. He mounted the coach and instructed his driver to take him home.

CHAPTER TWENTY

It was after midday prayer that Cardinal Parejas' helper announced Tomas de Torquemada was paying a visit.

"Please show him in immediately," he instructed.

"I'm not surprised to see you," Cardinal Parejas said, welcoming his guest, "I was expecting you."

"Queen Isabella advised me of your two visits yesterday and I came here to tell you that I am extremely disappointed in your comments about the Inquisition."

"What is there to be disappointed about?" the Cardinal asked. "Must we torture women in the most beastly way?"

"It's all very simple," Torquemada said. "They are sinners, therefore they are headed for hell. What difference does it make if their hell starts on earth?"

"I regret to tell you, but I'm planning to report this brutal torture to the Pope. I do not believe the Pope will condone such inhuman methods," the Cardinal said.

"You are completely out of place. It's not your responsibility, nor is it your business to be concerned how I run the Inquisition," Torquemada spoke firmly.

"You can do what you please, and I will do as I please. I'm an appointee of the Pope, and if I find Catholic behavior that is entirely contrary to my religion, it is my duty to report it to the Pope. I don't see one reason under the sun that calls for torturing women. I think you had better study the scriptures again and refresh your memory about Jesus' preaching," Cardinal Parejas suggested.

"I will not sit here and listen to this nonsense," Torquemada shouted. "What kind of a Catholic are you? I will report you to the Pope."

"I think you had better leave. We have nothing more to talk about," the Cardinal shouted back. Torquemada spat on the Cardinal's floor and left. He got into his coach and screamed at the coachman, "To the Inquisition, quick."

The coachman had never seen Torquemada this mad before.

"Your Eminence, is there anything I can do for you? I've never seen you so upset."

"You can return to the Cardinal and kill him," Torquemada shouted, "He has given up all Catholic learning." The coachman hurried his horse and dropped Torquemada by the Inquisition's main entrance.

"Kill all the sinners in the basement. Send them to hell. Let them burn in hell as well as on earth," he shouted as he walked in. The priests complied.

CHAPTER TWENTY-ONE

Yossef and Elisheva stopped at Magdalena Castle, located about half way between Tarragona and Zaragoza. The Land Management Office was open.

"We'd like to buy or lease a farmhouse with a barn," Yossef said to the man behind the desk. The man looked up and smiled. "You two, you are children."

"We are not children," Yossef said, "We're sixteen and seventeen years old. Our parents were killed in a fire and we want to be farmers."

"What do you know about farming?" the man asked.

"We know very little, but we're planning to hire experienced help."

"This is fascinating. Two children want to start farming. You need a lot of money. I can lease you a farmhouse and a barn for one and a half gold dukat per year," he said.

"I'll give you one gold dukat," Yossef said, assuming the man was overcharging him.

"You are some bargainer," he said.

"I'll give you one gold dukat," Yossef repeated. "If you won't accept it, we'll go elsewhere."

"One and a quarter," the man said, "That's my final offer."

"Good day, Sir," Yossef said and propelled Elisheva away.

"Come back here," the man called, "You're a tough young man. I'll give it to you for one gold dukat on one condition."

"What is the condition?" Yossef asked.

"That you employ and house no less than five men."

"How big is the barn?" Yossef asked.

"It's big enough."

"Will I be able to arrange sleeping quarters in it?"

"Certainly."

"I'd like to inspect the farmhouse and the barn."

"Very well. Let's go. It's only half an hour away."

"We can use my wagon," Yossef said. "We'll bring you back and complete our arrangement if we like the house."

"I'm sure you'll like it. It's very large and has many rooms. The previous tenant had lived there over fifty years. He died recently and his wife was unable to farm the land. She left and joined her younger sister in Tarragona."

"Where will I find the help?" Yossef asked.

"I'll send them to you. We have experienced men in the village, but not enough work. I don't like it when too many people do not earn a living. They become a problem for Don Daniel, the Landowner."

They reached the farmhouse and fell in love with it as soon as they walked in. It was obvious the previous lady of the house had taken care of it. She'd decorated the house well and made sure it was in good repair. There was a water well outside the kitchen door. They found a sizeable kitchen with all the stoves and utensils, a large dining table and chairs. In the center of the house there was a large living room fully furnished with a sofa and armchairs. The house had four bedrooms. "Apparently a large family lived here," Elisheva said.

"It was when the sons lived here. For some unknown reason the three of them joined the army fighting the Moors and never returned," the man said. "The old widow left without taking any of her property. One day she took her clothing and left."

"Let's look at the barn," Yossef suggested. It was very large, built on a stone foundation. It was made of strips of oiled wood. It, too, was in excellent repair. "The couple who lived here surely were proud people," Yossef said. "They took good care of the property. I can assure you we will do the same."

"I like to hear that," the man said.

"Do you like this place?"

"Oh Yes. I do indeed. I'm anxious to get started. I believe we can still plant autumn seeds," Elisheva replied.

"You have a small vineyard in the back of the grounds," the man said. "The climate in this location is excellent for growing grapes for wine. You may decide to expand the vineyard. There is good money to be made in wine."

"We will certainly give it some thought," Yossef assured him. "We'll take this farm. We like it and it's conveniently situated between Tarragona and Zaragoza. We'll have two markets for our produce."

They rode back to the man's office. Yossef paid one gold dukat and got a receipt. He signed a paper stipulating he had leased a farmhouse, barn and twenty dunam of land for ten years with the right to renew for an additional ten years if kept to the satisfaction of the Landowner. They drove back to the house and unloaded their few belongings. A tour of the property showed the land was fertile. Vegetable plots were easily distinguished and a good irrigation system was in place.

"The old man did a great job here," Yossef admitted.

"We're lucky, this is a wonderful property. When our fight is over, I wouldn't mind settling here permanently," Elisheva said.

"Are you suggesting something?"

"I am. How do you feel about me?" she asked.

Instead of responding, Yossef took her in his arms and kissed her. She did not refuse. "I love you, Yossef," she declared.

"I love you, too. I have this strange feeling every time you touch me or I touch you."

They were awakened early the following day by the arrival of the manager from the Landowner's office. He brought with him six men, but introduced only one.

"This is Emanuel Garcia. He is an expert farmer. His parents lost their farm because of a conflict with the landowner several years ago. Listen to his advice and you'll do well."

"We're very pleased to meet you," Yossef said, somewhat surprised at his first name, "This is my sister. You may call me Juan Carlos and my sister, Rosa."

The manager left. Yossef directed the men to the barn. "Please arrange your sleeping quarters in this end of the barn, that is, if you choose to sleep here. If you wish to return to your families at the end of the day, feel free to do so. I shall buy a number of horses for that purpose." Four of the men preferred to return home, and two, including Emanuel, decided to stay on the farm.

"There is lumber and tools in the barn. Go ahead and build whatever quarters you want," Yossef said. He turned to Emanuel; "I'd like to tour the grounds with you and decide what to do with this farm."

"I'll go to the house and fix a few things to my liking," Elisheva said.

Each party went its own way. Yossef and Emanuel walked through the entire property.

"What do think?" Yossef asked.

"The soil and elevation is perfect for growing grapes. I would expand the vineyard to cover at least half the land. Within two years you'll have enough grapes to produce some of the finest wine in Aragon. The other half I would cultivate for growing wheat, vegetables, and fruit. I would also plant a small orchard of apricots, peaches, apples, and almonds."

"What will we need in terms of equipment and seeds?" Yossef asked.

"We'll need four oxen to plow. We won't have to buy the plows -- I saw a few in the barn. We'll need six or eight horses, seeds for wheat, and cuttings for grapevines."

"Very well, let's go and purchase the oxen and horses. I imagine that the cuttings will have to be bought immediately before planting."

"That's right. I am ready."

During the coming days, the men plowed the entire tract of land. Emanuel received the funds and went shopping for grape cuttings, as well as other plants and seeds. When he returned, the men concentrated on planting while Yossef and Elisheva carried water in their wagon and watered the new plants.

"The Land manager was right about Emanuel," Elisheva said over the dining table, "he seems to know everything about farming."

"I believe he's also loyal and a hard worker."

"Tomorrow is the twenty-ninth. I'll have to leave for Segovia. You've been so involved in getting plantings done before winter sets in that you never mentioned our obligations to the fight against the Inquisition," she said.

"It's not that I've forgotten our objective, or neglected it," Yossef declared, "We had time to cultivate the farm. If you leave tomorrow, you'll have plenty of time to reach Segovia." She kissed him. "I'll miss you."

CHAPTER TWENTY-TWO

November 1476

Your Holiness
Pope Eugene IV
Rome

> *As you're surely aware, our Church in Aragon and Castile has been carrying out its missionary duties in converting the Jews.   It is my intention to complete this mission before I die. I fully intend to purify the entire population of this country, erase heresy, and assure a clean and pure Catholic society for the future of our children.*
>
> *To date, I, the Inquisitor General, have not received your authorization. It is of the utmost importance that the people of this country, the Jews, Marranos and Conversos in particular, are made aware that I have your authority to conduct the affairs of the Inquisition.*
>
> *Furthermore, it is my opinion that final authority over the functions of the Inquisition should be given to the monarchy of the land. Differences of opinion between the Church and the monarchy need to be smoothed out. Our King Ferdinand and Queen Isabella of Aragon and Castile are devout Catholics. If given your authority to head all Catholic affairs in these countries, I shall be in a position to force them to carry out the wishes of the Church.*
>
> *As the Queen's confessor and counselor, I exert great influence on her thinking. Your providing the Crown with the requisite authority will enhance my work significantly.*
>
> *I am sending this request with one of my trusted assistants, and hope to have your response when he returns to Toledo.*

> *Yours Obediently,*
> *Tomas de Torquemada*
> *Inquisitor General for Castile and*
> *Aragon*

CHAPTER TWENTY-THREE

David and Anna set out to seek their farmhouse somewhere between Toledo and Segovia. They stopped in a number of villages and Castles and finally settled on a house in the small village of El Mola. The scribe to the Marquis of Toresa, who had passed away, had owned the house they bought. In the back of the house the scribe had built a large carriage house for his wagon and horses.

"This is not the best of situations," David said, "but it will have to do."

"We should try and lease some land from the Marquis and cultivate it otherwise the locals will be talking about us," Anna said.

"That is exactly what I intend to do. Let's clean the house and make it livable." The next few days saw them strip the house of all its accumulated dirt and antiquated furniture. Anna washed the linen she found using water from the well in the center of the village. The kitchen had an old iron stove, which Anna estimated had not been cleaned in many a year. Eventually she learned that the scribe had lived by himself for many years after the passing of his wife. He had no children.

The Marquis' office leased an isolated tract of land to David for half a dukat, and he asked the proprietor of the trading post to help find experienced workers. David obtained permission to build a barn on the grounds, as there was no place to keep the animals and equipment. Once the laborers had been assembled, he drove to a nearby village and purchased lumber and other necessary materials.

"I'll be leaving for Toledo tomorrow," David announced. "On Saturday night Cardinal Gonzalez will commit suicide."

"I shall miss you terribly," Anna said. "What am I going to do without you?"

"I noticed a number of homeless children in the village, and since this house is rather large, perhaps we could give them a home," David suggested.

"That's a wonderful idea!" Anna said. "It will give me something to do, and I'll be helping those poor lost souls. Don't you wonder why the village priest doesn't do a thing about homeless children?"

"You see homeless children everywhere in Castile and Aragon. Apparently no one cares," David said.

"How's the Cardinal going to commit suicide?" Anna was curious.

"I don't know yet. I'll have to come up with something at the right moment."

"Obviously, you'll arrive in Toledo a day or two early. Where will you stay?" Anna asked.

"I know where my family's housekeeper used to live. I'm planning to look her up. She has been with our family for many years, long before I was born."

"Was she a Jew?"

"No, she is Christian, but she always regarded me as her son. I can trust her with my life."

"You have another mission to take care of in Toledo," Anna said.

"What's that?"

"You have to take the money out of the broken wagon in Zevulun's house."

"You're absolutely right. There is more money elsewhere, but it's dangerous to carry so much in one trip. I'll have to attend to it some other time."

"We need to arrange a safe hiding place in this house."

"I found the perfect place in the attic. I discovered it when we looked the house over."

"Very good."

"By the way, how did you know about Zevulun's money? I don't recall ever discussing it with you."

"I overheard you and Zevulun speak about it one night," she said.

"Very careless of us," David smiled, "not that I don't trust you, but in the event you are caught, they cannot extract from you what you don't know."

"You talk as though you have tens of thousands of gold dukats."

"That's right. It's a huge fortune."

"Why are we doing this? Wouldn't it be better if we took the money and left this country?"

"We'll have plenty of time to leave after we've defeated the Inquisition. That is, if we want to leave. I can assure you of one thing -- I will not leave until the Inquisition has been stopped and the Jews can live in peace and as equal citizens." David said emphatically. "I will never forgive the burning to death of my parents."

"I'm sorry I said those words to you, David. I'm with you with all my heart. Just for a moment my foolish heart was thinking selfishly of our love for each other."

"Our love will continue to flourish and even grow stronger as we accomplish one of the most difficult undertakings in history. Our campaign has just begun. I'm sure that the suicides of the Cardinals and the mix-ups created by the letters will bear fruit. From what I know of Torquemada, he's not going to give up easily. In our January meeting we'll find out about the results and make decisions about future operations."

"I'm terribly curious. How much money is hidden?" Anna asked.

"A great deal, my dear. Let it be. We'll have plenty left over when our battle is won," David kissed her. His kiss aroused her, and all of a sudden she was all over him. Her arousal had an effect on him he could not explain. Blood rushed to his temples and a sensation he had never experienced before captured his body and soul. They kissed passionately, and moments later the two of them were naked on the carpeted floor, body to body. Anna guided David into her.

"Push hard, my love," she said, and David's never ending love for sex began that day.

"I suppose this is how children are made?" David gasped.

"We need to get married," Anna said, "just in case I get pregnant."

"Aren't we too young for that?"

"Not for me," she responded. "If I do get pregnant, I want it to be legitimate."

"Our problem is that to get married, we'll need the priest, and our children will have to be baptized. I can't even think of having a priest touch my soul when it was men of the cloth who killed my parents in cold blood."

"What do we do?" Anna asked.

"We do nothing until the day comes when we surface. Then we can get married officially and name our children. Until such time we pray to God silently. I'm sure He will forgive us," David said.

"I suppose I'm thinking in womanly terms. You are of course right, my dear. We can certainly get married when our fight is over. If we have sons, they can be circumcised later."

"I hope we have many children. I was an only child. I always wanted brothers and sisters, but it never happened. I wouldn't want my son to be as lonely as I was."

"I love children," Anna declared. "I don't care if we have ten."

"You can have as many as you want immediately. Bring in the homeless. I could never understand how no one cares about them. Each time I see homeless children, my heart goes out to them. Perhaps one day we'll build a school for the homeless," David said.

"I'll begin as soon as you leave."

⊗⊗⊗

By the time David returned from his trip, the barn was standing and ready for its occupants. Anna took in eight children, five boys and three girls of different ages. David purchased oxen and plows and had the entire tract of land plowed and made ready for planting. As winter was at the door, he made a joint decision with his men to sow wheat, which they would harvest in late spring. They also decided to plan better use of the land during the winter.

Anna brought in the children one by one. Most of them had to be convinced to move in. They had been too long on their own, begging or stealing food, and were afraid of adults. But manage she did. She had them washed and cleaned, and dressed with new and simple clothing. Many of them had never worn shoes or boots before. The transformation of those children was a major accomplishment. She was very happy.

CHAPTER TWENTY-FOUR

Torquemada opened the meeting on a very angry note.

"Archbishop Carrillo, Bishops, and priests. I called this meeting because we find ourselves with a grave situation on our hands. It is grave on the one side, yet extremely simple on the other. I'm sure you notice how angry I am. I am not angry because a number of our members have died in mysterious ways. Death has hastened their joining our Lord Jesus Christ.

"During the past few months three Cardinals have committed suicide and one was murdered. At least two-dozen priests have been found with their throats cut. Two Bishops also died and their homes were set on fire. As I said earlier - they joined our Lord. I am sure they are happy.

"Our missionary obligation and the absolute need to cleanse our society from evil and human pestilence is the reason this meeting was called. It is our solemn duty to erase heresy from our society, yet how can we erase heresy if Jews live among us? They are the cause of all evil. We need to eliminate them from our society. The conversion of Jews began some time ago, yet too many have refused our offer. The stronger their refusal, the stronger our approach in dealing with them became. As a Christian, and a devout Catholic, I stand before you today, and tell you in no uncertain terms that Catholicism is the only way of life, and, I must stress, pure Catholicism at that.

"We have discovered that many Conversos and Marranos are still practicing Judaism in the secret of their homes. We have also discovered many Conversos and Marranos are secretly engaged in converting Old Christians to Judaist practices. I herby vow to you the Inquisition will continue to fight heresy, and in particular, will fight, arrest and sentence anyone who strays in any way shape or form from our Catholic doctrine!

"Also, during the past few months there has been a mysterious exchange of letters between many clergy. Yet when asked about those letters, every single clergyman has denied writing them. I find this extremely odd. If any of you have questions or are bothered by thoughts, this is the forum in which you may air your feelings. We have gathered here today because our work must continue under any circumstances. It is our duty to Christ, our Lord."

Torquemada took a deep breath and paused. Archbishop Carrillo rose from his seat.

"Inquisitor General, during the period you're talking about, I received three letters from different clergymen in Castile questioning the methods used by the Inquisition, particularly the torturing of people and the Auto-de-fe. What strikes me most is that two of the three writers are now dead. I would like to find out from this audience if others have received letters of a similar nature." More than a dozen hands raised. The Archbishop continued.

"Were the letters you received similar?" He faced the audience.

"Yes," was the general answer.

"I was afraid of that. It means there are many clerics among us who don't agree with your policies and methods, but are afraid to say so openly." He stared directly at Torquemada.

"Are you, Archbishop Carrillo, in agreement with my methods and policies, as you put it?" Torquemada ventured.

"I am not on trial here and I don't have to answer your questions. I am merely telling you what I believe the mystery is about. You are not the only priest who walks the ways of our Savior. Every one of us in this hall believes, preaches, and walks the ways of our Beloved. You are not the sole authority on Catholicism."

Torquemada's face turned red. "How dare you talk to me in that language. The Pope appointed me as Inquisitor General, and I have his supreme authority to carry out his mission the best way I know and believe. You are out of place with your statements," Torquemada raged.

"Rome is not a Dictatorship," the Archbishop said calmly. "The Pope uses various committees of learned Cardinals to help him make decisions."

"I don't care what the Pope does or how he runs his empire! Here in Castile I am the authority, and what I say goes," Torquemada shouted.

"Are you going to kill me too because I have a different opinion than yours?" Archbishop Carrillo asked.

"Are you saying I killed dozens of clergy?" Torquemada screamed. "You should be locked up."

"I have another question for you," Carrillo raised his voice, "Why are the Conversos still being hounded by your men? Do you really think a person, an individual can change his habits of generations by the stroke of a hand, or just because you put a sword at his throat? It took the Catholic Church over four hundred years after the death of Christ to develop."

"This Archbishop is doomed to burn in hell," Torquemada shouted. "If any of you wish to join him, I suggest you leave this meeting now."

"You are a blasphemy to the Catholic religion," Archbishop Carrillo shouted. "History will talk of you as a murderer and not as a pious clergy. You are the one who will find home in hell." He walked out of the meeting in disgust.

"Honorable clergy," Torquemada shouted over a chorus of voices, "I will continue to work for our Church and our beliefs. If any of you have a different view, I suggest you resign your priesthood. Any priest found disobeying my orders will be excommunicated and charged with crime against humanity, punishment for which is to be sentenced to Auto-de-Fe. Does anyone have any questions?" Not a single hand was raised, and the meeting closed.

CHAPTER TWENTY-FIVE

Zevulun was very excited. He left Torquemada's meeting with a feeling of accomplishment.   His friendly priest of the Church of San Christopher in Barcelona had told him about Torquemada's planned meeting. He decided to go and easily found his way into the meeting with all others. *"I wish I could see David and Reuven and tell them about our progress,"* he thought. And as if God had opened the gates of heaven, he was walking down the street towards his old home when David, dressed like a monk, came driving his wagon the other way. Seeing Zevulun, David almost passed out from joy. He stopped the wagon and jumped off.

"What an incredible surprise," David shouted and hugged Zevulun with all his might.

"I'm delighted to see you." Zevulun said. "Just this minute I was saying to myself, if I could only see David, and here you are. It's a miracle. Actually, what are you doing in Toledo?"

"I got the hidden coins out of your broken wagon. No one was there, so I walked around the back. I have it all in the wagon. Come with me. We have a lovely house in a village called El Mola, half way between Toledo and Segovia."

"We need to fetch Sister Maria," Zevulun said. "She delivered a letter to Gutierrez de Cardenas, the Queens counselor. It'll blow his mind when he reads it. Have I got news for you!. I'll have to tell you all about Torquemada's meeting when we get out of town."

"I spent the day searching for Nechemia's sons. I think I found them in the Catholic Academy. I found a few of my childhood friends whose parents converted and they directed me to the Academy. I told them I became a monk. I'm planning to go there this evening after supper. The dormitory seems to be open and possibly I can kidnap them," David said.

"Let me help you. Since I'm a priest, no one will question my being there," Zevulun said. "Let's go to the marketplace and find Miriam. She's dressed as a nun and can stay inside the covered wagon while we go looking for Nechemia's sons."

"Very well." Zevulun mounted the wagon and sat next to David. It wasn't difficult to spot Miriam, as she was the only nun in the market. She almost choked with happiness when she saw David.

"How did you get here?"

"I was on a mission in Toledo and ran across Zevulun. Isn't it wonderful?"

"Where are we going?" she asked.

"I believe I've found Nechemia's sons," David said. "We're going to get them. How is he?"

"He's a new man. He feels much better. I believe something is going on between him and Miriam," Zevulun said.

"You think you know everything," Miriam smiled. "I like him a lot. I think he's a fine man. It's unfortunate he had to suffer so much. If you can bring his sons, he will be grateful to you forever."

"The Catholic Academy is around the next corner. The dormitory is across the street from it. Go up first. I'll follow you if necessary," David said.

Zevulun climbed down off the wagon and walked into the dormitory building. A few minutes later he came out with two young boys by his side.

"Get into the wagon quickly," he ordered. "Get going!" He didn't have to say it twice. David whipped the horses and off they galloped.

"How did you find them so quickly?" David asked.

"It was easy," Zevulun said. "They had just finished supper and were on the way to their rooms. As the boys passed me, I couldn't help recognize one of them. He looks exactly like his father. He got his brother and off we went."

"How far can we go during the night?" Zevulun asked.

"I have become an excellent night driver," David said. "We'll go as far as we possibly can. Hopefully the sky won't be overcast and the moon will cooperate."

Miriam took care of the boys, who were very excited at the prospect of uniting with their father. Two days later they arrived in El Mola.

Anna greeted them with surprise and pleasure. She hadn't expected to see Zevulun and Miriam so soon and was enchanted when introduced to Nechemia's boys. She became even happier when David reported Zevulun's experience at Torquemada's meeting.

"The results of our letters are just as we predicted," she said. "This is marvelous. I wish the others could know about this meeting."

"If they befriended some of the clergy as suggested, they too might have the information. However, I suspect the clergy has been greatly shaken by Torquemada's remarks and will continue to pursue their goals even more vigorously than before," David said.

"I see your point," Anna said. "We'll need to expedite our attacks and create more confusion. Now that momentum has been created, we should keep up the pressure."

"We certainly will. In a few days I'll attend our own meeting in Barcelona, and I can assure you that we'll continue with more vigor than Torquemada."

CHAPTER TWENTY-SIX

By the thirty-first day of January, 1477, David, Reuven, Itzhak and Yossef arrived at Zevulun's house in Barcelona. Miriam and Devorah directed them to the farmhouse Zevulun had bought. Instructions were issued that in the future no one was to return to Zevulun's old house. The idea was to keep traffic to a minimum where the priest Carlos Ramirez was known to do his studies.

Itzhak was the last one to arrive, and could hardly wait to tell everyone about his new farmhouse.

"The Castle of the Marquis of San Cristobal, which is located exactly half way between Zaragoza and Tarragona, was looking for someone to take charge of a very large farm. An old widower, a second cousin to the Marquis, owned the farm. The old man had no children to continue his work and didn't want his farm to go to waste. The Marquis' manager took an immediate liking to Yael and me, and took us over to meet the old man. The old man fell in love with Yael and wouldn't let her out of his sight. He decided to introduce me, as his lost nephew and Yael as his personal caretaker. I didn't have to spend a penny, and we have an incredible shelter from which to operate. During the past two months or so I learned everything there is to learn about the farm and am in charge of the labor and sales. The old man is wealthy, and I suspect he'll leave everything to us as he doesn't particularly care for the Marquis."

The reunion of Nechemia and his sons was celebrated with great joy. "You cannot imagine my happiness when I found your sons," David said. "I am so glad you feel better."

"I feel like a new man thanks to you. I owe you a great deal."

"You don't owe me a thing. Reuven, you're awfully quiet."

"I'm desperate to know if anyone knows the results of the letters. I'm anxious to take the next step."

"I'm sure I'm speaking for everyone here," David said. "All of us are just as anxious as you, but we haven't seen each other in two months, and the excitement of being together is overwhelming."

"I'm sorry, it's just that I'm very impatient and want to get ahead. Marranos and Conversos have been attacked in every city. The priest I befriended told me that orders have come from the Inquisitor General to harass the Conversos. There has been a great deal of trouble in Valladolid and some in Salamanca. Mobs led by priests have attacked homes of Conversos, destroyed or looted their property, and in a few cases there were some killings, too. I want to discuss our future plans and develop a strategy. We must act and bring the Inquisition to its knees," Reuven said.

"Reuven, come take a walk with me," David suggested. The two of them left the house and strolled for a while.

"I'm delighted to see you." They hugged each other.

"So am I," David said. "Please relax. We have all day tomorrow to discuss our next steps. By the way, how and where did you settle?"

"As you know, Rachel was with me. She is a wonderful woman and was a great help to me. We rented a house from a farmer who isn't doing too well. This farmer is a very stubborn man. Everybody's telling him that the soil on his farm is mostly suitable for grapevines, but he refuses to take their advice. Instead, he planted citrus trees, and his results are devastating. Citrus trees need sandy soil, which is not available in the Valladolid – Salamanca area. As result, he has lost a lot of money and is in serious financial trouble. I have a feeling I'll be able to buy him out soon. Rachel has been working on him and says he'd be out in a matter of weeks. I told the Noble who owns the land and offered to replace him. I promised to pay cash." Reuven said.

"Where is it?" David asked.

"It's in the vicinity of San Jose and the landowner is non other than the famous Don Alberto de la Cruses."

"I never heard of Don Alberto de la Cruses," David said, "What made him famous?"

"He's said to have been the lover of King Ferdinand's sister."

"Does it make any difference for us?"

"Not one bit," Reuven said, "Just that he's a well known womanizer throughout the area."

"What is the situation with the Jews, Conversos, and Marranos in your region?" David asked.

"There have been some riots and mob attacks against our people, but not as horrible as I've seen and heard elsewhere. The friendly priest in the church I attend told me the 'horrible' news about the sudden mysterious deaths of Cardinals, Bishops and priests in Castile and Aragon. He is concerned because, as he put it, he was instrumental in inciting people in accordance with the Inquisition's guidance."

"Our approach was excellent. The suicides of the Cardinals and the barrage of letters must have created havoc. Zevulun attended the meeting of higher clergy called by Torquemada. He gave a fiery speech. A major conflict developed between Torquemada and the Archbishop of Toledo, Alfonso Carrillo de Acura, who stormed out of the meeting." David said.

"How did Zevulun find out about this meeting?" Reuven asked.

"His friendly contact in one of the churches in Barcelona told him about it. He went to the meeting mixing in with dozens of other priests. That's how I came to meet him in Toledo. I'd retrieved the money which he'd hidden in the broken wagon, and as I was driving off, I came across him. He went to his old house for the same reason. It was a great surprise and delightful meeting," David said.

"Finding Nechemia's sons was also incredible. I could barely hold back tears when I saw the three of them reunite," Reuven said.

"I have other news for you," David said, "Anna and I are going to be married. We can't do it officially as neither of us wants to be married by the church. If I can find a Rabbi, we'll do it clandestinely at home."

"Mazal Tov, David, this is wonderful news. I'm very happy for you. Anna seems to be a great lady. I like her a lot. I wish your parents were around to see this."

"So do I. And, speaking of parents, have you any news from yours?"

"I haven't heard from them since they left. I don't know where they are and they certainly have no knowledge of where I am."

"God willing, you'll reunite with them soon," David said. "Tomorrow we'll discuss our next steps. It's time to mount a major battle."

They reached the house and walked in. Zevulun was waiting for them. "Everybody has gone to bed. The two of you should turn in as well. Tomorrow we'll have a long day."

CHAPTER TWENTY-SEVEN

"Now that everyone is here, let's start the meeting," Reuven said. "However, before we begin, I think we should listen to Zevulun's report of Torquemada's meeting."

Zevulun described Torquemada's meeting in great detail.

"I'm convinced from what I heard that he plans to expand his activities. Just as I thought – Torquemada won't give up so easily."

"Neither will we," roared David. "I don't mind fighting Torquemada to the death."

"Please, let's not get overly emotional," Zevulun said. "We have a great deal of work ahead of us. We need to decide our next steps. Our first step was successful. The confusion we wanted to create materialized."

"I agree. I have a feeling we should continue with the letters. The pointing of fingers, the denials, and the distrust in each other should intensify."

"Itzhak is right. We should continue with the letters. Let's send a series of letters to Torquemada, say, one or two from each city, and a few letters from Torquemada to some clergy," Yossef suggested.

"In fact, we should have the same writers write to Torquemada every two or three weeks, with each message a little stronger than the last. Torquemada will start to excommunicate some of the priests, who will be extremely upset. They will become our silent allies," Zevulun said.

"The letter campaign should definitely continue. It was a great idea and we have proof it works. The more we infuriate Torquemada, the better. He may become more stubborn like pharaoh, but eventually he'll fall on his face," David said.

"I'm listening to you with great admiration," Nechemia interposed. "However, letters and confusion in the ranks will not do the job. You have to remember that Torquemada and those priests who are as zealous as he is believe deeply in their mission. They are following an ideal, and this ideal is Godly. Life and death don't mean a thing when you are dealing with God because they believe God will reward them for the mission they are carrying out. I think that along with the letters, we should stir up greater panic."

"How do you create greater panic?" David asked.

"In a number of ways. For example, Zevulun, who looks like a priest, should take over the podium in some major church on a Sunday mass and start preaching the exact opposite of what the parishioners have heard."

"How can Zevulun do that?" Reuven asked.

"Very simple. Minutes before the priest gets ready for his sermon, Zevulun enters from the rear and tells the priest Torquemada is in his office and wants to see him immediately. The priest is not sure what to do, and at that point Zevulun suggests that he take over the sermon. The priest enters his office and I disable him. Zevulun takes the podium and tells the audience that the Church has made a critical mistake in its dealing with the Jews. He tells them the truth and leaves through the rear. We'll have two or three wagons waiting in back and Zevulun will be smuggled away. We repeat this type of activity a number of times in different cities. The news is bound to reach Torquemada, who will be forced to take action. At that point we'll change our tactics and deal with whatever comes up. In the mean time our letters should continue, and I can see Torquemada going crazy."

"This is an outstanding idea," Reuven said. "Does everyone agree?"

"Yes!" was the unanimous call.

"How do we get Zevulun out safely?" Yossef asked.

"Quite simple," David declared. "Once he completes his sermon, he signals the choir to start singing, which is the tradition. He walks out through the rear door, and once in the priest's office, he takes off his priest's habit and gets into civilian clothing. One of us carries the sack with his habit in it and the two of us walk out through the rear of the building, jump in the wagons, and leave. No one will suspect a thing."

"I have a better idea," Zevulun said. "Once I finish the sermon, I walk out as you suggested, change my clothes, walk around the side of the Church and enter the front gate. Obviously, the service will be discontinued when the priest doesn't return and sooner or later the parishioners will start flocking out. At that point, I mix in with the crowd and walk away. A number of carriages are bound to be on the street waiting for their owners, and one of you can wait for me and pick me up the way the others are doing."

"This is real daring, but I think it'll work, since no one will suspect any member of the audience," David said. "By the time the priest wakes up, the entire congregation will be gone."

"We can try both approaches and see which works better," Itzhak suggested.

"All well and good, but I would also like to see some real damage inflicted on the Inquisition," Reuven said.

"Such as what?" David asked.

"I would burn down some of their buildings, the houses where their clergy reside, and family members of the priests. In each case we leave a note signed by some priest or other important member of the clergy saying he despises the brutality of the Church and the Inquisition and decided to burn them down," Reuven answered.

"To maximize results from this approach, it would be best if after the fire, the priest supposedly responsible disappears." David said.

"How do you make him disappear?" Yossef asked.

"Very simple -- we bury him," David said.

"I'd like to suggest that the same Sunday Zevulun delivers his sermon, we set a fire in another city, and the priest who left the message also vanishes. This way two events take place on the same day, each different from the other. Two weeks later we repeat these two events in two other cities. When the third event occurs, Torquemada will undoubtedly ask the Queen for help. After the third time, we should get together to re-evaluate our next strategy," Itzhak said.

"And meanwhile the letters should continue to flow," Yossef said.

"Very well. We're all in agreement as to our next step," Zevulun said. "Let's decide who does what, and where."

"I suggest we start two cities away from Toledo," David said. "By the time the news reach Torquemada, we will launch the second two cities on the other side of Aragon and Castile. Toledo should fall into the third set."

The meeting broke up. It was decided to meet again on the 15th of March in David's house at El Mola

CHAPTER TWENTY-EIGHT

"Your Majesty." Torquemada said giving Queen Isabella half a bow, "I received a letter from Pope Eugene IV two days ago. In his letter the Pope gives me complete authority to conduct the affairs of the Inquisition in Castile and Aragon. His Holiness also writes that he is considering giving the ultimate authority over the Church to the Crown in each country. Should the Pope decide on that change, you will become the head of the Church in Castile, and your husband, King Ferdinand, would head the Church in Aragon."

"Why is the Pope considering such a drastic change?" the Queen asked.

"Because there is great need to fight the spread of Protestantism. The Protestant faith is spreading in Europe like wildfire. Fortunately, it has not reached Aragon and Castile. The Catholic Church is the sole religious authority here. The Pope feels that his offices in Rome cannot accomplish much in this fight because he's so far away. He therefore relies on local devout members of the Crown to do his work," Torquemada replied.

"Does this mean I will have authority over you?"

"Yes, Your Majesty."

"In that event, you and I will have to discuss the ways of the Inquisition, and probably revise some of its functions," she said.

"I wish to remind you that you have not received authority from the Pope yet. Until then, I'm the sole authority over the Inquisition, and it will continue to function as it has in the past."

"You are in charge of the purification of the people within the Catholic religion, which is the greater part of my life. Yet I'm the Queen of this country and I have a great responsibility to the people and the Land. Your methods are continually destroying the sources of revenue for the Crown. If this continues much longer, our coffers will be empty," the Queen stated.

"Faith in our Lord and the purification of our people is more important than wealth. It guarantees reincarnation and safe travel in heaven with the angels. Life on earth is short, but life with Jesus is forever," Torquemada preached.

"I've been approached by an Italian navigator with a great dream. He told me that if I financed an expedition, he would travel west and discover India for us. If he is successful in his mission, the wealth he would bring back is immeasurable. It would also provide us with many colonies. And when that happens, your hands will be full with missionary work in the west," she said.

"Again, Your Majesty, the work for Christ under the Catholic doctrine is by far more important than any endeavor on earth. I will not reconsider the Inquisition's approach or methods in dealing with heresy or non-Catholics," Torquemada said firmly. "You, as a devout Catholic Queen, are obligated to carry out the will of Jesus, to love him with all your might, and to blindly carry out his work if you wish to stay out of hell. Just thinking about alternatives is improper, and you will have to confess your sins just like any other human being," Torquemada stated.

"You know my love for Jesus better than any man on earth," the Queen said. "Why is it that every time we speak about issues of State, you threaten me with hell?"

"In the eyes of our Lord, you are just a single human being of no consequence, like any other mortal," he answered.

"I can't accept that. Kings and Queens have to be received differently because they are the authority while on earth," she argued.

"You are wrong, Your Majesty. When you die, you are no different than anyone else."

"This discussion is getting us nowhere," she said. "I'm a devout Catholic and I shall continue to be so, yet I feel the need for a change. I can't help it. My intuition tells me that this man Columbus will bring us the west. I need the monies to do so. The Jews have historically produced the greater part of out tax revenues, and I can't have them destroyed. I have no intention of stopping their conversion, but I don't need riots and mobs running all over Castile, stealing and looting. One day that same mob may turn on me."

"You are building the road to hell," Torquemada boomed. "You are becoming blasphemous and I don't like it. We'll have to conduct a special session where you and I will talk about pure thinking and pure Catholicism."

Torquemada left and Queen Isabella felt extremely uncomfortable about her beliefs and thoughts. Her fear of hell was burning in her mind, and she grew restless. Yet Columbus and his strong case for exploration of the west seemed a great challenge she could not ignore.

"Go and bring this sailor Columbus to me," she ordered an assistant. "I must speak to him."

"Your Majesty, this letter arrived for you, and I don't know how to handle it. The subject matter is beyond me," the assistant said.

"Read it to me. I'm exhausted. Torquemada always leaves me with a heavy heart. He doesn't realize that I have a country to rule. He puts religion above anything else, but unfortunately it's impossible to let religion govern the Crown. He refuses to accept that human nature is imperfect and believes he can force humanity into pure Catholicism. I'd like it to be that way, too, but it will never happen unless you eliminate half the population of this earth. Please go on."

"Your Holy Majesty
Queen Isabella of Castile,
I am a simple person. I live with my wife and three children in a small Jewish neighborhood in the city of Bilbao. My family settled in Bilbao at least four hundred years ago. Like all my forefathers, before me, I am a silversmith. I make jewelry for women, which I sell at moderate prices and make a modest living. After years of struggling, I managed to buy a small house for my family.

We have lived peacefully in this area for many years. Suddenly, our lives have been turned around. Mobs are incited, for no reason that I can understand, to vandalize our properties and loot our meager belongings. I cannot recall in my lifetime any member of my family ever causing harm to anyone. Like many others, I have been a hard working man all my life.

I stopped one of the looters, whom I recognized as a client of my shop, and asked him why he was participating in a mob vendetta. He said that the priest, at Sunday mass, ordered his congregation to demonstrate against the Jews because they're destroying the pure Catholic morals of Castile.

Your Majesty, I cannot think of one deed that I or any of my neighbors and friends did that should bring about such a claim. I've been an observant Jew all my life, as my forefathers were. I respect the Catholic religion for what it is. I will admit I don't know much about it. The way I see it, I was born to a Jewish family, and you were born to a Catholic one. Each of us was brought up in the bosom of our respective religions. I cannot see how one people destroy the morals of another. After all, you surely will admit that the Jewish religion had been around for at least two thousand years before Christianity.

I am not saying, nor did I ever think one religion is superior to another. As little as I know about other religions, I am certain that all religions have the common good of mankind in mind. I am sure all religions preach decency, honor and respect, honesty and love for each other. I live by the Ten Commandments, which Moses brought down from the Sinai, and I am certain all Jews do the same.

What amazes me in particular is the accusation that Jews steal Christian babies, slaughter them, and use their blood for making soap. Your Majesty, if you investigate, you will find no such evidence. There isn't a normal person in this world that would kill an infant for its blood unless that person is mentally ill. The Jews are not isolated. The Jews are human beings made of the same flesh, bones, and blood as any other person on earth.

When the Black Plague killed thousands of people in Castile, the Jews were blamed for it. Jews died at the same rate as Christians did during those horrible years.

I am asking you, the benevolent ruler of Castile, the greatest monarch this country ever had, to bring the slaughter of innocent people as well as the destruction of personal property to an end. After all, Jesus was one of ours.

Your humble servant,

Ya'acov Halevi
Bilbao"

Queen Isabella remained sitting quietly for a few minutes deep in thought. "What do you make of this letter?" she asked.

"Your Majesty, it's not my place to express an opinion, however, the priest in my church tells us that Jews are evil people. They disgrace the fine fabric of our Catholic beliefs and society. In fact, this letter shows how tricky they are."

"What contacts have you ever had with Jews?" the Queen asked.

"Not on a personal level, Your Majesty, I wouldn't even think of it. The only time I see a Jew is when I enter a shop owned by a Jew."

"Have you bought merchandise from a Catholic shop?"

"Oh Yes, my Queen."

"Was your treatment any different?"

"No, my Queen. Both treated me nicely."

"Why do think your priest tells you Jews are evil?"

"I don't know. He certainly knows best. After all, he is a trained and ordained man. I'm sure he is telling the truth."

"Thank you, you may go. Leave the letter here. I'd like to read it again. Ask the King if he could join me."

Queen Isabella remained seated in her large armchair in deep thought. A few minutes later King Ferdinand walked in accompanied by one of his nobles. "What is it my dear?"

"I received this letter and I'm disturbed about what is happening in Aragon and Castile. Please read it. I'm too tired to read it to you. King Ferdinand sat down and read the letter.

"What is so special about this letter?"

"It speaks to the heart. It tells you about the life and desires of one man and it wouldn't surprise me if you asked every Jew to describe his life, he would write a very similar letter," she said.

"What has this to do with anything? Torquemada is convinced that to have a pure Catholic society, every man, woman and child should convert. Who says they should stay Jews for the rest of their lives? Torquemada knows more about these things than I do," the King said.

"I'm not suggesting Torquemada is wrong. I am suggesting the approach to conversion be reviewed and that mob incitement stops as well as the vandalizing of property, looting, and killing."

"Torquemada tells me Jews are evil and aim at destroying Catholicism. He told me that Conversos are teaching Catholics the practices of Judaism," the King said.

"This makes no sense. Christianity is about one thousand years old. When it started, there were only a few Christians, and look now -- there are millions all over Europe. The Jews have not increased as we have. To this day they remain a small minority and a productive one at that. You cannot dismiss the fact that over twenty percent of all taxes in our countries are paid by Jews while they hardly make up two percent of the population."

"That's because most of them are merchants and traders and profit from dealing with the population."

"Aren't there any Christian merchants?" Queen Isabella asked.

"Of course there are, but Jews seem to be superior. Even this monarchy depends heavily on Jewish tradesmen," he said.

"I'm told by various members of our staff that many needed items cannot be found anymore in Castile. The merchants who dealt with them disappeared. Also, our revenues have declined significantly."

"The Christians will have to learn, and eventually they'll take over new opportunities," the King said.

"This will never happen. The Jews have a network of families and businesses across many borders and that is why they're successful. They speak other languages, are better educated, and live by their religion."

"This is a Catholic country, and so it should remain," the King said.

"Is anyone questioning it? This was a Muslim country for hundreds of years until we kicked them out, and even though they tried to convert the population to Islam, they failed. I have a feeling we will fail in converting the Jews."

"Thousands have already converted, and I'm told that every day sees more Jews convert."

"Do you know why these people converted? They convert because the Inquisition forces them through torture, harassment, threats, vandalism, and mob violence. Do you really believe a converted Jew relinquishes the religion he's embraced since the days of Moses with one stroke?"

"This is getting far too complicated. Torquemada tells me we have no reason to judge this issue, and we should leave it entirely in his hands. He has written to the Pope for direction."

"The Pope wants to transfer the ultimate authority over the Church to us, the monarchs," Isabella said. "I'm very concerned about it because as a devout Catholic, I may fall victim to the theories of Torquemada, which do not take in account the problems and issues of State."

"I'm sure we'll have many more opportunities to discuss these matters with Torquemada," the King said.

"This is what frightens me," the Queen declared. "He knows too much about my personal weaknesses and is using it against me."

Queen Isabella rose and left the room in a slow and pensive mood. She was unhappy.

CHAPTER TWENTY-NINE

Reuven and Yossef left for Zaragoza as soon as the meeting broke up. Zevulun sat down and began writing his sermon. He wrote and rewrote and finally handed the draft to David.

"Tell me what you think of it."

"It's brilliant. It will certainly confuse the congregation."

"I suggest we leave as well. We need to decide which Church to use and prepare ourselves. The key is a safe exit from the scene," Zevulun said.

They decided to take Miriam with them.

"I'll pack the clothing for you, Reverend," Miriam smiled. "Don't forget we have to meet Yossef and Reuven by the central fountain."

They reached Zaragoza three days later. It was well after noontime.

"Let's tour the city and decide on the Church," Zevulun said.

"I'm going to put on my monk's habit and make some inquiries," David stated.

"Good idea," Zevulun said.

David changed his clothing inside the covered wagon and emerged as a monk. He sat next to Zevulun on the driver's bench. The wagon stopped two blocks before the first Church they spotted. David got down and walked into the church.

"Good evening," he greeted a repairman at work.

"I'm visiting Zaragoza and was wondering which of the churches in this city is the most important."

"They're all important," the man replied.

"Which would you say is the most prominent on account of its priest?" David asked.

"I think Reverend Stephan Martinos is the most noted priest in Zaragoza," the man answered.

"Where would I find him?" David asked.

"His Church is on King John Street. It's called the Church of Santa de Guadalupe," the man said. David thanked him and left.

"Let's find John Street. Cover your head with the big hat so your gray hair is hidden." He changed into his regular clothes and stretched out on the bottom of the wagon. By the time they identified the Church of Santa de

Guadalupe, it was dark. They parked the wagon in a nearby orchard. Miriam slept inside the wagon while Zevulun and David camped in the open.

The morning brought with it a strong cold gust of wind. The blue sky gave way to gray clouds, which moved slowly in a westerly direction.

"This is a pretty good location for our wagon," Zevulun said, "Let's find a grocer and replenish our supplies. I'm hungry."

"So am I," Miriam said. "I slept very well last night. I suppose this sudden cold temperature was a big help. Fortunately, I packed plenty of blankets."

"You seem to be in another world," Zevulun wondered.

"I'm thinking about the pastor I'll disable. Don't you think he should disappear altogether?"

"Let's think about it. If the pastor is disabled for a while, he is bound to find out what my sermon was about. On the following Sunday, when we are gone, he'll tell his parishioners what happened and denounce the occurrence as another Jewish act of deceit. Therefore, we'd better kidnap him."

"What do you mean by 'kidnap' him?" David asked, "Take him with us?"

"Something like that," he answered.

"I agree with your line of thought that it would be better if the pastor vanished, but I cannot see any benefit in kidnapping him. He has to be eliminated."

"How?"

"Killing him," David said calmly.

"In cold blood? How could you?"

"In very cold blood. The very same cold blood they killed my parents. I can still see the priest who lit the wood and then stood watching them burn to death. Their screams didn't mean a thing to him."

"How do we dispose of his body?"

"Right after the sermon, we leave the city as planned. Once we are out, we look for the proper burial grounds. We should have no difficulty finding a place where the pastor's body can be dumped."

As if hesitating, Zevulun repeated himself. "The results of our work, and the sermon in particular, will be of greater value if the regular pastor is missing. There is no question about it."

"I can visualize the Mass without its pastor. Great confusion will take over. By that time, we'll be far away. The parishioners will surely talk to lots of people about the odd sermon they listened to."

"That's exactly the intention."

Wearing his monk's habit, David entered the Church. He toured the area around it, paying special attention to the rear of the building. The large door was wide open, but he chose not to enter. He returned to the wagon.

"Miriam, pretend to be looking for a cleaning job and look around. Map the layout of the rear in your mind."

Miriam entered through the open rear door. There were four doors, two on each side of the narrow corridor, one at the end. She opened the door slightly and saw the back of the Alter and the main prayer hall. She shut the door and knocked on the first door to the left. There was no answer. She opened the door and looked in. *"This is the Pastor's office,"* she thought, *"It makes sense for his office to be next to the prayer hall."* As she turned around, a young priest came out of an adjoining room.

"Is there anything I can do for you?"

"I'm looking for work," Miriam said. "I think this building can use a woman's touch."

"I'll ask our pastor, but I doubt he'll hire anyone." He knocked on the far right door and walked in. He left the door open and Miriam, following him, took a quick look inside the room. It was a kitchen/dining room combination. She heard some conversation, but could not make out what was said. The young priest returned.

"I'm sorry, but this Church cannot hire anyone, we simply don't have the funds. If you wish to volunteer your work, our pastor will talk to you."

"No, thank you." Miriam left. She walked briskly to the wagon and explained in detail the layout of the rear of the church.

"Good work," Zevulun said.

There were many wagons and coaches awaiting their owners when they arrived at the center market plaza. Shoppers, particularly women looking for fresh produce and meats for the coming Sunday dinner, crowded the plaza. They bought fresh food and returned to their wagon.

They talked while they ate and planned their Sunday venture carefully.

"Tomorrow we'll check and prepare our exit," David said. "In the meantime, there isn't much else we can do except check on the Jewish community, or what's left of it."

CHAPTER THIRTY

Mass at the Church of Santa Guadalupe began precisely at 10:00 o'clock Sunday morning. David's wagon approached the church building and made its way to the rear. Zevulun, in full clerical garb, David in a monk's habit, and Miriam wearing a nun's outfit entered through the back door. The door to the pastor's office was unlocked. They entered and left the door ajar. As the prayers began to wind down, Zevulun opened the door to the Church and motioned David in as soon as the pastor began walking toward the podium. David quickly approached the pastor and said in a low voice, "Father Martinos, a messenger from Tomas de Torquemada's office is waiting for you with a very urgent message. He wants to see you immediately in your office."

"I have to deliver my sermon. I'll see him later."

"You must see him now." David propelled him towards the rear door.

"Pardon me, I'll be right back," he spoke loudly to his congregation.

As soon as the pastor passed, Zevulun, hiding behind the door, entered the prayer hall. He headed directly to the podium.

The pastor entered his office and was disabled by David hitting his head with a heavy wooden rod. The pastor fell to the floor unconscious.

"My fellow parishioners," Zevulun opened his sermon, "Father Martinos was called into a meeting of vital importance with a messenger from the Inquisition. He asked me to replace him this morning. My name is Father Juan Jose Alarcon, and I'm a special emissary from Pope Eugene IV in Rome. You may wonder what that urgent matter was. It has to do with the brutal behavior of the Holly Office known as the Inquisition.

"During the past few years, you've been told over and over by your pastors that the Inquisition was established in order that we may purify our society of its ills. Heresy will not be tolerated anymore, you were told, and I am sure many of you have been called to the Inquisition and punished for whatever sins you have committed. However, with time, the Inquisition slowly developed the opinion that those minorities living among us are just as bad as heresy, if not worse. In due course, the Inquisition, through its many serving priests, began feeding you deceitful information concerning the Jews. Your pastor systematically fed you information, which is hateful and untrue. You were told Jews represent the devil. You were told Jews are of bad moral character; you were told Jews poison the purity of Catholic beliefs. You were told Jews killed Jesus and that they should be punished for it. You were told Jews steal Christian children, slaughter them and use their blood to make soap. You were told you must demonstrate against the Jews, vandalize their properties and loot their homes. In simple words the Church planted and developed your hate for the Jews. It reached a point where all the teaching of the Ten Commandments and our beloved saints was lost to hate and destruction. Tomas de Torquemada has gone too far in his direction of the Church. The Church, which Rome envisions is full of love, of teaching of love, respect, mutual compassion and charity. The Inquisition has turned murderous. It tortures people until they confess, they sentence people to jail for long periods without mercy and consideration of family, and the worst is that they burn people to death because they refuse to convert. Yes, we do want our society to become Catholic in its entirety, however, we need to convert people by reasoning, by showing them that our Jesus is the salvation, by acts of love and charity, and not by force, torture and vandalism.

"The Jews did not kill Jesus. It was the Romans who crucified him. The Jews stoned people who were sentenced to death. Crucifixion was a Roman practice. Jews do not steal Christian children. Jews do not use blood to make soap. In fact, soap is made from animal fat and not from blood.

"The Pope feels that the zealousness of the Inquisition has turned you, good Catholics, into sinful people. The Pope wants all that changed. The preaching of Jesus relate to love and charity, not to hate and destruction. The Pope wants you to repent for the sins you have committed under the direction of your pastor. The Pope wants you to oppose any pastor who preaches hate. Remember, high morality, forgiveness, love and charity is what Catholic life is about."

"May the Lord bless you."

He motioned one of the young priests and asked him to continue the service until Father Martinos returned.

Zevulun left through the rear door and shut it firmly behind him. He looked into the pastor's office, but saw no one. He quickly walked out.

"Get quickly into the wagon," David said, "and change your clothes."

The wagon started moving before Zevulun was inside.

"How was it?" Miriam asked.

"The congregation was stunned. I saw it in their faces. Unfortunately, I could not see the faces of the two young priests. My message was strong, as you know, and hopefully it will create a commotion among the people."

"We'll be out of the city soon," David said looking backward. "Please don't disturb the pastor."

"Where is he?"

"He is sitting at the other end of the wagon, sound asleep."

"Is he dead?"

"Very dead," Miriam said. "David did not have to kill him. The blow on the head did it."

⊗⊗⊗

An hour before dawn on Sunday, the eleventh of February, 1477, Reuven and Yossef broke four windows on three ground floor sides of the Inquisition building in Tarragona. Four containers of oil were poured in and set afire. By the time their wagon was half way out of the city, the entire building was in flames.

CHAPTER THIRTY-ONE

"**Y**ou are very troubled," Torquemada said as Queen Isabella made her confession, "You are not at peace with yourself."

"I can't help it," she responded, "I find it more and more difficult to cope with the news of killings and fires. Perhaps something is wrong."

"You must have full faith in pure Catholicism, Your Majesty," Torquemada beamed, "There is no other religion in this world worthy of discussion. Catholicism, and pure Catholicism at that, is the way of Christ. If you continue to have doubts, the road to hell is almost certain for you."

"You always frighten me with hell," the Queen said, "and each time I confess my sins you become more adamant and more threatening. You don't seem to understand, or want to understand, that as the Queen of Castile I must rule the people fairly."

"I do understand your position," Torquemada said, "But you don't understand mine. Actually, it's quite simple. You must believe in Jesus with all your heart and soul. You must...---"

Queen Isabella interrupted Torquemada; "I do believe in Jesus with all my heart and soul, but I can't find the way to the creation of a pure Catholic society."

"That is my responsibility, and I aim to achieve it by every means at my disposal. All I need from you, Your Majesty, is full cooperation and authority to carry out my work."

"I must admit that I'm bothered by torture and burning people at the stake."

"You have it wrong, Your Majesty. All those sinners are headed for hell and whether hell starts on earth makes no difference. In fact, the experience of hell is what I hope will bring those sinners into our fold."

"In that case, perhaps you can explain to me the discrimination against Conversos. Why are they hounded?"

"Most Conversos are found to be practicing Judaism in secret. If Jesus wants us to have a pure Catholic society how can these people who were baptized remain Jewish in their hearts? I have an obligation to eradicate heresy of any kind," he stated.

"I hear people say that those who converted are specified as New Christians and are considered of impure blood. If they were baptized and accepted conversion, they should be left alone. How can you have people convert by force, and how do you expect them to have pure Catholic blood. What is pure Catholic blood? It is said that your grandmother was of Jewish origin. Does that make you impure?" the Queen asked.

"How dare you, Queen or not, question my devout belief before our Lord?" Torquemada said angrily, and pointed at the statue of Christ on the Cross. "I am carrying out His work. You should worship the ground I walk on. I am your official Counselor and Confessor. I am the only cleric in Castile who understands your soul, and you are driving yourself directly into burning hell."

"Stop that! You always end your preaching by threatening me with hell. I can't sleep nights because of you. I'm a frightened woman. Please go now," the Queen ordered.

"I can't go before I help you clean your soul. Please look at me." He waited until Queen Isabella lifted her head. "The forces of evil have descended on you. The Jews you are defending have brought this trouble upon you. This is precisely what I am preaching about. Once the Jews are out of your life, you will be a pure Catholic. Why is it so difficult for you to understand? Only when our society is clean of the filth which pollutes our very lives will the road to paradise open. Think about this carefully. It's not the money or economic value that count -- it's your relationship with Christ. The Lord will provide if the Jews don't." With those words, Torquemada left the palace.

Queen Isabella remained alone in her chamber and cried. The fear of hell, and particularly burning in it, had her out of her wits. One of her assistants saw Torquemada leave and walked in.

"Your Majesty, you are crying. What did he do to you? Why do you let him bring suffering into your life? You are the greatest Queen Castile ever had."

"I'm torn between his words and the reality of life. I cannot possibly understand his extremism. If the Jews are the Devil, how come this Devil brought us Jesus Christ, our Lord and Savior? It's very difficult for me to see the Jews as the Devil. Every Jew I met was always a hard-working man. The Jews the Crown employed performed extremely well. I'm thoroughly confused and frightened at the same time."

"My Queen, you are the supreme authority in this country. He should live by your wishes and not the other way around," her assistant said.

"I'm frightened of his association with our Lord, and I'm frightened of hell. He is the only man who can keep me out of it."

CHAPTER THIRTY-TWO

David, Zevulun, and Miriam approached the Cathedral of San Rafael in Valladolid. Mass was about to start when they entered the Cathedral. They had to enter through the front since the rear door was locked. Due to the size of the Cathedral they managed to move forward a few steps at a time unnoticed. Zevulun went first and walked with confidence. David and Miriam followed a few moments later. The door to the back of the Chapel was on the left side of the Altar. Zevulun waited a few minutes and at the appropriate moment quickly opened the door and snuck in. He left the door partially open. When the pastor called for kneeling and the entire congregation was deep in prayer, David, who held Miriam's hand, pulled her hard and they ran through the door, closing it behind them.

"I hope no one saw us. Zevulun must be in the office."

As they entered the office, they found Zevulun being questioned by a priest.

"I don't believe I know you. Is there anything I can do for you?" The priest asked.

"Who are you?" Zevulun asked; "Why aren't you in the Chapel with the others?"

"I'm father..." he suddenly turned around as he heard David and Miriam come in. "Who are you, and what do you want?"

"I have come here to cleanse your soul," David replied, "and to deliver you to your Lord."

"You must be out of your mind," the priest said. "Do you know these people?" he questioned Zevulun. At that moment David pulled out the knife from his belt and stabbed the priest in the left side of his back. The priest fell to the floor without a word. David ran through the rear corridor and opened the door, which led to a large yard. In the meantime, Zevulun was listening to the prayers and waited for the right moment to step into the Chapel.

David brought the wagon as close as possible to the rear entrance and with Miriam's help undressed the priest, lifted him, and carried him to the wagon. Once inside the wagon, the priest was covered with a blanket. They returned to the office and waited for the pastor to arrive.

"I wish I could listen to Zevulun's sermon," he said.

The waiting was nerve wracking. David held the bar of wood firmly in his right hand and waited for the door to open. He instructed Miriam to sit in the big chair behind the desk so that as soon as the door opened, the pastor's focus would be on her. His parents came into view. Their screams as the fire raged around them were as sharp as could be. The hate in his heart grew by the minute. Suddenly the door opened and his senses returned to the reality of the moment. The pastor never knew what hit him. David's swing was deliberately hard. The madness of the moment and the rage that consumed him doubled the force of his swing. The pastor's head was smashed so hard that he flew forward and hit the desk. Miriam quickly got up. They pulled him out and loaded his limp body on the wagon.

"I've never seen you so mad," Miriam said as they drove off.

"While waiting for the pastor to arrive, I had a vision of my parents being burned to death. Their screams and the picture of the fire, as well as my inability to help drove me insane. The pastor walked in at that moment and broke my vision. My ever growing hate for these murderers accompanied by the vengeance I hold in my heart gives me this power at the moment of need."

"I'm afraid you'll carry that memory of your parents for ever," she said.

"We'll park around the next corner as planned," David said. "Zevulun will join us soon. It's a shame I can't listen to his sermon. I'd give anything to watch the people's faces."

"Zevulun has that look of a priest. His age, looks, and shiny gray hair create the picture of reality. I can't wait to complete our mission in Toledo in two weeks," she said.

"Let's get going," David said, "here comes Zevulun. "How did it go?"

"I think some of the parishioners were in shock. Some of the faces looked so grave I began worrying for a moment. I rushed out as fast as I could and took the priest's habit off as I was walking away."

"The more shocked they are, the better. This is exactly what we're after. I can see that facing them and watching their faces twitch is not so easy, but you are a great actor."

"Is the pastor resting in the back?"

"Yes, together with the other unknown priest."

"We need to get rid of the bodies as soon as possible," Zevulun said.

"We'll be out of the city in about thirty minutes. There are a number of small forests along the way. It shouldn't be long before we dispose of this filthy cargo."

"I wonder what the other priest was doing in the office during mass? Why didn't he participate in the prayers?"

"I don't think we'll ever know."

"Perhaps we should investigate our next target closer and better," Zevulun said. "Imagine what can happen if someone in the crowd of parishioners contradicts my sermon."

They traveled in a pensive silence for a while. The outskirts of the city came into view as the last few houses almost touched one of the forests. There was little traffic on the road – mostly incoming. They did not see anyone behind them or in front. As soon as the road passed by the woods, David drove the wagon off the road and into the forest. The ground was flat and the trees were dense. Twice he had to maneuver hard to get his wagon through. David stopped when he saw another one parked in a small opening. There were no horses or people.

"It looks as though this wagon was left here a long time ago," Miriam said. "Look at the dust and dirt covering it."

"Someone abandoned it. I wonder why?"

"Let's take a look," David said. He jumped off the wagon and climbed on the other. He was back on the ground within an instant.

"There are two skeletons inside."

"Let's give them company," Zevulun said. "Apparently we are not the only ones who seek to hide corpses."

Zevulun and David undressed the two priests and threw their naked bodies on top of the skeletons.

"Aren't we nice to the priests?" David smiled. "We gave them company for the duration."

"Let's get out of here before dark," Miriam suggested.

"How right you are. Come on, David, you don't have to say Kaddish." They laughed.

⊗⊗⊗

In the city of Bilbao, that same night, a fire consumed the Inquisition building.

CHAPTER THIRTY-THREE

"**Y**our Eminence, we investigated the three suicides of the Cardinals as you instructed. We interrogated everybody connected with the Cardinals' residences the best we could," said the spokesman of the two priests. "Cardinals Cardenaz and Cardinal Gonzalez are sure suicides. Cardenaz's right hand was clutching the knife, which he held as he fell over it. The suicide took place in bed and there was no sign of violence. His manservant, housekeeper, and other members of his staff said they could not understand why he committed suicide. The two priests who worked closely with him said he was very disturbed by a number of letters he had received. The two of us read all the letters and we brought them with us. The letters are indeed very upsetting. However, it's very hard to understand why he committed suicide, just as it's hard to believe that the letters caused it. According to the entire staff, Cardinal Cardenaz acted normally and nothing unusual happened that day.

Cardinal Gonzalez's suicide was more bizarre. He had lodged a sword between two chairs and fell over it, just as King Saul did during the battle with the Philistines. No one was in the room. His manservant found him the next morning. The household was in shock because the Cardinal was always in good spirits. When we investigated his office, we found in one of the drawers three letters similar in tone and subject matter to the letters we found in Cardenaz's house. We brought those letters with us for you to see.

The suicide of Cardinal Avila is the one we couldn't figure out. His body was found on the ground floor early in the morning. On top of his body was his manservant, his hand clutching the knife that was embedded in the Cardinal's heart. The manservant was also dead. Apparently, there was a stab wound in his back, but no knife was found. We came to the conclusion that the Cardinal tried to kill his manservant. In the ensuing struggle the manservant got hold of the knife and killed the Cardinal, then collapsed over his body. The household stated that they never witnessed any bad feelings between the two, and as far as they knew the manservant was very happy in his job. He was a devout Catholic and served the Cardinal with much respect and admiration. Why the Cardinal wanted to kill him is a mystery.

Torquemada sat silently and listened to the report. "Did you find any letters in Cardinal's Avila's house?"

"Yes, Your Eminence, similar letters were found in his office. Here are all the letters. Each bunch is separated with the name of the Cardinal on top."

"Please leave." He took the letters. The priests left and he read every one of them. When he finished reading, he jumped out of his seat and roared for his secretary to enter.

"What happened?" his secretary asked, "Did these priests do any harm?"

"Read these letters and you'll understand. Every one of them is written by one clergy or another, and all behind my back. I want every one of these priests brought before me. Send messengers immediately with instructions for them to appear in my office with haste. I must get to the bottom of this. The work of our Lord must continue without interruption."

The secretary took the letters and left the room. Torquemada got up, left the Inquisition building, and ordered his coachman to take him to the palace.

Queen Isabella was in session when he arrived. The throne room in which she gave audiences was filled with people. When she saw Torquemada approaching her armchair, she lifted her hand, motioning everybody to be quiet.

"What urgent matter brings you this morning, Your Eminence?"

"I have a grave matter to discuss with you," Torquemada replied.

"Please leave the throne chamber," she spoke to the audience. "Wait in the room next door until I call you." The Queen's two assistants led the people out and the sentries closed the doors behind them.

"What is it?" she asked.

Torquemada reported the findings of his investigators. He also told her about the letters that were found.

"What do you mean, "the same theme"," the Queen asked.

"All the letters resemble the ones you and I received during the past few months. Every one of them is blasphemous," Torquemada said.

"What do you want me to do?" she asked.

"I'd like you to instruct your Chief of the Guards to place sentries at each of our houses of Inquisition and Churches in all major cities. All holy places should be guarded around the clock."

"I don't know that we have this many men available. Don't forget we're fighting the Moors in the south."

"I've told you many times that the Lord's work is far more important than anything else on earth. It's more important than food, shelter or living," Torquemada stated.

"You are right," she said, "I'll call the Chief of the Guards as soon as I finish with the people waiting in the other room."

"Thank you, Your Majesty." Torquemada left.

Two young priests were waiting for him in his office when he returned. "Who are you and what do you want?" he roared. "I have enough trouble for one day."

"Your Eminence," the younger of the two said, "I apologize for the intrusion, but something very peculiar happened in our Church and we didn't know where to turn. The Bishop and the Cardinal our Church reports to have died."

"Very well, what is it?"

"A few weeks ago our pastor was called into his office in the middle of the Sunday morning prayers, in fact, just before he was ready to deliver his sermon. Another priest showed up, one I've never seen before. He went directly to the podium and delivered his sermon. He opened his remarks by telling the parishioners that he was a special emissary from Rome. Everything he said negated all our teachings and beliefs. He left immediately after the sermon, but our own pastor never returned. We haven't seen him since."

"Has your pastor disappeared before for any reason?" Torquemada asked.

"As far as I can remember he did leave once for about a week, but then returned and said his mother was dying," the young priest said.

"Is it possible he went away for a similar reason?"

"It has been about four weeks now that he's gone. He would have sent word, I'm sure. But we received no messages."

"Who conducted the prayers in his absence?"

"The two of us alternated."

"What did this mysterious priest say in his sermon?"

"Every word he said was related to the Jews. He said the Jews did not kill Jesus, that they are not the Devil, and all the stories about kidnapping Christian children for their blood were nonsense. In fact, he said the Pope was unhappy with the way things are going on here, and there is need for change."

"Anything else happen in Zaragoza I should know about?"

"Your Eminence surely is aware that the Inquisition building was destroyed by fire."

"What?" Torquemada screamed. "How come no one notified me? I know nothing of it. When did it happen?"

"The same day our priest disappeared. I suppose all the priests residing in the building perished in the fire," the young priest said. "I hope you won't think badly of us for coming to you."

"Not at all. In fact, I will say a special prayer for your courage. Return to your Church and carry on. You must disregard the sermon of this mysterious priest from Rome. I don't know of any priest sent by Rome. In your next sermon you must tell your parishioners that this mysterious priest was mad, completely out of his mind. You must iterate that every word he said was the word of a crazy man. In fact, you may say he wasn't even a priest. Our Lord will reward you for it. Now go." Torquemada brought the meeting to an end and summoned his two closest assistants.

"I want you to listen very carefully to what I'm about to say."

Torquemada repeated the news he had just received from the two young priests. "I want you to go to Zaragoza immediately, find another building so that our operations do not stop. I will make arrangements to send young men from our seminary to help you. We must restore the Inquisition in Zaragoza with great dispatch. Do whatever needs to be done to acquire a house suitable for our work. We must continue the work our Lord ordered without fail."

"Your Eminence," one of his assistants said, "there is another priest waiting outside to see you. He just arrived from Valladolid. He arrived while you were receiving the priests from Zaragoza."

"What does he want?"

"He told us something identical to what you just heard about Zaragoza."

"What do you mean, something identical to Zaragoza?" Torquemada asked in a high tone.

"The priest who heads his Church disappeared together with another visiting priest. The sermon was as blasphemous, and the Inquisition building was destroyed by fire that same Sunday."

"What?" Torquemada screamed. "There is a conspiracy against the Church! I have to get to the bottom of it."

"Your Eminence, could it be that one or more of the priests who wrote all these letters have conspired against our Lord?" one of the assistants asked.

"At this moment I don't know what to think," Torquemada shouted. "It could easily be the Devil in the Jews who is killing our men and burning our houses."

"With due respect, Your Eminence, all the Jews we have known have never been violent. Look at the way they surrender to torture and look at the tens of thousands who converted."

"Their conversion has not changed them from being Jewish in their hearts. Too many Conversos practice Judaism in the secret of their homes. We will never purify the blood of our society as long as they are with us. And furthermore, I cannot overlook the possibility that Jews or Conversos are behind these disasters. We must arrest a number of Conversos in every city in which this alleged priest from Rome delivered his sermon. Interrogate every one of them and torture them if you have to until you get the answers we are seeking."

"We'll send some of our most devoted men to Zaragoza and Valladolid. We can always use the civil jails for interrogation purposes," one said, "and while we are investigating, one of us will identify the proper houses to re-establish the Inquisitions' buildings. We shall leave immediately."

"By all means. For your information, I've asked the Queen to post sentries at each one of our Churches and Inquisition buildings."

Torquemada summoned another helper and instructed him to call a meeting of all the priests in Toledo. "I want every last priest in this city to attend this meeting. You can tell them anyone who fails to show up will be excommunicated." The helper ran out.

CHAPTER THIRTY-FOUR

David and Zevulun met Reuven and Yossef at Toledo's Plaza Mayor, as planned.

"We noticed two sentries guarding every Church we passed," Reuven said. "Word of the sermons, the disappearing priests and the fires must have reached Torquemada. This will make our work more difficult. Let's find a quiet place where we can plan our course of action in this city."

"At least we know our work is producing results," Zevulun said. "While the two of you are resting by the fountain, let me visit the Church across the plaza."

"Good idea," David said. "We'll wait for you by the wagon. It's better that we aren't seen together."

Zevulun left, and the three of them walked back to David's wagon, which was a few blocks away. Miriam was very happy to see them and greeted them warmly.

"Let's sit inside the wagon," David said.

Zevulun returned almost immediately. He was very excited. "Torquemada called for a meeting of all Toledo priests. This meeting will be held in the Inquisition building tomorrow morning. The priest I talked to was very irritated. He knew about the disappearance of his colleagues in Zaragoza and Valladolid as well as the fires. Even his Church, which is relatively small, is guarded by sentries."

"How did you present yourself?" David asked.

"I told him I'm on holiday in Toledo and am anxious to tour the Queen's palace."

"Very good," Reuven said. "While you are in the meeting, we'll canvass the Churches and the two known Cathedrals and decide which one to target. Let's drive out of here and find a quiet place in the park or the forest next to it." Yossef and Miriam sat on the driver's bench while David, Reuven and Zevulun sat in back. Miriam stopped near a food store and bought provisions. The wagon was parked a few yards into the forest, entirely out of sight. Miriam prepared the meal while they talked.

"I have an idea," David said. "I actually anticipated a change because obviously news of the fires and missing priests has been circulated. Since I expected a change, my mind has been working on a new approach."

"Go ahead," Reuven said, "so far your vision and your stamina have been of major help. I thought I would be the strategist, but you certainly beat me to it. I'm very happy about it since you seem to have an analytical mind."

"Let's not fuss about who thinks what or does what. All of us put our heads together for a common goal," Zevulun said, "David, please continue."

"We'll have to get Nechemia as we'll need help. My house in the village is not that far and perhaps Miriam can go and get him. The plan I devised is actually quite simple. The sentries who guard each house of prayer will have to be immobilized. If you noticed, in each Church and Cathedral there is a foyer between the main entrance and the Chapel or prayer hall. In Cathedrals this foyer is quite large. Miriam, dressed in nun's habit, will bring the sentries a cool drink, which will be doctored. Within minutes the two sentries will be lying on the floor sound asleep. She will retrieve the keys from them and lock the front entrance to the Cathedral, followed by locking the second door leading to the Chapel. In most Cathedrals the foyer has a small side door through which she will exit after taking off the habit. Miriam mingles with the praying public and leaves at the end of the prayers when they leave."

"When does this operation begin?" Yossef asked.

"It begins moments after the Sunday mass starts. Meanwhile, the four of us enter the Cathedral from the rear and secure the door leading to the chapel. The same procedure we used in the earlier operations follows with just one change; when Zevulun returns, that door gets locked so that no one can exit from the rear. As soon as we enter from the rear, we canvass the entire space behind the Chapel and eliminate anyone we find. When the priest who was relieved by Zevulun comes through we take him out and load him onto our wagon. One of us stays behind until Zevulun exits and locks the door. We mount the wagon and depart. Miriam will find her way to the village on her own."

"What about Nechemia?"

"We need him to set the Inquisition building on fire. It is important that the pattern stays the same," David answered.

"But the Inquisition building will surely be guarded," Zevulun said. "How will he handle it on his own?"

"When Miriam goes for Nechemia, she can also bring Anna with her. Anna can help Nechemia. The sentries would be delighted to receive a tasty drink in the early hours of the morning," David said.

"Where do we go after the operation?"

"We return straight to my house in the village," David said.

"And the dead priest?"

"Like before, we dispose of his body while on our way."

"This plan sounds practical, but we need to check the Cathedrals and some of the largest Churches to determine which one to use," Zevulun suggested.

"Each one of us investigates in another direction in the city. We convene here after dark and spend the night. Tomorrow we continue. Miriam can be on her way to my house in the village," David said.

"Very well," Reuven said, "let's begin. I suggest we leave one at a time. We'll meet here after dark."

CHAPTER THIRTY-FIVE

The Cathedral of Santa Maria la Blanca was packed with worshipers on Sunday, the eleventh of March, 1477, David estimated at least three hundred. Miriam, in a nun's habit and wimple, came out of the Chapel as soon as the prayers began. She gave the sentries metal containers and poured the cool drink. The sentries gulped the drinks and returned the containers. It took but a few minutes and both of them were on the floor. Miriam pulled them into the foyer and closed the front gate. In the pocket of one sentry she found the keys and locked the gate. The prayers were in high gear when she locked the door to the Chapel. She took off the nun's habit, stuffed it into her sack, and joined the praying crowd.

Zevulun got off the wagon first and entered through the rear door. Moments later, David, Reuven and Yossef also alighted and entered the building. One manservant and a housekeeper were found in the small kitchen next to the dining room and were knocked out. They came across no one in the offices or any of the other rooms. Zevulun opened the door to the Chapel and left it ajar.

"I'm surprised no sentries were posted at the rear of the building," David commented.

"The Crown is short of manpower;" Reuven said, "Remember, they're fighting the Moors in the south."

"I hope the Moors keep them busy until we're done with our work," David said.

"As far as I know, the Crown's forces are making progress."

Zevulun opened the rear door and rushed into the Chapel. David hid behind the door, and as soon as the pastor walked through, he shut the door and slammed him on the back of the head. The pastor collapsed without a word. Yossef and Reuven carried him out of the Cathedral and loaded his limp body on the wagon. David put the key to the door he'd retrieved from the kitchen into the lock and waited. Zevulun's voice carried his message loud and clear. Suddenly, David heard one man shout at Zevulun.

"You are a liar and a traitor! It's impossible that the Pope sent you." Zevulun voice mounted a higher tone, "Sit down and be quiet. Who are you to interrupt my sermon?" But the man did not quiet down. He kept on shouting and managed to get other people in the audience to support him. David was beside himself. He didn't know what to do. He looked through the open door. A number of men started to march toward the podium. Zevulun shouted and instructed them to return to their seats, but to no avail. David locked the door and calculated that the lack of egress would delay anything that might happen. Miriam, seeing what was going on, rushed to the side foyer door and locked it from inside. The sentries were still sleeping on the floor. She quickly opened the front gate, got out and locked it from the outside.

David ran to the wagon and told Reuven and Yossef what had happened. The three of them ran back in, and as they got close to the Chapel door, they heard a tremendous argument in progress. The door's handle was being tried over and over without success.

"What can we do?" David asked nervously.

"There isn't much we can do," Reuven said.

"Let's find priests' habits and put them on." Yossef ordered. "We'll open the door and rescue Zevulun. The crowd doesn't know who we are."

"Excellent idea," David said. They located priests' habits, put them on and opened the door. The sight they saw was not a pleasant one. Zevulun's habit had been torn off and two men held him tightly. Without hesitation, David shouted, "What is going on here?"

"This man is an imposter. His blasphemy is beyond words," one of the men responded.

"Who are you?" David beamed at Zevulun.

"I am Father Carlos Ramirez," Zevulun answered, "and I'm the Pope's emissary."

"Where is our pastor, the Reverend Jose Carreras?" a man asked.

"He was called urgently to His Eminence Tomas de Torquemada's office. He left the Cathedral a few minutes ago," David answered. "We'll take this man to the Inquisition. They will find out the truth."

"Who are you?" one of the men shouted.

"The three of us are training to be priests at the Theological Seminary. We came by to visit with Father Carreras," David said and grabbed Zevulun's arm. He quickly elbowed Yossef, who grabbed Zevulun's other arm, and both of them propelled him out the door. As soon as they left, David threw the door back and locked it. The men inside the Chapel were pounding on the door and screaming as David, Zevulun and Yossef left the Cathedral.

They mounted the wagon and left in a hurry.

"The front gate is locked," Miriam said to their surprise.
David turned his head. "I thought you were going to leave on your own."

"When I realized what was happening, I decided to lock all the doors, figuring you'd locked the rear one. With everyone locked inside the Chapel, our escape will be secure," she said.

"Excellent thinking." David whipped the horses to greater speed.

"How long before the Cathedral is freed?" Yossef asked.

"There's no telling. It could be minutes or hours. I want to thank you for rescuing me. I didn't know what to do except argue with them. Only four of them questioned me. The rest of the congregation sat still in their seats."

"It was bound to happen sooner or later. Thank God we managed to get you out safely. David has the mind of an eagle. He can come up with answers at an incredible speed."

"Do we leave the city or help Nechemia tonight?"

"We'd better leave. Once the Cathedral is opened, the authorities are bound to search for us. Nechemia and Anna will find a way to take care of their job. They have been forewarned about the sentries," Reuven said.

"The number of sentries posted at the Inquisition may be significantly beefed up after this episode," David said.

"I wouldn't worry too much about Nechemia. He's full of venom and he is a clever man."

"I hope so for Anna's sake," David said. By mid afternoon he drove the wagon off the dirt road into one of the many orchards dotting the landscape. Deep inside the orchard they dumped the pastor's body and covered it with leaves and dead branches. He continued to drive the wagon parallel to the road for a while and emerged when no other traffic was in sight. He kept driving his horses hard until darkness fell.

Nechemia and Anna arrived in Toledo on Thursday afternoon, the eighth of March, and checked into a local inn. Anna insisted on two separate rooms, which they received without any difficulties. They left the inn soon after and toured the Inquisition building area. As they approached the building they saw four sentries, two posted by the main entrance, one in the right alleyway, and one on the left. Nechemia decided to check the houses behind the building.

"Do you think the back might be the easiest way to penetrate?" Anna asked.

"I don't know yet," he said, "I hope so." They found three private homes in back of the Inquisition building. "Let's wait and see who lives here," Nechemia said. "If we're lucky, we'll be able to get across through one of these yards."

"I see trees in the back. Let's walk into the yard. Hopefully no one will accost us. And if somebody does, we can apologize and say we entered the wrong house by mistake," Anna said.

They walked into the yard belonging to the center house and found their way to the rear wall separating the properties. The wall was Anna's height. Nechemia hid behind a tree and looked in.

"There's one sentry in the back," he whispered, "He's seating on a chair."

"How will we get in?" Anna asked, "And don't forget, we'll be carrying containers filled with oil."

"The sentry will be quite sleepy when we get here in the early hours of the morning."

"I certainly hope so."

"Let's hire a coach before it gets too dark," Nechemia said. He held Anna's arm and they walked out into the street.

They stopped the first coach that passed and asked its driver to take them to the central market. Nechemia bought three containers filled with oil and loaded them onto the rear compartment. He instructed the driver to take them to a house he had seen near the road as they'd entered one of Toledo's gates. He knew it would be dark by the time they got there. That was exactly what he wanted. There was a long driveway in front of the house, and Nechemia instructed the driver to stop near a shed.

"Please help me unload the containers," he requested. The driver jumped promptly off the coach.

"Lift this one first." The driver never rose. Nechemia's knife sank into his back tearing the heart vessels apart. He pulled the man off the driveway and left his body behind a tree. He mounted the coach, and drove it out onto the dirt road and back to Toledo.

"Why did you have to kill him?"

"We cannot leave witnesses." They parked the coach near their inn and walked in. After a light meal, they went to their rooms. Nechemia made sure the innkeeper and the kitchen help knew they were retiring for the night.

It was well past midnight when Nechemia knocked gently on Anna's door.

"I've been ready all night," she said, "I didn't want to go to sleep." Making sure no one was in sight, they snuck out of the inn. The coach was precisely where they'd left and the horse was munching grain left for him on the ground. Nechemia drove the coach carefully around the Inquisition building and stopped in front of the center house in the back. They carried the three containers of oil to the wall in silence. Nechemia looked over the wall. The sentry was sound asleep. He went to the end of the wall and jumped over. Step by step, as slowly as possible, he advanced towards the sentry whose snores were audible. Holding his knife at the ready, he advanced noiselessly. The sentry never knew what killed him. Nechemia's knife slit his throat with one stroke. Anna lifted the containers and passed them to Nechemia, who instructed her to stay behind the wall. To his surprise, he found the back door unlocked. He walked in and dispensed the oil in three different locations. After setting the fire, he jumped over the wall, and off they went in their coach, which he abandoned about an hour's walk from the inn. Dawn was breaking as they returned to their rooms. The skies were red when they looked out their windows. The building was on fire.

After an early breakfast, Nechemia ordered a coach to drive them to the marketplace. He bought various items and provisions and instructed the driver to take them to the coach terminal. An hour later they joined four passengers on a coach headed for Segovia.

CHAPTER THIRTY-SIX

"Your Eminence, Your Eminence," the young novice priest shouted as he entered Torquemada's house, "The Inquisition building is on fire." Torquemada jumped out of bed.

"Did the sentries catch the perpetrators?" he asked.

"I don't know, Your Eminence," he replied, "I was told to call you. Fortunately, one of the priests was awakened by the smell and heat and woke up the others on our floor. He told me to call you." Torquemada got dressed and followed the young man to the Inquisition building. By the time he got there, the entire building was in flames. It looked as though the flames reached heaven. The sky above was red. A number of priests were standing outside, some of them in nightgowns, watching the fire.

"I shall kill with my own hands the man who set this fire," Torquemada screamed. "Where are the sentries?"

"I'm right here, Your Eminence," the sentry in charge responded.

"Did your men see who set fire to the building?"

"No, Your Eminence, I questioned every one of my men. They didn't see a soul. One of our sentries is missing. I don't know where he is. I'm sure we'll soon find out," he answered.

"Where was the missing man's post?"

"He was guarding the rear door," the man responded. "If you ask me, I'd say the fire started from within the building."

"I'm not asking you," Torquemada snapped.

"You may think what you wish, Your Eminence," the man said, "but I can vouch for my men. They are alert and trustworthy. When they said they saw no one, I believe them."

"Let me know when you find your missing man," Torquemada said, and walked away. He called the priests and students who were standing outside.

"Any of you know what happened at the Cathedral of Santa Maria la Blanca yesterday?"

"I heard the parishioners got locked in the Chapel for hours before they were rescued," one of the seminary students said. "I was told an unknown priest took over from the regular one at the sermon and declared he was the Pope's emissary. He went on to denounce our policies and beliefs, at which point some men in the audience began to question him. An argument followed, and three parishioners tried to detain him. The rear door opened and some other priests walked in, saying they would bring this priest to the Inquisition building. They grabbed him, dragged him out and locked the door behind them. When the parishioners tried to leave through the main gate, they found it locked, too."

"What did the sentries do while all this was going on?" Torquemada asked.

"The sentries were found sleeping on the floor in the foyer."

"Something is seriously wrong," Torquemada shouted, "but I can't put my finger on it. I want those sentries brought before me immediately. Go find them."

"I haven't the faintest idea how to locate them," the student said.

"Check with the guard in charge at the Queen's palace. Go immediately and tell him I sent you. Also, tell him I want to see him right away," Torquemada was still shouting. "Was everyone saved from the fire?"

"We don't know."

"I was quite lucky to have gone home last night. On many occasions I sleep in the Inquisition building. The Lord has spared my life for a reason. He wants me to continue with my work," Torquemada said.

"Your Eminence is right. The Lord certainly wishes you to continue," one of the young men said.

"Do any of you know how many of our clergy were in the building last night?" No one knew. Torquemada began to pace. He was worried; the number of unexplained events was mounting, and he didn't have a single clue. He was particularly bothered by the letters, which carried authentic seals, yet their writers vehemently denied having written them. Why did three Cardinals, men appointed by the Pope, commit suicide on the same night? Who was the priest who had delivered sermons denouncing his work? And where were the pastors who vanished at the same time? *I need to acquire a new building -- my office was completely destroyed,* he said to himself. *"I have to see Queen Isabella."*

CHAPTER THIRTY-SEVEN

Nechemia and Anna arrived in Segovia and headed directly to the Inquisition building. The building was located at the end of a large plaza, which at one time had served as a flower market. There were two fountains in the center of the plaza, a number of old oak trees in-between them. They sat on one of the benches facing the building.

"This is such a beautiful building," Anna said, "It would be a shame to burn it."

"Burn it we will," Nechemia said emphatically. "If beauty had anything to do with it, they wouldn't be torturing people to death in it."

"I didn't mean we shouldn't set it on fire," Anna said, "I just meant that it was a shame."

"There are two sentries in front of the main entrance. I would think the building is guarded day and night just like the one in Toledo," Nechemia said.

"Let's check the back," Anna said.

"I don't think the back of the building is as accessible as the one in Toledo," Nechemia said. "I can see from here that the wall around the building is much higher, and it looks as though the building behind the wall abuts with the building up front."

"If that's the case, we'll have to use the front entrance."

"How do you propose to do that?" he questioned.

"I'll approach the sentries and play up to them. I'll take the first one ripe for action to the side of the house. The sentry remaining by the entrance will most certainly keep looking at the two of us as we walk away and disappear into the alley. That's when you come from the other side and take him out. I'll keep the sentry occupied while you pour the oil and set the fire. And after you've done that, you come to my rescue. It shouldn't be difficult -- I'll have his pants down," Anna said.

"This is too much of a risk. I'd like to think of another alternative."

"You don't have one short of attacking both of them from the front."

"You just gave me an idea," Nechemia said. "Listen to this. We buy or rent a coach and park it a few blocks from the building. When we're ready, you drive the coach and stop in front of the entrance. You call the sentries. I'll be hiding in the rear luggage compartment. As the sentries approach the coach, I lunge from the back and stab the one to your left, and you stab the one to your right. They'll be taken by surprise and we'll be rid of them in no time."

"I have a better and safer idea. Let's use the same technique Miriam used in Toledo. We mix a strong sleeping potion into a hot drink. I'll deliver it with the Bishop's compliments. Within minutes they'll be sound asleep on the floor."

"You're right, this is far safer and actually quite easy. Let's do it that way," Nechemia said.

They walked back to the terminal and hired a one-horse coach. The oil and the potion were purchased and the drinks prepared. They drove the coach toward the plaza, parked in one of the side streets, and waited.

It was past midnight when Anna drove the coach slowly towards the Inquisition building. Nechemia walked alongside the buildings and stopped a block away. He watched the coach carefully as it stopped in front of the building.

"Officers," Anna called, "the Bishop instructed me to deliver hot drinks after midnight. Please come and get it." The sentries accepted the drinks with pleasure. Anna drove off, circled the buildings, and joined Nechemia. By the time she arrived, Nechemia reported that the two sentries were sitting on the floor. They drove to the front of the building. Nechemia unloaded the oil containers and walked in. Anna remained in the driver's seat watching. He came out a few minutes later, mounted the coach and off they went. They stopped on the other side of the plaza and watched the flames as they intensified. The coach was returned to its stables early in the morning, and they left Segovia with the first coach for Toledo.

CHAPTER THIRTY-EIGHT

"Your Eminence, this letter was delivered last night," the Chief of the Guards said. Torquemada took the letter and opened it. It read;

"Your Eminence,
Tomas de Torquemada,
Chief Inquisitor

We wrote this letter because we want to take you out of your misery. You must be wondering about the recent occurrences, the suicides, deaths and fires in your organization. You know that this situation cannot continue because the forces of Christianity are working against you. You, Tomas de Torquemada, have behaved like a butcher. Jesus Christ our Lord, must be turning in his grave not knowing how to stop your madness. Jesus taught us love, mercy, forgiveness and charity, while you are teaching us hate, torture and murder, and you are using his name to do all these atrocities.

You, Your Eminence, are a beast. We do not want you as part of the Catholic Organization. You are putting us to shame. You will make us remembered as the butchers of history. The only reason we are not killing you is that we do not wish to treat you the way you treat others. However, if you do not change your character and persist in your ill-mannered blasphemy of Christ, we shall kill you in the same way you killed others, by Auto-de-Fe.

Take this as a warning.

The True Catholic Movement

"Who brought this letter? I must catch the person who delivered it," Torquemada blasted.

"I'm sorry, Your Eminence, this letter, addressed to you, was found on the floor at the main entrance to my office. No one saw who delivered it," the Chief of the Guards said.

"I want you to instruct your men to be on full alert at all times. You had guards at the Cathedrals and Churches as well as at our various houses of Inquisition, yet the enemies of Christ fooled them. I will have to report your failures to the Queen. I don't believe she will like to hear of it," Torquemada said.

"I'm afraid it's not all that simple. Our best men are fighting the Moors in the south. We had no alternative but keep the recruits that are unfit for battle in the cities. The Queen is fully aware of our predicament."

"I told the Queen and I shall tell you as well, the work for Christ has today and always will have priority over anything else. Nothing in the world is more important and vital than the purification of our Catholic society. There is nothing more valuable than to live for Christ, and the only way mortals like us can achieve it and find ourselves in heaven with our Lord is to cleanse our society from all the elements of evil. The Jews, the Muslims, and even the Conversos are of bad blood, which poisons our devout Catholic citizens. The battle against the evil and blasphemy must and will take priority over anything else." Torquemada walked away.

"I'm ready for your confession," Torquemada said to Queen Isabella as she walked into her private chapel.

"Before we begin," the Queen said, "you should read this letter addressed to me. It arrived yesterday."

The Most Honorable Majesty
Queen Isabella of Castile,

Being the oldest of all Bishops in Castile and Aragon, I've been approached by a number of clergy demanding that the Inquisition be dismantled and that the beastly behavior against Jews, Conversos and Marranos stop.

The practices used by the Inquisition defame our Lord and Savior, Jesus Christ. It is inconceivable that men of the cloth torture fellow human beings. It is inconceivable that men of the cloth tell people lies and incite mobs against various minorities. Don't forget, Your Majesty, mobs can also turn against the Crown.

I plead with you, put a stop to Torquemada's madness. Any human being can be a devout Catholic. The degree of devoutness is up to our Lord to judge and not any human being on earth. Who said Torquemada is the most devout Catholic in the world? And who made him the judge of all people?

Even if he was appointed, who gave him the right to abuse others in the name of our Lord? The truth of the matter is that he is defaming our Lord. How do you expect any Converso to accept Jesus if the example set is one of torture, harassment, vandalization, and discrimination? What are those people to think of Catholics?

All the people we want to convert have been taught in their religion to love one another, be merciful, forgiving, and charitable to the poor. What do we show them? The force of deceit, of lies, of torture, and hate!

Your Majesty, the man you confess your sins to is an imposter, for he cannot be pure at heart. He isn't a loving Christian and definitely not a lover of Christ. Bring his rein to an end for the sake of Catholicism and humanity.

Regretfully, I must bring one additional matter to your attention. Look at the number of clergy that have died in recent months, some by suicide, others murdered. I feel confident that Torquemada eliminates anyone who stands in his way or anyone he believes is not as devout as he. You must admit that he is mad. Why don't you ask him if he killed any of the clergy?

Your Obedient Servant
Bishop Emanuel de Armand
Bilbao

Torquemada's face turned red with anger and he screamed, "I'm mad, am I? I, the only man in Aragon and Castile who is a true believer in Jesus and the only man who wants to purify the blood of our Catholic society is blasphemous to the Church? This accusation is madness. Do you believe for one moment that I set fire to my own buildings?"

"I don't know what to think!" the Queen said. "All I know is that suddenly I'm in the middle of a religious war, a war I don't want to fight. I must admit that I, too, have doubts in my heart about the methods of the Inquisition. I have told you that in the past."

"You will burn in hell if you continue to talk like this." Torquemada raised his voice. "I shall not be able to help you. Remember, the Pope appointed me General Inquisitor. The Pope knows my value to the Catholic Church. The Pope also passed unto you the authority over all Catholic affairs in this country; why don't you make the decision?"

"I'm afraid. I don't sleep nights. I see visions of hell and of fire. I am lost. My soul is lost." Queen Isabella held back her tears.

"I'm the only priest you ever had who soothed your heart and soul. Confess your sins to me and our Lord will save you from the fires of hell," Torquemada said.

"Is it true that you killed your own clergy?" she asked.

"I only had one man killed," Torquemada said, "Archbishop Alfonso Carrillo de Acura, because he was blasphemous in front of dozens of priests I had called to a meeting."

Queen Isabella confessed for hours. Her fear of hell was overwhelming. On his way from the palace, Torquemada stopped at the office of Chief of Guards, "The Queen wishes you to bring to the palace Bishop Emanuel de Armand from Bilbao. Send a coach immediately, and send for me when he arrives."

CHAPTER THIRTY-NINE

David's house was full. Reuven, Zevulun, Devorah, Miriam, Rachel, Nechemia, Yossef, Elisheva, Itzhak, Yael, and, of course, Anna were all there.

"I wish I could see Torquemada's face when he received the last letter," Itzhak said. "I'm sure he was called to the Queen when she received hers."

"The confusion we set out to create has become reality. It hit Torquemada hard. I think the priests themselves are worried about the deaths, disappearances, and fires that have hit in every city around the country," Reuven said.

"Don't forget the people who heard Zevulun's sermon. They're bound to be confused, too," Miriam said.

"The question is, what are our next steps?" Yael asked.

"I think we should attack individual priests everywhere. Let's scare them out of their wits," David said.

"How?" Yossef asked.

"There are a number of ways. We could post letters to their homes telling them the consequences of hell for priests. We can keep eliminating them one by one," David replied.

"We should publicize The True Catholic Movement in the streets. If we succeed in doing that, Torquemada's battle for purification of Catholic society will run into endless trouble. I feel certain that many Catholics are not aware of the behavior of the Inquisition against others and would not condone brutal behavior," Zevulun said.

"I doubt you'll find many Catholics who believe otherwise. I think the Church managed to poison their minds a long time ago," Elisheva said.

"All of you are trying to be too nice to your enemy," Nechemia said. "I agree with David. We should eliminate the priests one by one all over the country. It's bound to create a revolution from within."

"I agree. However, I would start with the priests who work in the Inquisition and later follow those who just spread the word through deceitful sermons," Reuven said.

"Is it decided then that we pursue this route?" David asked.

"Let's pursue it on three fronts," Itzhak suggested. "First, elimination of priests working for the Inquisition. Second, letter posting, which we'll post in public places, and third, letters to priests serving various Churches."

"I would like to suggest that the names of the priests working for the Inquisition be publicized upon their death and that the priests who work in the various churches be kidnapped and disappear. This will truly create panic among the clergy and will drive Torquemada out of his mind," Elisheva said.

"Why not kill Torquemada?" Rachel asked.

"It may be too soon," Reuven said. "I'm sure the day will come when we burn him to death. Meanwhile we should continue to harass him with letters. The constant stream of deaths of his men and the disappearance of priests will certainly affect him."

"It may also affect the recruitment of men for the priesthood," David said.

"Speaking of burning Torquemada at the stake, I would suggest leaving this decision open. If we do our job correctly, the Catholics themselves will burn him to death. We should continue our work covertly, placing the blame on a Catholic organization. The more dispute develops within the Catholic hierarchy, the more successful we will become," Reuven said.

"This discussion is extremely fruitful," Zevulun said. "I'm also coming to the conclusion that we should sway public opinion and reduce Torquemada's ability to recruit new members. It's the Queen I'm worried about. I have a feeling Torquemada controls her soul."

"Then she should be bombarded with letters, and perhaps we should also write to King Ferdinand, trying to create a new source of conflict," Rachel suggested.

"I agree," Itzhak said, "I'll prepare letters to the Queen and King."

"Should we continue with Zevulun's sermons in other towns and villages?" Miriam asked.

"The villages are of no consequence. The cities have more enlightened people. It's time we find real priests who disagree with Torquemada."

"Excellent thought," David said. "If real priests change their approach, stop inciting the masses and start telling the truth, we'll develop allies within the Catholic system."

"We agree that we need to sway public opinion and that we continue to harass the Crown. Since the Pope gave the ultimate authority to the Crown over all religious matters, it's imperative that we soften them up. At the same time we have to locate priests who will help us. I therefore suggest that Zevulun and I immediately start to look for such priests in major cities. The two of us are the most experienced with religious matters in this group. Others, like David, Nechemia and Yossef should continue to harass priests who work in the Inquisition by whatever method they want. Also, Torquemada is bound to build or requisition buildings to replace those that have burned down. Disrupting that effort should also pay off." Reuven said.

"I suggest that our farms be cultivated and developed to set an example," Nechemia suddenly interjected.

"I'd like to concentrate on Toledo since it's the seat of the Crown and government of Castile," David said. "It is also Torquemada's headquarters. The more we annoy him, the better."

"Excellent thought," Reuven said, "I'll join you. The two of us can operate as monks."

Airing of thoughts and ideas developed a plan of action, which was about to be implemented.

CHAPTER FORTY

28TH of March 1477

Her Supreme Majesty
Queen Isabella of Castile,
Have you asked yourself who is God? Have you asked yourself why all religions put the fear of God into our hearts? If we are taught to love each other, to be forgiving and be charitable, why is it that we're not willing to love and forgive those among us of different faiths? Do any of the scriptures tell us to be cruel to strangers? Who is to say that we are the best? Who is to tell us that we are right and all the others are wrong? Can man declare himself God and state that he knows best? More than God?

Your Majesty, have you thought about these things? What is heaven and what is hell? Who defined what heaven is and what hell is? If we are to forgive others for their sins, should they be sent to hell? Are any of us free from sin?

A scholar once said that to err is human, but to forgive is divine. Aren't all humans on this earth alike, made in the image of God?

Based on Torquemada's theories, a man has committed a sin by simply being of another faith. Let me ask you; are the Protestants in the north not considered Christians? According to Torquemada they have no right to exist on this earth. Do you agree? The Jews have been on earth for nearly three thousand years. Their only sin is that they wish to remain Jews. They lived on this earth long before Christ was born. In fact, the Jewish religion was the only one that believed in God and not a statue or other hand-made item which the ignorant people of the world worshiped. Isn't it the Jews who brought us Jesus? Were the Jews who lived in Jesus' time sinners?

It seems to us, the writers of this letter, that it's high time we stop the mad and brutal behavior of the Church. It seems to us that every man should be let alone to live his life as he chooses. The Jews and the Muslims around us have been good citizens, hard working people who always paid their taxes to the Crown like anyone else. In what way do they contaminate Catholic blood? The Jews are educated people because their race places great importance on literacy. Can we Catholics claim the same? What are we doing to educate our people?   Absolutely nothing.   It seems we thrive on keeping our masses poor and ignorant.

Your Majesty, we are not trying here to defend the Jews.   We are trying to better our own ways, which have reached the rock bottom of decency. The writers of this letter, who unfortunately have to remain anonymous, plead with you to view life in an enlightened way.   You don't get sent to hell just because you are not a Catholic, nor are you sent there for treating other human beings with decency.

If you want to convert others to Catholicism, let our Church demonstrate that we are better people, better human beings, caring human beings, and that Jesus Christ is the true redeemer.

Finally, you may wonder why we do not publish our names.   The reason is that Torquemada kills anyone who disagrees with him.   Archbishop Carrillo disagreed with him during a conference and that same night the Archbishop was murdered.   In fact, Torquemada threatened his audience, quite severely, before that conference came to a conclusion.

It is our opinion that if Torquemada was not an ordained priest, but an ordinary citizen working for the Crown, you would not tolerate his attitude and superiority complex.

Your Obedient Servants,
The True Catholic Movement

28th of March 1477

Your Supreme Majesty
Ferdinand King of Aragon,
The attached letter was sent to your wife, Queen Isabella of Castile. The letter speaks for itself. Our main reason in addressing her is that Tomas de Torquemada resides and works out of Toledo.

In this letter we raise many issues, however, our main concern is restoring civility to our Church. The torture, the killings, the vandalization of property, hate, and discrimination must be abolished. We have to return our people to decency.

Torquemada talks of purifying Catholic blood from all elements of impurity. It cannot happen while we engage in burning people to death, by building hate and destroying people's lives. As long as the Church does those things, it is the Church which is the sinner, because it negates everything it teaches.

We urge you to discuss these matters in great detail with Queen Isabella. If there is hell somewhere below us, we are afraid that you will end up there precisely because you did not take steps to stop the madness.

Your Obedient Servants,
The True Catholic Movement

CHAPTER FORTY-ONE

"These letters bring up many questions we must discuss," King Ferdinand stated. They were sitting in their music room listening to two entertainers playing ancient guitars.

"I didn't know you received a letter from the True Catholic Movement, too," Queen Isabella responded. "Do you have any idea who is behind it?"

"This is the first time I've heard of it. It's the contents I'm worried about."

"I'm scared to death. Torquemada has been my confessor and counselor for many years. The Pope appointed him the Inquisitor General. Who am I to believe, Torquemada or a bunch of priests I've never heard of?"

"I can well understand their concerns," the King said. "Torquemada has no human blood in his veins. He feels far too superior in matters of Church, and I'm convinced no one can create a pure society. The world began with Abel and Cain. The Bible is full of war and killing stories. History also demonstrates man as a stubborn and stiff-necked person. Change can be achieved by reasoning and proof, not by violence. Man looks at violence as a challenge for new violence."

"What are we to do?" the Queen asked.

"It's not a simple matter. We've been brought up to be good Catholics," the King said.

"No one is asking us to be bad Catholics. On the contrary, unknown priests tell us that the behavior of the Church is inhuman and contradictory to its teachings. The trouble is, I don't know whom to believe. Torquemada tells me that I'll end in hell for merely thinking about changing anything. I don't want to burn in hell," she shivered.

"My dear, you will never end in hell. You are the most thoughtful and generous person I know. You rule your people well," the King said.

"According to the letter, I'm not doing my job right if I continue to allow the torture, killings and other atrocities in the name of religion. How can I not think about these matters? After all, I am the Queen of Castile. It is my duty to think, but Torquemada doesn't permit it."

"May be you should consider changing your confessor," the King suggested.

"I'm afraid."

"This is the problem. Too many people are afraid of Torquemada. He rules with an iron fist and puts the fear of hell in everyone's heart. Perhaps we should consider removing him," the King said.

"Torquemada says there isn't a thing on earth that matters except being a pure Catholic. How can you be a pure Catholic if you spread disaster on others? I think I'm beginning to answer my own questions and those of the unknown priests."

"How do you know they are priests?" They could be a bunch of clever Jews or Conversos."

"Anything is possible. However, they've written words of wisdom, and we must decide what to do."

"The truth is I'm afraid to. Who are we to judge Torquemada, even if we don't share his opinion?"

"Will it sound wild if I suggest we discuss this entire issue with one of the Chief Rabbis in this country?" she asked.

"I believe you'll create an everlasting enemy in the man you call your confessor."

"If you read the Bible as closely as I have, you'll agree that God gave preference to kings. We are King and Queen, therefore we have the ultimate right to behave like supreme rulers."

"But you said you are afraid of Torquemada...."

"I am. In fact, I've been sleeping very poorly lately because of his pronouncements and threats. I don't want to burn in hell. We need to find a solution to this problem. In reality the problem has many faces. Further complicating matters is the fact that the Pope gave us, the rulers of Aragon and Castile, the power to make religious decisions based on doctrines of the Catholic Church. We therefore need to decide which doctrine to pursue -- Torquemada's, the violent approach, or the humane one of charity, compassion, and forgiveness."

Since the Pope appointed Torquemada as the Inquisitor General, who is he accountable to?" the King queried.

"The problem you just outlined is my dilemma. Who do I believe and trust? Torquemada tells me he is the ultimate authority on Catholicism. Am I to accept his word for it when so many priests seem to disagree? All the letters I, and members of the cloth have been receiving point to unrest within the Church, and also demonstrate that they are afraid of him. He is a killer, there is no doubt about it," the Queen declared.

"Then what do we do?"

"We get Torquemada in here and discuss these issues face to face."

"I've heard that tonight there's an Auto-de-Fe taking place in the Plaza Mayor. Have you ever watched one?" the King asked.

"No, I haven't. Have you?"

"Me neither. I think we should take a look," he suggested.

"If we go there officially we'll be swamped with people and it will legitimize the entire affair. I'm not sure we ought to do that," the Queen said.

"Perhaps we should go in disguise," the King suggested.

"Let's do that. I'm very curious and would like to watch the process," Isabella said.

"What do you propose to wear?" he asked.

"You wear the habit of a priest and I of a monk. The hood will hide my blond hair and most of my face," she said.

"That's fine. I'll send word to Torquemada and request he visit us tomorrow morning."

CHAPTER FORTY-TWO

"Have you noticed the crowds heading towards Plaza Mayor?" David asked.

"It's usually the sign of some major event," Reuven said. "Let's follow the crowd."

"Look, there's a priest and a monk walking in front of us. Let's engage them in conversation," David said.

They walked a little faster, but the crowd thickened and slowed them down. By the time they caught up with the priest and the monk, the crowd had stopped moving. Suddenly the priest began to push people aside and made his way to the front line. The monk followed.

"Let's stick to them." David pulled Reuven by his hand.

They were soon behind the priest and the monk. The crowd was roaring. David craned his neck. What he saw in front of him made him go rigid. A huge Auto-de-Fe was being prepared. A large freight wagon was unloaded of its kiln and lumber. Two priests piled the wood up around a large platform. The noise kept growing. When the wood was in place, one of the priests gave a signal; eight men and women were marched to the platform and were tied to the center mast. The crowd grew wilder by the minute. The screams and shouts, the cursing and the joy gripped everyone. All the priests but one moved back and formed a loose circle around the platform. The priest who was left behind lifted a container and poured liquid on the wood. When he completed the entire circle, he lit the kiln, and as if lightning had struck, flames leaped up. The five men and three women tied to the center mast screamed as the fire began to roast their bodies. The crowd was yelling with joy. "Burn to hell! Burn to hell!"

David and Reuven were struck by the shock of the fire and the screams, which overpowered the noise of the chanting crowd. David began to relive his own horror of events. Suddenly the monk in front of him fell to the ground. Without thinking, David bent down to help the monk up, and to his amazement, as he lifted the limp body the hood fell off and the face of a beautiful blond woman was revealed. The priest who stood next to the monk was so absorbed in the sight in front of him that he hadn't noticed the monk's fall.

David motioned to Reuven, covered the blond's head with the hood, and both of them carried her to the rear.

"Why is this woman masquerading as a monk?" Reuven asked.

"I don't know. Something peculiar is going on here. We must find out," David said.

"Who are you?" he asked the blond, slapping her face gently. "We have to bring her out of her faint. Go find some water."

Reuven went off and returned with a small container of water borrowed from a bystander. He poured water over her face and signs of life returned.

"Where is the King?" the woman asked, semi conscious. David looked at Reuven. "Could this be Queen Isabella? She looks familiar."

"Then the priest she was walking with must be King Ferdinand," he said.

"You are Queen Isabella. Why are you masquerading as a monk?"

"Please take me out of here right away. If I stay here another moment, I shall die," she spoke in a low voice.

"What about the King?" David asked.

"Send your friend and tell him I have gone to the palace. That is if he can be found," the Queen said.

David grasped her arm and propelled her away from the plaza. "I can't walk this fast. I'm out of breath. Let's sit here for a moment. I need to rest."

She sat down on the edge of a small stone-fence and looked at David.

"What were you doing here tonight? You're so young."

"My friend and I are visiting Toledo. We come from the Monastery of San Cristobal near Barcelona. Why are you masquerading as a monk?" David found his voice.

"I wanted to see what the Auto-de-Fe is about. I've never witnessed it before. Now that I have seen it, I am appalled by it," she said. "Please accompany me to the palace. I am frightened. The vision of the fire and the screams from hell made me faint. Please hold my arm…. I feel faint again."

"Don't be afraid, I'll take you home."

"Where is the King?"

"At this moment I don't know. I sent my fellow monk to look for him. When you fainted, there was a priest standing next to you, but he didn't notice your fall. We didn't want to disturb his concentration. We knew how important the Auto-de-Fe is," David lied. "How come you and the King had to disguise yourselves? If you had come in your official carriage, you would have lent this event much credibility."

"You are too young to understand," she blurted. "I need to sit down again. I'm very tired."

David and the Queen, looking like two monks, sat down on an old broken stone wall. The Queen was extremely uneasy. David felt her pain through holding her arm.

"Why are you shivering? Was the scene of the burning sinners too much for you?"

"It was the picture Torquemada conjured of hell. He keeps telling me all those who are not pure Catholics at heart will end up burning in hell. I'm afraid of hell."

"There's no reason for you to fear hell," David pronounced firmly. "I believe that Torquemada himself will end up in hell."

"You, a monk, believe that?" she asked astonishingly.

"You see, Your Majesty, the two of us are in disguise also. I'm not a monk. I watched my parents burn to death just like the event you were watching a little earlier. My parents were good people, honest, hardworking, charitable, and decent citizens of Castile. Their only crime was that they were Jews. Torquemada believes he can abolish Judaism for the sake of purifying all Catholics, but he is wrong. You punish people for crimes against society and not for being religious. Belonging to another faith, or simply being of a different opinion than Torquemada is not a crime or sin. The Jewish people came to earth over two thousand five hundred years ago, and they will be around long after Torquemada is gone." David made a stand.

"You must hate me," Queen Isabella said.

"No, Your Majesty, you are wrong. I do not hate you at all. All of this and what is happening in our country is the result of one fanatic person," David said. "You are still shivering."

"Because I saw the picture Torquemada drew – burning in the fires of hell."

"God has always provided for kings and queens. As a devout Catholic, I assume you are well versed in the Bible. You have many privileges as queen. No God in heaven would send you to hell for doing what you believe is right. God is a God of mercy, a God of love, and a God of peace. It is people who abuse his command and take his words to extremes, thinking that He wants them to. They operate in his name. Think about this for a moment. If God created man in his image, as the Bible says, why would he want to destroy it? Is the image of God an image of hate, torture, or murder?" David asked.

"You seem to be a very wise young man," the Queen said, "How old are you?"

"I'm fifteen years old, Your Majesty," David replied. "You stopped shivering."

"I feel much better listening to you," she declared. "I'd like you to live in the palace. I need to balance my religious environment. Would you do that for me?"

"I'm honored, Your Majesty, but I am a Jew, and I don't believe your Catholic friends will like this idea," David said.

"I'll be the only one who knows you are a Jew," she announced, "not even the king. I'll provide you with room and board and you may go and come as you please. When I need you, I'll send for you. Do you agree?"

"On condition that I keep my disguise as a monk and your solemn promise not to report my faith to any one," David said.

"You have my word of honor," the Queen said.

"What if Torquemada hears about me?" David asked.

"I'll tell him you are my personal guest. However, I'll always let you know when he comes to the palace. Remember, I see him every Friday morning for my confession," she said.

"Are you going to confess about meeting me at the Auto-de-Fe? David asked.

"I won't tell him a word about you. You are going to be my young balancing monk from now on," she said, getting up. "Let's get going. I feel much better now."

As they approached the side entrance to the palace they spotted the King and Reuven. King Ferdinand was very happy to see Isabella.

"I was worried about you. I had no idea what happened to you. This young monk told me that you fainted and were escorted to the palace. Thank you very much for attending to my wife. How can I repay you?"

"There is no need to repay me. Your wife invited me to live in the palace for a while. I'll spend my time wisely in your private chapel," David said. He really meant for Reuven to get the message.

"Tell our Prior that the Queen has asked me to spend some time in the palace." Reuven was shocked but recovered quickly.

"I surely will," he said. "Will I be able to see you?"

"Of course, any time," the Queen said.

Reuven bid them farewell and left. The King opened a hidden side door and led the way into a garden which led to their private rooms. The Queen called one of her maids and instructed her to arrange a room for the Monk.

CHAPTER FORTY-THREE

T orquemada was fuming. He held a letter which had been delivered late at night. No one saw the messenger and no one could say for sure where it came from. He sat down on the wooden chair and read it again.

Your Eminence
Inquisitor General
Tomas de Torquemada
Toledo, Castile.

> *It pains us to watch our brethren die. The men who decided to devote their lives to Jesus have lost their souls as well as their true mission in life. What is it that drives you? We keep wondering. What is it you think you will accomplish in your lifetime? In complete truth, we pity your soul. Your beliefs are misguided. Why do you believe you can eradicate a race of Jews, Conversos and Marranos? Even if you had the largest army in the world, you couldn't reach such a goal.*

> *In case you didn't realize, Castile and Aragon are not the only kingdoms on earth that harbor minorities. You can find them all over Europe, the Middle East and Africa. In fact, your misguided beliefs would turn every one of the people you seek to eliminate into a bigger enemy of yours. But what sorrows us more than anything else is your turning young men who want to seek our Lord, devote their lives to Him, and become priests, into murderers. How can you face this reality? How can you see your way through life making men of God behave like hardened criminals?*

> *There is obviously something critically wrong with your character, just as there is something crucially wrong with the way you believe in Christ.*

> *By the way, who is your confessor? Do you have one? We don't think so. The fact is, you do not have a confessor. The fact is that you consider yourself above every one else in the Catholic hierarchy. We strongly suspect that in your heart you feel you are superior to the Pope. Tomas de Torquemada, you are a sick man, and don't forget, a mortal one.*

> *If we were Christ, sitting in our heavenly chair by the pearly gates, when you arrived, we would probably want to tear your body apart piece by piece for your deeds on earth. But we are good Christians. We've been*

taught to love and forgive; therefore, we would have you repent for all the crimes you've committed.

We suggest that you start reading the Bible again, the Old Testament and the New Testament. Read it with love and caring in your heart, not with vengeance and a doomed mission which no one asked you to undertake. As hard as we want to believe the possibility, we feel you are mentally unable to change because there is no love in your heart. You are an evil man and unless you can change and demonstrate the will to work for the betterment of mankind, the day will come when we burn you at the stake.

Finally, we do not believe that you are the authority on heaven or hell. You disgrace both.

The True Catholic Movement

"I must find out who's behind this movement," Torquemada thought. *"I'll eliminate them one by one. Who do they think they are? I am the man who will be remembered as the savior and the purifier of Catholic blood."*

He rose from his chair and called two of his assistants. "Do you believe in Jesus Christ?" he yelled.

"Of course, Your Eminence, why such a question? We have devoted our lives to Christ."

"I want to recruit as many young men as possible to the priesthood. We are short on manpower. We must continue our effort to cleanse and purify all Catholics from the evils of the Jews and the Moors. It is our Godly duty. Death is not what we're fearing. Death brings us closer to Christ. After death we live with him. Are you afraid to die for Christ as he died for you?" Torquemada blasted.

"Oh! No! Your Eminence, our lives and the life of Christ are one. As far as we are concerned Christ is alive."

"Take some young men working or studying in our seminary and travel to all the cities around us to recruit people to work and fight with us in the name of Jesus," Torquemada said.

Torquemada's assistants left and he strolled to the building being converted into his new Inquisition home in Toledo. He observed the work and was pleased. He returned to his temporary housing, which had a large basement that was used as his torture chamber. His small army of priests was interrogating Conversos suspected of practicing Judaism in secret.

CHAPTER FORTY-FOUR

Zevulun took to the road accompanied by Nechemia and Rachel. They traveled from city to city and village to village throughout Castile and Aragon. Stops were made at every Church and Cathedral they passed. Zevulun introduced himself as Father Carlos Ramirez, escaped from Cordova. He had managed to develop a convincing routine. Nechemia and Rachel waited in the wagon for his return.

"I'm Father Carlos Ramirez of Cordova," he introduced himself. "I recently escaped from the Moors and somehow managed to get to Rome. The Pope was very anxious to learn about the difficulties of the Church under the Moors and granted me a long audience. During the course of our conversation, the Pope revealed he was unsure about the role the Inquisition was playing in Castile and Aragon. He asked me to interview priests, such as you, in various parts of the country. He wants to know how you feel about the functions and methods of the Inquisition."

His introductory remarks always opened the door to a free discussion, which in due course Zevulun turned into a message of hope.

"What is it you'd like to know?" the priest responded.

"As you surely are aware, we are in the process of converting the heathen to Catholicism. The heathen have no religion, have no God, and believe in nothing. In order that we may convert these people, we try to fulfill their lives with a Godly message. We tell them about Christ, we tell them about God and we preach the values of good Christian living. The work of conversion is simple and straightforward. However, when it comes to people whose religion is Jewish or Muslim, we have to deal with educated men and women. The conversion work is more complex and difficult, for these people have had their religions for centuries before Christ. The question the Pope is mostly concerned with is whether Jews and Muslims have to be forced to convert. The Pope feels that very little, if anything, is accomplished by force. Religion is a matter of spirituality and deep beliefs nurtured by customs and old habits. Generation after generation is born into each of the existing religions. To switch from one to another is a matter of education, not force. What is your opinion?"

"I really haven't thought about it at all," the priest said. "I take orders from the Bishop in this area and carry out my work without the slightest of doubt. I was taught to accept instructions from above without question."

"The Pope fully understands that. In fact, it has always been the policy and spiritual belief of the Catholic Church to accept the gospel as presented and without question. However, the Pope feels the Catholic Church has reached a fork in the road to conversion, a fork which His Holiness considers a matter of grave importance. Hence, his desire for feelings and opinions of the priesthood."

"I'm having a very hard time in creating an opinion. I'm merely a servant of the Lord. My knowledge is insignificant. My Bishop and Archbishop are the final authorities as far as I'm concerned," the priest said.

"The Pope is fully aware of this, however, he is seeking your help. Am I to tell him that you wouldn't consider assisting the ultimate Catholic authority?"

"It's not that. It's my inability to form an opinion," he said.

"Explain to me then what you do to prepare for your Sunday sermon."

"I usually pick a subject from one occurrence or another in this community and seek passage in the scriptures that fits it," the priest said.

"That requires thinking and analysis as well as creating an opinion. "The question the Pope wants answered is whether you, as a priest, feel conversion should be made willingly, or by torture and force?"

"This is difficult for me to answer since I don't know or understand the theological issues behind it."

"Please put aside theological matters," Zevulun pleaded, "just think of conversion in its simplest form. Think of me for a moment as a Muslim. I want to convert you to Islam. How do I go about it? Do I reason with you by means of educating you about Islam, or do I torture you to death and force you to convert by means of torture and threats."

"I would rather die than convert," the priest said.

"That's exactly is my point," Zevulun said. "If our objective is to convert you, we wouldn't want you to die. We would want to exhibit to the world that you converted. However, you stated that you would rather die, but since it does not solve our problem, we take you to a dark basement and torture you until you collapse. The pain and suffering of inhuman torture will cause you to state that you are willing to convert, but deep in your heart you hate us because we abused your body and soul. You end up converting on the surface, just because you want to stay alive, but in your heart you have never converted, and keep on practicing your old religion in secret."

"I think I'm beginning to see what the Pope means," the priest said, "I've never thought about it before. Of course, I had nothing to do with conversions. All I had to do was to direct the anger of my parishioners against the evils of the Jews and the Muslims."

"Wouldn't you say that inciting good Catholics to behave abominably against these minorities is preaching hate? Is that what Catholicism is about?" Zevulun asked.

"I was instructed to tell my parishioners Jews are the sons of the devil, that they steal our babies and use their blood in making soap, and more," the priest said defensively.

"We are back to the same question and concern the Pope has. Is this the right way to win them over?" Zevulun said. "I would like you to think about this for a moment. First, have you or anyone you know, in your lifetime, seen or caught a Jew stealing and killing babies?"

"I can't say I have, nor have I ever heard of any babies of my parishioners or others in this city reported missing. Perhaps it happened in another city," the priest said.

"Let us say it did happen in another city. Can you blame every Jew in Castile for a single act of violence? Furthermore, I can tell you there isn't one Jew in any of the many jails in Castile or Aragon. Every act of violence and crime is committed by our own Catholic people. It is a very sad truth. Converting Jews and Muslims to Catholicism is not going to cure the bad element within our own. Only education will," Zevulun said.

"I believe I'm beginning to understand what you mean. It seems we are blaming the Jews and the Muslims for our own ills. It's the conversion issue I'm not too clear about. Why does the Catholic Church want every person on earth to become Catholic? The world we live in survived quite well before we appeared on the scene," the priest said.

"Now you are using common sense," Zevulun said, "This is precisely why the Pope has me talk to the priests in Castile outside the main channels."

"I'll admit this is the first time I've allowed myself to think. Until now I accepted everything as if the Almighty sent it. You are right. We should be permitted to use our God given brain. Using our brains and thinking should not make us any less worthy Catholics. If we direct our thoughts to areas of need, we would do better for our communities," the priest concluded.

"Then you agree that torturing people in order to convert them is a poorly devised mechanism that can only work against us in the long run?" Zevulun said.

"I believe you are right. If we want to convert people, we should show them that we are better. We should educate them about our religion and move them gently in our direction. Violence begets closed-mindedness and the desire for vengeance," he said.

"I have a feeling the Pope will be very pleased with your reaction," Zevulun said. "I shall put in a good word for you when I return to Rome. I might even suggest that he transfers you to Rome for a few years to see for yourself how concerned the Vatican is with brutalism and violence."

And so went the interviews Zevulun conducted with the priests he

Visited during the coming months. However, not all priests agreed with him. It was late June when the group met in David's house in the village of El Mola.

CHAPTER FORTY-FIVE

"**I** met over two hundred priests in ten cities and dozens of villages. About half were willing to listen and actually discuss matters of conscience and about half wouldn't. The two schools of priests are quite identical, each group in its own way. The major difference between the two is wanting to be of open mind or blind devotion with no thinking. My feeling is that a seed of mistrust was sown and that sermons relating to hate and violence will stop or be reduced significantly. I've heard from a number of the priests that Torquemada has called for regional meetings to be held throughout the country. His first meeting is going to be held in Toledo next week. Regrettably, I cannot attend these meetings, as I will be identified as the priest from Rome. In fact, I'm planning to disappear for a while." Zevulun opened.

"This is an excellent report," David said. "There's no question we're making progress. Perhaps Reuven or myself can sneak into a meeting dressed as monks."

"Let me go -- masquerading as a priest," Nechemia said. "Monks will look out of place in a priests meeting. You also look too young to be a priest."

"That's fine," Reuven said, "I have plenty to do. David, tell us about your experiences in the palace."

"Before I continue, I'd like to suggest that Zevulun travels to Lisbon. I started to make contacts with our family there, but had to stop on account of developments here. This will enable Zevulun to drop from sight for a while and will help us cement the relationship we wanted to develop."

"This is an outstanding idea. I'm sure Devorah would love to join me."

"So that's settled," David said. "Leave as soon as you can."

"Please continue with your life at the palace," Itzhak said, "I can't wait to hear about your relationship with Queen Isabella."

"Let's not call it a relationship -- otherwise Anna will get jealous," David laughed.

"Did you tell her you are engaged to be married?" Anna asked.

"What a story that will make -- a monk with a bride!"

"Tell us about the palace," Yael said, "we're all anxious."

"I'm sure Reuven filled you in about the events of the night that brought us together with royalty," David said. "Upon our return to the palace, I was given one of many small rooms in the building. My room is close to the Queen's private chapel, and from time to time she comes to see me. We always met in my room as it's out of the way and private. Two days after I moved in, she came to my room after supper and told me about a meeting she and King Ferdinand had with Torquemada.

Torquemada reported that the man named Yaacov Halevi could not be found in Bilbao. He stated that there never was a Yaacov Halevi living in Bilbao. His investigators could not find anything about the True Catholic Movement or who was behind it. He stated said all the letters were fake and a conspiracy against the Church. The conversation went more or less as follows:

"I received a letter from the True Catholic Movement, a copy of which was sent to the King," Queen Isabella stated. "The basic gist of the letter, as all previous ones relates to the same issue, namely, the brutal and inhuman behavior of the Church, and the Inquisition in particular. You have told me many times that it is not up to me to think, but to accept the wish of Jesus. I can't help but think that Jesus, who was the symbol of love, would not want us to torture and kill in his name."

"You have it all wrong," Torquemada said, "Precisely because Jesus was about love, caring and forgiveness, we must make our society as pure as he. It is our solemn duty to him and our future generations that our society is truly Catholic in every sense of the word. Our blood must be pure of the Jewish devil. They are the people who blaspheme Jesus. They do not believe in him, therefore, they do not deserve to live. By living next to us, by working for you they contaminate our souls, and we cannot become as pure as Jesus.

"Furthermore, you are sinning by merely thinking differently. You are a sinner when you question my knowledge and authority. Even the Pope recognized my knowledge and appointed me Inquisitor General. Is the Pope wrong? If you don't change your thoughts and repent, you will burn in hell for eternity. Is that what you want?"

"Why is it that you always threaten us with burning in hell?" the King asked. "The Crown has been appointed by Rome, too, and made the supreme authority of the Church in this country. How can you expect us to run this country without thinking and taking into consideration the needs and problems of the people?"

"It seems that we always end in a circle on this subject," Torquemada said. "There is no kingdom but the kingdom of our Lord. You, the Queen, or I do not matter, but only the betterment of our Catholic society. We are obligated to strive for that. My entire work is dedicated to clean the air we breathe from foreign dirt and of foreign messengers from hell. The Jews and the Muslims will have no place in heaven. I can assure you they are headed directly to hell when they die. When we burn them at the stake, they are getting a preview of their future in hell. You must believe in that. If you don't, you are doomed as the rest of the sinners."

"You always put the fright of hell in me and my soul. I am sleepless, I am restless and I am scared. I am the Queen of Castile. Why should I be scared?"

"You are scared because you hesitate. If you would devote your entire being to Christ, you wouldn't be scared and you'll have no fear of hell," Torquemada continued. "I will take my leave and would ask you to dwell on my words. The kingdom of heaven is the one and only kingdom."

Torquemada left, and so did the King. He seemed worried and upset. While he was a firm believer in Christ and a devout Catholic, he could not grasp the concept that there was one kingdom only. *"Is my kingdom a mirage?"* he asked himself.

Queen Isabella sat pensively in her chamber and after a while sent her maid to find me.

"My dear Monk," she said, "How many kingdoms has God created?"

"God has created two kingdoms. The one on earth, which we live in, and the kingdom of heaven, which is the hereafter," I told her. "Some people believe that there exists but one kingdom, the kingdom of heaven. But we are on earth for a purpose; otherwise we wouldn't be here. God, the father of all prophets and saints, rules the kingdom of heaven. The kingdom of heaven is an eternal one. The earthly kingdom is a transitional kingdom. We are born into it and die in it. Yet, while we live, we are part of the kingdom. We make it the way we want it to be. All that God expects of us humans is to live by his commandments while we are guests on this earth. Think of it as an elementary school; once you graduated, you are brought into a higher level. Perhaps God is testing us while we are in the transitional stage; however, God does not have a hell into which he throws the people he doesn't like. God and the prophets threatened people so that they would behave, maintain good morals, and live in harmony. God is not the one who created religions -- man did.

"If you understand and accept that, you do the best you can to be a fair ruler, one concerned about her people. There are too many citizens who are being used and abused by the Church and by the nobility. Give the people education and help them out of superstition. Teach them to love each other, respect each other, and love their country.

"Yet no one will be able to change man's nature. The Bible is full of stories about the nature of mankind. That is why the Jews have the Talmud, which is the book of laws. Sins and crimes have been committed by many men, and when caught, they were sentenced to punishment by the courts. You, me, Torquemada, or anybody else on earth is not going to change that. If Torquemada believes he can create a nation of pure people, he is more than mistaken. It has never happened throughout history, and it will not happen in the future. He must be stopped because he creates hate, distrust, and turns good people into bad ones."

"You are a very clever young man," she told me. "Yet I'm scared of hell and burning in its fires."

"There is no hell. You have nothing to fear. If you follow God's commandments and if you insist that the priests in their Sunday sermons concentrate on preaching these commandments and help people attain the required level of performance you'd have bettered their lives. You must understand that preaching hate and tearing people apart, you cannot reach harmony. The fact is, when you preach hate, one day that hate turns against the very people who preached it in the first place. Preach love, not hate. Preach respect for your fellow man and you will be respected in return. Preach charity, and the soul of the giver shall be redeemed by his mere actions. Preach forgiveness, and peace will reign," I told her.

The Queen got up kissed me and left my room without saying another word. Her silence meant a great deal to me. She understood my message. I had a feeling she had regained her self-confidence. A few minutes later she returned. "An Italian sailor named Columbus has been asking me to finance his trip to India. I think I will. I'm determined to find new frontiers for our people. Perhaps it will take their minds off the religious fervor."

CHAPTER FORTY-SIX

"My fellow priests," Torquemada opened the meeting he had called for the Toledo region, "there are traitors among us. There are priests and perhaps even members of the Archdiocese who have ceased to believe in the work of Christ. These cowards are afraid to identify themselves and engage in discussion. They are writing letters, some of which were addressed to the Queen and King and even to me. They call themselves 'The True Catholic Movement'. I ask you, what are we? What am I? Aren't we all true Catholics? They are spreading the word that our methods are harsh. I ask you, what is harsh when you deal with sinners? What is harsh when you deal with part of our society that blasphemes our beloved Jesus? What is harsh when those who converted are found praying to their old Gods in secret? What is harsh when those who are on their way to hell begin their journey here on earth?

"I'll tell you what's harsh -- it is the desire to live for and die for Christ our Savior. There isn't one single matter, there isn't one single issue, and there isn't one single reason on this earth more important and valuable than to live for Jesus. Each one of us here, as individuals, or all of us together as a group, don't mean a thing. The only significance is to guide our society to purity, to Catholic purity of soul, heart, and deed. All the generations to come must be of pure Catholic blood. We are the tools that have begun this process. And there will be others who will follow when we have passed on to the heaven of our Lord.

"Is there anyone in this crowd who thinks differently? Is there anyone in this crowd who knows something about the clandestine movement? Is there anyone in this crowd who has any information which might help me in my work?"

One of the priests raised his hand. "What have you to say?" Torquemada asked.

"Your Eminence, a few weeks ago I was visited by a priest named Carlos Ramirez. He told me he was sent by the Pope to investigate the methodology of the Inquisition in Castile and Aragon. He was trying to convince me that dealing with the Jews, Conversos and Muslims should change. I turned him down flatly and told him you are our guiding light and we would follow you to the end."

"Has anyone else in this audience been visited by this Carlos Ramirez?" Torquemada asked.

About two-dozen priests raised their hands. "I assume that you refused his remarks," Torquemada said. "Does any of you have an idea where this man is?"

No one responded. "From now on, if any of you come across this man, detain him and send for the sentries. We must catch this imposter. We must bring to an end any opposition to our holy work. I'm going to make sure that all our churches and cathedrals are properly guarded day and night. We must guard our properties from these sinful lunatics. I have no doubt they will burn in hell. Any one of you who is instrumental in capturing the imposters will be rewarded handsomely. And remember, we, and no one else, are the true Catholics. I want our work to continue as usual. Your parishioners must be reminded over and over that the Jews, Muslims and Conversos are the devil among us, and it is our intention to continue to strive toward a pure Catholic society."

Nechemia raised his hand. "What say you?" Torquemada asked.

"Your Eminence, I don't think anyone in this audience questions you and the truth. All of us desire a pure Catholic society. The question that has not been brought up here is the method employed to achieve this goal."

"Where is your church?" Torquemada asked.

"My church, Your Eminence, is in a remote part of Castile, near the Portugese border. I was visiting Toledo and heard of this meeting, and obviously wanted to attend it, as I am your most devoted servant."

"Perhaps you care to explain yourself about the 'method'," Torquemada said.

"I have not had a visit from this Carlos Ramirez, but from what I heard some of the priests attending this meeting saying prior to your arrival, it seems the issue was the method by which to achieve our goals. In other words, could we get better results by educating the sinners, by exhibiting our true beliefs and convincing them that Catholicism is far superior to Judaism or Islam? You said Conversos practice their religion in secret. Might that be because they were forcefully converted? I think it would make sense if we enlightened their minds rather than kill them."

Torquemada remained silent for a few minutes. The audience was silent. Most of the priests in attendance thought that this outspoken priest would soon be excommunicated. No one ever dared speak words to Torquemada he did not like to hear. "What is your name?" Torquemada asked, "and in what village is your church?"

"My name is Adolfo Cutinga de Santander, and my village is Santa Clara," Nechemia responded.

"Arrest this man, hold him down, and someone call the sentries," Torquemada exploded. The priests sitting next to Nechemia jumped and held him tight. He couldn't move. The sentries who guarded the front entrance to the Cathedral grabbed Nechemia and took him away.

"This meeting is over," Torquemada announced. "Remember our Lord and follow his mission. We will not fail. Jesus blesses you all."

From where they were hiding, David and Reuven watched Nechemia being hauled away.

"Let's follow the sentries and see where they're taking him," Reuven said. "Fortunately, it's late afternoon. I hope Torquemada has other things on his agenda. We'll have to rescue him tonight -- otherwise he is a dead man."

"We don't know if he'll stand the torture. He may betray us," David said. They followed the sentries and Nechemia from a distance and soon enough they arrived at the new building being built for the Inquisition. "The upper part of the building is not ready yet," David said, "I have to assume the basement is complete. Look, there are two guards by the front entrance, and piles of building materials all over the place."

Reuven developed a plan which he outlined to David.

"What if we are stopped?" David asked.

"We tell them that Torquemada instructed to bring him to another location," Reuven said.

"And what if it doesn't work?"

"We fight our way in and out."

CHAPTER FORTY-SEVEN

Having procured two sentry outfits, David and Reuven returned to the Inquisition building and parked their wagon in the shadow of a house across the street. They saw two priests enter the building. A few minutes later, two priests came out. Two sentries were guarding the front entrance, talking to each other. The sun had set, and no other traffic was noticed going into or out of the building.

Reuven got off the wagon and walked diagonally across. David drove the wagon towards the building as soon as he saw Reuven getting to the side building. He whipped the horses hard, but when he was almost to the entrance he stopped the wagon abruptly. The sentries jumped from their places and approached. Reuven, like lightning, struck the sentry on David's left. He fell to the ground. David's knife went through the second sentry's side, slicing his heart in two. He jumped off the wagon and helped Reuven drag the two bodies behind a pile of cut stone. A minute later they ran down the stairs to the basement. There was one door only. Other open areas were blocked with heavy strips of lumber. They opened the door. Three priests were in the room. With swords taken from the slain sentries, in hand, David and Reuven approached the priests who were working over Nechemia.

"Move over," David screamed at a third priest eating his supper at a nearby table. The priest came over immediately.

"Release this prisoner," he yelled; "Who told you to torture him?"

"No one. We were told Torquemada wants to question him personally. All we did was prepare him," one of the priests answered.

"Release him, now!" David screamed. The priests obeyed instantly. As soon as Nechemia was freed, two of the priests were killed. The third priest stood horrified in his position.

"Move toward the table," David ordered. The priest moved over. "Place your hands on top of the table," David ordered again. His sword came down like a butcher's knife and cut both hands off. The priest fell to the floor, senseless with shock. David pulled out his tongue and cut it. "Bring me the pail of water," he ordered Reuven, who wordlessly obliged. David poured the water over the priest's face and slapped it until he woke from his faint. "Listen carefully," David said. "We are members of The True Catholic Movement. Tell that to Torquemada, and tell him that he is next on our list."

David turned around, "Let's go!" They left the building, jumped onto the wagon, and departed. David drove the wagon around some of the buildings, returned to where he was parked before their attack, and stopped.

"Why are we stopping here?" Reuven asked. It was the first time he or Nechemia had spoken after David's brutal attack on the priest.

"I want to see Torquemada. I want to have the pleasure of seeing him leave his new house of Inquisition, mad as a madman," David answered.

Nechemia, who wanted to thank his friends for rescuing him, kept his mouth shut. He wasn't about to start a conversation when David was in that kind of a mood. Reuven decided to keep quiet, too.

They had sat in silence for about an hour when a dozen or so priests came passing by.

"The man up front must be Torquemada," David whispered. "I wish I could kill him this instant." He was right. The man was Torquemada, and was followed by his butchers. They disappeared from view as they entered the building. Their silhouettes danced on the walls as they walked down the stairs. A few short minutes later, Torquemada's party came streaming out of the building. Torquemada's screaming could be heard across the street as he emerged from the building.

"Let's get out of here," Reuven poked David's side.

"I hate these people with passion," David said, "I could kill them one by one."

I hope to God that one day I will have the pleasure of frying Torquemada as he had done to so many innocent people." Nechemia spoke for the first time. "Thank you for rescuing me. I will be obliged to you for the rest of my life."

David responded, "Nechemia, you owe us nothing. We are all in this war together. We will fight together, and if we have to, we'll die together."

CHAPTER FORTY-EIGHT

David stopped the wagon a short distance from the secret entrance to the palace. He changed into the monk's habit. "Torquemada is going to behave just like the Pharaohs of Egypt did two thousand years ago. He is not going to give up easily. I suggest that each of you move into different cities and murder priests who come out of any Inquisition building. All these killings must be made at night and preferably in the priest's home. Do not take risks. There is no point in any of our people being caught. There are enough priests everywhere. No one in our group should kill more than one priest in any city. Kill and leave town. Go to the next. This way we'll drive Torquemada crazy and the priests will be afraid of their own shadows. Return to the first city a few weeks later. We have to create chaos within the priesthood." David didn't even wait for an answer. He suddenly turned around. "Reuven, ask Anna to meet me each Sunday at the Church of Redemption in Toledo after mass. I'll be sitting on a bench behind the church in its small cemetery in my monk's habit."

"He is a remarkable young man," Nechemia said, "You, too, Reuven. I love you both. David is right; we should continue to eliminate priests who work for the Inquisition. The day will come when they will ask themselves how come only Inquisition priests are being killed."

"The real revolution will have to come from within Torquemada's organization," Reuven said. "There is no question. We are making significant progress."

CHAPTER FORTY-NINE

Who did this to you?" Torquemada asked the priest.

"Two sentries walked in on us just as we were putting the arrested priest in chains," the bandaged priest answered. Torquemada could barely understand him. The wounded priest was reeling from pain.

"Can you describe these two sentries to me?" Torquemada asked.

"They were young, but so are most of the sentries the Chief of Guard recruits these days. The experienced soldiers are sent to the front."

"What did they look like?" Torquemada kept at it.

"I can't exactly tell because their heads were helmeted and everything happened so fast," the priest said.

"Where they the sentries that guarded our building," he asked.

"No, Your Eminence," another priest answered. "The sentries guarding the building were found dead behind a pile of construction stones. Their swords are missing."

"Was anything said by these intruders I should know about? Torquemada directed at the wounded priest.

"They said they were members of the True Catholic Movement and that I was left alive to tell you."

"I want every Converso tortured until someone confesses knowledge about this movement. We must get to the bottom of it. I'm going to speak to the Queen about the latest events tomorrow," Torquemada stated.

"Your Eminence, it appears the movement comes from within our organization. I don't believe any Converso is involved," one of the priests said.

"I can't believe there's anyone among us so brutal as to kill his own fellow priests. Only the most devout Catholics have joined our ranks, only men who wished to devote their lives to Jesus. It has to be someone from the outside. We must make every effort to find these monsters. They are the True Sinners. We must eliminate this disease so we can proceed with our mission unhindered." Torquemada said.

"Please forgive me Your Eminence, I don't mean to argue with you. In fact, I worship the ground you walk on, but I have this gut feeling that some of our Catholic friends are not as devout as you believe they are," another young priest said.

"If you investigate hard enough, you'll soon find out the truth," Torquemada said.

"I hope and pray it's not one of ours."

"I take it from your comment that we should investigate every priest. Perhaps one will lead us to the truth," Torquemada grasped

"How do we split the investigative work among us?" a priest asked.

"I'd like to think about it and plan a course of action," Torquemada said. "I'll give you my decision in a day or two."

Torquemada went to his temporary home. He had two young priests accompany him and was silent most of the way. The latest events were annoying and the more he thought about them, the further away he was from their source. *"Is it possible that some priests disagree with me? I must find out."* For the first time, he began to doubt.

CHAPTER FIFTY

"I miss you so much I could die," Anna said. "I'm very lonely even though I have so many orphans to look after." They met behind the church near the cemetery.

"I miss you, too," David said. "I can't wait to take you in my arms and kiss you. Unfortunately, I can't do it in daylight while I'm in a monk's habit. How is the orphanage coming along?"

"I have more children than I can handle in our house. We'll need to do something about it."

"Talk to the Landowner's office and ask them to allocate a tract of land so we can build an orphanage."

"Do we have the money?"

"We certainly do. Ask the office to recommend a builder and get the ball rolling. Make sure the house is big enough and has all the facilities for boys and girls. Every time I see homeless children, my heart bleeds."

"Rachel and Miriam are very helpful when they are there, but I'll need more help as the number of children grows."

"Just get the help. There is no reason for you to worry about money. I'll see that you have enough."

"The priest in our village's church offered to help. Shall I accept it?"

"Absolutely. However, if he utters one word against the Jews or Conversos, I want you to kick him out. Should such a thing happen, just tell him you oppose any preaching which includes hate for other human beings."

"Tell me about life in the palace," Anna said, "I'm very curious."

"I think the Queen is in love with me. I don't mean the kind of love you and I have for each other, but rather a motherly kind of love. She is fascinated by my open mind and ability to make sense of real issues. What she is really missing is a good Jewish education. Torquemada has put the fear of hell in her heart and it's driving her crazy. He is not a man who will compromise. He is a radical in every sense of the word. He is obviously taking advantage of being the Queen's confessor and counselor. The Queen is a woman with a simple soul. She was not brought up in royalty and lacks the fundamental education most members of crown have gotten. She is a devout Catholic, but is driven in the wrong direction. I believe she senses that and has the need for balance. She found that in me by accident. Since I've come to the palace she sees me about once a week in my room. Our meetings are kept secret from Torquemada. She told me that the only one who knows about my real reason for being there is her personal maid, who has been with her since childhood."

"Does the Queen know you are a Jew?"

"Yes, I told her when I saved her from the crowd, the night she fainted watching the Auto-de-Fe."

"And the maid, does she know that, too?"

"The Queen specifically told me the maid was not told. The maid knows I'm there to give the Queen fresh advice in order to get a different perspective than Torquemada's."

"I'm very uneasy about all this. You're in the devil's nest. What if Torquemada finds you out?"

"I'm much younger than him and can fight my way out."

"I'll die if anything happens to you."

"Nothing will happen to me," David said. "This is quite an experience. It sharpens my wits and gives me the opportunity to work on the Queen's mind. Perhaps through my words she'll come to see the light. Let's call it part of our revolt against the Church. The only difference is that this work is nonviolent."

"You said she looks you up once a week. When is that?"

"Usually on Fridays, immediately after Torquemada's departure. Every time he sees her, he upsets her tremendously. Her fear of burning in hell is very real. I'm trying by every means I know to get that fear out of her mind. If not for that, I would have had her on our side."

"I have an idea," Anna said. "Get her involved with the orphanage. Let her see all those poor abandoned children face to face. Perhaps the reality of life in hell, while on earth, will help her change her mind. I understand she can't have children -- is that true?"

"Your idea is very interesting. Let me think how to go about it."

"How do you bring me into the picture?"

"The Queen is a very practical person, and she listens to me. I'll find a way to get her involved. You'll need to get Nechemia out of the house. When she comes to visit you, if she does, that is, she should only see women. And if she asks who is financing this operation, tell her my father left some money before he was killed. You can tell her of the plans to build a special orphanage building so all the poor abandoned and homeless children can find a home. Get the local priest involved. It'll make him feel good, and the children can get a Catholic education. After all, they all come from Catholic families. When the orphanage is built, make sure the plans include a chapel."

"Why are you doing all this?" Anna asked.

"First and foremost, let's not forget it was your idea to save homeless children, which is something I admire in you. Secondly, it gives you a noble thing to do, especially while I'm away. And thirdly, I feel in my heart that one day we'll be able to tell the worlds of Castile and Aragon that it was the Jews who saved the hundreds of abandoned children and gave them a Catholic education and upbringing."

"I see your point. You are convinced that one day we will be free to practice our religion in the open."

"Absolutely, that day will come, and I believe in the not too distant future."

CHAPTER FIFTY-ONE

Your Majesty
Queen Isabella
Of Castile,

We, the members of The True Catholic Movement, wish to thank you for taking the time to read our letters. All of us without exception feel rather badly that we have to take action anonymously. We wish it weren't the case. However, Torquemada is still on the warpath, and if caught there is no question in our minds that he would have us executed in his usual way, by Auto-de-Fe.

We want you to know we are a group of senior clergy who oppose violence. We do not believe now, nor did we believe in the past, that the Catholic Church would ever achieve its objective of converting men and women to Catholicism by violent means. The more we read the scriptures and the more we study about the life of our Lord Jesus Christ, we cannot but come to one conclusion, and that is, His mission was made in the most non-violent ways. We fail to understand the need for violence. Only an uneducated, evil man can have his fellow men tortured and burned to death. It is inhuman to set a living person on fire. Hell is not on earth, and if it is, then the man who authorizes such killings is the devil himself.

Being of another faith is not a sin. It is simple ignorance of our better Catholic ways of life. If we are so determined to convert the others, let us show them that we are better. At present, we only show them we are worse than animals. No wonder the men and women who converted under fear of torture and death practice their religion in secret. In their hearts they still feel that their religion is superior. Can you blame them?

Perhaps you can talk to Torquemada. Whenever one of us opens his mouth, he is killed or arrested. In fact, just a few days ago we rescued one of our men who was arrested and readied for torture by Torquemada when he asked pointed questions at a meeting he held for priests.

You have to trust our just cause. Violence begets violence, and blood is shed for absolutely nothing.

Your Obedient Servants
The True Catholic Movement

"Read this letter," Queen Isabella told David. "What is your opinion?"

"I couldn't agree more," David said, "Violence does beget violence. Also, violence can get out of control. The Church fed misguided information in order to incite people. Once incited mobs are formed, they can turn on you one day. There is no telling what a mob can do. It is dangerous for the monarchy to allow mob power to exist."

"How do I stop Torquemada? I'm afraid of him."

"Reason with him. Try to put God's fear in him if you can."

"You don't understand. He doesn't fear God or death. He believes that God sent him to do his work. The more I tried in the past, the harder he became. I can't explain it, but I fear him terribly. There are many nights I cannot sleep without seeing myself burn in the fires of hell."

"You will never burn in the fires of hell," David said emphatically. "You have not hurt a fly."

"What shall I do?"

"Do something good. There is a house in the village of El Mola, about six or seven hours ride from Toledo. A young woman lives in that house. Her name is Anna. She takes in abandoned children and gives them shelter. There are so many homeless children roaming the streets of every city who turn to crime because that's the only way they can feed themselves. I heard that Anna wants to build an orphanage to house these children and give them a good Catholic education. Devote yourself to doing good. It will offset the evils of Torquemada," David said.

"You may be right," the Queen said, "but how will she be able to finance the construction, and furthermore, she doesn't own land on which to build. I'll travel to El Mola and speak with the Landowner."

"That's very noble of you," David said. "My father left a few gold dukats, which I gave her for the purpose of building an orphanage."

"You are absolutely right. I need to balance violence with some good deeds and there is nothing finer than to help poor homeless children. I'm going to check if there are any children in our jails," the Queen said, "I have been so removed from the people."

"Don't blame yourself. You've been involved in fighting the Moors and getting them out of Castile. It's time the conquerors were defeated," David complimented her.

"You are a very wise young man. One day you'll be the light of Castile. I will see to it if I'm still alive."

That day, while David was having his midday meal in the kitchen, he overheard about a big Auto-de-Fe planned for that night. He could never understand the joy of seeing people burn alive. *"What can I do to stop it?"* he asked himself.

CHAPTER FIFTY-TWO

David left the palace and walked towards Plaza Mayor. In the center he saw the round platform where the victims would be burned to death. Rows of wood were stacked in a large circle around the platform, and on one side were four large buckets filled with oil. He stood at a distance and watched, his mind racing. The solution to his problem became clearer as his eyes focused on the buckets.

He walked briskly towards the shops at one end of the plaza and purchased four containers. He waited until dusk and moved the containers to the water fountain near the Auto-de-Fe platform. He filled them with water and dragged them to the platform. He then removed the oil containers and poured the oil in a large circle around the platform, about ten feet away. Crowds began to appear from all sides. David disposed of the empty containers. He then took off his monk's habit, rolled it up, and tied it around his waist. He took his knife from the sack on his back and shoved it inside his belt. The crowds grew, as did the noise and the shouts. It was totally dark when four priests marched a group of people to the platform and tied them neatly to the center post. One of the priests tried to light the wet wood without success. At that moment David lit the oil he'd poured around and within moments the priests and their victims were inside a circle of fire. Completely baffled by the fire behind them, the priests began running in every direction. In the meantime, David ran from priest to priest and stabbed one after the other. The chaos was tremendous. No one knew what was going on. David rushed to the platform, cut the ropes, and freed the victims. "Run after me," he screamed. He jumped through the fire followed by the eight prisoners. The fire and the smoke distorted the scene the crowd was expecting. Screams and shouts were heard from every corner as the crowds jostled to get away from the fire. David pushed and ran until he reached a house at the other end of the plaza and hid in its shadows. He quickly put on his monk's habit, jumped over the fence connecting to a house behind and walked back to the palace. He entered through the King's secret passage and settled in his room, completely exhausted.

Shortly before dawn the Chief of Guards was summoned to the scene of the failed Auto-de-Fe. Four priests lay dead on the stone floor. The platform and the wood were intact. The Chief was puzzled.

⊗⊗⊗

Torquemada was awakened by a sentry.

"Your Eminence is wanted in Plaza Mayor immediately," the sentry said.

"In the plaza?" he asked. "Why? What for?"

"I don't know, Your Eminence, the Chief of Guards instructed me to bring you there."

"Very well, wait for me by the door. I'll be right out."

Twenty minutes later Torquemada faced the four priests laid neatly one next to the other on the stone floor.

"Are they dead?" he asked.

"Yes, Your Eminence, they were stabbed to death hours ago. Their bodies are stiff and cold," he responded.

Torquemada looked around and saw the platform and unused wood.

"There was supposed to be an Auto-de-Fe here last night. What happened?"

"I have no idea. I was told that a huge fire suddenly circled the platform. The crowds pulled back in panic, screaming and yelling. By the time the fire died, all the people were gone. A passerby found the bodies of the priests and alerted a nearby guard. I was hoping you had an idea what happened here last night," the Chief said.

Torquemada grew agitated and began shouting.

"I asked the Queen to provide sentries to guard us, and all I get is dead priests on every step. This senseless killing has to stop. If you can't deal with the situation, you'll be replaced and hung like a traitor."

"I don't have to take insults from you," the Chief said. "I don't have an army here, and even if I did, I wouldn't know who the enemy is."

CHAPTER FIFTY-THREE

"Your Majesty," one of the Queen's assistants addressed her in her private chambers.

"Torquemada wants to see you immediately. He said the matter he had to discuss with you was of great importance. Today is not his regular day. Shall I ask him to return on Friday?"

"No, I'll see him. Ask him to wait." She deliberately kept him waiting.

"What can be so urgent?" she asked as she walked into her reception room. "I have a full agenda this morning."

"Someone foiled the Auto-de-Fe last night and killed four of my priests. All the prisoners escaped. I need more protection from the Crown." He was very angry.

"I don't have extra men. We're in the midst of great battles in the south. I'm receiving favorable reports from the front. Our men are pushing the Moors back. I have a duty to reconquer our peninsula. We are sick and tired of foreign occupation. This is my priority."

"I've told you over and over that work for our Lord takes priority over everything. Nothing in this world should come ahead of that," he said angrily, his voice rising.

"I am the Queen of Castile! Stop telling me what to do! It is my duty as the monarch of this nation to liberate it from foreign conquerors. The Lord would not dispute the right of man to be free. Our war against the Moors has nothing to do with your work. If you need an army, go and recruit one yourself! The Crown's coffers are emptying out at a very rapid pace thanks to you."

"Why thanks to me?" Torquemada's anger doubled.

"Because you are getting rid of my best tax payers, the people who fully supported my liberation efforts," she responded.

"You are sinning with every word that comes out of your mouth. Your road to burn in hell is guaranteed," he shrieked.

"Don't come here on Friday. I don't wish to see you anymore. If you set foot in this palace, I shall have you arrested," the Queen shouted, and left the room. She walked directly to David's room and knocked on his door. She walked in without waiting. David closed the door and offered her a chair.

"What happened? You're very upset."

"Torquemada is driving me mad. Don't be surprised if I commit suicide one day." She was beside herself.

"Please calm down. Tell me all about it. Don't get upset, you're the ruler of this country. You dictate what you want done."

"Torquemada again threatened me with hell. I can't take it any more. I have constant nightmares about it. This man is making me mad."

"Listen to me, Your Majesty, you are the Queen and ruler of Castile. You happen to be a devout Catholic. You believe firmly in Jesus Christ, attend prayers when needed, celebrate all Christian holidays and act in a proper Christian manner. Torquemada is an extreme radical for whom nothing exists apart from religion. While religion is of great importance so is life and all that comes with it. There is a life to be lived by you and your subjects. The duty of the Church is to preach the teachings of Christ and to guide the people into proper living. Imagine for one moment what would happen if every person on earth put the Church and religion ahead of anything else. There would be no crops, no food, no love between man and woman -- the earth would be bleak. Torquemada is very wrong. You must understand this and head in the right direction. In fact, if I were you, I'd get rid of him because he is liable to destroy you," David said.

"I can hardly get over what a wise young man you are. I wish I had your wisdom," she said. "The truth is that today I literally threw him out and told him if he sets foot in this palace again, I will have him arrested. I can't take him any more."

"That was very wise of you," David said. "The man is a lunatic. Let him practice his extremism elsewhere."

"The problem is I'm afraid of him. His remarks surface at night when I'm sleeping. I have a feeling he'd want me dead."

"You are the Queen. He should be afraid of you. Unfortunately, he is only afraid of his Lord. I suggest you post reliable guards in the palace. I suspect he might try to harm you. Your current guards are untrained and useless. I can tell by looking at them. You need well-paid mercenaries who cannot be intimidated by religion."

"I will do that immediately. Thank you very much for your advice. You're right! I am the Queen of Castile and a good Catholic. There is no reason under the sun why I should worry or fear hell." She finally saw the light.

"I'm delighted you grasped my reasoning."

"Let me order my coach and we'll travel to El Mola and visit with Anna. I need to do a good deed. Meet me at the carriage house. I'll be there shortly. I have to cancel all meetings for today."

Isabella, Queen of Castile, made a sudden about face.

CHAPTER FIFTY-FOUR

Itzhak's route took him to Bilbao, Salamanca, and Leon. Upon arrival in Bilbao he checked into a small inn near the city's main stable and trading post. His two-horse wagon now securely stowed he went about his business of tracking down priests working for the Inquisition.

The new Inquisition building confiscated from Jews who had fled or disappeared, was in the center of the old Jewish quarter. He had a difficult time finding a good hiding place to observe the building from. Finally, after many tours around the area, he noticed a huge oak tree. As soon as it got dark, he climbed the tree and watched.

Candlelight flickered in various windows. On occasion he noticed a face or two, but no one entered or left the building. As it got darker, he descended and walked over towards the building. He stopped about a block away and stood under a tree. Two sentries stood by the main entrance. He waited until a priest came out. As soon as he passed, Itzhak followed him from a distance. Some passerby greeted the priest. He didn't have to walk far. The priest entered a small house, and moments later, candlelight appeared in one of the windows. Itzhak waited across the street until the light went out. It was close to midnight when he made his move. The front door was locked. He walked around the house and found two windows open to let in fresh air. He looked in, adjusting his eyesight, and realized he was peering into the bedroom. The priest was standing in a corner praying in front of Christ's statue. Itzhak watched until he finished his prayers and went to bed. A while later he heard gentle snoring. He climbed into the window and entered the room. He approached the bed cautiously, knife in hand. The priest was sound asleep when Itzhak slit his throat. He wiped the knife on the bed linen and left a note.

"The road to hell begins when you decide to work for the Inquisition. This is the sad ending for priests who spend their lives torturing and killing innocent men and women instead of preaching love, the Ten Commandments, forgiveness and charity. Our Lord Jesus Christ did not ask anyone to kill for his namesake. If you continue in your crooked religious path, your ending will be the same.

(-) The True Catholic Movement"

Itzhak left the house the same way he entered. He looked right and left, the street was dark and deserted. He proceeded to his inn and slipped into his room unobserved. He couldn't sleep. His mind kept taking him back to the slaying of the priest. *"What a shame we have to kill ignorant priests,"* he thought.

He knelt by his bedside, facing east, and prayed. *"Oh God of Judah and Israel, I hope you will forgive me for taking the life of another man. I wouldn't have had to had you not let these religious fanatics torture and burn our people at the stake. Please help us win this battle as you gave us victory at Jericho. Our people should be able to live in dignity and equality without fear of these Satans. Help us bring this fight to a successful ending soon. You are the God of mercy, you are one!"*

Itzhak left the next day for Salamanca. However his work took a different turn. He found the Inquisition house guarded by sentries as well as several young priests. It was the first time he had seen priests with drawn swords in their hands.

The Inquisition building stood next to a Church facing a large plaza in the center of which was a huge statue of one of the kings of Salamanca. There were houses crowded all around the plaza. He sat on the ground, leaning against the stone base of the statue, and observed the Inquisition building. A number of people were dragged into the building and a few were taken out, bound with ropes. He decided to follow and see where those people were taken. One priest led the way and two priests followed on each side of the small group, long knives at ready.

They marched for some time until they reached a large barn on the outskirts of the city. The men was untied, given shovels, and instructed to dig. *"They're digging a grave"* Itzhak said to himself, *"How can I stop it?"* He looked frantically for a place to hide but could find none. The inside of the barn was wide open, no walls or structures of any kind. On the outside, where he stood, he saw no one. He got an idea. He knocked at the entrance and waited. Soon enough one of the priests came out. Itzhak jumped at him and slashed the hand holding the long knife. The knife fell to the ground. Itzhak pointed his knife at the priest's chest.

"Turn around." The priest turned without a word. Itzhak picked up the priest's knife, which was twice as long as his, and instructed the priest to walk into the barn. The knife touched the back of the priest's neck. As they reached the group, Itzhak screamed,

"Drop your knives or I'll kill this priest!" He did not have to wait for an answer. The men who were digging swung their shovels and hit the priests who had turned to face Itzhak. The priests were on the ground before they knew what had hit them.

"Take their knives away," Itzhak yelled as two of the priests started to get up. Two more shovel hits and they were unconscious.

"Who are you?" One of the men spoke.

"I saw you dragged out of the Inquisition building and decided to follow. As soon as I realized that you were digging your own grave I decided to take action."

"You saved our lives," one of the group exclaimed, "I don't know how to thank you. I have no money."

"I don't need your money. I'm one of you," Itzhak said.

"You mean you're a Jew?"

"Just like you."

"How can we repay you?"

"There's no need for repayment."

Introductions followed. One of the priests began to moan and wake up. Itzhak took a shovel and hit him hard on the head.

"What do we do with these priests?" one man asked.

"We kill them," Itzhak replied.

"I've never killed a man," he said.

"We can bury them alive," Itzhak suggested. The men picked up the shovels and resumed digging. When the grave was ready, Itzhak spoke.

"Undress the priests and put on their habits. It will give you safe passage to your destination." The priest's habits were soon removed and their bodies thrown into the common grave. To assure they were unconscious, Itzhak gave each another blow with a shovel.

"If you are willing to fight, let's march into the Inquisition building tonight and eliminate everyone in sight. Perhaps we can save the lives of others who are jailed there," Itzhak said.

"We've never done anything like this in our lives," a man named Moise said.

"Neither have I," Itzhak said, "but someone has to fight back, don't you think?"

"I don't know if I can do it," Moise said.

If you won't join me, I'll have to fight all by myself," Itzhak said, not wanting to mention his group and its mission.

"Good luck to you." He walked away.

"Come back here," Moise pleaded, "all this is new to us. We need to talk more about it."

"There isn't anything to talk about," Itzhak said. "There is need for action. Either you're with me or not. I'm not forcing you. Do as you please."

"You can't fight the Inquisition by yourself," Moise said, "it's ridiculous. There are thousands of them."

"And there could be thousands of us if we rose and fought back," Itzhak said. "We are allowing them to take us like sheep to the slaughter. Look at you, you were taken to a distant barn and instructed to dig your own grave. I bet that if we dig here, you'll find many other graves of good Jews who disappeared. Look here," Itzhak pointed to fresh dirt in one location after another. "I wonder how many good Jews are buried here?"

"Itzhak is right," Moise said, "If they can kill us like flies, why can't we kill them? I'll go with you. I've never killed another human being, but by God I will."

"You understand that there is no backing out. Once we're in the Inquisition building it's kill or be killed," Itzhak said. The men who had put on the priests' habits looked exactly like the group of priests who had marched in. "Let's get going. Hold the knives under your garments. We'll enter the Inquisition building after dark. The sentries won't know the difference. Once we've killed everyone inside the building, we'll call them one by one and eliminate them, too."

Darkness had begun to fall when a group of priests entered the Inquisition building. Itzhak was held as a prisoner. The sentries didn't bat an eye. Once inside the building, they walked up to the third floor and went from room to room. No one there. They descended to the second floor. In one room they found an old priest. Itzhak took a rope he'd taken from the barn and tied the old man. He then cut a large piece of bed sheet and stuffed it into his mouth.

On the ground floor they found two priests in an office. Itzhak slashed their throats before any of his accomplices could move.

"Let's check the basement floor." He led the way. One of the men vomited. "I can't do this."

"Stay here and wait for us," Moise said and followed Itzhak. The other rooms were dark.

"Every one must be in the basement," Itzhak announced. "Let's move cautiously. We cannot afford to be outnumbered." The sentries were still by the front entrance when they passed toward the staircase. They walked down the stairs slowly. No one was in sight. On the basement floor Itzhak opened the first door to a sight of horror. He shut the door and turned around facing Moise.

"Tell me, how come you weren't tortured?"

"I told them I'd give them enough money to build two Cathedrals if they didn't torture me. They checked with the man in charge and agreed. I told them I would deliver the same amount of gold for each of my friends. They agreed to that, too. Yesterday I took them to the hiding place and gave them all my money, close to a thousand gold dukats."

"The money must be in this building then," Itzhak said. "Let's look for it when we finish our work. Go in and tell one of the priests that the sentries want him. When he comes out I'll kill him. We'll put the body of the dead priest in an empty room and continue until they are all dead.

Moise went into the room and soon enough one of the priests came out. Itzhak's knife went through his heart. The men dragged his body to one of the rooms. This process was repeated several times. When it came to the last two priests, they walked in as a group and held them at bay.

"Release the victims from these machines," Itzhak ordered. The men complied immediately. "Now tie these two animals in their stead." The two priests were undressed and tied to the machines. Itzhak began to operate one of them and Moise took to the other. Their screams were music to Itzhak's ears. "Let's leave them like this until they're found tomorrow. I doubt they'll survive. Let them feel the pain and agony our people do."

"They left the basement after completing a thorough search. The money was not there. Once on the ground floor, they repeated the routine used in the basement. Ten minutes later the three sentries and two priests guarding the building were dead. Itzhak posted two men at the entrance and they went on a hunt for the money. They found the box containing the gold dukats in a closet. Itzhak asked them to wait. He ran up to the second floor and entered the room in which they had left the old priest.

"We represent The True Catholic Movement," Itzhak said. "I want you to remember this because tomorrow you'll discover that every priest working in this hell of the Inquisition building is dead. The True Catholic Movement will not rest until all violent actions are stopped. Do you understand me?" The old man nodded.

"If you promise not to scream, I'll take the cloth out of your mouth." The old man nodded again. Itzhak took it out. The old man breathed deeply.

"Who is the True Catholic Movement?"

"It's a group of priests who oppose the use of violence against innocent people. It's not the function of the Church to torture and kill people. It's not the function of the Church to incite good Christians against minorities using lies and deceit. Tell that to your friends. Anyone who participates in the destruction of true Catholic values will be killed." Itzhak walked out, joined the others, and left the building.

"What are you going to do?" Moise asked.

"I have other cities to go to," he responded.

"Can we come with you? We have nowhere to go. We couldn't possibly return to our homes."

"I'd be delighted. My wagon is at the trading post near the highway."

"What is your next target?"

"The City of Leon."

CHAPTER FIFTY-FIVE

Anna was shocked when a coachmen walked into the house and announced the arrival of Queen Isabella. She was even more shocked when she saw David come in with her in his monk's habit.

"This is Anna, my fiancé," David announced as he and the Queen entered. Anna began to bow, but the Queen stopped her.

"There is no need, my dear," she said, "I decided to pay you a visit and see for myself what you're doing for homeless children. I want to learn more about your project and see how the Crown could help."

David took over as he noticed Anna was still in shock.

"Anna wants to build a house large enough for hundreds of orphans and homeless children. She has most of the money for the construction, but she needs the land, and the noble who is the landowner around here won't give her permission."

"This is absurd," Queen Isabella said. "This noble is none other than Julio Caregna de Cervantes. I know him well. I will speak to him as soon as we leave. May I sit down?"

"Of course," Anna apologized. "I'm overwhelmed by your visit. Please sit here."

"David told me all about you and your circumstances. I'm afraid that I'm guilty of not paying attention to the miseries of our orphaned and homeless children. I will send my best builder to help you build the house you need. I will also make provisions for you to receive a monthly allowance from the Crown to support the cost of running this facility," the Queen said.

"I don't know how to thank you," Anna said.

"There is no need to thank me. It is my Christian duty to help the needy. David told me about your parent's demise, and I'd like to express my deep sorrow. I hope and pray the Lord will reward you for the good deeds you're doing. How many children do you have now?"

"At present I have nine children ages four through eleven. Children occupy every room in this house. As soon as I have proper facilities, I'll gather every child I can and give them shelter and education. The local priest offered his help, too."

"Do you have a plan for the house you wish built?" The Queen asked.

"I need a building that can house over a hundred children. I need separate rooms for boys and girls, a large kitchen, dining room, playrooms and schoolrooms. I suspect that when this project becomes known, it will be swamped with newcomers," Anna said.

"You're absolutely right. I don't know of any facility in Castile that caters to abandoned children. I'll help you any way I can. David, let's go to Caregna's castle. It's not too far from here. I suspect we'll have to spend the night there as it will soon be dark," she said.

"We'll stop here tomorrow morning," David said.

"Yes, we'll stop on our way to Toledo. I'm sure Caregna will come see you immediately," she said.

The Queen and David left El Mola on their way to the Castle.

Count Julio Caregna de Cervantes could not believe his eyes. One of his footmen ran in and announced that the Royal coach was approaching his castle. He rushed to the entrance and ran down the stairs. The Queen's coach pulled in and came to a stop.

"Your Majesty, I'm deeply honored by your visit," he said, bowing down as Queen Isabella alighted. "Please come into my home."

"I'm afraid we'll have to spend the night in your castle. It's too dark to drive back."

"I'll make all the arrangements for a most comfortable stay, Your Majesty," he said and spoke briefly to one of his footmen.

"Please follow me to the drawing room. As soon as your room is ready you'll be able to freshen up."

"Is this monk with you?"

"Yes. Please arrange a room for him too."

Queen Isabella did not waste any time. As soon as they sat down to dinner, she said, "The reason I'm here is because you have a tenant in El Mola who wishes to build a home for abandoned children. I'd like you to donate a parcel of land near the village for that purpose. I will send my best builder to build the house and school. You won't have to bother with that expense. The Crown will contribute a monthly allowance for its upkeep and I expect you to support this effort as well. There are hundreds of orphaned and homeless children wandering the streets of our cities. Unattended, they turn to criminal activity in order to survive. By giving them a home and education we'll significantly reduce the number of prisoners in our jails. I am told that probably half our prisoners are under age eighteen."

"This country has had abandoned children for centuries. Why the sudden change?" he asked.

"Because it's time we acted as Christians are supposed to act."

"Very well, Your Majesty, I will make all the arrangements tomorrow morning. I have plenty of land next to the village unsuitable for farming. It might as well be used for a school," he responded. "I'm very curious, Your Majesty. I have never seen you with a monk before, nor have I seen any monks in your palace," he said.

"This monk is helping me. As you surely are aware, most of my retainers are in the south helping the war effort. The time is ripe for change. In fact, there is a navigator who wants to travel west to discover a shorter route to India. There is nothing west of us except an ocean. Do I embrace change or do I throw out his request? Sometimes I feel in my bones that a great change is coming. Doing a good deed will help me, and probably you, too," she said.

"If this is your wish I will abide by it. When we meet in heaven, I will tell you if it worked," he joked.

CHAPTER FIFTY-SIX

Moise tried in vain to find out who Itzhak was and why he was so determined to fight the Inquisition. Itzhak was as close mouthed as could be. His answers were always the same, "Someone has to fight those killers. It might as well be me."

They reached Leon in a day and a half. They decided to park the wagon in one of the many parks and forests surrounding the city. Itzhak put on his monk's habit and walked with Moise into the city while the others stayed behind. Itzhak could not figure out why the others in this group were so quiet and non-communicative.

"I can't make out these men," Itzhak said as they left the forest. "They hardly talk not even among themselves."

"They're traumatized," Moise said. "One of them will open up from time to time, but the other five are mentally sick. I don't know exactly what the Inquisition priests did to them, but I managed to bribe our way out. At least that was what I thought at the time, however, had you not shown up, we would have been killed and buried in that barn."

"Are you familiar with Leon?" Itzhak asked.

"I've never been here before. My business always took me to coastal cities."

"What business were you in?"

"I was a wool trader. I bought wool from the farmers and shipped it to manufacturers in Barcelona and Valencia. Occasionally, I shipped wool overseas."

"My father was also a trader, but in metals," Itzhak said.

"I'm going into this Church to ask the whereabouts of the Inquisition. Please wait for me here." Itzhak walked into the Church. He came out in a couple of minutes.

"Follow me, but stay behind at least twenty to thirty paces at all times. Should something occur, you're on your own." When they reached vicinity of the Inquisition, Itzhak began touring the area, its side streets, the rear and front of the building. There were sentries both front and rear, standing with swords at the ready. It was quite obvious that there was tension and that the sentries were forewarned.

Itzhak decided to wait until nightfall. When darkness descended, he joined Moise at a nearby house.

"I sense vigilance I haven't encountered before," Itzhak said. "Let's wait until some priests come out and go home. We can always kill them there."

They waited a long time before a priest came out. Two sentries they had not seen before accompanied him. Itzhak and Moise followed far behind. When the priest reached his destination, he entered a house and the sentries posted themselves by the front door.

"Let's check around back," Itzhak said; "perhaps there's a way in from the rear."

They circled the block of houses and entered the yard of the house directly behind the priest's home. Two sentries were standing guard at the rear of the house, too.

"He must be an important priest to have so many sentries guard him," Itzhak whispered.

"How do we get in?" Moise asked.

"I have an idea. I'll walk over to the sentries up front and offer them two gold dukats if they vanish. If they take the money, we're home free. If they don't and try to arrest me, I can easily outrun them. Meanwhile, you enter the house and kill the priest."

"What makes you think they'll accept the money?"

"One gold dukat is what this man earns in two years, if not longer. I think they'll take the money."

"What if only one of them accepts your offer?"

"I'll tell them there's no deal."

"I think it's too risky," Moise said.

"We have to reach a decision if we want to kill this priest."

"How about I go and ask for directions? I'll tell them I'm lost and while they tell me how to get to the highway inn, you sneak in and kill the bastard," Moise said.

"Sounds good to me. The house is completely dark now. Go ahead," Itzhak said.

Moise walked slowly and Itzhak followed closely behind.

"Who goes there?" Moise heard one of the sentries call.

"I'm a visitor in this city and I'm lost." Moise approached the sentries.

"What are you doing outside at this hour anyhow?"

"I was visiting my old sister who lives around here and lost track of time. I thought I knew the way to my inn, but I seem to be going in circles."

"Which inn are you staying at?"

"I'm staying at the Highway Inn on the road from Bilbao," Moise said.

"That's simple enough," one of the sentries said, "let me show you." Suddenly, a sentry guarding the rear showed up on the side of the house. "What's going on here? I heard voices."

"This man is lost. I'm showing him the way."

If not for the darkness, the sentry could have stepped on Itzhak where he was crouched on the ground. The sentry walked back, and as he did so, Itzhak leaped and stabbed him in the back. The man fell to the ground without a sound. He quickly looked over his shoulder and saw the two sentries standing at the corner showing Moise the way. He ran into the house and came face to face with the priest, holding a candle.

"Who are you? What do you want?" the priest asked. "You're far away from your monastery."

"I got lost and requested permission to ask you for directions," Itzhak answered recovering from the shock of the encounter.

"You can spend the night here. It's too late to be walking around an unfamiliar city," the priest said. "I just finished my prayers. Let me show you to a room you can sleep in. Follow me." As soon as the priest turned, Itzhak's knife went through his heart. Itzhak pulled a note from his inner pocket and placed it on the priest's chest. It read:

"The work of The True Catholic Movement continues. This message goes to all priests engaged in torturing and killing innocent men and women. If you continue in your brutal, inhuman, and unchristian work, your body, too, will be found dead and your soul will be on its way to hell."

"Who are you?" shouted a sentry. "Where did you come from?"

"I'm a guest of your client. I'm going home," Itzhak said, walking rapidly away. The monk's habit momentarily confused the sentries.

"Wait," they shouted. But Itzhak started running and disappeared from sight. He looked back. No one was behind him. Moise emerged from behind a fence.

"Did you kill the priest?"

"He joined his maker. Let's go back to the wagon."

CHAPTER FIFTY-SEVEN

It was almost midday when Queen Isabella stopped at Anna's house.

"I have good news for you," she said. "You'll receive a large parcel of land for your orphanage and home for homeless children. As soon as I return to Toledo, I'll engage our master builder to build this house. I will also authorize the Crown's treasury to pay you one gold dukat every month to cover the cost of running this institution. I'll pray to Jesus for your success."

"Thank you, you are very generous and kind. I shall not fail you," Anna said. She wanted to kiss David, but that was not possible. David and the Queen left immediately.

"I'm relieved," the Queen said. "I feel much better. I want to thank you for bringing me here and your confidence in me. I will not divulge your true identity. I promise."

"There's no need to thank me," David said gently, "A good deed is always beneficial to the heart. You'll need to find a way to stop the persecution by the Inquisition. God did not bring people into the world and gave them life so that one fanatic individual would destroy his work. You must believe in God, for he is merciful, and you must believe me when I say that there is no hell down there. God did not create hell. God created paradise - the Garden of Eden. Man created hell for his own selfish reasons."

"I'm fascinated by your wisdom," Queen Isabella said. "You speak gems, not evil. You preach goodness, not brutality. I love you, and I love your mind."

"The biggest obstacle to decency in Castile and Aragon is Torquemada. You need to end his career. People lived in greater harmony before he appeared on the scene. Commerce was booming and our citizens had work and earned a living. The Crown collected taxes and was well off. Today, tens of thousands are unemployed and are easy pray for Torquemada's lies and deceit. Mobs rule the streets of most cities and mobs are dangerous because they can be used for anyone's bad intentions, even against your monarchy. Also, preaching in the churches should concentrate on the good of man, not turn people against minorities. When the Hebrews left Egypt after four hundred years of slavery, God told Moses to treat the minorities as they treat themselves. There is no change in God's message," David said.

"You are absolutely right. I've already kicked Torquemada out of the palace. If he returns, I'll have him arrested. But stopping him is not a simple matter. The Pope appointed Torquemada Inquisitor General. I need to think this out so I don't get in trouble with the Papacy," she said.

"You're a wise woman and Queen. I'm sure you'll find the way. Would you mind if I went back to Anna with your master builder? I'd like to help put the plans together. I'll only be gone a few days."

"By all means do so. I want the children's project to start immediately. Once the building is ready, I'll have all the homeless children brought there. The children are our future. I will not fail them anymore. I hope the Lord forgives me for neglecting them."

"Your redemption is found in the will to do good. God is on your side," David said as they pulled into the palace grounds.

A message from an assistant awaited the Queen. Her personal maid said a letter had arrived to be read immediately. The Queen sent for her assistant who came with the letter in hand.

Her great Majesty
Queen Isabella of Castile
Toledo

The powers of heaven are greater than those of man. You have defied the power of our Lord who wishes us to become one nation, pure in Catholic blood, and purged of Jews and Muslims. You have become a blasphemy to the Church I serve and to Christianity in general. If you cannot put the work of the Lord ahead of anything you do in life you do not deserve to be the monarch of Castile.

I have told you over and over that your thinking is impure, which will result in your burning in the eternal fires of hell. As Queen of Castile and as an appointee of the Vatican, you represent the Pope and the doctrines of Catholicism. You have failed in both. I shall so advise Pope Eugene IV.

I know you claim to be a devout Catholic, but so far you have not proven to be one. As Queen you should set an example to the people, but you do not.

I am willing to give you one more chance to improve your behavior and to embrace our Lord in the true meaning of our Catholic faith. I will be awaiting your call.

Tomas de Torquemada
Inquisitor General

"Ask the monk to come over to my private chambers immediately," the Queen shouted at her assistant.

David came running.

"What happened?"

"Read this letter," she instructed. David read the letter several times. He was pensive for a few moments.

"The man is definitely insane. First, he insults the Crown, and secondly, he has no consideration for mankind. Can you imagine what humanity will turn into if every person on earth is denied the right to think or discuss any subject but the Lord? The Lord gave us a brain for a reason. He wants us to use it. Without a brain we are no different from any beast roaming the forests.

"As Queen of Castile you must make judgments. You must decide matters of life and death brought before you by your constituents. You are obliged to think of the future of your nation, its safety and welfare. There is no way under the sun you can think that nothing matters but your work for the Lord. The fact is that by doing your work as a monarch, you are providing for all the people the Lord gave life to. You are an extension of the Lord -- don't you ever forget that! I believe this was the reason the Pope gave you the ultimate authority over the Church in Castile. Your authority is superior to that of the Inquisitor General. Therefore, I suggest you have him arrested and tried for blasphemy against the Crown."

Queen Isabella sat quietly digesting David's remarks. She rose from her chair, walked over to David where he was standing near the window, and took him into her arms, kissing his cheeks on both sides.

"You are indeed a very wise young man. You seem to be able to put everything in the right perspective. You are right, of course. The Pope gave me the ultimate authority over the Church. Torquemada writes to me as though I was his adulterous wife. He dares to insult me and threaten me as though I were a street criminal. I will have him arrested immediately. The problem I see, however, is that he has many followers, priests he cultivated through a system based on fanaticism. I know I'll have to deal with this problem, but am not sure how at this moment."

"I suggest that Torquemada's arrest is kept quiet. Let his colleagues think he disappeared. In the meantime, you call all the Cardinals, Archbishops, and Bishops in Castile and Aragon to a meeting in the palace. I'll write the speech for you. Of course, you may correct it as you please. Once you get all the top clergy to agree with you, they will instruct the army of priests operating throughout the country what to say and how to behave. If you find any renegade priests you have the right to excommunicate them," David said.

"I will take your advice." One of her assistants walked in. "Ask the Chief of the Guard to come here immediately," she ordered.

"He may have gone home, Your Majesty. It's quite late."

"Send someone to his home. I want him in my chambers as soon as possible. She looked at David with great appreciation. "I'll be ever grateful for your advice. I should have gotten rid of him a long time ago." There was a knock, and the door to the Queen's private chambers opened. The Chief of Guards walked in.

"Your Majesty," he said, "I was about to go home when you called. What can I do for you?"

"Take some of your best and most trusted men and arrest Tomas de Torquemada. I want him jailed in an isolated cell until further notice," the Queen ordered.

"I can't arrest the Inquisitor General!" the Chief said; "He's a man of God."

"I, not Torquemada, am the superior of the Church in this country! Now go and put him under arrest for blasphemy against the Crown, and if you won't do it, I'll have you arrested as well for disobeying my orders."

"I will obey your orders, Your Majesty, with pleasure, but I have to warn you that his arrest may cause serious disturbances among the clergy."

"Take him away discretely. Let his followers believe he disappeared. Leave a note saying he went on a trip, but do it immediately. The cover of night will be helpful. Take some men and wear civilian clothes when you take him in." The Chief left totally mystified and Isabella rang the bell again. Her assistant walked in promptly.

"I want a letter of invitation to go out to every Cardinal, Archbishop, and Bishop in Castile and Aragon asking them to attend a meeting in the palace on the first day of next month. Make sure all letters are delivered by special couriers within a week," she ordered. David was still standing by the window on the far side of her chamber.

"I believe I will have a good night's sleep tonight. Thank you again. I'll let you know when Torquemada has been put in jail."

David left the Queen's chambers with delight in his heart. He wanted to jump and sing Halleluiah, but restrained himself. *"I need to notify my people, but I can't leave the palace,"* he thought. *"On Sunday when Anna comes to meet me at the Church, I'll send the word."*

CHAPTER FIFTY-EIGHT

Yossef arrived in Zaragoza on a rainy day. His journey from El Mola was damp and wet. He checked into a small inn and rested an entire day. He wanted the weather to change, but it didn't. It seemed the drizzle would never end. He finally gave up, covered himself with a large woolen blanket, and went out.

The rain poured down relentlessly. He entered a Church on his way and pretended to be praying. There was no one else in the Church. The pastor passed by and greeted him.

"It's nasty outside," he said.

"It sure is," Yossef said. "My cloak is all wet, so I decided to come in and pray."

"I don't recall seeing you before. Do you usually pray in this Church?"

"No, I'm visiting Zaragoza for a few days. I'm interested in old castles because I plan to be a builder when I grow up. I was told there are beautiful castles in this city."

"Yes, indeed," the pastor said, "but unfortunately the weather is of no help to you."

"I can wait a few days, I'm in no hurry," Yossef said.

"I'll pray for good weather." The pastor left.

Yossef waited a while, but rain kept coming down in a slow unending down pour. The skies were gray. Yossef thought the clouds would reach the ground at any moment. He bought food and returned to his inn.

Finally, on the third day of his stay, the sky cleared somewhat and the rain stopped. He went to the Inquisition building and wandered around, acquainting himself with the surroundings. Sentries were guarding the main entrance. He decided not to wait until dark, but returned to the inn, took out his monk's habit, rolled it carefully and stuffed it into a sack.

He stopped at one of the Churches and headed for the rest room. No one was there. He put on the monk's habit and hood and tucked his knife securely in his belt. He walked slowly, as most monks do, with head lowered, and approached the Inquisition building. He walked up the two steps, passed right by the unconcerned guards, and entered the building.

"*Whom do I kill in this building?*" he thought. He decided to check the basement, where every Inquisition building housed its torturing machines. He opened the first door he came across and was surprised to find no one. He proceeded to the next door and opened it cautiously. A priest and a mechanic were building some sort of machine. The priest heard the door open and turned around.

"Who are you looking for?"

"I've never been to an Inquisition building before and I'm curious what it's like. There was no one on the ground floor, so I came down here."

"Where are you from?" the priest asked.

"I'm from the San Cristobal monastery in Barcelona," Yossef responded.

"Let me show you around," the priest said. As he came out of the room into the semi dark hall in the basement, Yossef took out his knife and held it at the priest's throat.

"Tell me, what kind of a machine are you building?"

"Don't kill me," he pleaded, "I have done no harm to anyone."

"How long have you been a priest?"

"I was ordained last week."

"Have you tortured anyone yet?"

"No, I haven't."

"Have you watched anyone being tortured?"

"Yes, I have."

"How did you feel about it?"

"I think it's disgusting. I don't have the physical or mental strength to torture people."

"Why are you here, then?"

"I was told I'll burn in hell if I don't do my duty to Christ."

"And you call this 'the duty to Christ'?"

"I don't know. I'm totally confused."

"How old are you?"

"Twenty."

"I'm only sixteen."

"What are you doing here?"

"I've come to kill one of you."

"Who sent you?"

"I'm a member of The True Catholic Movement."

"What's that? I've never heard of it."

"We are fighting the Inquisition because of its brutal inhuman behavior. Look, I can't stand here and talk to you all day. Enter this room and lock the door. If you come out before the hour is over, I'll have to kill you."

The young priest leaped into the room and locked himself in. Yossef walked up the stairs and entered the first doorway. A priest was sitting at a desk writing.

"Can I help you?"

"Yes," Yossef answered, "Do you work here?"

"Of course. What do you want?"

"I'm curious to know how many Jews you've tortured and killed in this building."

"We don't keep numbers, we just get rid of the sinners who refuse to convert. What's it to you anyhow?"

"I'll tell you what it is to me," Yossef approached the man, pulling the knife from his belt, he brought it up against the priest's chest. "To me you are a murderer of innocent people, a disgrace to Catholicism and Christianity in general. Ordinary murderers are sentenced to death and die in prison. I'll give you the privilege of dying in this office." He pushed the knife into the man's heart. He took a prepared note and left it on the desk.

"The True Catholic Movement sentenced this priest to death for the torture and killing of many innocent Jews. Let it be known that any priest participating in brutal and inhuman behavior will be subject to the same termination."

Yossef went down the stairs and out of the building. The sentries respected his monk's habit, and asked no questions.

CHAPTER FIFTY-NINE

"Honorable Cardinals, Archbishops, and Bishops," Queen Isabella opened the meeting, "Thank you for coming so promptly. I called this important meeting because we have a major problem on our hands, a problem that keeps growing and growing. I suspect that if I let the present situation continue, it will bring down our entire country.

"The problem as I see it is that some of us have been seeking to create a pure Catholic State, and in doing so have caused members of the clergy to engage in brutal behavior toward minorities and some Christians as well. When I say brutal behavior, I mean the torture of human beings and burning them at the stake when their sole crime was being of another faith.

"In analyzing the problem I'm faced with, I came to a number of conclusions. First, let me touch upon the existing objective, namely, the creation of a pure Catholic blooded society. You know and I know that this is an impossible dream. There always have been and always will be strangers among us. Not a single nation in the world is free of minorities. Over the past centuries many people migrated from country to country for personal reasons, or were forced to do so. Frankly, I don't believe this will ever stop. Furthermore, even among us Catholics there are different degrees of devoutness. How deeply every Catholic immerses himself in the religion is a personal decision. Who is to dictate the exact level of religious life and purity?

"If we want to convert others to Catholicism, it is up to us to show them our religion is superior. There are many ways we can demonstrate the better side of Catholicism. But this wasn't what we did. We allowed the creation of an Inquisition which forced people to convert. Most of those people refused so what did we do? We arrested them and began torturing them to the point of collapse. The weak ones, which are the majority, converted, but continued to practice their religion in secret. The stronger people, those who refused to convert, were tortured and burned to death. Apart from this misconception, we've been harassing the converted because we were told that their blood is not pure enough for our society, so even the converted remained impure.

"On top of all that, our clergy who serve in hundreds of Cathedrals and churches around the country have been instructed to tell their parishioners that Jews were responsible for the death of Christ, that they steal Christian babies and use their blood in soap making. Also, that Jews represent and believe in the devil. All these preachings are pure lies, and you know it! The Jews did not kill Jesus, for he was one of them when he lived in the land of Israel. It is a known fact that Christianity developed hundreds of years after his death. Furthermore, the Jews do not steal Christian babies, and for your information, soap is not made from blood. And finally, the Jews do not believe in the devil. Speak to any Jew and you'll find out the truth. The point I am trying to make is that we lied, we cheated, we bad-mouthed people just because they are of a different faith to a point that good Christians formed mobs and began vandalizing and looting Jewish neighborhoods. The truth of the matter is that Jews are hard working people, good taxpayers and valuable citizens. Look in any jail around the country and tell me how many Jews are there. You won't find one, while thousands of prisoners are our own flesh and blood Catholics.

"If all the information and thoughts I've presented to you seems confused, it is because we have strayed from the work of our Lord. Holy men of the church are engaging in murderous behavior. How can a man ordained to be a priest torture another human being to death? How can men who were ordained as priests light a fire under another man and watch him burn to death? I am convinced that Our Lord Jesus Christ is wondering how this sort of behavior is happening on earth.

"Regretfully, we owe most of this disaster to one man, Tomas de Torquemada, who was blackmailing me with threats of hell for years. Torquemada is a fanatic and has to be stopped. I want to bring back law and order into our lives. We are in the midst of a war of liberation in the south. We cannot have another internal war for a reason that is beyond us all.

"Torquemada has been arrested and is in isolation. He will not disrupt our lives any more. I want you, the main force of the Church, to instruct your men to preach the teaching of our Lord, to love thy neighbor, to respect your fellow man, obey the Ten Commandments, to strive to high morality, integrity, honesty and good morals. I want the Church to return to the work of the Lord in honesty and truth, not in lies and deceit.

"A few weeks ago I met a young girl of sixteen who took into her home a dozen abandoned, orphaned and homeless children. She gave them a home and takes care of them. She enlisted a local priest to help educate them. This is the kind of deed that will demonstrate the quality of Catholicism. This girl has received a parcel of land and is now building a house and school where hundreds of homeless children will live and be educated.

"Castile and Aragon are in the midst of joining forces. There is no need for us to have two separate countries. As my husband is the King of Aragon and I am the Queen of Castile, and since the nobles, landowners and citizens of both countries seem to like the idea, I will use this quorum to announce the amalgamation of our two countries. My husband is making this same announcement in Segovia this morning.

"Both of us have decided to change the path of evil in our country to a path of love and friendship. I want your support and cooperation. Are there any questions?"

"Which city will become the Capital city for the new country?"

"Toledo will be the Capital City."

"What are your plans for Torquemada?"

"I plan to keep him in jail until he repents or dies, whichever comes first."

"I don't believe he will ever change."

"In that case he will have to remain jailed for life."

"Shouldn't we consider this entire issue from a theological point of view?"

"The only theology I know is the proper interpretation of Christ's wishes. He did not leave a legacy which directs us to brutality."

"What about his disciples? Some of them did."

"Even if some did, does that mean we should follow ideas or thoughts that occurred over a thousand years ago? Just take a look at what is happening around you. People rejoice at the sight of an Auto-de-Fe. I went to watch one, a while back since I had never seen it with my own eyes before. I can tell you, it is sickening to watch people burn to death. I fainted and a young man helped me out. He is the one who opened my eyes to reality. But what bothered me most was that our citizens, and there were thousands of them at the plaza, were having a great time celebrating an event of extreme brutality and inhuman behavior of ordained priests. People need to rejoice from the good things in life, not from murder."

"What if Torquemada is right?"

"How can he be right? How are you going to isolate people, a whole nation? Are you going to interview every citizen as to his ancestry? What if a man is from an old-line Catholic family and the wife is not? Are you going to separate them? Where to do you send the wife? And then their children - who and what are they?

"Torquemada's objective is as elusive as what is beyond death. The people of this earth have different beliefs as to what happens to us after death. Torquemada seems to be the only one who knows exactly where hell is. I'm sick and tired of his threats, his beliefs, his conduct, his doctrines, and his Godly superiority. Torquemada cannot be right. Torquemada is a very sick man."

"Have you brought this matter up with the Pope?"

"I don't have to. The Pope is the one who appointed me, as monarch of this country, the ultimate authority over the Church. It is my decision. All I can hope for is that you see the light and follow my desires."

"You do have a valid point about the behavior of our ordained men. The use of force, torture, murder, of lies and deceit should not be our tools of trade. I agree we need to reach the heathen by friendly and cordial means. Yes, we should set an example to the world, an example of fraternity, good morals, and proper behavior."

"May I conclude this meeting, then, knowing that I have the full and complete cooperation of all branches of our Church?" the Queen asked.

There was a unanimous vote of confidence and acceptance of Queen Isabella's request.

"Before you leave, I want every priest or theological student working in every house of Inquisition transferred to different churches in your districts. I will close every Inquisition building and return it to its lawful owners. Any priest who disagrees with you should be excommunicated. I want the names and addresses of every such priest; as I may consider deporting them. In fact, I am about to authorize an exploratory mission to India, and I might send those priests to far lands."

The meeting broke up and the Queen returned to her chambers.

"Call in my monk," she ordered her assistant. David, who was anxiously waiting in his room, came running.

"You won, my dear David. Thank you for opening my eyes. All members of the Church's hierarchy have agreed to the change. Each one of them will hold meetings in their districts and give out new instructions. My biggest problem is what to do with Torquemada."

"I suggest you have him deported. Send him somewhere he couldn't easily escape from," David suggested.

"I expected you to suggest I have him burned at the stake as he had done unto thousands of others," the Queen said.

"The decision is yours," David said, "I would rather see him suffer for the rest of his life."

"I will have him deported as you suggest, but with one little change. I'll have one of our navy ships drop him off on an isolated island far from civilization."

"Didn't you say you were going to finance Columbus's expedition to India? Have him go with Columbus and let him dispose of Torquemada on any island he comes across at the end of his journey," David said.

"That's what I'll do. On another subject, I would like you to oversee the dismantling of all Inquisition operations throughout Castile and Aragon."

"That is very commendable of you, but I think I'm too young for such an important position. I have a friend a man by the name of Zevulun ben Yishai. He is much older than me. He used to work for my father before he died. He would be perfect for the job," David said.

"Very well," the Queen said, "I will have my assistant prepare the order."

"Zevulun should be returning from Portugal any day now. Anyway, it will take a while before the Cardinals and Archbishops prepare and dispatch all their instructions."

"I don't know your last name," the Queen said.

"My last name is Abulafia. My ancestors came from Egypt soon after the Moors conquered the Iberian Peninsula. My family's business covered a large territory from Constantinople to Tangier and various major cities in Portugal, Castile and Aragon. Of course, the business in Castile and Aragon was closed down. My cousins' parents who ran the Barcelona branch escaped the Inquisition and settled in Constantinople or Alexandria. I'm sure they'll be delighted to return to Barcelona," David said, "Perhaps, with Zevulun's help I'll be able to revive my father's business in Toledo."

"I'll give you all the help I can," the Queen said.

David left the Queen's chambers and went to his room. He danced around the room until he collapsed from fatigue.

CHAPTER SIXTY

"My darling, we won," David shouted as he entered his house in El Mola. "The Inquisition is dead. Queen Isabella ordered the dismantling of the Inquisition and the return of the Church to humane behavior."

"Calm down," Anna shouted back and grabbed David in a long hug. "Tell me all about it."

They talked for hours in great excitement.

"How do I recall all of our people in different cities?" David asked. "We must stop our fight immediately or the Queen might encounter a backlash."

"If I'm not mistaken, we had planned to reunite here in ten days. It would take that long for the Church to notify all branches. Stop worrying. Everyone will be on the road in matter of days."

"The Queen told me she used your 'orphanage-care' as an example of good Catholic behavior. She must have forgotten we're Jews," David said humorously.

⊗⊗⊗

The days passed quickly, and finally all the young fighters returned to the nest. The house in El Mola turned into a house of joy.

"I'm delighted we won't have to kill anymore," Elisheva declared. "It's amazing that once you've killed your first victim, the second and third become routine. I suspect the priests must have experienced the same feelings."

"I'm happy for all the Jews in the world. Perhaps now we will be able to live in peace," Reuven said. "I'd like to travel to Constantinople, find my parents, and bring them back."

"By all means," David said, "Do that. If they return perhaps they can teach me my father's trade and I can revive the family's business in Toledo."

"I'm sure they'll want to return," Reuven said, "after all, our families have lived here for generations, and we have our pride."

"What is to become of the rest of us?" Rachel asked.

"You will continue to live with us. We are one family. The construction of the orphanages and schools will begin soon. There will be plenty to do for us all."

At that point Zevulun walked in.

"I haven't seen such happy faces in a long time," he declared. "What is the occasion?"

"The Queen has appointed you as her representative to oversee the dismantling of all Inquisition operations in Castile and Aragon," David shouted, "We won."

"Are you pulling my leg?" Zevulun asked. "Come to think of it on the last leg of my journey to Toledo I overheard conversations which made no sense to me. Now I understand. You must tell me all about it."

David recounted his story with much enthusiasm.

"I have a feeling that the Queen's observance of the Auto-de-Fe is the straw that broke the camel's back, as they say. Yet, somehow she listened to my words. It was her visit to El Mola that made her realize good should reign over evil. You and I are going to Toledo first thing tomorrow morning. I will introduce you to Queen Isabella and she'll give you written authorization to act on her behalf. I believe she wants to dismantle the Inquisition as soon as possible and have the country return to normal life," David stated.

"I will be delighted to accommodate her," Zevulun declared.

"By the way, what did you find in Lisbon? How are our fellow Jews faring over there?" David asked.

"First let me tell you about your family. It seems that two or three generations ago the key Abulafia personality in Lisbon got into a business disagreement with your grandfather, may he rest in peace, and since then the personal relations with the family in Castile and Aragon cooled off. Apparently the Barcelona branch sided with your grandfather. No one seems to know what the dispute was about, so I suggested they forget the whole thing and renew their relationship with you. Now that we're rid of the Inquisition and all its discrimination against the Jews, it will be so much easier to reconnect the families. In reality they were quite distressed at the separation. I would suggest you travel to Lisbon as soon as feasible since I'm sure good business can be developed for the reestablished Abulafia Company in Toledo. You can count on me to help achieve that," Zevulun said.

"You will help me in family matters once the Inquisition has been destroyed," David said. "The Inquisition's demise comes before anything else."

"You'll need plenty of funds to restart the business," Zevulun said, "I'll give you what I have."

"There's no need for it. I do appreciate your offer. I have all the money my father left me and it is substantial. In fact, this gives me an idea," David said.

"Which is?"

"I'll buy the Inn where the money is stashed and give it as a present to Nechemia and Miriam if they marry and make a new family," David said, "and then there is the money hidden in my parents old house. I'll pay any price to regain that house. This house in El Mola can become part of the Orphanage organization."

Anna joined the conversation.

"David and I are planning to get married as soon as we can find a Rabbi. We would very much like to get married in one of the Toledo synagogues."

Shouts of happiness and words of congratulations flew from every side. "Mazal Tov!"

"You may extend the good wishes to us, too," Itzhak said. "Yael and I are also contemplating marriage." Cries of happiness took over the entire household, and when the joyful noise quieted down a bit, Yossef looked at Elisheva and took her hand.

"Will you marry me?" Elisheva almost passed out. She lost her voice for a moment. When she could speak again, she whispered, "Yes, I will."

Yossef grabbed her and kissed her passionately. The crowd turned wild with unprecedented joy.

"I will need financial help to build our wine business," Yossef declared. Reuven and David looked at each other and spoke simultaneously, "We'll provide all the funds you need."

In the early hours of the morning the house quieted and everyone found a spot to sleep. But they didn't get much sleep, for early the next day heavy knocks were heard on the front door.

"I'm looking for Senorita Anna," the man said. "I am Master Builder Jose Calderon de Medina. Queen Isabella instructed me to design and build an orphanage and school for you," he stated.

"Please come in," Anna said. "The trouble is I have many guests and I don't have a chair to offer you. Most of us were sitting on the floor."

"Let's walk outside. I'd like to see the grounds where you want the buildings," he suggested. Anna and the builder left. David and Zevulun got ready to journey to Toledo. Reuven turned to David.

"If you don't mind, brother David, I'd like to take the first ship to Constantinople. My parents may be there, and if not, most probably in Alexandria. You know where my money is. Take as much as you need. I'll be back as soon as I can. I hope my parents will want to return with me."

"Go find your parents," David said; "perhaps there's a girl you can marry in Alexandria. We need to bring as many children as possible into the world. We have to replenish the number of Jews." They hugged and kissed each other. Reuven bid farewell and left for Barcelona.

"I'd like Nechemia to come with me," Zevulun said. "Dismantling dozens of Inquisition buildings is a major job and I'll need all the help I can get."

"I'll assist you for a while, too," David said. "I just have to participate in this God sent work. I wish my parents were alive to see this day. I shall rebuild the Central Synagogue in Toledo and dedicate it to them. By the time we complete all the work, the orphanage and school buildings will be complete and I'll be free to help Anna in the tremendous job of running this institution, apart from starting my father's business. I know it's a large order, but I will have to work on all fronts."

"Let's get going," Zevulun said, "I'd like to reach Toledo by tomorrow morning and perhaps the Queen will receive us immediately."

"I'm sure she will, " David said, "She's very excited about the future and wants the bad times to be behind her."

Before leaving, David gave Yossef a pouch full of gold dukats.

"Go with God's blessing and build your home. I want the first bottle of wine you produce, don't forget." They hugged each other. By the time Anna returned with the builder, most of the guests had left. David was waiting on the front porch.

"I'm going with Zevulun and Nechemia to Toledo. I'll return as soon as I can." He kissed Anna and they left. Rachel and Miriam were left with Anna to look after the orphans and plan for the day when the orphanage would officially open its doors.

CHAPTER SIXTY-ONE

"**I** am delighted to see you, my dear David," Queen Isabella said as he and Zevulun walked into the throne room.

"You look wonderful, Your Majesty. I'm delighted to see you with a relieved face. This is Zevulun ben Yishai. He's the man who would help you dismantle the Inquisition."

"I'm deeply honored, Your Majesty," Zevulun said and bowed. "I will carry out your orders without delay."

"Our newly appointed Archbishop, His Eminence Raul Garcia de Uria, has already issued walking papers to all priests working in Inquisition houses throughout Castile, Aragon, and Leon. Every priest has been assigned to one local church or cathedral. By the time you reach the Inquisition houses, you should find them unoccupied. Please dispose of the contents and see to it they're returned to their lawful owners. If the owner was Jewish and cannot be found, the house should be sold and the proceeds go towards the cost of building the orphanages and schools," the Queen said.

"I'll prepare a report for each of the buildings as I dispose of them."

"David told me much about you," the Queen said. "You must miss the Abulafias."

"Indeed I do, Your Majesty," Zevulun said, "They were fine people."

"I know. David's father was a very important merchant in Toledo. I understand you plan to revive your father's business," the Queen said to David.

"I'm planning to do that as soon as Zevulun has completed his work for the Crown. I will need his help since no one knows the business better than he," David said.

"I wish you luck. Of course, it goes without saying that the Crown and the government will renew its purchases from the Abulafia Company. Indeed, we always received the best merchandise from your father," the Queen said. "On another matter, Columbus will be leaving on his exploratory mission in a few days. I've instructed him to imprison Torquemada on board his lead ship and have him released when he reaches India. Let him convert the natives of India. I also issued a decree forbidding Torquemada to return to Castile."

The Queen gave Zevulun her written authority to carry out his job throughout the kingdom. They left the palace elated.

"There is a great deal of work to be done. With God's help I'll complete it in a few months."

"I'll help you around Toledo. After that you and Nechemia are on your own. My first mission will be to buy back my parents land and rebuild the house. I plan to live in it for the rest of my life. While you are gone, I'll buy the inn in Azulas for Nechemia and Miriam. I'll make an offer its owner cannot refuse."

EPILOGUE

Zevulun's work in dismantling all Inquisition buildings in Castile, Aragon and Leon was much easier than he anticipated. By the time he reached the first building he found it empty. All priests except one who was left to care for the buildings until taken over had gone to new locations. The Archbishop responsible for the territory made certain each priest was sent to a far away city or village. Zevulun and Nechemia found good records in most town halls and former owners of the buildings were easily identified. In some cases the owners were Jewish and could not be located. Those buildings were auctioned off and the proceeds were dispatched to Anna. By the end of the year, all Inquisition buildings had been eliminated.

David bought the Azulas Inn as well as his parents' former home, which had burned down. He immediately hired a builder who was commissioned to rebuild the house, no expenses spared. He also saw to it that all ten Toledo synagogues were restored to their original condition. The tremendous construction and rehabilitation undertaking brought new prosperity to the Toledo area, and Queen Isabella arranged a special reception to honor David.

Anna and David were married by one of the surviving Rabbis and soon moved into the Abulafia's rebuilt house. The loyal Abulafia housekeeper returned to serve David and Anna. She said she would not have it any other way despite her age. She promised David to serve his family for the rest of her life. Anna gave birth to a healthy baby boy who was named after David's father.

David removed the hidden monies from the Azulas Inn, which was given to Nechemia and Rachel. The Inn was renamed 'The Reconquista Inn'. Nechemia's sons joined them soon and completed their Hebrew studies at the reopened Judaica School run by Rabbi Shimon be Yossef. Anna received David's mother's jewelry he had hidden in the trunk of a tree.

Anna supervised the construction of the orphanage and school building in El Mola until she gave birth. Rachel took over at that point. Both buildings and the dormitory built next door were large enough to house over one hundred children. The local priest, with the help of his Bishop, brought in teachers and nuns to help run the institution. Rachel remained in overall charge. Word was sent throughout Castile, Aragon and Leon about this orphanage and the Queen insisted that all abandoned, orphaned and homeless children have proper shelter and education. The El Mola institution was named 'Anna's Home for Children'.

Anna's Home for Children soon filled up and the Queen, who was a regular visitor, ordered the construction of similar facilities in four other major locations throughout her territory. Anna was appointed by the Queen to supervise and manage all these facilities.

David reestablished his father's business with Zevulun's help. Letters were sent to all suppliers overseas and locally as well as to all old clients. Reuven found his parents in Alexandria and the reunion was celebrated with much fanfare. The entire Egyptian branch of the Abulafia family was there. Immediately following the big party, Reuven and his parents departed for Barcelona. Reuven's father was surprised that the fortune he had entrusted to Reuven was hardly touched.

Yossef and Elisheva prospered as their wine industry developed and grew to become one of Castile's major producers. The young couple was married and soon twins were born, a boy and a girl. They named their children Anna and David.

Itzhak and Yael decided to leave Castile and moved to the Holy Land where Itzhak studied and became a religious teacher of Talmud. They, too, prospered and had many children.

Columbus left with three ships to find India. Thomas de Torquemada was jailed on one of the ships and kept in isolation. After a harrowing journey, Columbus reached one of the West Indies islands, mistaking it for India. Soon he discovered the South American continent and the Queen's forces conquered much of it. Torquemada was freed in the land of Peru and had a ball continuing his missionary work among the heathen Indians. He authorized the killing of all men he said were the bearers of sin. He died soon after from malaria he contracted in one of the jungles in Peru. Queen Isabella was relieved when the news of his death reached her months later. The Queen's coffers began to fill with gold from South America and her monarchy became one of the richest in the world.

The Conversos and Marranos abandoned their newly forced religion and returned to practice Judaism. Synagogues throughout the country were filled with men, women and children, as was the custom in the past. The church openly repented to all its parishioners and all sermons directed to tolerance, love, and the ways of Christ.

Thomas de Torquemada had failed....